Always Will

A FORT BENDER NOVEL

LAYNA JAMES

ALWAYS WILL

Cover Design by Maldo Designs

Chapter Headers by Kim Cavrak, Spiritofebullience.com

Ornamental Breaks by Amanda Webb, @LegendsofAukera

Custom Artwork by Lindsey Cargal, @artfullylinzee

Developmental Editing by KS Editing Services

Editing by J. Berry Editorial

First Edition: September 2025

ISBN: 978-1-963567-06-9 (eBook)

978-1-963567-07-6 (Paperback)

978-1-963567-08-3 (Hardcover)

ALWAYS WILL is a work of fiction. Names, places, and events are either the product of the author's imagination or used fictitiously. Any resemblance to persons, living or dead, places, or events is entirely coincidental.

Printed in the United States of America

www.laynajames.com

What if alone isn't the only way?
Lay down your armor and rest.

CONTENT NOTES

ALWAYS WILL is intended for adult readers 18+. The story depicts explicit language and open door scenes. Other themes to be aware of:

- Adoption
- Alcohol use
- Child physical abuse/neglect (off page, but described in reference to the past)
- Domestic violence (not between main characters. Off page, but described in reference to the past)
- Fatphobia from parent
- Foster care (mentioned in reference to the past)
- Parental estrangement
- Parental mental illness
- Pregnancy
- Pregnancy complications: subchorionic hemorrhage/hematoma
- Stalking (not between main characters)

Fort Bender
N
W
E
S
THE BLUFFS ESTAT
FORT BENDER
VISITOR'S CENTER
AND MUSEUM
LIBRARY
MAIN STREET
CRYSTAL BEACH

ER BOTANICAL GARDENS
SHOWER TREE LODGE
YOUTH CENTER
FORGET ME NOTS
FORGET ME NOTS
WILLIS NEIGHBORHOOD
CAMP BENDER
WALLER TREE FARM
RRIS ORHOOD
BENDER ELEMENTARY
BENDER SECONDARY
HERBERT'S HOLE

TWO YEARS AGO
WILLA

I *never should have come home.*

HOME? THAT'S A SUPREMELY LOOSE DEFINITION FOR Fort Bender, California. Crystal Beach is one of the few things I love about this place, but the spiced ocher sunset glistening off the shore doesn't set me at ease like it usually does. Neither does the Northern California breeze, or the camera strapped around my neck. Not with my mother's shrill rebuke replaying in my head.

To berate me behind closed doors is one thing, but cornering me in front of family friends while I shot their wedding was humiliating. She damn near ruined Chase and Kayla's photos. It was completely uncalled for, no matter how much she disagrees with my life.

I'll never come back.

Securing my camera on the tripod at the edge of the pier, I hope to capture the golden hue glistening off the waves before I lose my light. *I've already lost it, but this place sure as hell won't help me get it back.*

Peering through the viewfinder, I shut out the noise and focus on the paradoxical sea. The crashing tide, forceful and demanding, yet flowing with serenity. Whitecaps kiss the shore, enchanting the wind with a soothing melody—a mighty calm with the power to destroy. *I need to be like the sea.* I pause, peace washing over me as I marvel at the ocean, wishing I could bottle this feeling and take it back with me to LA.

"*Semper Paratus,*" a voice says from behind me. I jump and almost knock my tripod over. Too-friendly Trevor sidles up next to me, his loosened tie flapping around the lapels of his champagne hued tuxedo. "It's Latin for—"

"Always Ready. I know." I roll my eyes at his dimpled smile and the way the sun illuminates his warm sepia skin. He's been trying to get my attention all weekend. I've managed to curve him every time, except for now.

"Just sayin', don't worry. If you fall in, I got you..."

"The only thing I'm worried about is who will pay for my camera if you make me knock it into the water."

"You sure that's all you're worried about? You're staring at the waves like you wish they'd take you away..."

I *do* wish they'd take me away. Erase every decision I've made that led me to the hell I just escaped back in LA. But that's none of Trevor's business. We're barely acquaintances. "I was just lost in thought."

"About?"

I sneer at the annoying lilt to his voice. *He's so damn aggravating.* What is it about people seeing me with my camera that makes them think I want to have a conversation? Just because I don't plaster a smile on my face like he does, doesn't mean I need to be checked on. I was doing just fine out here by myself. "It's not important."

"Try me."

Squinting at him, I chew on my lower lip. Even with irritation sizzling in my chest, something about the way he's looking at me makes me want to share. "I was just thinking about the water." I drop my eyes and turn back to the waves. "Did you know the crystals here used to be glass bottles?" He nods and takes a step toward me. "I was lost in thought over all these jagged pieces of glass—rough around the edges—viewed as garbage that was only worthy of being dumped into the ocean. They were meant to be forgotten, but the waves swept them up and breathed new life into them. Molded them. Gave them a sparkling new purpose. The ocean turned them into gems people come from all over just to witness. They had no value until they were completely changed. It's sad, really." I'm breathless by the time I finish, having lost myself in the ocean's beautiful transformation process. I glance at the tall man next to me, the sunset casting gilded rays over his auburn hair.

"Gems, huh?" His hazel eyes are plastered on my face as if he doesn't see the waves at all. It sets me on edge, and I look away, wringing my hands to distract myself.

"See? Not important."

"Sounds like it is... Sounds pretty heavy too."

"Yeah, well, not more important than me getting this shot." Whipping back to my camera, I peek through the viewfinder. "If you'll excuse me."

He lets out a breathy chuckle behind me, and I try to ignore the tiny current beating in my chest. "I'll take the hint...but, Willa?" He clears his throat. "Maybe it's time to let go."

Yeah right.

His footsteps retreat, and I suck air into my lungs, finally able to breathe now that I'm alone again. I snap a few test shots, adjust my camera once more, and take the photo. *What would it be like to let it all go for the first time in my life?* No. There's too much to figure out, too much riding on my success, too many people rooting for my failure. I glance down at the camera screen. The motionless blur of the waves under the setting sun is frozen in time, exactly as I want to remember it. As much as I hate coming home to Fort Bender, this moment makes it all worth it.

CHAPTER ONE

WILLA

Present Day

"Don't be scared, Mo..." I send a reassuring smile to my photography intern right before I turn off the lights. "Crank that ISO up." Apprehension scrunches her bronzed features as the Framed Orchid logo on the wall bathes the studio in a lavender glow.

"But the grains, Willa..." Monique's dark, curly pigtails dangle when her head falls back with a groan. "*The grainnns.*"

I snort at her zombie impression as my arms settle across my chest tightly. It's already September. Her internship started weeks ago. I'm not letting her put this natural lighting assignment off again, and she knows it. If I didn't have to drive to San Diego in the morning, we'd stay as late as she needs.

She slides a pleading glance to my junior photographer. "Cara—"

"Nope." Cara laughs, juggling her gaze between us before tossing a sleek platinum blond ponytail over her shoulder. "Don't drag me into this..." The light from the large studio window catches her golden-brown skin just right, and I resist snatching my camera from my desk to capture it. We're running out of time as it is.

Cara repositions the overstuffed dragon—Mo's photo subject—on a stool, tapping its head back into position each time it droops forward. "Emily, can you toss me the double-sided tape?"

"Yep!" Drawers open and close at the front desk while Emily mumbles, "Tape...tape...taaape...?" *Figures*. My receptionist/assistant does her job well when it matters, but she's also the ambassador of space case town.

"Next to the phone, Emily," I call over my shoulder, then turn back to Mo. "Look at me. *The grains* can't hurt you. Just take a few test shots and see which you like better. You can't edi—"

"*Edit a photo you never take*." Their resounding droning makes me wince, and it's quickly followed by murmured apologies.

"It's fine." I wave it off, breathing deeply until the ringing in my ears fades. "I'm just saying, you can't master the skill if you don't actually take the picture."

"*Ughhhh*. I know. But it feels wrong." She gestures to the window. "It's too bright outside. Professor Reinert's judgy voice is in my head..." Clearing her throat, she mimics his pretentiously deep tone. "Only an amateur would introduce noise and granularity to a photograph."

Can't believe he's still touting that shit. "Yeah, well, we're not outside, and he was a prick when I was a student too..." My wince has nothing to do with the volume of her guffaw. "Don't tell your adviser I said that. What I mean is, there's an artistic time and place for everything, even if shit-for-brains says there's not..." At this point, Cara and Emily are laughing too, and I crack a smile. "Don't tell anyone at TAILA I said that either."

I graduated from The Art Institute of Los Angeles (TAILA) a decade ago. Improving my craft while among some of the greatest photographers in the country was invaluable, as well as learning how to navigate artistic spaces as a Black woman. Barton Reinert *tried* to make my life hell. Passive aggressive praise, overly harsh critique, unjustified failing grades—it would have made most people wither. But I'd just escaped the purgatory my parents had me trapped in and wasn't going down without a fight. I raised so much hell, his efforts to prove my incompetency drove me straight to winning the prestigious Hartney Arts award three years in a row. There was nothing he could do about it; my work spoke for itself. Now he propositions me at every department mixer and covertly asks me to join his lectures through other members of the internship board. My answer is always no to both.

The phone rings, and Emily clears her throat before answering. "Thank you for choosing Framed Orchid Studio. This is Emily. How can I help you?" A wide smile lights up her pale face as she tucks a chunk of black hair behind her ear. "Oh, hi, Mr. Renner."

"See!" Monique's eyes squeeze shut when she gasps ominously. "He *knows.*"

"Barton Reinert wouldn't dare call this studio again." I snort. The memory of him fumbling over his words after I cussed him out the first time still gives me a rush. "That's likely Kyle *Renner*, confirming his family's session next week. Now focus. We're almost out of time."

"But—"

"Mo, *girl. Woosah.* Breathe." Cara abandons the floppy dragon, marches up to Monique, and grips her shoulders. "No one's lying in wait here. You're just trying out different settings to see how light affects the picture. Have we steered you wrong yet?"

Mo shakes her head but makes no effort to step toward the tripod.

Cara sighs dramatically, turning to me with a gleam in her eye. "She's not gonna master natural lighting."

"Nope." I tut, catching on immediately. "She's not."

Mo's face falls as she shifts on her feet. "...I'm not?"

"Nope." Cara smiles and shoots me a knowing glance.

"W-what am I gonna do then?" Her worried eyes shift between me and Cara.

I nod toward the camera in her hand with a smirk. "Not only are you gonna master it, you're gonna make it your bitch."

Her eyes widen comically. "My b-bi—"

"*YOUR BITCH!*" Cara calls, shooting her fingers in the air. I wince at her loud imitation of an air horn, but no one notices this time.

"Be-otchhhhh," Emily adds a second too late, which gets Mo laughing.

I cock my head at my intern, eyebrows raised. "Say it, girl."

"But—"

"Say it. Say it. Say it," Cara chants playfully.

Mo stops midrebuttal when I raise a finger in protest. She nibbles her bottom lip, and I cup my hand behind my ear, waiting. A timid grin creeps across her face as she whispers, "I'm gonna make it my bitch."

"Damn right." I smile back. That confidence brightening her eyes is exactly why I do this. I glance at the clock again. "Cara's going to finish up your session, but I'll be right at my desk if you need me... Just. Try. It." I poke her shoulder to accent my words. "The worst that happens is we repeat the session. And maybe a visit from Reinert."

Monique's eyes widen and shoot to the door, as if saying his name is an instant summons.

"Only kidding." I laugh. "No Professor. Embrace the grain. Just explore and see what works. You got this." Her wary face breaks my heart, but pride stitches it back up when she straightens her shoulders and adjusts the settings on her camera.

It's the third year of my partnership with my alma mater for this internship. Providing Black, Indigenous, and POC photography students a supportive in-studio experience has been one of the most rewarding things I've ever done. There were only a handful of us when I went, and the unspoken demand for excellence was stifling. My internships were surrounded by stuffy assholes who were impressed with my work until they saw my face. Once Framed Orchid made it big, I knew I wanted to give a safe studio experience to other TAILA students so they wouldn't have to struggle like I did.

Rebuilding their confidence at the beginning of each semester is necessary, but frustrating. They've already had heavy doses of the objective side of photography. My goal is to remind them that art can still be subjective amid all the rules. Most of my interns come to me completely gutted, terrified to make mistakes. I get it entirely. When you're marginalized, perfectionism is expected everywhere. Even a tiny slip-up could be a death sentence for their budding careers. So no matter how pissed I get at the powers that be, I'll always encourage plenty of trial and error in this space. This is their safe place to fail and fail again, until they learn to fly.

THEY'RE STILL FUCKING HERE? THE SQUEAL FROM THE masonry saw hits my ears before I put my purple crossover in park. Construction workers mill around the two homes closest to the parking lot. My head falls back with a groan as I look across the bungalow court at my solitary craftsman-style cottage at the other end. I bought one of the first reconstructed units a few years ago, and it's perfect for me. Small, cozy, and quiet...for the most part. The only thing I don't like is how long it's taking for them to finish the other units.

All construction is supposed to be wrapped up by 5 p.m. daily, so I usually don't have to deal with the piercing shriek of metal on stone. But here it is at six, with no signs of them stopping. Grumbling obscenities, my shoulders scrunched to my ears, I gather my things and scurry past the chaos through the tree-lined courtyard. There are only four rows of homes, but by the time I reach my door, my head is pounding from the noise. I snatch the potted purple orchid waiting on my coir doormat and tap the keypad, slamming the door behind me with a huff. *Silence*. Well, mostly.

It's not that I can't handle any noise. If I know beforehand, I can disassociate to cope with it. But loud and unexpected shoots dysregulation through me so fast I want to curl into a ball and dissolve. Between that, my rigid routines, and hyper-focusing on my interests, my therapist has her theories about me. That's one reason I'm already packed for my trip tomorrow. Since I insist on going, she encouraged me to take the evening to prepare for the music festival chaos my sister talked me into.

Flipping the lock, I leave the house dark as my breathing slows, focusing on the farmhouse-style wooden beams outlining my vaulted ceilings. There's enough light from the transom above the door to read the card hanging from the brown pot in my hands.

Happy (early) Birthday, Will! Hope this gets to you before your weekend getaway.
—Sam

I smile as the pounding in my head dissipates, dropping my camera bag on the mocha microsuede sofa on my way to the kitchen. My best friend, Samson, owns a flower shop in Fort Bender and regularly sends me plants like I'm not horticulturally hopeless. Flora enters my house with the hope of a thousand suns, only to leave as withered mulch. It infuriates me to no end that I can't figure out the plant life cycle. Spite drives me to keep trying.

ME

Thanks for the flower, dork. Aren't these things super hard to care for?

SAM

Didn't you get accepted into 3 Ivy Leagues,
nerd?

ME

For math, not marigolds.

SAM

😂 Touché. I'll send a care sheet. How's the
Dracaena trifasciata and Monstera?

ME

Translation, I beg.

SAM

Stripey Leaves and Holey Hearts...

In the dumpster with the cactus and aloe...

ME

See! My names make much more sense.
Stripey and Holey are currently taking a nap.

A dirt nap.

SAM

You didn't water them enough, did you?

Guilty.

ME

They only liked bottled water from the titties of
Antarctic icebergs. I had no chance.

SAM

Maci says that's not a thing.

Giggling as a picture of my one-year-old goddaughter's scowl fills the screen, I set my phone on the counter. There's no drainage hole in the bottom of the pot, but since I'll be gone all weekend, it'll probably need the extra water. I run the faucet over the silvery orchid roots until water flows down the sides, spilling some on the herringbone hardwood. Grumbling, I set the pot on the windowsill above the sink, wipe up the spill, and shift into decompression mode.

Tabletop fountain. Vanilla wax warmer. Light over the stove.

I grab my camera bag from the couch and stick it in the small bedroom turned editing studio at the front of my house, then slip back through the kitchen and down the hallway to my room.

Stretchy pants. Hair off my neck. Yoga mat.

Retracing my steps back to the kitchen, I cue up my version of a mindfulness playlist on the record player, breathing out the stress as soft R&B eases through the wireless speaker. It's fascinating, really—the invisible force of sound. How something so innocuous has the power to soothe or torment. Enhance or defile. Establish or ruin. It's astonishing.

With the flip of a switch, the gas fireplace ticks to life—the last step in my routine. I settle on my mat on the living room hardwood and take a cleansing breath. My eyes fall closed. I'm finally at peace. *My therapist might just be right.*

CHAPTER TWO

TREVOR

"So, hypothetically, if I didn't save my field report for the week, how bad would that be?" Caleb—one of several new associates on my sales team—leans over the metal chair in front of my desk, squinting at the glare from the window as he fidgets with his cell phone.

Frustration puffs through my lips, and I turn to close the blinds behind me to hide it. "Depending on how hypothetical we're talking, pretty bad, Caleb. Did you check your drafts?" I try to keep the edge out of my voice, but there's been something with him every week for the last month.

"Yeah…" He checks his buzzing phone. "But, uhh"—he taps the screen—"I forgot to"—he fucking laughs—"uh, forgot to use…" When he finally looks up at the exasperation on my face, he slides his phone in his pocket with a nervous grin. "Sorry. I forgot to use the new form in SalesUp, so it didn't autosave."

SalesUp is our Customer Relationship Management (CRM) software. Our bread and butter for data organization. We've made Fridays in-office days to keep our team up to date with all our contracts each week. But it's hard to do that when Caleb refuses to use the damn tools he's been trained on.

"Which form did you use?" He better not say the sample

template again, or I'm sticking him on mail duty for the foreseeable future.

With a grimace, Caleb shifts on his feet, tossing his black hair out of his eyes. "...The blank sample template."

Sighing, I hang my head. *Of course he did.* Why use a pre-populated form that autosaves to the company server every thirty seconds? What sense does *that* make? Nope, let's manually enter every-*damn*-thing into a sample template. "The whole reason we created the new forms was to make it easy for you to avoid mistakes like this."

"There's no way to recover it? Like, from the cloud or something?"

All I can do is blink at him. How he thinks I can pull an unsaved form out of thin air is some kind of logic I can't get behind. But Big, Angry Black Man is a label I've worked hard to avoid in my HR file, so I stifle my annoyance. "...Did you save it to the cloud, Caleb?"

"Uh, no."

"Then no." I turn to my double monitor and open his field file, only to be smacked in the face with another problem. "Where are the rest of your daily reports? I'm only seeing the clients from Monday and Tuesday." It's Friday. If he tells me he didn't make any progress after I met him on the job this week, I might lose it.

"So...how bad would it be if I forg—"

"Never mind." Leaning back in my leather office chair, I lace my hands behind my neck, squinting against the pounding in my head. Our department secures contracts for EdTechU's virtual whiteboard planning systems with universities and school districts in the Bay Area. Building professional relationships by workshopping directly with administrators, teachers, and students through the life of the contract put EdTechU on the map.

Organization on our part is vital, which is why my comanager and I have streamlined everything for our associates, fine-tuning the basic corporate CRM to fit our needs. EdTechU has always encouraged its employees to adjust the given tools to match the learning styles on our teams. With this new cohort being so green, we made the entire reporting process as easy as click, drop, submit. *At least, I thought we did.* But clearly, we needed to add in some digital hand-holding on top of traveling across the area to provide them with on-site support during the week. I tap over to my managerial view in SalesUp, find his Field Reports folder, and bring up the correct recording form on my second monitor. "How many contacts did you make this week?"

"Uh, twelve...or twenty-one. Eleven?"

My hand settles over my mouth to hide the tension setting into my jaw while watching him try to recall a week's worth of information. The weight of his mistake seems to sink into lines on his forehead, and the more we talk, the more his shoulders slump. I'm not trying to be hard on him, but he's got to step it up before performance reviews. "Hey—"

"It was...twelve. It was twelve."

I chuckle at how absurd this all is, down to him using his fingers to count the contacts from memory. "Okay, take a breath, and have a seat. We'll figure it out." I turn my screens toward him as he wiggles the chair closer, sitting with a huff. "This is what I documented from our time on Tuesday." When I slide my keyboard to him, his eyebrows knit like he's never worked a day in this office before. "Caleb, bud, redo the form. I'll watch, to make sure you don't miss anything. It won't have all of your data, but for your sake, it's better than nothing."

He nods and breathes out his relief. "Thanks, Trevor. Won't let it happen again."

Doubt it. Shaking my head, I check my watch. I can *almost* call it a day, and I'll still have enough time to hit the gym before catching my flight to San Diego. Meeting my friends for an end-of-summer music festival is the reward I deserve after dealing with Caleb's shit today.

The rapping on my office door pulls my attention from the rookie tapping away on my keyboard. "Hey, Trev." Chase, my comanager and one of my best friends, peeks his head in my office. "They're waiting for us in the conference room."

Damn, I totally spaced the call with the LA office. Might have to skip the gym after all.

"Hey, Caleb, do me a favor." I clap his shoulder on my way out, and he freezes. Chuckling, I head to the door, calling over my shoulder, "Save those when you're done."

"He used the sample again, didn't he?" Chase asks, swiping fingers through his sandy blond hair. We fall in step down the hallway.

"Three times, on three different days. I think we gotta pull them for another training intensive."

"Sounds good to me, man. The team hasn't struggled like this since our first year here."

As we round the corner, I catch a curvy, power-suit-wearing head of caramel curls walking through the conference room door. She doesn't see me, which is good, considering the instant sneer that takes over my face. I'm tempted to dip out of this meeting entirely. It's not like I don't need to leave soon anyway. Chase can fill me in on Monday.

"Was that—?"

"Looked like it." I resist the urge to turn around, steeling myself before walking into the room. Even after all these years, the sight of Marla Rhodes still sets my teeth on edge.

"Come on, Wills. Aren't you even a little excited?" Ashlie asks Willa. I slide into the booth next to Hunter, and we bump knuckles. Willa wrinkles her nose as her head shakes, her deep amber skin glowing under the warm lighting. She gathers her black and brown twists over her shoulder, and my mouth goes dry. Beautiful doesn't even begin to describe her.

From her full, pouty lips to the almond shape of her eyes, the soft-ness of her thick curves, Willa's inimitable.

"Hey, sorry I'm late." I smile at the arguing sisters, who barely acknowledge me. Glancing back at Hunter, I whisper, "What's that about?"

"Who the hell knows anymore?" The deep-set scowl on his face as he adjusts his glasses tells me he's about to bolt. His sienna-toned skin is pulled taut over his knuckles as he cracks them and nods toward the bar. "You want a drink?"

"Nope, I'm good with water."

"After listening to these two all day, I need several." His elbow jabs me until I scoot off the bench. When he gets to the bar, he slumps into a stool, a clear sign he's not coming back anytime soon.

"Hey, Trev! How was your flight?" Ashlie's golden-brown coils bounce against her amber cheeks as she turns toward me.

"Not too bad. Hey, Willa." I hold up a few fingers, and Willa gives a tight-lipped grin before burying her head in her phone. *Damn...*

"Don't mind her. She's mad at me for convincing her to come."

"I'm not *mad*. I just know I won't have a great time."

"Come on now, Gem. You might be surprised," I say.

"I doubt it, *Dimples*." She rolls her eyes, and my heart skips a beat. "Not with the way Hunter and Ashlie maul each other every chance they get."

"You could stick with me: handsome and hands-off." I draw an *x* over my heart with a finger and flash her a smile.

Willa's eyes narrow. "Hard pass."

Ouch.

We stay like that, me smiling and her glaring at me for a few seconds, before her phone buzzes and steals her attention away. Willa acts like I bother the hell out of her most of the time, but I've always been enamored. She's beauty and brains, all wrapped up in an introverted high-security package. I've had this crush for years, which is a little embarrassing to admit at thirty-two. Pining isn't a habit of mine. I never hesitate to go for what I want in life, but she's in a class all her own.

"Don't waste your breath, Trev," Ashlie says. "Once she makes up her mind, it's a wrap."

Willa side-eyes her, and I bite my cheek to stifle the smirk creeping across my face. Willa's the epitome of snark, and it does things to me. I've asked Ashlie repeatedly if she's seeing someone, and the answer has been no for a while. According to Ashlie, the last guy fumbled Willa so badly, she's sworn off relationships completely. I don't know a lot about it, but I know one thing: if the time ever came where I could have a chance with Willa, I wouldn't let it slip through my fingers.

CHAPTER THREE

WILLA

The frequency of sound can kiss my entire ass. This iterating rattling from the oversized speakers sets my teeth on edge as I scan the outdoor venue, plotting my escape. I've done clubs and concerts before, but only when the stars align and my mood matches my mindset. A weekend music festival clearly meets neither of those requirements. It's too much. *I need to get the hell out of here.*

Smoke fills the air as the sweaty throng sways around me, high off their asses. The sustained baseline lulls them into a trance, while it sends me over the edge. Every single one of them has contributed to my decision to call it a night. I've been outside all day, and now that the sun is down, my body is screaming for solitude. My sole reason for coming to the San Diego Tunes Festival left the stage over an hour ago. I should have gone with her.

I've forced myself to power through to justify the gaping hole left in my Europe or Bust fund, but fuck all of that right now. The holidays are right around the corner. I'll make it back with the uptick in family photo sessions.

My lavender sundress, which seemed like a good outfit choice this morning, clings to the sweat trickling down my spine, touching me in all the wrong places. I'm ready to toss it in a fire and crawl into the sweatpants waiting for me in my room. As I peel the dress away from my lower back and smooth it around my hips, I'm jostled forward, and my eye twitches. This bitch-ass lothario has bumped me from behind three times, trying to get my attention. I'm about to go off, when a fourth bump solidifies my decision to head back to the hotel. That, and my growing headache from the weed wafting in the breeze. Trekking across the sandy beach in the dark is a small price to pay to get away from this chaos.

"Hey, I'm heading back." I turn to my sister, who's swaying to the repetitious droning like it's fixing her life.

She leans in to hear me, dewy amber skin glistening with sweat, and rolls her eyes. "I'm surprised you lasted this long. You want Hunter to walk you back?" She tilts her head to her spectacled fiancé, who taps away on his phone as he bobs his fresh fade to the beat.

"No, I'm good. You two have fun."

"You sure? Or I could text Trev. He'd *love* to walk you back..." Her eyes fall closed as she lets the music course through her, missing my scowl. Trevor started the day with us, but I haven't seen him in a few hours. His corny ass would walk me back in a heartbeat, that's for damn sure. I suspect he's had a misguided crush on me for years, based on his attempts at grade school teasing. He calls me *Jim* for fuck's sake, which I'll never understand. So I ignore it and him. I'm not interested in the do-gooder Eagle Scout type, no matter how nice he is to look at.

"I don't need a damn escort, Ash. I'll be fine. See you in the morning."

She cuts me with a glare mid-sway. "Miss me with that attitude, girl. I'm just looking out for you."

"I know. Sorry." I blow out a breath and grimace. "The noise is getting to me."

"It's called 'music.'" A smile creeps across her face, and I brace myself as she slips an arm around my waist, pulling me into the side hug she knows I'll hate. "Happy birthday, Wills."

She suggested we come to this festival for my birthday and lured me in with my favorite singer, Sienna Raine. Seeing her perform live was once-in-a-lifetime amazing, but this environment is the furthest thing from my scene. Crowds have a way of making me never want to leave my house again, and retreating to my quiet hotel room will be a welcome solitude. I'm ready to drown in peace and quiet.

Weaving through the horde, I breathe easier as I get farther from the speakers, but the low vibrations taunt me across the sand until I've almost reached the pavement. Only then do I look up at the stars and pause. *Breathe. Release the tension.* Kicking off my gladiator sandals, I let the gritty sand between my toes bring me back into my body. I don't know how long I stand there wiggling my feet, but a buzzing on my hip snaps me out of it. Reaching into my mini sling bag, I grab my phone.

Her wide-eyed face lights up my screen, and I laugh, despite myself. She's the most expressive baby I've ever seen, and I've seen a lot in the studio. But she's a tiny spitfire already, a girl after my own heart. I love her to bits. A FundsForMe banner slides right over her perfect wisps of brown hair.

Sam: $200 for the birthday girl. I know you didn't get your-self anything. Go wild and buy a week's worth of sweatpants ☺ 🤍. JK. Europe or bust!

I smile at his message because he's right—I didn't. Being a business owner himself, Sam knows how hard it is for me to spend money on myself. I like to put everything back into the studio, and that's part of the reason business has grown so much these last few years. That, and getting a few high-profile clients who leave me raving reviews and send constant referrals my way. Momentum is on the fast track, and I've given all I have to Framed Orchid. It's my baby. My home. I shoot off a text to Sam.

ME

Ah, so the "Plant Daddy" to "grey sweatpants" pipeline is real.

SAM

How about neither of those things.

ME

Aww, come on! You can don some grey sweatpants, stick a rose between your teeth, and gyrate to one of those viral TickTech dances. The ladies will love it!

SAM

Sounds scandalous, Will. That life is behind me. I'm more of a Mimosa pudica these days.

ME

Love Mimosas. I'm in.

SAM

Mimosa pudica: The Shy Plant

ME

Thanks for the gift, dork. Please don't send me a scaredy plant.

You're welcome, nerd. Try to have a little fun
out there, yeah? You deserve to let loose.

He's probably right about that too. Even though we live nine hours apart, Sam's always looking out for me. We've been friends since high school, never anything more. He's been there in the wings since I escaped to LA over a decade ago, offering support when my family refused. I wouldn't be where I am without him.

I look up at the star-smattered sky with a wistful smile, wishing I would have taken a quick trip to see him and Maci instead of paying to be miserable on the beach. My phone goes off again, and I look down, expecting another picture.

Happy Birthday, sweetheart.

Don't think I forgot...

My stomach drops. *Sweetheart.* This bastard is the only person who calls me that, and I haven't spoken to him in years. I'm ready to throw my phone in the ocean.

CLASSICAL MUSIC DRIFTS ACROSS THE HOTEL LOBBY from the piano bar. The serenity that washes over me halts my determined steps. I contemplate continuing to my room, but the lilting of the keys draws me in like a moth to a flame. It's calm and soothing, and after the chaos of the music festival, I could use some relaxed entertainment. I stand in the lobby, conflicted for several minutes while my dress chafes my underarms from the drying sweat.

After a quick shower, I'm sitting at the bar, drinking a Lemon

Drop martini that matches the sleeveless sundress I changed into. The dim warm lighting sets a sultry mood throughout the room, glinting off the liquor bottles lining the wall. Sighing, I take another sip. That text message rattled me more than I'd like to admit, but I try to let the alcohol convince me it didn't. Drinking in a bar by myself probably wasn't what Sam had in mind when he said to let loose, but what he doesn't know won't hurt him. Besides, it's *my* birthday. A little indulgence could be just what I need...

Okay, a lot of indulgence. The longer I sit, the more relaxed I feel, and one Lemon Drop turns into two. Classical music changes to sultry jazz. My scowl has shifted to a soft smile. This doesn't happen often, but I've been enjoying the music in the bar for a couple of hours now. I've worked too hard to get where I am in life, and I didn't do that by partying and drinking. I like schedules. Routines. And I prefer my *own* company to anyone else's. But tonight, I indulge.

The blue lighting on the stage illuminates the petite brunette singer who joined the pianist about an hour ago. I sway to the music, drink in hand, like I didn't just criticize every single person on the beach for doing the same.

"This seems more your style, Jim."

I'm bumped from the side, triggering the fury I've worked so hard to extinguish. I half expect it to be that dude from the beach, except no one but Trevor calls me that stupid-ass name. My head whips around right as he slides onto the high-back barstool next to me. Even with him sitting, I have to tip my head back to look at him. "Are you by yourself?" he asks. Nodding, I take another sip of my drink, stifling the groan in my throat. *Social butterflies make my damn head hurt.*

Trevor's my sister's friend, but I wouldn't call him mine. Not that he hasn't tried—he's friends with everyone. It probably bothers him that I don't consider him one, but he talks too much for my liking. And he's too nice. Like helping old ladies across the street and saving the world in a single bound with his glistening biceps nice. I don't care what anyone says, no one is that damn happy all the time. I'd hurt his feelings so fast.

Trevor's head falls to the side, those dimples sinking into his cheeks as he smiles. The familiar pang of annoyance doesn't hit my chest like I'm expecting. "Why are you sitting alone in a bar on your birthday, Jim?"

Spoke to soon. "Because I want to, *Dimples*," I say, flipping my twists behind me. His olive-green Henley complements his sepia skin, prominently displaying the nautical tattoo sleeve down his left arm. As much as I try not to, I salivate at the veins rippling through his muscular forearm when he slides his elbow onto the bar. *This is just biology.* An attractive man sits down next to you and your body reacts. It's normal. Evolutionary. And it doesn't mean a thing, no matter how much I want to climb him like a tree right now. "Why are *you* sitting alone in a bar on my birthday?"

He chuckles. "I'm not. I'm sitting with you."

"Again, I ask *why*?"

"I saw you when I walked in and thought I'd say *hi*." There's a fucking twinkle gleaming from his eyes like he jumped right off the silver screen to crowd my space at the bar. "So, hey, Willa. Happy birthday. How's it going?"

The rusted hair color works for him, and with those hazel eyes —accented by a thin scar through his right eyebrow—he's a towering Adonis with an auburn drop fade. The subtle waves don't hurt either. This man is fine, okay? I can't lie and say he's not. And that's the very logical reason I spill some of my drink when he winks at me. No sooner than the drops hit the bar top, he reaches for my napkin and wipes it up.

See? Too damn nice.

Batting a hand in the air, I turn back to my drink. "I'm good, Trevor. No need to worry about me. You can move along to someone more interesting. I'm just fine here by myself."

"What makes you think I want to talk to someone else?"

"Oh, please." I roll my eyes and take another sip of my drink, which must be going to my head, considering the words that fly out of my mouth. "Look, I know you have a crush or whatever, but trust me. I'm not your type. This place is crawling with the kind of women you like. There's no need to keep me company. I'm good."

"Type? I don't have a type."

"Yeah, *okay.*" The mocking in my voice oozes with sarcasm as I squint at him. He does, indeed, have a type. *Case in point: my sister.*

Goody-Two-Dimples keeps that friendly smile as he crosses his arms, and my eyes drop to his corded biceps. Most guys would be long gone by now, but he looks amused. "Since you think you know more about myself than I do, tell me. What does my type look like?"

"My sister, for starters..."

He lets out a good-natured belly laugh, as if that fact is illogical. "Pulling out one example of someone I went on a couple of dates with years ago hardly makes 'a type.' You always so quick with your assumptions?" He taps his fingers on the bar top as he watches me.

They might all be friends now, but Trevor dated Ashlie a couple of years ago, before she got together with Hunter. That's a whole other story in itself, but I guess he's technically right. They went on less than a handful of dates before deciding to stay friends. However, people are predictable, and dating patterns are easy to spot. Ash is short, slender, and perkier than a cup of morning coffee. It's safe to say that's who he goes for—my opposite. I'm taller than most men I meet, my thighs rub holes in every pair of jeans I own, and I polish the Fuck Off sign stamped on my forehead daily. Not that I particularly enjoy comparing myself to my sister, but when you grow up hearing everyone gush about all the things you're not, old habits die hard.

Clearing my throat, I reach for my glass. "I don't assume. I observe and assess. It's perfectly fine to have a type, Trevor. Everyone does."

"Oh?" His eyebrows arch over the amused glint in his eyes. "So what's yours, then?"

"Easy. Stuffy and pretentious, with just a smidge of condescension." I lift my drink to my lips. "Oh! And about a decade older than me." My last relationship flashes through my mind, and I grimace. Even after two years, I don't speak his name. He's a partner at one of the biggest law firms in LA and an entire asshole who I couldn't get enough of until it was too much. If mansplaining were a person, it'd be him. The one before him wasn't any better, being a hedge fund manager. Same brand, different flavor. I'm fully aware I have issues, but I'm working on them. It is what it is.

Trevor shrugs. "Well, I guess there's a first time for everything. I don't have a type."

Lips scrunched, I glare at him before scanning the room. *I don't have a type* is something you say when you want people to think you're open and accepting, but no one's really like that. Everyone has a type. I know I'm right about this, and I'm determined to prove it to him.

"Okay, her," I say, thumbing over to a woman who fits my previous description to a T. She's gorgeous. Petite, with a long, curly ponytail bobbing behind her as she chats excitedly to the people at her table.

He glances and tips a shoulder. "She's alright."

"*Alright*? She's an absolute smokeshow. You mean to tell me you wouldn't have made a beeline over to her if you saw her before you saw me?"

The tip of his tongue juts into the corner of his mouth as he studies me, nodding slowly. I've got him completely pegged, like I do with most people. He knows it, and so do I. "I saw her when I first walked in, Jim." Leaning in, he slides one of my twists over my shoulder and smooths it down my back with the rest. A disloyal shiver travels through me, but I trap the ensuing gasp behind my lips. "She's not the one who caught my attention tonight. You were..." The briefest flash of heat sparks in his eyes before he smiles that Boy Scout smile, and my smug resolve disintegrates like cotton candy.

I take a gulp from my glass and immediately choke on the last of my drink, unsure if the swirling in my head is from the liquor or the chiseled angles of his clean-shaven face. He chuckles as he sweeps my hair to the side and claps me on the back, leaving his hand on the bare cut-out of my dress while I catch my breath. My first instinct is to lean in to his warm touch, but an efficient hit of oxygen snaps me out of that. *Fickle-ass hormones.* "Your flirting won't work on me. I'm not that drunk."

Trevor laughs again and drops his hand to my lower back. My traitorous thighs clench, all but soothing the sudden pulsing between them while my body hijacks itself. All I can think about is the trail of lingering heat as tingles zing down to my toes.

"If you say so," he whispers in my ear. The smell of Christmas, all clove and citrus, lingers as he turns back to the bar, leaving me to deal with the throbbing between my legs. "So...what are we drinking tonight?"

"*We?*"

"Yeah. No one should drink alone on their birthday. What's in your glass?" He slides his hands over the bar top and damn it all to hell if I don't notice how big they are.

CHAPTER FOUR
TREVOR

My shoulder tension eases with each sip of this tart cocktail. I wasn't feeling the music festival, so I left early to shower off all the sand and sweat, hoping it would fix my attitude. It didn't. The news I got from work yesterday has clawed its way into my mind, putting a damper on the entire weekend. Finding out your cheating ex is working for your company again lands you two Lemon Drop martinis deep with a third in the wings. I'm not a big drinker, but this has just enough sweetness to go down easily, taking my mind off the curly haired tornado I have to deal with on Monday.

I'd wandered into the bar tonight as soon as I heard the jazz music, hoping the crooning performance on stage would wash away the bullshit from work. Finding the quiet brown-eyed goddess was just a bonus—one I quickly snatched up. When I saw her sitting alone at the bar on her birthday, I had to see what that was about.

"See. These are good, huh?" Willa asks.

"Not too bad. You've got pretty good taste."

"*Okay, Trevor,*" she scoffs, slapping her hand on mine and giving it a squeeze. She's had enough to drink that she talks to me uninhibited, her nervous rambling growing cuter by the second.

Willa's usually feisty as hell, so watching her reservations melt away puts a smile on my face. Her laugh shoots beams into my sour mood, threatening to light me all the way up inside. "Oh, shit! I'm holding your hand..." Her eyes flash as she whips her fingers to her chest, covering them up with the others like I'm trying to snatch her hand from her.

"See, I knew you liked me," I tease with a wink.

"Oh, please. You wouldn't be able to handle me, even if I did."

"Sounds like a challenge, Gem."

With a snort, Willa looks back toward the singer on stage. I've learned enough about her over the years to know there's more than meets the eye. I don't know what all of it is, but I can appreciate it. She doesn't like people in her business, and as open as I try to appear, neither do I. I'm selective. Everyone can think what they want while I move in silence and live my life. People have their ideas about me, and I let them.

Except for her. The punch to my gut after she made the comment about "my type" still chafes. *Comments...* She's actively trying to pawn me off on several women in this bar, almost like she's convincing herself she knows me better than I do. But all these women look the same, and none of them hold a candle to the one in front of me. She's focused on them, while I'm drooling over her confidence. Her drive. Her intelligence. Don't get me started on her thick thighs. I like powerful women, and right now, she's holding a helluva lot of it.

Willa's yellow dress clings to her deep amber skin—tight at the top, puckering in at her waist, and flowing over the swell of her hips. She gets better the more layers I peel back, and as amused as I was at the beginning of the night, I really think she has no idea of the effect she has on me. She's fucking amazing.

Crossing one long leg over the other, she takes another sip and turns to me. "I didn't take you as a picky one. And why are you being so quiet? You're always talking." She tosses her waist-length twists over her shoulder.

When I brushed that same shoulder earlier, her soft skin almost made me forget everything that had pissed me off yesterday. *Almost.* If I'm more reserved than usual, it's the anxious rancor rattling around in my stomach from learning the news about Marla. I had no idea she was even back in California. It's been four years, and I'm pissed that one glimpse of her in that conference room made me see red. Holding grudges isn't my thing, except for this one. I've tried to let it go, but the resentment still stands.

That's the only reason I accept the next drink the bartender slides my way. I thank him, and he throws me an icy glare, mumbling something that sounds a lot like "piss off" under his breath. He stomps across the floor in a huff, stopping to wipe up the scattered piles of sugar used to line the rim of our drinks. Murmuring something else I can't hear, he shakes his head, but the giggling beauty next to me steals my attention.

"I'm not picky. Or quiet." I laugh, sliding my gaze back to hers. She smiles, and I admire the curve of her cheekbone as I take another sip of my drink.

"I don't believe you."

"You don't have to." I shrug. "I'm just watching you have the time of your life comparing yourself to every other woman in this bar. I didn't want to interrupt."

"I'm not—"

"You're getting off on trying to hook me up, aren't you?" I tease.

Her eyes narrow. "Don't make this weird."

"You started it, sweetheart." I wink, loving every bit of her flustered banter.

"I'm not your sweet—"

"So let's say you *do* pick a lady for me tonight. You gonna tell me what I should do to her in bed too?"

Her mouth drops open, eyes wide.

Bold? Yes. But it's been a long-ass day, I'm feeling plucky, and her unfettered rambling is turning me on. It's like I'm arguing with a feisty, curvaceous encyclopedia. Leaning in, I whisper, "You can tell me, Willa. I know how much you like control..." I take a drink, hiding my smirk as confliction mars her disdain.

"I'm not comparing myself to anyone. Why would I do that?" The words tumble out as she tries to explain away the last hour. Her tongue darts to wet her lips, and all of my attention falls to her plump, kissable mouth.

A twitch in my boxers and just enough alcohol leads me to ask, "You want to be my type *so bad*, don't you?"

"I—no. Obviously not." She waves a hand in the air like she's unbothered, but drops her eyes to the black bar top. Her long, dainty fingers curve around the base of her glass, catapulting my imagination to those painted fingers tightening around me. "We both know I'm not your... I could never be—"

She gasps when I grab the leg of her stool and pull it closer, too stunned to move away as I lean in. The sweet coconut scent in her hair seizes my chest as I slide an arm across her back. Crowding her space gives me a hint of her desire and raw nerves, and it takes all the control I have left to resist slipping a kiss on her bare shoulder. "You don't need to compare yourself to them."

She shakes her head, keeping her eyes down. "I'm not..."

"Good." I curve my fingers around her chin—turning her head until she looks at me—and dip my head to hers. "You're timeless, Willa," I whisper. "There's no comparison."

An audible gulp rolls down her throat before her lips are on mine. I drop my hand around her waist to bring her closer, savoring the soft tug her teeth perform on my lower lip. My silly little crush is about to be pulverized into a million seeds of infatuation, all because of her velvety lips. She palms the back of my head, and we're all lemon and tongues as my heart beats out of control in my chest. She whimpers when I slide my hand up her thigh, and I'm about to invite her upstairs when she steals words right out of my mouth.

"Take me to your room," she whispers around my lips.

Nodding, I dig for my wallet, pulling away to slap some bills on the bar. She grabs her purse, gives me one flirty look over her shoulder, and saunters toward the exit. Stumbling over the stool with no logic to my name, I hurry to catch up to her, and we meet at the elevator. Once the door shuts, she closes the distance between us.

CHAPTER FIVE

TREVOR

I tap the fourth floor and whip Willa around, pulling her against me. She sucks in a hiss of air as my lips course down her neck.

"Shit, you're good at this," she muses. My surprised chuckle sends her lip between her teeth. *That was an inside thought.* It might be the first compliment she's ever given me. If this is how I go down in the history books, I'm about show her just how good I can be.

"Grab my shoulders." The words hardly leave my mouth before her arms circle my neck; legs wrapped around my waist. Her dress rides up as my hands skirt her thighs, grabbing a fistful of bare ass. *Fucking hell.* This goddamn woman is trying to kill me. A shameless moan rumbles from my chest when I crash into her soft lips, set adrift in a cloud of coconut and fantasies come to life. Her fingernails graze my scalp, and I pin her against the wall, dazed by my matchless desire to sink into her right here in the elevator. Then the doors slide open with a ding, and a poor housekeeper gets an eyeful.

Willa slides down my body and silently fixes her dress. I have to resist pulling her against me when she brushes the strain in my jeans. With our gazes locked, my thoughts move at warp speed as the awareness of who this is and what we're doing seeps through the haze. *I need to slow this down. She means more than this.*

But when the housekeeper steps out on the third floor and the doors close, Willa presses into me, sliding fingers over my shoulders as she guides me to her mouth. A jolt races down my spine, but that brief loss of contact sobered me just enough to slip a little sense back into my body. This is my friend's sister. A friend who I dated once upon a time. There aren't any lingering feelings there, but it still happened. *Do I bring it up?* I don't know what rules there are about this, but a conversation should probably be had, despite my hand wandering under her dress.

"Willa," I mumble as I pull back. "Uh—we're friends."

Her eyebrows dip as she licks her lips. "We're not friends, Trevor."

Damn.

The elevator dings, and I follow as she steps onto the fourth floor. Slipping my fingers around her wrist, I turn her to face me. "Okay, well, we're friend*ly*. And I'm friends with your sister, who I dated."

"Are you still hung up on her?" she asks, slapping a hand on her hip.

"No! Not at all. I just—aren't there rules against this? Ash isn't going to disown you?"

Willa laughs, and I'm confused. I'm really not trying to be responsible for another estrangement between the sisters.

"Oh, you're *serious*?" Her giggles simmer as she shakes her head, eyes wild with amusement. "You give yourself too much credit. I'm grown, and I don't need her permission to fuck a grown-ass man."

"Uh...okay. Fair enough. But we've been drinking..."

"I know exactly what going back to your room entails, and I asked you." She waves a hand between us. "I'm not drunk, Trevor. Are you?"

She has a point. This is the most clearheaded I've been all day.

The longer we stare, the more I want to pick her up and make a mess of her right here in the hallway. I shake my head slowly.

"Now, if you don't want to anymore, that's another story." Crossed arms settle over her chest, and she cocks a hip. "Are we doing this or not?"

I must take too long to answer, because she rolls her eyes and turns the opposite direction, reigniting my desire to feel her skin against mine. Grabbing her elbow, I pull her back, losing my mind at the devilish smirk on her face. I jerk her hips against mine, my dick jumping at the shiver that travels through her. "We're doing this," I whisper, stealing a kiss. It's been a hot minute since I've been with anyone, especially someone with this much moxie. Someone I want a chance with. *Don't fuck it up.* "I just want it to be known that I don't do thi—"

"I don't care." Swallowing the rest of my sentence with eager lips, she pushes me against the wall, claiming my tongue until she's had her fill. She lifts an expectant eyebrow, and I spin her around, grinding into her ass so she can feel what she's doing to me. The sexiest whimper eases from her lips as she throws a heated gaze over her shoulder. I grab her chin and kiss her hard, then propel her a few doors down to my room.

She whips her purse over her head and damn near climbs me like a tree as soon as we're inside, latching on like she did in the elevator. We clumsily fall on the mattress, a tangled mess of legs and arms, while we claw at each other's clothes.

"I don't do this," I murmur against her neck, nudging the strap of her dress down her shoulder as I straddle her. For whatever reason, I want her to know I don't drunkenly take women to bed like this. She needs to know she's special.

"You always talk so much?" She gasps on the last word when I grip her dimpled thigh and pull her slick heat against me.

"Usually," I say, nipping at her ear. "I just...don't do this..."

"You think I do? I barely leave my house." Her hands are at my zipper, and I can't tell if she's teasing me with how long she takes. Fingers brush against my dick, and I buck into her, letting out a moan. She giggles and touches me again, getting another rise out of me. "You wanna stop?" she asks.

"Not a chance." This playful side of her is driving me wild. I can't get enough, needing to taste every inch of her soft skin as my lips work across her collarbone.

She meets me with an eager kiss, abandoning my zipper as she clutches my hips. "Then shut up and get a condom, Trevor."

Yes ma'am. I hop off the bed, whip off my shirt, and dig into my bag. "You always this bossy?" I ask.

"Usually."

I tear into the foil as I step out of my jeans and boxers. When I turn around, she's propped on an elbow, her mouth hanging open.

"Shit. You're—"

"Extremely fucking happy you're in my bed right now? Yeah..." I take a step closer, amused by her widened eyes. "You wanna stop?" I tease.

"Hell no." The awe in her voice as she watches my dick bob is the ultimate confidence boost. I palm it, giving a few tugs as I strut toward the bed. She slowly licks her lips. "I shouldn't be surprised you're so..."

"Gifted?" I offer.

"That's to be determined."

Fucking kill me dead with that look in her eyes right now. She's already wrecking me, and I haven't even sunk into her yet. The skirt of her dress falls to her waist as her legs spread wide, bearing her glistening pussy to me. *Goddamn glistening.* I'm kneeling on the bed, rolling on protection faster than anything. Grasping behind her knees, I tug her toward me. Her gaze stays fixed on me the entire time, burning hotter as I tease her opening with my tip.

"Mmm, that's it." She sighs, eyes rolling back in pleasure. A sudden arch in her back makes her dress ripple around her waist as if it's begging to be ripped off. The visual is immaculate, but it stays on...for now. I grip her hips and find my rhythm, dropping kisses along her neck. Stroking inside of her feels so good I can't form thoughts, words, sounds. She said I talk too much, so keeping my mouth shut is for the best anyway. She moans in time with each thrust, clawing mementos into my back I hope never fade. "*Fuck*, yes…" Her legs cage my waist, and she pulls me against her. My head falls back in ecstasy as her pussy clamps around my dick, the urge to rut deeper at odds with the need to go fast and hard. Her warmth, her assertiveness, her skin against mine, it's all driving me crazy. But tapping on my shoulders brings my eyes back to hers.

"Why are you so quiet all of a sudden?" She huffs.

"You just said I was talking too much…"

"Yeah, well, now you're not talking enough. I'm starting to freak out."

I stop mid-thrust. "Willa—"

"No! Don't stop—just…talk." She rolls her hips in encouragement.

A smile quirks my lips. *This woman loves her some control*. I'm not opposed to giving it to her either, if that's what she actually wants. I'm not convinced it is though.

"Don't look at me like that. This isn't a control thing. Just talk…and move."

I pull out completely, hating myself a little for the guttural sigh she lets out. But the surprised yelp when I lift her and slide her over my lap more than makes up for it. She traps her lip between her teeth timidly but doesn't move. "Well, don't be shy now. Climb on, and go for a ride."

Raw lust flares in her gaze as she shifts to her knees, guiding herself back around me until sinking to the hilt. Her eyes fall closed, and when she finds her rhythm, she smiles. I fucking shatter on the inside. Willa, the dress, being inside her, it's all mind-blowing, but that smile is the cherry on top. Whatever spell she's been casting all night has officially wrecked me.

"That's it, beautiful. You take what you need from me." I rock with her, meeting her hips slowly with thrusts of my own.

Stars dance across my vision as she bounces on my dick. I'd close my eyes and get lost in her, except they're stuck on her hardened nipples cutting through the thin fabric of her dress. She's so fucking sexy right now, grinding her swollen clit into me for relief. Like a queen on a throne, making sounds I'll log in my memory bank for a rainy day.

Sliding my hands up her thick thighs until I'm gripping her waist is like a wet dream. I love the way she preens under my touch, caressing her own breasts while she rides out her pleasure. I could watch her do this all damn night. "You feel amazing, sweetheart. Don't hold back."

"*Don't* call me sweetheart." She leans forward, blessing me with a feverish kiss on my lips. I grip the back of her neck and drown in her, drifting straight into the rocks from this siren's addictive song. She's intoxicating, and I'm drunk on all that she is. "I'm gonna..." she breathes around my lips before tipping her forehead against mine.

"That's it, baby. Use me as long as you need. Lose control." She closes her eyes, her lips parted, pulling me closer to the edge with each moan. I have no doubt in my mind she took my words literally, completely losing herself as she rides me to completion. "Let go, Willa," I whisper in her ear. The series of shudders that roll through her as she cries out is a prize all its own. Gripping her hips, I piston into her, finishing just seconds after. There's a moment, mere seconds, where our eyes lock and the walls between us disappear. A silent acknowledgment that she needed this release as much as I did.

Her forehead rests against mine with a sigh, and she whispers, "I should probably go." But I'm still buried inside of her, and she doesn't seem in a rush to change that.

Stay. Give me tonight. "Is that what you want?"

"...It's what I *should* want."

I tighten my grasp on her hips. "Tell me what you really want, Willa."

Confliction clouds her expression as her stare dances with

mine. *Stay*. I don't dare say it, in fear that it'll run her off, but the word echoes in my mind. I need more of her. More than tonight. Her lips brush mine, whispering, "I want your tongue all over my body."

My dick springs back to life. "Lose the dress."

Sitting on her knees, she pulls her dress over her head, and I just admire the view for several seconds. I don't even blink, not wanting to miss a thing as I take in everything from those inquisitive brown eyes to the teeth holding onto her lower lip. The swell of her ample breasts, the soft curve of her belly, and the faint mocha stretch marks adorning her full hips—I can't stand it anymore and reach out to touch the jewel in her belly button.

"What are you waiting—?"

I flip her down on the bed, effectively stealing the words from her. "You always talk so much?" I tease, reaching between us and tossing the condom. A giggle slips from her lips when I nibble her ear, and I dive right into the coconut haze. "I'll get you there, but I need you to do something for me." She gasps, arching into me as I take my time kissing down her body. Sucking each perfect peak. Licking every delicious dip. I reach her thighs and breathe over her center, my mouth watering at the thought of devouring her. But I hold her there until she looks down at me with that sassy eyebrow raised. "Use my name when you say *please*."

Her eyes flash with desire, but just as quickly, she catches herself and sets her mouth in a scowl. We stare at each other for several seconds. If I'm right about her, she'll do it. "Please," she whispers.

I tilt my head. "Please, what?"

Her tongue swipes across her lips painfully slowly before her defenses fall and vulnerability seeps into her expression. "Please make me come on your tongue."

"That"—I tut, sliding a knuckle through her slit—"is not what I asked for." I circle her clit slowly, and her head drops back with a groan. I'm playing with fire now, but she's so elusive, I need to know if I've figured her out.

A heavy sigh later, she pins me with her stare, enunciating each word. "Please lick my pussy until I'm screaming your name, *Trevor*."

Goddamn, the mouth on her.

"Gladly." I grip her hips and pull her to me, relishing in her taste as if she's a long drink after a scorching day. She squirms under my tongue, her moans growing louder as she claws at my head. Reckless abandon, at the mercy of my mouth. *I knew it.*

As much as she might pretend to, Willa doesn't like being in control. She craves the freedom of letting go, and I'll gladly give it to her.

ME

Can we talk about last night?

WILLA

That defeats the purpose of a one-night stand...

We don't need to talk about anything. It happened, and we can forget about it.

ME

Please? Over breakfast?

WILLA

I'm already headed back to LA. Really Trevor, don't worry about it. We're good.

CHAPTER SIX
WILLA

My phone dings right as I decide to lock it inside my computer desk. Emily and I are the only ones in the studio this morning, so I can't even blame my employees for my distraction today. Ironclad focus at work is a superpower I pride myself on, but everything has been stealing my attention. I take another impulsive peek at the screen as I turn off the sound. Passport Application Received sits at the top of my inbox, sending a flurry of excitement through me. *I'm actually doing it.* This dream of photographing my way through Europe is really happening. *All thanks to Trevor...*

His stupid smile flashes in my head, and I sneer. I'll never admit it out loud, but I've been working toward this trip ever since he told me to "let it go" at Crystal Beach a few years ago. He planted the seed, and he was righ—*Whatthefuck?*

I set my phone on my desk for the umpteenth time, pushing it away for good measure. It's hazardous to my mental health, *clearly*. Never in my life have I thought about that man so much. *Maybe I'm getting sick.*

My phone buzzes again, and it's in my hands before I realize it.

ASH

Spook Fest tickets just went on sale.

ME

What does that have to do with me?

ASH

Commmme withhhh ussssss! It'll be fun.

Fun like a punch in the ovary, maybe. I think I've officially reached the age where staying my ass at home is more appealing than noise and nonsense. *And one-night stands...*

Goddammit it. I press my lips together as if I wasn't just biting the lower one. It does nothing to stop the memory of Trevor's tongue mapping my body. Doesn't erase the warmth of his hands eclipsing my thighs like I'm some dainty maiden. Won't undo the shudder traveling down my spine at the thought of him whispering in my ear—*Ugh. Let it fucking go!*

It's been weeks since I lost my mind in San Diego, and those fucking dimples have been a prominent part of my dreams ever since. I wasted three full days trying to get back into my routine after that night. It's pissing me off that I *still* can't control my thoughts. Maybe it's guilt from blowing him off the morning after, or maybe I was lonelier than I realized. Either way, I'm sick of the reminder that I let myself get out of control. Too much followed me home from that trip, including the sand I keep finding in my house. Lesson learned. It won't happen again.

ME

I'd rather scoot my bare ass over every cactus in Death Valley.

ASH

😒 You're too young to be this grumpy.
Speaking of...

Mom wants to know if you're coming for Thanksgiving.

ME
Ooh, totally!

ASH
Really?!

ME
HELL NO.

ASH
Please, Wills? It might be different this year.

ME
Golden Child says what?

ASH
😔 Don't call me that…

Despite the three-year age gap, it's always been clear my younger sister is the preferred child. Even our names scream favoritism. Ashlie got the cutesy, popular moniker, while I was saddled with the drab *Wilhelmina*. My parents claim it's a namesake from some distant grand relative—that I should be proud—but I don't give two shits. No one gives a child this name unless she's expected to be holed up in a library with no social life.

Enter me: the shy, chubby genius. Our parents focused on my path to the Ivy Leagues, while remaining adamant about clearing all possible obstacles in my sister's path. If she even looked like she would struggle, they jumped to her aid. But that's not Ashlie's fault; she's had her own issues with them. I'm just in a weird mood.

Sighing, I shoot off an apology and stick my phone in my desk. That's my whole reason for this vacation to Europe. I'm pent up and making bad decisions because of it. Doing something just for me is long overdue. I've started talking with potential guest photographers for the studio, and already gave a heads-up to TAILA. Once I replace the money used for the festival, I'll be ready to pick a date and find accommodations. It'll be a trip of a lifetime.

"Ms. Willa, can I have some chocolate now?" five-year-old Maddie Johnson asks. She's been eyeing the candy bowl since she came in. Between her afro puffs and the black and purple tutu, I can't decide which is cuter. The Johnson family has been coming to me since before she was born. They're always the first to schedule a Halloween session, so I've gotten to see each one of her adorable costumes through the years.

"Let's make sure it's okay with your mom first."

"Mommy, *please*! I smiled in every single picture."

She did. Even the serious ones feature a toothless vampire-ballerina grin—much different from her usual pout.

Mrs. Johnson nods while her husband chats with my assistant. I slide the candy bowl over, laughing at the elated jumps exploding out of Maddie. Even as an infant, she was full of sass and attitude. It's always been in the back of my mind that if I ever had a little girl, she'd be exactly the same.

"I'll get the sneak peeks back in forty-eight hours, but I just have to show you this one. It's too cute," I say, whipping the camera strap over my head. As soon as I turn the screen toward Shawna Johnson, she covers a cackle. Maddie took my direction to be "fierce" and went fully vogue.

"She's obsessed with that new modeling show on NetVids. I keep finding my makeup in her backpack."

"Ooh! She. Is. Ready." I snap my fingers with each word, *Z* formation.

"And then some! Thanks, Willa. We'll be back for our Christmas card."

They walk to their car, and my heart nearly explodes when the chocolate-covered kiddo turns and waves at me. I wave back with a smile and head to my desk to edit.

October is officially the start of my holiday family photoshoots, and all the toddlers zooming around my little studio today have been shredding my ovaries. Watching them grow into their personalities is a bonus that makes my heart squeeze. The missing teeth, the squeals of happiness, and even the puppy dog eyes when they find my candy bowl make for a fun and rewarding work experience.

Walking back to my desk, I can't help but feel proud. Life is exactly how I dreamed it would be. My client following is steadily growing. I have employees I can trust. I'm even planning on advancing Cara to a lead photographer position when I go to Europe. There's nothing I would change about any part of my life right now, but a break probably should've happened a while ago. I'm comfortable, and now it's time for me to give over some responsibilities after doing it all for the last several years.

Scrolling through the RAW files from the Kimball's shoot has my eyes misty. *What the hell?* This is the fifth time today where emotion has tried to leak down my face. I'm no crier, no matter how attached I get to my clients. I'd blame PMS, but I just had my period a week ago. Maybe getting older is turning me into a sap. You get a minute over thirty-one and everything in your body goes haywire. *Another sign I need a break.*

My stomach growls as I open my photo editing program. Since my bookings have been back-to-back this afternoon, I've eaten nothing except for a granola bar on my drive to work. I just want to get these sneak peeks ready, and then I'll dig the peanut butter crackers out of my bag.

"Hey, Willa, what's $92.56 times three?" Emily asks from the front desk.

"$277.68," I mumble around the stylus hanging out of my mouth.

"Thanks. And what's $143.00 divided by seven?"

"$20.43, rounded up to the nearest penny."

"Cool. And $26.50 plus—"

"Emily, find a calculator." I reach for my stainless-steel water bottle, and even though I just filled it up, the water tastes tinny already.

"You're faster than a calculator, though."

"But I pay *you* to use a calculator. I've had to fiddle with the saturation three times on this photo because of you." I shake my head like she's the reason I've been distracted all day. *Why's it so hot in here?*

"You're, like, a genius though. I'm trying to work smarter, not harder."

Rolling my eyes, I focus back on the screen in front of me. She's not wrong. I taught myself to read by age three and surpassed everyone in my gifted classes by second grade. But I didn't speak much as a child. I'd rather click through grainy photos on the old slide projector or read classic novels than play outside. *Moby Dick* was less frustrating than making friends. My parents were fine with anything that kept me out of their way, so they didn't see any issues back then. I learned to hide most of my social problems by leaning into bluntness and sarcasm by the time I reached middle school, but my parents still expected me to play the "studious older daughter" role.

When we moved from Vegas to Fort Bender, I was the perfect overachiever with a 4.3 GPA. I was a polyglot on the fast track to pre-med during high school. The only parent-approved extracurriculars were college courses and accounting club. In their eyes, books and straight *A*'s were the only companions I needed. But when it came time to apply to universities, I couldn't do it. It wasn't what I wanted for myself. Everything I'd worked so hard to achieve was my parents' dream. When I gave it all up, they insisted I was throwing my life away and refused to support me in it. They still don't. But even after a decade long estrangement, I regret nothing. I'll take studio time over organic chemistry any day of the week.

"Is it hot in here?" I ask, more to myself than to Emily. The AC is running, but I'm still dripping sweat under my arms. My heart's beating a little fast too. I pull at the collar of my dress repeatedly, trying to fan my face. Maybe I'm catching that flu that's been going around. One downside of working with young families, they bring chubby cheeks and all their little germs.

"Nope. Thermostat's where it usually is."

My stomach rumbles, clearly missing the memo that I have more important things to worry about. I ignore it, checking the time on the digital wall clock. *Thirty minutes until my last family.* Another swig from my water makes me gag, so I set it on the far edge of my desk while working the metal taste out of my mouth.

Edits, Willa. EDITS.

Shifting my attention back to my computer, I get as far as selecting the next file before my stomach gurgles. My thoughts drift to what food could possibly be in the fridge in the back, which reminds me the Craft family requested a smoky effect in their pictures. I'll need to have Emily grab the dry ice out of the freezer a little before they get—*Why can't I fucking focus?*

The sheer volume of my stomach's revolt gets me out of my chair. Fine. Whatever. Just a quick snack. *And then edits.* I take a step toward the front desk for my bag when black spots dance across my vision. Swaying briefly, I grab the back of my chair, blinking a few times to clear the haze. When I try to take another step, my head squeezes tightly, and I reach for my temples.

"You okay, Boss Lady?"

"I—yeah. I'm just dizzy, and I—"

My knees give out, and I crumple to the floor. The last thing I hear is Emily yelling my name and something clattering to the tiles.

CHAPTER SEVEN
WILLA

A bright light in my eyes wakes me, and Ashlie's voice whispers with Emily's. I blink to see a couple of paramedics, in addition to the one blinding me.

"Hey, Willa," the paramedic says. "Just lie here for a few minutes. When's the last time you ate something?"

"Uh, this morning." The blood pressure cuff on my right arm squeezes uncomfortably until a slow hiss of air eases out. I focus on the woman, lingering on her cornrows secured in a bun at the top of her head. Her name tag reads M. J. Thomas.

"Your blood pressure's a little low. I'll help you sit, then I want you to sip on something sweet." M. J. calls over her shoulder, "I don't think we need to take her in the rig, but I want her to be seen ASAP." She helps me into a sitting position and types on a tablet.

My eyes sweep around my small studio—the lavender walls, the black and orange Halloween backdrop in the back, my tidy workspace in the corner. Everything looks like it did before, aside from the four extra people. Emily is talking with another paramedic at the counter now, sliding worried glances at me every few seconds. I suddenly remember my last clients of the day and crane my neck to see the clock. My heart pounds in my chest as I try to stand. They'll be here any minute, and I still need to adjust my lighting and filters.

"No, girl." Ashlie comes toward me, carrying a can of orange soda and wearing her red director polo for the swim center. "Sit back down. Emily took care of everything. Your clients have been rescheduled. Just relax." She squats and hands me the drink.

"What are you doing here?"

"Didn't you write the employee handbook? Emily followed protocol and called your emergency contact." Her eyes scan over me, eyebrows dipping with worry. "Good thing I'm just down the street. I beat the paramedics here. Why aren't you eating, Wills?"

"I got caught up in editing." I pop the tab and take a drink. It's cold and fizzy but isn't sweet. "And I haven't really been feeling well all day. I think it's the flu." The next sip tastes like ass-tainted soap, and I scrunch my face. "Here, taste this." I stick the can under her nose.

"Nuh-uh!" She juts her head back as she pushes the can away. "You're not giving me the flu... What's wrong with it?"

"It tastes like soap. And smells like sewage."

Her lips scrunch, skepticism falling over her face. "I'm gonna take your word for it. Let's get you to the doctor."

M. J. and Ashlie help me stand, my vision fluttering as soon as I'm up. They hold me steady until the room settles, and I turn toward my desk to gather my things.

"Nope. Doctor." Ashlie pulls me toward the door. "Emily will bring all your stuff to you tonight."

"Ash, just let me transfer some files to my tab—"

"No, Willa! You just passed out on the floor. Get in the damn car."

I whip my head back to my sister. Her playful sass is gone, replaced by a furrow between her eyes and a hard set to her jaw. Ashlie and I have been rebuilding our relationship over the last few years. We've gotten to a good place for the most part, but when we disagree, heads roll. Right now, though, with that look in her eyes, I think she'll drag me to the car kicking and screaming if I try to challenge her. And with the way I'm feeling, she's likely to whoop my ass despite the five inches I have on her.

"Yeah, okay. Just let me grab my ba—"

"Already got it, girl. Come on."

"I JUST DON'T GET WHY THEY MADE ME PEE IN A CUP. Watch, they'll come back in and tell me it's all in my head and ask if I've thought about losing weight." The rough paper crinkles underneath my legs as I shift on the rigid exam table. I'm comfortable with my curves, but doctors never find it funny when I tell them *thick thighs save lives*. No matter the illness, a woman can't have any other ailments as long as she carries a little weight.

"They make everyone pee in a cup, Wills." Ashlie doesn't even look up from the magazine she's flipping through while she chides me. She's used to my ranting by now, but I can't let it go.

"Not everyone. Every *woman*. And I told the nurse I just had my period."

"Okay, girl. You march out there and tell the doctor how to do her job. I'll wait right here." Her head falls to the side, but that teasing look is back in her eyes.

"I'm just *saying*, doctors always think a woman is pregnant or fat. She can't possibly have any other health problems. I didn't eat enough today. Might be getting sick. I'm fine."

"Whew. You're fun when you get hangry. Here." She hands me the crackers from my bag, and my mouth waters. "Eat these and calm your ass down."

A quick double tap on the door after it opens is the only warning we have before the doctor comes in. *Why even knock if you've already opened the door? What if I was changing in here? What kind of hospitality is that?* You knock, and you wait for someone to say they're ready before you come in.

The tall Asian woman with graying hair slides the glasses from the top of her head and sets them on her nose. "Hello... Willa Willis?"

"Hi. What's the point of knocking?"

"Willa!" Ashlie gasps, wide-eyed. "Sorry about her, doctor. The flu has clearly made her lose her mind..."

The doctor laughs, shaking her head. "Don't worry about it. Moodiness comes with the territory. I'm Dr. Clifford. Are you comfortable discussing your results with your..." She gestures to Ashlie.

"Sister." I nod, my face twisting quizzically. "Yeah, it's fine."

"Well, in that case, your flu should resolve in about nine months. Congratulations!" She hugs the clipboard to her chest, bouncing on her feet like she's proud of her nonsensical diagnosis.

"What kind of flu is that?" I ask, glancing at Ashlie and back. Her mouth has dropped open as she stares at the doctor. It takes me a couple more seconds before it hits me.

Dr. Clifford tilts her head slightly. "You're—"

"Pregnant? No." I scoff, batting away the completely ridiculous notion with a shake of my head. "I'm not." My eyes search the doctor's face for the joke. Ashlie put her up to this or something.

"Yep. It explains the fainting and your lowered blood pressure. Have you had any cravings? Weird tasting food?"

"No, because I'm not—"

"Earlier she said her soda tasted like soap," Ashlie says. I shoot her a wide-eyed threat. *Narc.*

"Ah, yeah, that can happen as hormones change. Cravings, altered taste, aversions. It's all very normal for early pregnancy."

"I'm not pregnant. I just had my period a week ago."

"Mm-hmm, and was it lighter than usual?"

"I—yes..."

"How long did it last?"

"Just a couple of days. But my periods are always short." My voice lowers each time I open my mouth with a rebuttal. The checkered vinyl flooring blurs as my eyes rove, searching for the logical response I'm supposed to have. None of this makes any sense, and yet, it's crystal clear.

"That's all perfectly normal. Egg implantation can cause bleeding. Do you have an established OBGYN?"

My eyes lock onto my sister, whose face has gone pallid as she stares back at me. Hands shaking, I nod numbly at the doctor.

"Great! Follow up with your provider. They usually want you to wait until you're eight to ten weeks along. Do you know when conception would have been?"

"Yes," I whisper. I know exactly when. My birthday, after a night of unforgettable dick. I've tried to push all memories of that spontaneous night out of my head, as well as the man responsible for them. That's how a one-night stand is supposed to go. You have an out-of-character, earthquaking, body trembling experience, and leave it there. Trevor's the only man I've been with in months. He's the only one it could be, and now, he's responsible for so much more than memories.

"Good. I'll let you gather your things. Just check out at the front desk when you're ready. And congratulations, mama!" The doctor closes the door, leaving me shocked and petrified as the weight of her words settles in around me. *Mama? No.* That title has no place in this room. Mama is a woman back home, who's disappointed in everything I do. Mama is critical and callous. Mama is the only example I have of motherhood, and I don't want to be anything like her.

I'm still clutching the bag of crackers, now pulverized from my grip as I tremble on the paper-topped table. My eyes track the cracks on the floor tiles. I almost forget I'm not alone when Ashlie touches my arm.

"Wills, is it Carter's?"

"Huh?"

"Carter. Is he the...?"

A tear falls down my cheek as I shake my head. And then another. My breath hitches in my throat several times. I can't control it, nor the pressure in my chest squeezing tighter by the second. *Me, pregnant?* This can't be happening. I drop the crackers and knock my phone off the exam table, trying to catch them. *A solo trip to Europe.* That's what I'm supposed to be planning for right now. Just me, my camera, and the breathtaking views overseas.

And now, a baby.

I look at my sister with wide eyes, and she smooths her hand down my back, saying something I can't hear. My stomach heaves. The buzzing in my ears grows with the need to run and hide, but my body is trapped in place.

"Willa, hey. You're panicking. Look at me." She boxes my head in her hands, forcing me to look into her eyes. "Just breathe. Follow me. In through the nose. Out through the mouth...again. In...out. Good." The calm in her stare is my only lifeline right now. I don't dare look away. She pulls me off the table and leads me to the sink. Cold water flows over my fingers when she plunges them under the stream. The room finally eases back into focus, but she keeps my hands underwater until my breathing slows.

Pregnant? With a baby?

Water flings in the air as I turn and cling to her, violent sobs racking my body.

"Hey, you're okay. It's okay." She rubs my back, wrapping her comfort around me while I process how this could have happened. *We were safe. We used protection. This shouldn't be happening.* I'm supposed to be saving for a once-in-a-lifetime excursion through Europe, not diapers and wipes.

Ashlie doesn't pull away until I do, and even then, she keeps her hands on my shoulders. It only takes a few minutes for the tears to stop, but I still feel like I want to throw up. Because I'm *fucking* pregnant.

"Do you know who the—"

"Trevor." I glance at her, then the floor after I see the shock on her face.

"How dare you?" she whispers.

"Excuse me?" I scoff, pushing away to snatch my phone off the ground. "You have an entire fiancé. Why do you care?"

"I'm not mad about *that*! Marry him for all I care. But how could you not tell me, Wills? We're sisters."

Taking a deep breath, I look up at the garish fluorescent tube lighting. "I don't know. We were drinking, it was my birthday, and I just wanted to let loose for once. It wasn't supposed to follow me out of San Diego."

"Didn't you use a condom?"

"We did, but I guess it broke..."

"Was it good? Do you like him?" Ashlie gasps and steps toward me. "Are you even going to keep the baby?"

"Of course I'm keeping the baby, Ash. Even if I have to do it on my own." As shocking as this news is, I have no question in my mind about that. I've always thought I'd be a mom someday, I just thought it would involve a syringe and donor number 752. Figured I'd raise a child like I do everything else, on my own. I never imagined the other half of the equation being in the picture.

"You have to tell him, Willa..."

I know this. He wanted to talk the morning after but I blew him off, mostly from embarrassment. Not that I regret our tryst; I don't. I'm adult enough to acknowledge I enjoyed everything we did that night. But morning has a way of putting things into perspective. I didn't want to make something out of nothing. Now though, it's a gigantic something that I absolutely need to talk to him about. It wouldn't be right to keep this from him.

"You won't have to do it on your own, you know? Trevor won't let that happen."

"You think I don't know that?" I snap.

Her eyes narrow as she sucks her teeth. "I'm blaming the attitude on hormones, but don't think I won't go off on you, Wills. You're not *that* pregnant."

"Ugh, I'm sorry," I say, my face falling into my hands. She's right about Trevor. In the years I've known him, he's always the first to jump in and help. As soon as I tell him, he'll be all in. The perfect partner to lean on. But leaning on him—on anyone— that's the part that has me terrified.

CHAPTER EIGHT

TREVOR

Frustrated doesn't begin to cover the pent-up agitation I've been ignoring for weeks. Willa made it perfectly clear she wasn't interested in anything else after our night together. What choice do I have, other than moving on? Going through the motions—out with friends, random dates from the MeetCute app, the gym—whatever keeps me busy, really. This is my new normal for the time being. My head isn't in it, but sitting alone in my quiet apartment has never been good for my mind. Neither has wallowing in self-pity. I'll be alright as soon as I figure out how to get over someone who was never really mine to begin with. A mirage I can't seem to shake. Needless to say, I'll be spending the evening throwing weights around the gym after work.

My sister's name pops up on the screen as my phone skitters across my desk, snapping me back to the handful of incorrectly submitted proposals on my computer screen. I rub the headache forming behind my eyes and sigh. I'll call Maya back after I fix up this document.

This report has enough errors to warrant a team intensive on corporate expectations. *Again.* Tech sales generally has a high turnover rate, but with the way Chase and I run things, our associates advance to higher positions instead of leaving the company. It's a good ego boost, except for cohorts like this one where most of our associates are brand new to the industry. After seven years, I forget how much of a learning curve there is. But training comes with the territory as a manager, and despite all the tedium in the beginning, the teaching aspect is one of my favorite parts of this job. They'll catch on eventually; I just need to pick up the slack until then.

I duplicate the document to use as a nonexample, polish up the inaccuracies, and submit the corrected form for processing. A text buzzes through as I stretch the muscles in my neck and shoulders, leaning back in my leather office chair. Friday afternoons at EdTechU are pretty slow, and it's close enough to the end of the workday that I feel the fight against procrastination leave as I pick up my phone.

BIG SIS

Answer your phone, T.

ME

So you can guilt me into coming home for Thanksgiving? Not gonna happen.

BIG SIS

Come on. You could surprise Mom. She'll do that Jazz Hands squealing thing when she cries. Pure entertainment.

ME

I'm sure she can save the Jazz Hands for Christmas…

BIG SIS

I'm gonna put Hazel on a video chat with puppy dog eyes.

ME

Not gonna work…this time.

A video call pops up on my screen, and I instantly smile at the picture of my sister dressed in pink scrubs, hugging my niece. She *would* pull out the big guns to get me home to Nebraska twice this year. Maya is an OBGYN back home. Why she opened her practice in that hellhole is beyond me, but she's doing well for herself. My thumb hovers over the video icon, but a knock on my open office door stops me from answering.

"She's pregnant, man." Chase smiles from the doorway, his blue eyes glinting as he struts across the room. His navy EdTechU polo and khakis match mine.

"Who? Kayla?"

"Yeah. We found out last night." He runs his hand through his dark blond hair and blows out a breath. "It still doesn't feel real." The cheesy grin stretched across his face almost hides the tired lines around his eyes. "I was up all night stressing out."

"Bro, that's amazing!" I abandon my phone on the desk and pull him into a hug. He and his wife have been together for so long, this next step doesn't surprise me at all. "Congratulations. How's she feeling?"

"She's grouchy as hell." He grimaces, but it only lasts a second before the smile overtakes his face again. Kayla doesn't play around as it is. I imagine pregnancy hormones will amplify her Type A tendencies, but Chase is built for fatherhood. He'll rock at it. "I need to skip poker night tomorrow."

"I doubt that'll be a problem." I chuckle when he flips me off. Chase and I have a weekly game night with some of my buddies from the Coast Guard. His poker face is as horrible as his strategy. "How far along is she?" I ask.

"Eh, not too sure. Her first appointment isn't for a couple of weeks. We're not really sharing the news yet, but she wanted me to ask if you could get some prenatal recs from your sister."

"Bet. I'll shoot her a text right now." Grabbing my phone off the desk, I type out the message and slip it in my pocket. "And I'll keep it to myself."

"Thanks, man." Chase slumps into the seat in front of my desk. "You, uh, checked your email?"

Shaking my head, I move back to my computer and tap the keyboard, scanning over my inbox once the screen lights up. My stomach drops as soon as I click the corporate newsletter and see the rosy-cheeked menace in all her glory—my worst nightmare. *My ex: the company's newest training supervisor.* I tip my head back with a groan.

"Explains why she was in the building a few weeks ago..." Chase drums his fingers on his leg, flashing his teeth in a nervous grin. "She'll be around."

He had a front-row seat to that entire relationship and its demise. Helped me deal with the fallout too. *My hell*, what an evolving shit show this is turning into. The woman is destructive. "I'll deal with her when I have to, as little as possible."

"She's overseeing flex trainers too..."

Fucking fantastic. I've been considering moving to a corporate trainer position for a while now. I love traveling, and being on the road most of the week soothes that wanderlust. Ever since me and Chase were first invited to teach our sales methods at the LA office a few years ago, I've enjoyed getting my feet wet in a trainer roll. We run such a well-oiled machine here, but flex would be perfect for me. With Marla in charge, I'm not sure I want it anymore.

Scrubbing my face with both hands, I groan again. As I sit up in my chair, someone clears their throat from the hall. Chase looks over his shoulder right as I shift my eyes to the doorway, and there she is—Willa—wringing her hands together. Her waist-length twists are flecked with golden brown, just like the last time I saw her. Those soft lips I've been dreaming about are smashed into a line so tight they're pale. A black leather jacket hugs around her mustard yellow turtleneck, and an olive-green skirt outlines the curve of her hips down to her knees. She's stunning, despite the tension in her face. I'm dying to talk to her, but I don't move, afraid the mirage will dissolve into the ether.

"Hey, Willa! What are you doing here?" Chase doesn't miss a beat, walking across the room and pulling her into a hug. He knows about the night in San Diego. She wouldn't talk to me after, and I needed someone to confide in. He won't say anything though, except maybe to Kayla. But she won't say anything either.

Willa's rigid as stone in Chase's embrace, just staring at me. *How do I start this conversation?* The morning after a one-night stand is one thing; I barely knew what I wanted to say then. Add in several weeks and way too much overthinking, and I have no idea how this is supposed to go. An apology would be a good start, I think. There's not a regretful bone in my body about our time together, but I don't have hotel flings. I should have had the balls to ask her out before sleeping with her. She deserved more. I need her to understand that, but the words are stuck in my throat. So she stares, and I stare right back.

"I...shouldn't have come." Willa shakes her head, turns on her heel, and hurries down the hallway. I'm out of my seat as soon as I realize she's taking off. She came all this way to San Francisco—to *my* office—to see me. It's clear she's ready to talk about that night. Pushing past Chase, I spot Willa at the elevator and jog the short distance to catch her. The doors slide open as I'm reaching out toward her, and she scurries inside, pressing the *close* button frantically.

"Willa, wait! Please, don't leave." I slip my hand between them, triggering the sensor to keep them from closing.

"You're working. I shouldn't have come here like this."

The elevator beeps angrily as I stand between the doors, prompting me to take a step forward and let them shut behind me. Being back in an elevator with Willa sets my thoughts swirling with memories of the last time we were in one together. I swallow the thick lump clustering in my throat and take a step toward her. Her back presses against the wall as she looks down at the floor. "I don't know why I came here. This can wait. You're at work."

"It's fine," I say with a smile. "I can take a break. Don't worry about it..."

The elevator settles on the main floor, and she slides past me so fast my head spins. Her brisk walk to the revolving doors sends me jogging after her again, catching up in a few steps. "No," she says over her shoulder, determined to make it outside. "W-we can talk later. It's fine. I'm sorr—"

"Willa." I grab her elbow right before she reaches the doors. "Don't apologize. I can take a break. Just...come back up so we can talk." She turns, looking right into my eyes. Whatever that emotion is on her face claws at my heart. She looks terrified, near tears, and I do the first thing I think of—wrap her in my arms.

I don't think she's much of a hugger. She tries to pull away at first, but I hold her to me anyway, and eventually, she hugs my waist. Her body shakes as she trembles against me, her tears soaking through my polo shirt. "Shh, it's okay. I've been wanting to talk to you too. I told you I don't do stuff like that. It's been eating me up inside, thinking you hate me for what happened."

She pulls away, shaking her head. "No, this isn't..." Taking a swipe at her face, she steps back and jams her hands into her jacket pockets. "Trevor, I'm pregnant."

Huh?

She's standing in front of me, but steadily being pulled farther away as the bustling lobby fades to fuzz around me. Her lips are moving, and yet, I hear nothing besides the echo of the last word she said. *Pregnant?* I scan her entire face, blinking rapidly when I don't find an ounce of humor. My stomach drops, the taste of bile rising in my throat.

It's not until she snaps in my face a few times that I'm transported back to the lobby. "Did you hear me?"

My hands shake as I take a deep breath. "Y-you're...and I'm the...?"

"Yeah, Trevor. You think I'd come all the way to San Francisco if it wasn't yours? You're the only one it could be."

"But how? We used a c—"

"Condoms break. Leak. Microtears. I don't fucking know. They're only, like, 98 percent effective. It happens." Her snappy attitude is a quick switch from the sobbing she was doing seconds ago, but I'm still stuck on the pregnancy part. We were careful. We did everything right. Looking into her eyes, the only thoughts rolling through my mind are all the improbabilities. I believe her completely, but the chances are so minuscule, I just need a minute. My hand finds hers, and I dazedly pull her off to the side. I don't realize I'm holding onto her so tightly until she tugs her hand away and shakes it. "We can take a DNA test."

"For what?" The stupid question slips from my lips before I can filter the thought.

"A random woman says she's pregnant with your baby, and you don't want a test?"

"From a random woman? Yeah." I turn to her. "But you're not one."

"Yeah, *okay*." She scoffs.

"Willa, I've seen the kind of person you are. You're blatantly honest. If you say the baby's mine, I believe you."

"I..." Her jaw hinges as if she's waiting for words to fall out on their own, then her eyes drop to her lap. "I really need to pee."

"Yeah. Yep." I shake my head to knock the last few tendrils of shock out of my system and place my hand on her back as I guide her to the restroom. Waiting on the bench outside the door, I try to make sense of my rapid thoughts. *Willa's pregnant. I'm the reason she's pregnant. It's my fault. I'm responsible for ruining her life. Shit. She must hate me for it. I need to make this right. There's no way in hell I'm letting her deal with this alone. I have to figure out how to make it as easy as possible for her, how to care for her. I need to—*

Willa steps out and sits next to me, not attempting to say anything else. It only takes one sideways glance at her curled-in frame before I'm on my feet. "Let me grab my things. I'll be five minutes, and then we can go talk. Please, don't leave."

I wait for her to nod and take off for the stairwell, checking over my shoulder when I get there before jetting up to the second floor. I just need to move, do something with the energy coursing through me. Willa's pregnant. I'm the father. We have things to figure out, but I need her to know she's not alone in this.

CHAPTER NINE
WILLA

The drive to Trevor's apartment is quiet. Nope, worse. *Silent.* He turned the radio off in his SUV as soon as he slid in the driver's seat, and neither of us have said a word. *How do you open Pandora's box when it should have stayed hidden on the shelf?* Once he pulls into the parking garage and cuts the engine, we inhale simultaneously.

I haven't been able to look at him since I erupted into tears in his arms. Talk about awkward. Weeping over client photos is one thing, but sobbing in the arms of your one-night stand because he knocked you up is another thing entirely. I couldn't get ahold of the tears before they fell. I'm embarrassed, to say the least. This whole situation is embarrassing. I'm used to being called a screwup, but it took thirty-one years and one drunken night for me to feel like it might be true.

"Come on, Jim," he says, reaching for his door handle. I take another couple of breaths, and by the time I reach for mine, he's already opening my door, offering his hand to help me out. Once I'm safely on the ground, he doesn't let go, despite my tugging.

Trevor's place is neat, organized, and bare. He has no pictures or artwork on the walls. No knick-knacks scattered around the few books on the built-in mahogany shelves. Not even a throw blanket or pillows on the dark leather couch. There's a TV on the wall, a desktop in the corner, and a whole lot of white space. I'm surprised the windows have curtains.

He slides his wallet and keys onto the white granite countertop in the kitchen and walks toward the fridge. "Are you hungry? Thirsty? If I don't have it, we can order in. You need lots of snacks when you're..."

"Pregnant, yeah. I got the whole spiel last week when I fainted at work."

"You what?" He abandons the fridge and rushes to my side. "You fainted?"

"Yeah. That's how I found out I was pregnant. I passed out at work. Ashlie had to take me to urgent care. She knows, by the way, which means Hunter does too."

His face twists like I'm missing the point. "I don't care who knows, Willa. Are you okay? What did the doctor say?"

"I hadn't eaten all day, and my blood pressure was low. It's all better now." Even as I'm saying it, he guides me to his naked couch and plops me down on it.

"You can't stand too fast. Your body's redirecting all your—"

"Yeah, I know. *Slow down. Eat snacks. Sleep when the baby sleeps.* I got it. How do *you* know all this stuff?"

"My sister's an OBGYN." He smiles, and it strikes me this is the first one I've seen from him since I shared the news. I've never seen him go this long without it. He must really be freaking out inside. "She made me watch a ton of medical documentaries with her growing up. I could have gotten an honorary degree."

"Cool." I give him a sarcastic thumbs-up and scan the empty room again, suddenly realizing how much I don't know about this man. By the looks of his apartment, he might be a serial killer. "Why haven't you decorated? Did you just move in?"

"Nope. It's been"—he blows out a breath—"two years now? I'm hardly ever home, so it feels like a waste of time."

"It's weird, Trevor."

He chuckles. "Yeah, I've heard that before. My sister had to force me to decorate my room growing up. When I moved out after high school, it just never seemed that important. Military life helped with that too." He sits on the couch next to me, flexes his fingers, and slowly reaches for my hands. "Look, I've been trying to figure out how to start this conversation. So I'll just... Are you... do you want to keep the baby?"

"Of course I do," I say with a bite to my voice, trying to pull my hands free. "If you don't want to be involved, that's fine—"

"Whoa. Hey. I didn't want to assume. It's your body, and I'm trying to be supportive. Have you had your first appointment yet?"

"It's on Thursday."

"Okay. I'll fly out Wednesday night."

"What? No." I shake my head emphatically. "You don't need to do that."

"Willa—"

"This thing is smaller than a blueberry. The appointment will only be, like, ten minutes long. I can handle it by myself."

"No." He shakes his head.

"What the hell do you mean, 'no'?"

"Willa, you're not doing any of this alone. I'm as much responsible for this as you are, and I have a duty to take care of you while you grow our child."

Our child. There's no hesitation from him. No reticence. He said it so casually, as if it's absurd for me to think he wouldn't come to my first appointment. Like I should know he's all in. "It's fine. I'm used to doing things by myself."

"Well, not this. Not with me. Whether you like it or not, we're doing this together. I'll fly into LAX on Wednesday night and drive you to the appointment on Thursday.

"So you're my handler now?" Heat flushes through me as I scowl. "I'm pregnant, not dead. I can drive myself."

"No."

"Trevor—"

"Nope. I'm flying out, and I'm driving. Find a way to cope with it."

I'm speechless, mouth hinged open as I stare at his dimpled smile. He's not being rude about it, but the assertive way he keeps shutting me down has me reeling. This man is determined to drive me crazy for the next nine months, and because he's half of the speck of life growing inside me, I don't have any other choice but to let him.

CHAPTER TEN
TREVOR

ME

How are you feeling?

WILLA

You already asked me this morning. I'm fine.

ME

Do you need anything?

WILLA

Again, no.

ME

You sure?

WILLA

Holy hell. You doing this for 9 months?

I *'m going to be a dad.* It's a title I've always looked forward to, but I've wanted to make sure I was ready. Growing up in foster care puts a different perspective on the whole parent-child relationship. I know all too well how things go when you don't get it right the first time, and I'd never wish that on anyone.

It's been less than a week, and despite the initial shock, cold feet never crossed my mind. I won't fail this child or Willa. *Espe-*

cially Willa. The only thing I'm worried about is how she's handling everything. The woman is a steel vault; I can't get any information out of her. She's been vague about how she's feeling, but after days of checking in on her, I finally annoyed her enough to get appointment details.

"Any questions?" Marla stands in front of the glowing projector screen. The EdTechU office complex in LA has several instructional rooms. This one is set up like a university lecture hall—tiered seating with elongated tabletops anchored into the navy carpeted floor. Today, we're bombarded with fresh sales tactics by the harbinger of headaches. This Wednesday morning meeting has dragged on into lunch hour, her voice grating on every *single* one of my nerves. Avoiding eye contact with someone for three hours isn't easy, but I've coasted through training without so much as a glance.

Chase lounges in his chair next to me, switching between taking notes and playing games on his tablet. I've resorted to shading in the empty space inside my tattoos with my pen. Distraction at its finest. "Okay then, we'll break for lunch and pick this all up at two," Marla calls over the sound of folding chair seats banging closed.

As much as I've hated sitting in this meeting, the timing worked out perfectly. We got the call to come down to the LA offices for the week on Monday. This is something we do a few times a year as guest trainers, but this time, they asked me and Chase to present our streamlined process for gathering sales reports. I jumped at the opportunity to be closer to Willa. Now I won't have to request any time off for her appointment tomorrow, and I'll have the chance to take care of some of her needs before I have to leave too.

"You ready?" Chase tucks his tablet under his arm and pulls out his phone. "Hunter's meeting us in the lobby."

I shake my head to clear the post-meeting haze and smile. "Yeah. Get me out of here."

As we near the door, I try to slip by unnoticed, but a hand on my arm stops me. I'm forced to make the eye contact I've been avoiding, if only to look good in front of the suits in the back of the room. Between my size and the color of my skin, I'm always trying to keep it professional in corporate spaces. But she's really testing that resolve. "Trevor, hey," Marla says. Her caramel-colored curls are pulled back, olive skin peeking through her black blouse. "Can I grab you for a sec?"

Chase pauses at the door, waiting for my nod before he steps into the hallway. "Uh, I kind of have somewhere to be," I say.

"This'll be quick. Promise."

Like her promises hold any weight with me. Still, I let out a long sigh and step over to her. "What do you need, Marla?"

"How are you, Trevy?"

Nope. Not doing this here. Or now. Or ever, for that matter. "I really have to get going..."

"I don't want this to be awkward, working together." She takes a step toward me, and I step back on instinct.

"Don't call me that, and it won't be."

"Okay, yeah...sorry... I just wanted to let you know that we have a flex position opening soon, and your name has come up several times for it." Her hand reaches toward me but stops midair. "I know how much you like to travel. Just thought I would pass on the information in case you're interested."

Blinking at her, my mind battles the excitement of a possible promotion with the dread of welcoming a whole lot of instability into my life. Even without knowing it, Marla's already trying to blow up my life again. I'm in the direct path of destruction and need to escape this walking tornado. "Uh, okay. I have to go..." I give her a tight-lipped grin and walk right out the door, trying to shake the immediate pounding in my head. It only took her five minutes to ruin my day.

We pile into Hunter's car and head to lunch, rapid-fire logistics spinning in my head the entire way. *Diapers, medical bills, a college fund. Working in San Francisco while Willa's in LA. Inserting myself into the life of a less than enthusiastic co-parent.*

As much as I've entertained this promotion at work in the past, adding interstate travel most days of the week doesn't sit well with me right now. The money will be there when all of this settles, but it isn't a huge concern for me, anyway. I've done well for myself between savings, investments, and having all my education paid for from my time in the Coast Guard, so I don't have any debt. That's all before taking the trust fund from my grandparents into consideration. Promotion or not, Willa will want for nothing, if I can get her to communicate with me.

"Is Ash meeting us for lunch?" Chase asks Hunter as we sit on the Lunch-a-Bunch patio. I barely remember getting out of the car and walking into the red-brick restaurant. Enclosed in a black steel lattice fence, the elongated patio is peppered with round bistro tables. Water glasses and a bread basket sit atop the green tablecloth next to vinyl menus. The fall breeze feels nice after being stuffed up in that conference room all morning, but my mind is still reeling.

"Naw. She went to check on Willa."

That snaps me out of it. "Wait. What's wrong with Willa?"

"She's been sick all week. How the hell do I know this before you do?" Hunter's eyes narrow. "Bruh, don't let me find out you're a deadbeat."

With how chaotic this has been, all of our close friends know about the baby now. Ashlie told Hunter the same day Willa passed out at work, and I filled Chase in on everything that happened on our flight to LA. It's nice not having to keep it a secret from them, but we haven't told our families yet.

"What kind of sick?" I shake my head and dig my phone out of my pocket. "Like morning sickness?"

"More like all day sickness. According to Ash, Willa can't keep anything down."

"Shit. Okay. She's been curving me all week. I had no idea." I type out a text to Maya, under the guise of morning sickness advice 'for my friend, Kayla.' After I hit send, I look up to them staring at me. My mind has been all over the place today, so I'm sure I missed another part of the conversation. "What?"

"I mean, I knew you had a crush on Willa, but you went from secret admirer to secret baby like a sonic boom. How did that happen?" Hunter asks.

"It's not a secret." I shake my head. "Does it matter?"

"Yeah." Hunter snorts. "What's going on? Are you trying to be with her?"

I would if she'd let me anywhere close. I'd lay everything at her feet if she wanted it, but the only proximity I've gained has been by imposing myself into her life. It's not sustainable. She's fiercely independent, and I'm clawing my way through it to show her she's not alone. "I'm trying to take care of her and the baby. She just won't let me."

Hunter laughs. "Good luck with that. She's a force to be reckoned with."

Chase blows out a chuckled breath, clapping my shoulder. "Yeah, man. Hang on tight. She and Kayla get along for a reason."

CHAPTER ELEVEN

TREVOR

I juggle a couple of grocery bags as I walk through the courtyard toward Willa's house. Knocking on her door sends a sudden ripple of anxiety through me. I didn't tell her I was coming. She would have refused. And she definitely didn't ask for anything in these bags. She could be allergic to...well, all of it. My heart pounds, increasing to rapid thrashing when the lock jiggles. I'm nervous as hell.

Willa cracks the door and scowls at me. "What are you doing here?" A purple hair scarf is tied around her head with her twists flowing out of it behind her. I can just make out the hem of an oversized TAILA T-shirt hitting her bare thigh through the door gap.

"I brought you some stuff. Can I come in?"

She groans, reaching for her stomach as a retch rolls through her body before she takes off for the kitchen sink. I let myself into her dark entryway, the only light coming from the TV and the small glow above the stove. Running water competes with the garbage disposal as I close the door, then slip off my shoes. The mechanical whirring hides the sound of her heaving, but the violent lurch of her shoulders as I enter the kitchen is obvious. I line up the bags on the countertop, next to a bottle of cleaning solution, mouthwash, and paper towels.

Grabbing the entire roll, I stand next to her and sweep her twists off to the side. Her poor body looks exhausted, clutching to the edge of the sink, knees half bent like they're struggling to keep her upright. I dip a folded paper towel into the water flowing from the faucet, squeeze, and flatten it out over the back of her neck. She goes rigid at my touch until a sigh slips past her lips as she gives in to the coolness. Only then do I place my hand on her back. "Why didn't you tell me you've been sick, Gem?"

"What can you do about morning sickness?" she says through ragged breaths, cupping water in her hand to rinse her mouth. The paper towel falls when she tries to stand straight, but she instantly curls back into herself and turns toward the darkened living room. She collapses on the sofa with a groan.

"Be here for you, for starters. Willa—"

"It'll pass. It's fine."

"Okay, well, I brought some things to help. You up to try them?"

"I'll try anything to stop feeling like death warmed over."

Chuckling, I pluck a bag off the counter and follow. Despite her joking, she looks horrible. "Any allergies, beautiful?"

"Yeah. Babies, apparently. I thought I wasn't supposed to be miserable until the end."

"Here, try this." I hand her a ginger lozenge. "Have you been able to eat anything today?"

"No." She rolls on her back to look up at me. "The only thing staying down is ice water."

Digging into the bag, I grab the clamshell holding acupressure wristbands and sit on the arm of the couch, right above her head. "Wrist," I say.

She squints at me, not moving a muscle.

"Please."

Slowly, she raises her arm in the air, eyes skeptically watching mine. I slip the band on her wrist, lining up the plastic disk with the pressure point below her hand. "Other wrist. When was the last time you ate something, sweetheart?"

She raises her other arm in the air. "Last night. And it all came back out. I'm scared to eat anything else."

"Sit tight, Gem." I start for the kitchen.

"Ugh, can you stop with the names?"

"What?"

"*Sweetheart. Beautiful. Gem.* Just use my name like a normal person."

"Sure thing, Willa." Laughing quietly, I rummage through the other bags on the counter. I didn't even realize I wasn't using her name, which probably means something I'm not going to think too hard about right now. I reach for my next remedy, opening it while heading back to the couch. She needs something—anything—in her stomach. "Here, Willa."

She scowls at the bag like it's a rabid squirrel. "...Chips?"

"I'm about to make you some soup, but see if you can handle a few, swee—Willa."

Her indignant stare bores into me as she reaches inside and places a chip in her mouth. How she does it in slow motion is beyond me. *Shit. Not now.* She feels like garbage, just threw up in the sink, but the way she slides the chip on her tongue sends my attention straight to her lips. Closing her eyes, she fucking moans like it's the best thing she's ever tasted, and despite knowing it was exclusively for the snack, my body reacts anyway. *What the hell is wrong with you?* This is the worst time for a semi but, luckily, the darkness is my friend. I clear my throat as a distraction. "Good?"

She snatches the bag out of my hand so fast, I draw back to keep all of my fingers attached. The foil rustles as she quickly demolishes the chips, but even with her attention long gone, I'm still feeling the effects as I walk back into the kitchen and adjust myself. *Calm the fuck down.* I flip on the light and get to work. Spraying the sink and counters with the bottle of cleaner, I wipe everything down with paper towels, disposing of them in an empty grocery bag at my feet. After using soap and the hottest water I can stand to wash my hands, I turn around to find Willa watching me from the couch. "Everything okay, Ge—Willa?"

"Did you just clean my kitchen?"

"You've been puking in it. Didn't think you wanted the extra flavor in your soup. Is that okay, Will—"

"*Ohmygod*! Stop saying my name." She sits up straighter, cocking her head to the side.

I laugh, a little surprised it took her this long to catch on. "You just told me to use your name..." I tease.

"Yeah, but now you're being a smart-ass."

"Okay, so what do you want me to call you?"

"Anything you want. Just stop being weird."

"Okay...bossy."

Her glare only makes my smile grow as I wink at her, turn my back, and search for a pot.

WILLA SUCKED DOWN THREE BOWLS OF POTATO SOUP and a ginger soda so quickly, I contemplated running back to the store for more. Right now, she's lounging against the arm of the couch with her eyes closed and a sated smile on her face. Her defenses have fallen enough that sitting next to her doesn't feel like a one-way trip to a lion's den.

"Thanks, Trevor," she says on a sigh, fiddling with the wristbands on her arms. "How did you know these would work?"

"I asked my sister."

Her eyes fly open in a panic. "You told your sister I'm pregnant?"

"Nope. Told her it was for a friend. But we should tell our families pretty soon, considering our friends already know."

She takes a deep breath, heaving out a forceful puff of air. "I was going to wait until Thanksgiving to tell my parents..." Her teeth sink into her lower lip as she wrings her hands. I've met them before, a couple of times when tagging along with Ashlie and Hunter. They're intense, but friendly enough, in my experience. I don't have many details about her strained relationship with them, but it involves her choosing a different path for her life than they wanted. I imagine this kind of news won't go over well with them at all.

"I'll come with you...if you want."

"You're not going home?"

"Nope. I go home once a year, at Christmas. I usually tough Thanksgiving out on my own."

"Oh. Why?"

Because I hate Heritage, Nebraska, and try to spend as little time there as possible. Some of my worst memories are tied to that place. The trapped feeling I get whenever I'm home makes me want to take a flying leap.

"It's...just not my favorite place. Let me come with you to Fort Bender. We can tell your parents together."

Willa nibbles her lip for several seconds as she thinks. I spend the time gazing at the arches of her eyebrows, the slope of her nose, the outline of her lips—I can't help but admire all that she is. Too quickly, she lets out a sigh and shakes her head, etching over my reverie

"Hey." I place my hand on her foot. "We're in this together. Let me support you."

A grimace scrolls across her face, but it's gone by the time she looks at me. Her head falls back on the couch, and she nods as a yawn stretches her jaw.

"Yeah?"

She yawns again, eyes drooping closed as she rolls to her side and curls her legs in. "Yes, Trevor. Come to Bender." Another yawn, and she mumbles, "You might as well see the dysfunction in all of its glory." A couple of deep breaths later, she's out like a light.

The bags under her eyes are so dark, it's clear she hasn't slept while she's been sick. I can't stand the thought of her waking up with a sore body on top of a sour stomach, so I stand from the couch and scoop her in my arms. She murmurs something when her head flops against my chest, but stays asleep as I walk her down the hallway. Besides a small bathroom, her bedroom is the only other room on this side of the house. As I settle her under the pintuck comforter, the pale moonlight streaming through the window casts peaceful shadows over her face. *She's so damn beautiful.* I press a kiss to her forehead, just because it feels right.

After tucking her in, I grab her phone and some snacks from the kitchen, and leave them on her nightstand, closing the door softly while backing into the hallway. Then I clean up and settle on her couch. I'll sleep here tonight, just in case she needs me.

CHAPTER TWELVE

WILLA

There's a bag of potato chips on my nightstand. I've been staring at it since I woke up, not daring to touch it, or the water, or the ginger candy. My phone is suspect too. I don't remember coming to bed last night, which means that man carried me to my room—pregnancy wristbands and all—and left me a bag of chips. I'm not sure how I feel about that. The only reason I'm reaching for the candy right now is because of the sour plume bubbling in my stomach. But I'm not touching the chips. I draw the line at the chips.

Slipping the wristbands off, I head into my bathroom. It takes me all of three minutes and a gag on my toothbrush to run back to my bed and put them back on. Whatever magic these things have, I need them.

I breathe a sigh at the relieving pressure and get a sudden craving for potato soup. It's the only thing that sounds good as I grab my phone and make my way to the kitchen. As annoyed as I was when Trevor showed up unannounced, I have to admit he knows what he's doing. I feel a little bad for keeping him in the dark, but seriously, how was I supposed to know he was a morning sickness aficionado? And efficient at cleaning up, apparently.

My kitchen is spotless. I've been sick for days, just leaving everything out on display while my energy waned. Right now, my white quartz countertops sparkle, the stovetop glistens, and there's a lemony fresh scent coming from the sink. The roll of paper towels is back in its holder, the garbage can is empty—I'm pretty sure the floor has been mopped. The last flower hanging from that poor purple orchid in the window even looks perkier. *I really need to try and save that plant.* There's a note tucked under a can of ginger ale:

Leftover soup's in the fridge. See you at 3:00. —Trev

My stomach grumbles as I read the word soup. I'm so hungry, my feet are on their way to the fridge before I realize where I'm headed. As I wait for the microwave to finish, I marvel at the tenacity of this man. Without my asking, Trevor came to my house, eased my nausea, carried me to bed, and cleaned my mess like a goddamn superhero. And he wasn't mad about any of it. I know I should have told him I was sick when he asked how I was feeling on Monday. And Tuesday. And yesterday. But I don't do needy. The thought of asking anyone for something when I'm sick makes me want to crawl out of my skin. Hell, asking anyone for help with *anything* makes me feel inadequate.

I learned at an early age that asking for help was a waste of my time, since people are determined to believe being book smart means you have no struggles in life. By people, I mostly mean my parents. Any problems I had growing up were met with:

"*You'll figure it out.*"

"*You're not trying hard enough.*"

And my personal favorite, "*We don't have to worry about you.*"

By the time I graduated from high school, I'd had enough and walked away. My parents told me I was on my own and not to come to them for help. I haven't. I've worked my ass off for everything I have right now—my car, the studio, this sparkling clean house with a mortgage in my name. I don't want to get used to having someone in my space, offering to help me. Not when the help has a time limit.

Using a towel, I pull the hot soup from the microwave and walk straight to the couch. The plush throw blanket I usually have draped across the back is folded on a cushion with military precision. I look around the room before I sit. Everything else in here has been tidied up too. From the magazines on my glass coffee table—arranged in a neat little stack—to the remotes lined up next to them. When I wrap the throw around my legs, the smell of Christmas elicits an exasperated sigh. I pull out my phone.

ME

You didn't have to clean my house…

TREVOR

I think you mean, "Gee, thanks, Trev. You're so kind. And funny. And handsome."

ME

👆 Thank you 👆 for cleaning up. And for dinner. It was nice.

TREVOR

Oh, so you DO like when I'm nice to you…

ME

Don't push it, Dimples.

TREVOR

My bad, sweetheart

ME

Trevor, the pet names…

TREVOR

You started it 😊

Feeling any better?

If I say yes, will you promise to never clean my house again.

LOL! Nope.

THERE'S A KNOCK ON MY DOOR AT 2:55 P.M., AND ALL MY nausea rises in my throat. I don't think I'm ready for this appointment. *What if something's already gone wrong and I've stressed everyone out for nothing? What if there's more than one in there? What if—*

Another knock has me on my feet, smoothing out my dress before I open the door. Trevor has a computer bag slung over his navy blue EdTechU windbreaker, and he's wearing the biggest smile. I can't help but roll my eyes. "You ready?" he asks, stepping back so I can lock the door.

I nod silently and follow him to his rental car. Having no control over what's going on inside my body is one of the most stressful things I've ever experienced. After spending the morning reading statistics on early pregnancy loss, I'm mostly convinced I'll walk into this appointment and be told the worst.

Trevor heads straight to the passenger side, opens the door, and waits well after I've settled into the seat. Sneering, I reach for the seat belt, pausing with it halfway across my body. "I know how to close the door, Trevor..."

"So do I." He winks and stands there like a damn car salesman. Rolling my eyes at his amused laugh, I click the buckle and pull out my phone to send the clearest signal that I'm already done with him. As soon as he starts the car, a super cheesy '90s boy band song fills the cabin. I'm talking love, fire, desire, and all that bullshit.

"You're kidding, right? You don't actually listen to this…"

"What you got against my music, Jim?" He laughs.

"Nothing. I just think all the lovey-dovey lyrics are gonna make me puke in this car," I say with a straight face. "Change it. Let's see if that helps."

He shakes his head, smiling as he presses a button on the radio. Another love song comes on. This one might be worse, talking about wedding vows and cherishing forever. I groan, and he laughs while backing out of the parking spot. "It's a playlist," he says.

"So it's just '90s love songs, all the time?"

"Nope. Sometimes they're from the '80s and 2000s." He glances at me as we drive down the street, and his smile falls. "Speaking of puke, how are you feeling today?"

"Better. As long as I keep these things on my wrists and a candy in my mouth, I'm okay."

He nods as he maneuvers onto the freeway. Neither of us say anything else. Nearly twenty minutes later, a blond nurse introduces herself as Mandy while showing us back to a room. After taking some blood, she hands me a white sheet and instructs me to undress from the waist down. My heart stalls.

"W-we're not just answering questions?" I thought *maybe* we'd do an ultrasound on my stomach at the most, but I never once thought about needing a pelvic exam.

"This is a dating scan," Mandy explains. "The baby is too small to see over the belly. We'll have to use the internal transducer for accurate measurements. It's like a little wand that—"

"Yeah. Got it," I say, glancing at Trevor. He doesn't look fazed one bit, lounging back in a chair with his arms crossed.

"The doctor will be in shortly." She smiles and slips out the door.

"You knew about this?"

"Yep. Pretty standard."

"Well, could you turn around or something?"

He laughs and grabs a magazine from the table next to him, opens it up, and covers his face.

"What's so funny about this?" I ask, slipping out of my panties and placing them in my purse. He's seen me in less, but the garish lights in this exam room are making me feel self-conscious about my choice in underwear.

"Nothing." His muffled voice lilts with amusement.

"No. Say it."

"You're just real cute when you get flustered."

"I'm not flustered. I'm agitated. And hungry," I grumble, sliding onto the exam chair and positioning the sheet over my waist. I didn't even think about bringing snacks with me. The only things in my purse are gum, ginger candy, and my phone. "You can look now."

Trevor closes the magazine and digs in his computer bag, then walks over to me, unwrapping a granola bar on his way. "I have a few other things if you're still hungry. We can grab some food afterward too."

"I don't want to eat all of your snacks."

"They're not my snacks. I brought them for you." He meets my scowl with a smirk. As I start to tell him how unnecessary it is for him to feed me, he sticks the granola bar in my mouth. "Eat. You'll feel better, swee—Willa."

I'd argue, but this basic-ass granola bar is the best thing I've ever tasted. Demolishing it in three bites, I smack my lips for good measure when it's gone. I'm about to ask for more when there's a knock on the door. One that *stays* on the other side until I say, "Come in."

Dr. Quentin is about fifteen years older than I am, a straight shooter, and speaks her mind freely, which I deeply appreciate. She walks into the room with a bright white smile gleaming from her mahogany face. Her curly brown hair is secured on top of her head with a claw clip. She doesn't even glance at the man in the corner, her attention solely on me as she looks over her glasses. "Willa, Willa, Willa. You are full of surprises."

"Hey, Doctor Q."

"You told me you were done with that Carter guy." She waggles her finger at me, but the smile remains. I had plenty of visits with her when I found out my ex had cheated on me the first time. And the second time. By the third time, she was as fed up with him as I was.

"Oh, I am." I clear my throat and point behind her. "This is Trevor."

Turning on her heel, she cocks her head at him before walking over and sticking out her hand. "Nice to meet you, Trevor." He takes her hand with a smile. "Now"—she flips her attention back to me—"what ever happened to using protection?"

"We did." I shrug and give her a nervous smile.

"Mm-hmm." She tucks her chin, scrutinizing me over her glasses again as she walks toward her stool. I can't blame her. If it wasn't happening to me, I wouldn't believe it either. "Well, I guess you two get a pass, then. Let's see how far along you are."

"Eight weeks, exactly," I say without hesitation.

She laughs. "You *would* know exactly when you conceived. You're sure this wasn't planned?"

"Not. At. All." I shake my head.

Dr. Quentin whips her head back to Trevor. "And you plan on being involved the entire time?"

He chuckles and nods. "Yep. If she'll let me."

"Willa, you better let this man take care of you." She repeats her finger waggle. "Any morning sickness?"

"Nothing too bad..." I lie. Now that I'm feeling a little better, the past few days feel like an overreaction. I don't want to seem weak so early on, and with this being a surprise, I definitely don't want to look like I can't handle my responsibility.

Trevor clears his throat and walks across the room to stand next to me. "Uh, yeah, she's been sick all day long since Monday."

"Ooh, he's tellin' on you!" Dr. Q teases, slipping on blue nitrile gloves. "I like him. Let's do this ultrasound so you two can get out of here." She slides a condom on the transducer and squeezes lube over it. "You ready for me to bring my rowdy kids to the studio next week?"

"Of course. I've got some of those sparkly Santa hats your girls liked last year."

"They'll be all over that! Here we go." She nods toward the screen.

Trevor's hand is on my shoulder before the image comes up, squeezing reassuringly when I gasp. The tiny figure lying in the large black oval is wiggling away. It's surreal that I'm watching something happening inside my body and can't even feel it.

Dr. Quentin points at the screen. "That's your little gummy bear. There's the head and spine. And here is the yolk sac. Let me click in some measurements, but everything looks good."

I turn to Trevor, whose eyes are sparkling as he stares at the screen, lips slightly parted. When he glances at me and smiles, something inside me shifts. Not the baby, obviously, but something tight grips my heart. This is really happening. We're having a baby together. *Holy shit.* My hand has found its way up to his on my shoulder, and I don't move it once I notice. This feels okay, for now.

"You're right. Eight weeks," she confirms. "Would you like some pictures?" My eyes snap to hers, and I nod, still speechless. She prints off three and hands them to me, smiling at my trembling fingers when I take them. "Congratulations, you two! Get started on a prenatal, lots of fruits and veggies, and I'll see you back in four weeks."

Dr. Q shakes our hands and heads for the door, leaving me alone with Trevor and pictures of the dancing gummy bear. Glancing over my shoulder, I find Trevor watching me, homed in like he's stuck in a daydream. I hold the pictures out to him, assuming he's waiting for his turn to marvel at the ultrasound. He doesn't take them. Heat fills my cheeks as his eyes rove all over my face, but looking away from him right now feels impossible. Breaking the silence seems wrong too. After an eternity, he releases a breath. "You're amazing, Willa. I hope you know that." His gaze falls to the floor, and he walks to the corner of the room for his bag, then heads toward the door. "I'll wait for you in the hallway."

CHAPTER THIRTEEN

TREVOR

Willa hands me the ultrasound pictures while we walk through the parking garage. I'm awestruck, studying the black-and-white images. I had a part in creating that little life kicking around inside of her. The most amazing woman is sacrificing herself to bring a part of me into the world. She deserves uncomplicated calm. Softness. *Everything*. And I'll *give* her everything, but I doubt she even considers me a friend at this point. I'm still her sister's friend who knocked her up and ruined her life. I need to change that.

"So...I was gonna hit up a bookstore after getting you some food. Do you want to come with me?"

"For what?"

"Books, Willa..." Smirking playfully, I ignore her glare and help her into the car. "I thought it could be a good bonding experience."

She rolls her eyes. "Don't you think it's a little too early to start bonding with the baby over books?"

"I'm talking about us. There's science behind reducing stress during pregnancy." She likes facts and statistics. Maybe appealing to her logic like this will help me wiggle my way into her good graces. "If we got to know each other better, it would be good for the baby."

"For the baby?" she asks slowly, eyeing me. "This sounds like a date."

"It can be a date, if that's what you wanna call it." I wink and close her door before she protests.

I'd love to date Willa. Even before our night in San Diego, I would have taken her out in a heartbeat if I thought she was interested. I love how her brain works. She observes people. Tries to understand them. She's snappy, sarcastic, and smart as hell, with a deep well of empathy she pretends doesn't exist. Behind that wall, I'm convinced she has a big heart, surrounded by overgrown wildflowers, waiting to be tended to. I'm stubborn enough to forge a direct path with an arsenal of kindness and dedication—starting with dinner and books.

After satisfying Willa's Taco Chime craving—and making a quick stop for gummy bears—we walk into Board 'n' Books. My hand brushes against hers as I reach forward to open the door, sending goosebumps down my arms. Those same warm tingles that coursed through me as she held my hand at the doctor's office threaten to light up my insides. I don't even think she did it on purpose, but when she grabbed my hand and squeezed, I had the first spark of hope that she might not completely hate me for all of this.

Her eyes perk up as soon as we hit the first bookshelf, and I grab a hand basket in preparation. After seeing her book collection last night, I had a feeling she'd love this. *Another point for Trevor.* She heads right to the lifestyle section and pulls her phone out, taking pictures of several of the titles before sliding them back on the shelf. I watch her flip through and return a couple more before I say, "Get whatever you want, Gem. I'm buying."

She turns to me and shakes her head. "Um, no. You're not buying me books."

"Why not?"

"Because books are expensive. I can find all this information online."

"So you're not taking those pictures to come back later and buy them on your own?" My eyes narrow, and she sighs as I grab the book she's trying to slip back on the shelf.

"So what if I am?"

"Willa, you want the books." I drop it in the basket. "Get the books."

"No. It's too much. I have no self-control in this place."

"Get what you want, or so help me, I'll buy one of every single book in this section."

"Yeah, *okay*." Her sarcasm puts a smile on my face as I take a step backward and reach for the shelf. "Trevor, you can't threaten me with paperbacks..."

"Hardcover, then. I don't care." Another step back, and I grab a few books off the shelf, throwing in everything from pregnancy nutrition to weekly milestones. Her eyes widen with each thump as I pile them into the basket. A panicked squeak accents her voice each time I ignore her heightened protests.

"Are you—you're serious?"

I look her dead in the eye as I pull out another book and drop it in. Her scowl morphs into amusement, and she rushes forward, grabbing my hand. "Okay. Fine. I'll get some. Just...chill." Without looking, she snags a book and shoves it at me. "Here. Happy? I got a book."

"You realize we're only having one, right?"

Willa's eyes drop to the bright pink cover titled *How to Survive Multiples* as she chews the inside of her lip. A giggle slips out of her, and she hides her face behind the book. A tiny snort is followed by more laughter as she turns away from me. The whole interaction is so ridiculous, I can't do anything other than grin at how tickled she is. She tucks the book back onto the shelf and, in that time, a somber look falls over her face. "Are you nervous?" The vulnerable tremble in her voice prompts me to step toward her.

"Hell yeah, I'm nervous. I didn't sleep at all last night."

"Me too." She lets out a shaky breath, her gaze dropping to the floor between us. "And I think I've been using it as an excuse to shut you out." She takes a step toward me and puts her hand on my arm. "I think you were right, though. Becoming friends is going to be the only way to survive this."

I clutch my chest, sighing dramatically. "Thank *God*, Willa." She pushes on my shoulder, but a smile slides on her face. "Now get your books."

"Okay, but I'm only getting two."

"I saw you snap pictures of at least ten. Get them all."

"Fine, three."

"Five."

"Seriously, Trevor? You're going to fight me on this?"

"Notice how I haven't emptied the basket yet? I'll walk to the register right now..."

Willa rolls her eyes and plucks a few books out of the basket, swapping them for others on the shelf. "What are you getting?" she asks.

"Oh. Nothing. I have my sister on speed dial for all things baby related. This trip was just for you, Gem." I chuckle as her jaw hinges to the floor. Turning on my heel, I walk to the register before she can take back anything—a book *or* our budding friendship. If that's the kind of relationship she wants, I'll take it.

"So how is this supposed to work?" Willa asks as we settle on her couch. The books from the store lay scattered across her coffee table. "You're in San Francisco."

"For now, I plan on flying down for all your monthly appointments. And I'll check in with you every day, get you anything you need, but you *have* to tell me what's going on. I'm so serious,

Willa." I place a hand on her arm. "Anything. Even if the wind blows dust in your eye or you're craving chocolate at midnight. I want to know everything."

Willa nods, staring at her lap.

"And the closer we get to the due date, I'll look into working remotely from the LA office."

"Sounds like you've got it all figured out..." she murmurs, wringing her hands. Her eyebrows dip as she scans the floor.

"Hey." Grabbing her hand, I encase it in both of mine. I expect her to pull away, but she doesn't, instead, shifting her gaze to my face. "Talk to me. Let me in."

She sniffs and shakes her head. "What if something happens?"

"Something like what?"

"I don't know. Like, what if the baby kicks for the first time while I'm driving and I freak out and crash the car?"

"Then I'll be on the first flight out to make sure you're okay."

"What if something goes wrong with the baby?

"I'll drop everything to get here, and we'll handle it together." I squeeze her hand for reassurance, but she scoffs.

"That can't be your solution for everything, Trevor."

"Try me," I say with a smile.

"Okay. What if the baby has seventeen toes and they want to operate before birth?"

I laugh at that one until I see the tears brimming in her eyes and choke it back. "Hey. Come here." Pulling her toward me, I wrap my arms around her right as the first tears fall.

"I'm sorry. This is stupid. I don't cry. I shouldn't even be crying."

"It's not stupid. Your world is on its head right now. Worry is warranted."

Willa buries her face into my chest, imprinting the light coconut notes on her skin into my senses. Stroking her back, I pull her closer to tuck her head under my chin. She fits so perfectly there, and I bite my cheeks to rid myself of the impulse to kiss the top of her head. "What if I come down on the weekends?"

Her stuttered sniffles shake her body against mine. "I can't let you do that. It'll cost so much."

"Let me worry about the cost. I'll fly out on Fridays after work and head back on Sunday nights. And I'll enlist Ashlie and Hunter to check in on you during the week. How does that sound?"

"It sounds like I'm about to be everyone's problem..."

"You're the furthest thing from a burden, Willa. You're worth every single effort."

CHAPTER FOURTEEN

WILLA

Despite me telling him not to, Trevor changed his Friday flight to Sunday and stayed in LA last weekend. Bursting into tears after my appointment sent him into overprotective hyperdrive. With another bad wave of morning sickness that had him fussing at me to lie down every five minutes, I'm surprised he actually left. He made me swear, pledge, and promise to call if I needed him to come back. I think we both know that won't happen.

Sunday night is when the nightmares started. I've had them every day since. They always start out as bright, sunny dreams with a precious bundle of joy in my arms. But just when I get comfortable, a crack of lightning cues the skies to darken. I look down at a faceless baby girl before she's ripped from my hands in a windstorm, floating just high enough that I can't reach. It doesn't matter what the dream is about. For the past five days, they've all ended the same, with me waking up soaked in sweat and tangled in my sheets. I'm too scared to fall back asleep at that point and have gotten into the habit of bundling up in front of the TV until daybreak. I'm fucking exhausted.

So tell me why, instead of curling up on my sofa, I'm at the vanity concealing the dark circles under my eyes, all just to suffer at Ashlie's Halloween party. She and Hunter recently bought a house and thought the holiday was perfect for a housewarming party. This long-ass week is never-ending. It's Friday, it's chilly outside, and all I want to do is curl up in my sweatpants and fall asleep. Except I can't because I'll just wake up screaming again. My phone buzzes on the marble vanity underneath me, causing me to smear my winged eyeliner for my goddess costume.

TREVOR

Just got in. You sure you don't want me to pick you up?

ME

I'm good. I don't think I'll stay too long.

TREVOR

Everything ok?

ME

Yeah. I don't usually last long at parties. I'll see you there.

In true Willa fashion, I haven't told him a thing about the nightmares or the exhaustion. Admitting I'm terrified of going to sleep like I'm three years old makes me cringe inside. He can't do anything about it, anyway. Vivid pregnancy dreams are normal; I looked it up. Hopefully, it'll pass soon, just like the morning sickness.

For fuck's sake. My phone rattles like I'm getting a call right as I pick up the eyeliner.

UNKNOWN

Hey beautiful...

I know you're getting these.

You ever going to answer me?

Now I'm exhausted *and* livid. It's an unknown number, but my ex has been playing this game for years. The only reason I haven't fucking blocked him is because he'll take satisfaction from any reaction I give him. He always has. My past attempts to block his ass resulted in three new unknown numbers torturing my phone day and night. The police claimed the numbers were untraceable, that they couldn't do anything unless it escalated. He's too smart to do that. At least this way, he knows the messages are going through, and I feel in control.

After fixing my eye makeup, I wrap a black rope belt around the waist of my shimmery gold dress and reach for the gilded headpiece hanging on the bathroom doorknob. I have to say, for how unenthusiastic I feel right now, I love every aspect of this costume I threw together. It hugs my curves just enough to make me feel sexy while leaving an air of mystery. Scanning myself in the full-length mirror on my bedroom wall, I take a deep breath. *Why do I do this to myself?* I grab my keys and head for the door. The sooner I get this over with, the sooner I can come back home and enjoy the rest of my night.

"GIRL, *FINALLY*!" ASHLIE RUSHES ME AT THE FRONT door, sounds of laughter floating into the entryway. Her skeleton bodysuit looks hand painted, the bones drawn on her face already smudging. I don't even have time to admire the updates she's made to the huge open concept living room before she pulls me through the pods of people socializing. She doesn't stop until we reach the *U*-shaped kitchen, packed with more guests. Glass cabinets line the white walls, drinks are scattered around the butcher block island, and finger foods crowd the marble countertops. *The perks of marrying the son of a multimillionaire.* With wide eyes, she tips on her toes to grab my shoulders. "I have a problem."

"What's up, Ash?" I grit my teeth, wincing at the music

blaring from somewhere in the house. *I won't make it an hour in here.*

"Well, we may have gone overboard with how many people we invited tonight. None of the games I've planned will work."

She *would* be panicking about how to entertain guests who are perfectly capable of entertaining themselves. I point to the oversized sectional covered with people in the living room. "It seems like everyone's happily preoccupied. Crisis averted."

She rolls her eyes. "For now, maybe. But I need ideas on how to keep the night alive. I don't want people talking about me in the break room for throwing a trash-ass party."

"How old are you again?" I try to ignore the urge to twitch at the music. It's so loud, I feel it shaking my insides.

"Girl, do you have any ideas or not? I'm freaking out here."

Dramatic ass. This isn't even close to a problem. She's a lot better than she used to be, but her people-pleasing tendencies die hard. "Pull out your karaoke machine and let everyone entertain themselves."

She gasps, cheesing so hard you'd think I just solved world hunger. "You're a genius, Wills!" Her shoulders shimmy as she pulls out her phone. After a minute, Hunter, in a matching skeleton costume, comes downstairs holding tablecloths, followed by Trevor, who's wearing a suit and tie.

As soon as Trevor sees me, he breaks out in a smile and comes to my side, placing a hand on my shoulder with a squeeze. "Hey. You alright?"

Nodding, I painstakingly mold my scowl into a tight-lipped smile. He squints at me until I relent. "It's just busy in here. I'm fine." I wave my hand up and down his suit to change the subject. "What are you supposed to be?"

"Oh!" Plucking sunglasses out of his pocket, he slides them on his face. Then he opens the lapel of his jacket, flashing a badge. "I'm a federal agent. At your service, Ms. Aphrodite." He finishes the look with a self-satisfied grin. I roll my eyes, despite the smile trying to make an appearance.

Ashlie turns to Hunter, batting her lashes. "Love, can you set up the karaoke machine? Please?" She flits off to the living room, expecting him to handle it.

The way Hunter clenches his jaw and purses his lips, I just know Ashlie has been driving him crazy all day, setting up for this party. "Come help me, bruh," he says, whacking Trevor on the arm. Trevor gives my shoulder another squeeze and follows him to the garage.

The song changes, and my head pounds as the bass rattles the windows. This is not sustainable, especially now that off-key singing is about to fill the air. It hasn't even been twenty minutes, but I need to step out for a breather.

I slip out the back door and drink in the cool night air. Once my heart rate slows, I walk farther into the backyard, taking a seat on the stone bench in the garden. *Why did I come*? I'm in no mood to be good company, and even though the walls of the house mute the music, I'm annoyed I can still hear it. Those fascinating sound waves, invisible but powerful, just irking my entire soul. I'm thinking about hopping the fence and heading straight for my car when the back door opens.

Trevor walks toward me with a bottle of water in one hand and a plate of food in the other. "An outside party for one shouldn't surprise me." He smiles. "You looked a little miserable in there. I thought food might help." Returning his smile, I make room for him on the bench. Food would probably be a good idea right about now. Snagging a taquito from the plate, I take a bite and tip my head up to the stars in the sky, savoring the taste with a moan. The doom and gloom gets a little less dire with every bite. "You gonna tell me what's wrong?"

I hate how well Trevor can read me sometimes. He found me outside—knew I was hungry before I did. We've seen each other all of five minutes today and he already knows something's up. "Nothing's wrong. It's just easier to think out here."

"Okay. What are you thinking about?"

I grab another taquito. "It's dumb."

"Try me."

"Sound waves," I say. Trevor chokes on his laugh, and I shoot him a glare. "See. I told you it was dumb."

"Nope. Just surprising. Who comes to a Halloween party to philosophize about sound waves except you, Jim?" He nudges me with his elbow, and a smile slides across my face.

"In my defense, I didn't want to come to this party."

"So why did you?"

Because I'll fall asleep if I stay home, and I'm scared of having nightmares. "It seemed important to Ash." I shrug. A partial truth that makes me feel a little better about keeping the dreams from him.

Trevor nods, and we sit quietly for several seconds before he cracks open the water and hands it to me. "So, tell me about the sound waves, Professor Willis."

Rolling my eyes, I take a drink while deciding whether to go full existential crisis on him. The eagerness in his stare hits me in a way it never has before. *Or maybe it's the sleep deprivation.* Whatever the hell it is, I angle toward him. "Sound has always fascinated me. It flows through air, ripples across water, vibrates the ground, snuffs out fire. How it's invisible to the naked eye but can penetrate almost anything—demanding to be acknowledged. You can be basking in peace and quiet, and the softest thrum will shatter the silence. Even locked away in isolation, feeling the most alone you've ever felt, the tiniest wave can find you—light you up with hope. Sound will travel to the ends of the earth and back just to claim you. It's amazing..." My gaze drifts to the stone pavers on the ground as my mind carries on with the thought, but I stop talking, mainly because I hear how unhinged I sound.

"That's not dumb at all," Trevor whispers. I glance at the faint shadow clouding his eyes. "I think it's a profound way to look at life. We spend so much time convincing ourselves that we're in control here, without stopping to consider the unseen forces acted upon us every minute of every day. We're drops in a bucket, no matter how much we pretend to be more."

He gets it. Not only does unserious, sparkle-eyed Trevor follow my inane path of thinking, he agrees with it. He verbalized it in a much cleaner way than I've ever been able to. Maybe there's a little more depth to him than I've allowed myself to see. Sighing, I look back at the night sky. "I think I'm going to head home." As soon as the words leave my mouth, my body floods with relief. I had no business trying to tough out a Halloween party tonight. I pat his leg and stand, but as I take a step forward, he grabs my hand.

"Want some company?"

Maybe it's the exhaustion, or the way he completely understood my rambling, but I think about it for less time than I ever have before with him. "Yeah. I think I do."

CHAPTER FIFTEEN

TREVOR

I close Willa's car door and tap the roof, waiting until she drives around the corner before heading back inside to say goodbye to Hunter and Ashlie. I'd leave my own birthday party if it meant spending more time with her. And after our conversation in the backyard, I have absolutely no interest in talking to anyone else for the rest of the night. Asking if she wanted company was a risky move, but I'm glad I took it. Her answer almost shot me to the moon.

Pitchy singing and loud laughter greet me as soon as I open the door to the Halloween party. Hunter's in the corner of the darkened room, drink in hand, likely taking a breather from Ashlie's requests. When I got here, she sent us upstairs to move a table, then immediately to the garage for folding chairs, and back upstairs for table linens. The karaoke machine might have been his last straw. He's fed up.

"Bruh, you good?" He bumps my knuckles in greeting when I lean on the wall next to him. "I was about to grab the 'do not disturb' sign for the back door. Looked pretty cozy out there."

"Yeah. Willa invited me over, so I'm gonna head out."

A smirk slides across his face. "I mean, I guess she's already knocked-up. Can't get into any more trouble."

"Nah, it's not like that." My face flushes because no matter how much it's not *like that*, I wish it were. "We're just getting to know each other."

"For now. Keep showing up for her, and she'll cave. Just watch, you'll be singing a different tune by the New Year's Eve party."

Chuckling, I shake my head. *Don't jinx it.*

"You wanna bet?" Hunter's eyes narrow, his smirk growing.

"You and your bets can stay the hell away from me, bro." I send a smile to Ashlie, who has wedged her way onto Hunter's lap. He stiffens, but a kiss from her relaxes his shoulders.

"Hey, Trev. You heading out?"

"Yeah. Gonna go check on Willa."

Hunter snorts and takes a sip of his drink. "New Year's, if not before."

"What's happening on New Year's?" Ashlie asks.

"Oh, just Willa and Trev doing the 'do.'"

Ashlie throws her head back and cackles. "Oh yeah, that's happening. One hundred percent. You're good to her. She's gonna crack."

"Look"—Hunter snorts, pointing at my face—"he can't stop smiling!"

"Aww." Ashlie puts a hand on my arm.

Heat creeps up my neck as I shake my head and glance down at the floor. "It's not like that."

She tilts her head, scrutinizing me with a raised brow. "You wanna bet?"

"Why don't you two bet with each other and leave me out of it?" I say through my laugh. Their eyes spark, and when they turn and shake on it, I can't believe I ever missed how perfect they are for each other. When we were tangled in a weird secret bet love triangle a few years back, I had no idea they were anything more than friends. Once it all came out, there was no denying they're meant to be. Bowing out wasn't hard at all, especially since I was already stifling a small crush on Willa by then. Watching them joke with each other about my sex life, I can't imagine them any way except together.

Ashlie slips Hunter another kiss and rejoins the karaoke crowd. "Looks like she's calmed down," I say.

"Thankfully. If she asks me to do one more thing for this damn party, I'm out the door right behind you."

Laughing, I clap his shoulder. "Thanks for the invite. I should get going."

"Alright, bruh." He nods, and I turn for the door. "Oh, hey, Trev?" I look over my shoulder, and his puckish grin prepares me for more bullshit. "Maybe use protection this time..."

Turning my back on him, I raise my middle finger in the air as his snickers follow me to the door.

"So, let me get this straight. You tease me for my '90s music, meanwhile you're sitting here watching teen movies from the early aughts?" I settle into Willa's couch, juggling bottles of water as she follows behind with a tray full of snacks. She's dressed in the same oversized TAILA shirt from a few weeks ago, with shorts this time.

"First of all"—she places the tray on the coffee table—"these are cinematic masterpieces. You can say you're watching a 'teen movie' and everyone knows the exact genre and time period you're talking about. And second, it's all about nostalgia."

"I didn't realize you were so passionate about remembering your awkward prom night..." I tease.

"Well, considering I never went to prom, I can guarantee it's not that." She settles on the opposite end of the couch.

"Why didn't you go to prom? It's a rite of passage."

"I was more of a bookworm, tutoring, no-social-life kind of girl back then. Doesn't exactly scream 'take me to prom.' Ashlie was the popular one. I was the know-it-all." She looks down and plays with her fingers before grabbing a cube of cheese. "And let me guess, you were exactly as you are now..."

"What's *that* supposed to mean?" I chuckle.

She points to the TV right as a letterman-wearing jock flips his hair, strolling through the cafeteria. "That."

"I mean, I played sports, but I did everything else too."

"Let me guess...football and basketball. Maybe track and field."

"And swimming. Choir, piano, theater, and debate club—"

Her mouth hangs open as my extracurricular list grows.

"—STEM, obviously. Oh, and farming club."

"Farming club?" She shifts to sit cross-legged on the cushion, eyebrows bunching.

"It's the Midwest. Even if I hadn't grown up on one, farms abound. Heritage was small enough that I did anything to keep me busy until I could get out. That's how I graduated from high school early. Nothing else to do." The way her face glitches makes me want to bite my lip. *Surprising her might be my new favorite thing.*

"I have so many questions..."

Slinging an arm over the back of the couch, I turn to face her. "Go for it."

"You graduated early? I didn't even graduate early."

"Yep. At seventeen and went right into the Coast Guard."

"People don't just graduate early, Trev."

Trev... My heart leaps to my throat. Everyone uses that nickname all the time, but this might be the first time she ever has. I can't help but smile. "Welp, I did. Wasn't that hard. Just a few extra courses in the summer."

"Yeah, *okay.*"

"What's your next question?"

"A Black boy growing up on a farm?"

I laugh. "Yep. I mean, when you're adopted by Black ranchers, that's kind of how it works out."

"*Adopted*? How did I not know you're adopted?"

"'Cuz you been keeping me away with a ten-foot pole." I reach over and nudge her foot with my hand, daring to leave it for as long as she lets me. "My older sister and I were in foster care for a while before our adoptive parents found us."

"That must have been hard," she says softly. The silken pads of her fingers slide over my knuckles, giving a subtle squeeze. It takes everything within me not to knit our fingers.

"I was five when the adoption was finalized, so I don't remember too much other than being excited to have a room of my own. My parents are great, though. It all worked out." Shrugging, I send over a half smile with my partial truth. There's more to it, but I always give a feel-good response when anyone tries to delve too deeply into my early years. In my experience, people don't actually want to hear the sob story of siblings found hiding in a closet amid domestic violence. Happy endings are better received. She holds my gaze as if she can see the shadows underneath my cover story, her thumb steadily stroking the back of my hand. The repetitive zing is hypnotizing. I never want it to stop. "What were you like as a kid?"

She moves her hand from mine, simultaneously blinking away our little moment. The double sensory loss punches me in the chest. "I was quiet, stayed out of the way, and did what everyone expected of me." The hollow drop in her tone is unbearable. Her eyes darken as if she's transported into a memory that isn't quite far enough away. That solid barrier she's kept in place around me has been a little more translucent tonight, but now, I feel her retreating into the locked away place she mentioned at the party.

"Hey," I whisper, squeezing her foot to bring her back to me. "Where'd you go, Gem?"

"Just..." Willa clears her throat and shakes the scowl off her face. "Fort Bender, California. If I know my parents at all, you'll understand completely before the end of Thanksgiving dinner. Just remember, you asked to come."

CHAPTER SIXTEEN

WILLA

TREVOR

Caught an early flight. Can I bring you lunch?

ME

Uh, sure? You know where the studio is?

TREVOR

I have this handy little gadget called GPS…

What sounds good?

ME

Veggie sub from Subbie's, hold the sarcasm.

TREVOR

LOL. Gimme 20.

Setting my phone to the side, I fiddle with the exposure on the Crockett family portrait.

"Working through lunch again?" Emily stops in front of my desk, tucking her short black hair behind her ear. She pulls the sleeves of her baggy cable-knit sweater over her knuckles.

I save the portrait and pull up the Brown family's file. "No. I have someone bringing me lunch."

"Ooh, like someone *special*?"

"Yes." The answer flies out of my mouth so fast, my hand slapping over my lips is almost comical.

Emily's face reflects my surprise as she leans over my desk. "The suspense! The intrigue! Tell me more..."

"He's just a friend." I stare at my screen, avoiding her gaze.

"A *special friend*, huh? Good for you, finally getting out there."

The tips of my ears burn as I try to focus on anything but the heat sliding up my neck. "I'm not *getting* anywhere. He's a friend —that's it. Not special or anything. Only a friend."

"Oh, okay. Got it. A super not special friend who turns the tips of your ears red. *Totally* just a friend."

Glaring over the monitor, I resist my impulse to crack a smile at my smirking assistant. She squints, staring me down, but a clearing of my throat has her snapping straight. "Okay, okay. I'm going to lunch now." She takes a slow step toward the door. "I won't ask anything else about your *special* friend." Another hesitant step. "*Or* decide to order in so I can meet him..."

"Emily, go."

"*Ugh*, fine," she says over her shoulder, quickening her pace. "You're always so secretive, Boss Lady. I promise I won't te—"

Emily bumps right into Trevor, smashing the Subbie's bag in his hand. "Ope! I'm sorry. You okay?" he asks, grabbing her shoulder while she steadies herself. The stretch Emily's neck has to make as she looks up at him is cartoonish.

"Whew! You're a tall drink!" Emily turns to me with no attempts to be subtle and says, "Good job, boss!"

I roll my eyes.

He chuckles and shakes her hand. "I'm Trevor. Nice to meet you."

"Emily... And I'm late for lunch. Bye!" She dips around him, flitting outside to her car.

"She's fun." Turning his smile on me, he struts to my desk, completely demolishing all my boss-mode attitude to goo as I melt down to my shoes. It's the dimples over the rugged line of his jaw, and the way his long olive Henley hugs around his shoulders. The sleeves pushed up his muscled forearms, with the tattoo snaking up the left side. Strong fingers clutching the white paper bag with my lunch in it certainly doesn't hurt. I'm eating it all up, and he hasn't even handed me my sandwich. "You okay?"

I snap to attention, ears burning again as I realize he watched me eye-fuck him all the way over here. "Mhmm." I clear my throat and look back at my computer screen. "I'm good."

"You sure?" He rests a hip on the edge of my desk. "Lookin' *pretty* hungry…"

I glance at the teasing slant of his lips, and my eyes get stuck. He winks, sending a rush of heat to my face. *Ass.*

With an eye roll, I snatch the bag from him. "Yeah. I *am* hungry. Pregnant here, remember?"

"Well, don't let me stop you." The amused twinkle in his eye holds me hostage as he bends to my eye level, plucks the sandwich from the bag, and hands it to me. His minty breath fans over my face. "Eat up, Willa." My chest seizes, breath gurgling in my throat as my gaze dips to avoid his stare, landing right back on his mouth. *That's worse.* I'm consumed by the vibrations humming through my body, unable to look away while he walks to the front desk for a chair. I try to keep my eyes to myself; I really do. But I take just a little peek at his barely laced work boots, and my gaze travels up to his ass in those jeans right as he looks over his shoulder, catching me in the act. Chuckling, he shakes his head while wheeling the chair over. "I meant eat the *food*, Jim. *Sheesh.*"

That'll do it. Jim breaks the spell, but I leave it alone. "Whatever." I hand him his sandwich. "Thanks for bringing me lunch."

"Thanks for letting me." We eat in silence for a solid minute before he clears his throat. "Can I have a little moment of insecurity?" he asks, looking down at his food.

"Umm." My voice is still husky, so I take a sip from my water bottle, expecting him to bring up the blatant simmering attraction between us. "Sure. What's up?"

"Uh…" He squeezes his eyes closed tightly, rubbing fingers across his forehead. *He's nervous*? "Do you hate me?"

What the hell? That's not even close to what I thought he was going to say. "Uh…no? Why would I hate you?"

He drags a hand down his face, shielding him from view. "I got you pregnant, for one. I'm pretty sure I bothered the hell out of you before then, and I just wouldn't be surprised if you hate me now. That night kinda changed the entire trajectory of your life."

"You're acting like I had no say in this." I take a bite of my sandwich and chew thoroughly before continuing, gathering my thoughts. *I know I've been frosty, but he really thinks I hate him?* "Wasn't I the one who told you to take me to your room that night? I'm the one who decided to keep this little gummy bear, and I'm actively choosing to change my own life. I don't hate you, Trevor, and I never have. I've made my own choices with all of this."

"Okay…but you don't like me."

"It's not that I don't like you." I sigh. "You're just…too nice."

"That's not a thing."

"It very much *is* a thing." I laugh, knocking my water off the edge of my desk to prove a point. He reaches over and grabs it right before it hits the floor. "See? Too nice. You're like a super-hero-boy-scout hybrid, and it just bothered me. I'm half convinced you stash a cape in your car."

"Let me get this straight. I'm too nice to you, and you hate me for it?"

"I don't hate you! You were just annoying."

He squints, but the smile teasing his lips gives him away before he laughs. "You're using past tense, which I'm going to assume is a good sign."

"Oh, you're still annoying." I nudge his foot and grin. "But I'm getting used to the 'nice' part. It's an adjustment."

"Yeah, well, buckle up, Jim." He misses my sneer at his use of *Jim* as he digs for the buzzing in his pocket, furrowing his brow when he sees the screen. "I'm just getting started…" he says distractedly. "Be right back." Pressing the phone to his ear, he struts to the front desk. I try to focus on my half-eaten sandwich, but whatever's happening sounds intense and keeps pulling my attention to him.

"Well." He sighs, striding back to me. "A pipe burst at the hotel I reserved. I don't want to be rude, but I need to scroll on my phone for a bit to find an alternative." He rubs a hand over his auburn fade and plops in the chair, staring at his screen with the same stressed look from when he asked if I hate him.

Seeing a tense Trevor unsettles me. I'm surprised by how much I don't like it. He's always so sure of himself. Easygoing and calm. And he's already done so much for me. *It's the least I can do.* "You could stay with me…"

"No." His eyes jump to mine, and he shakes his head emphatically. "You don't have to do that. I know you like your space. I'll be fi—"

"I want you to."

"You…do?"

"Why do you look so surprised?"

"I just found out you don't hate me five minutes ago. Gimme a minute to adjust," he teases.

I expect him to refuse, to pull his superhuman *I-can-handle-anything* bullshit. Instead, he rubs the back of his neck and nods. "Okay. I'll stay with you tonight. But I'm finding a hotel for tomorrow."

TREVOR

This couch is longer than most, but my head and feet hang off the ends as I try to get comfortable enough to sleep. I readjust my durag and turn toward the cushion, finding the perfect divot to wedge my shoulder into, when Willa shouts from her bedroom. I pause to be sure of what I heard, but after the second yell, I throw the blanket off and scramble to my feet. When I reach her door, the anguish in her voice is heart-wrenching enough that I don't even knock.

Willa's lying on her bed, head whipping back and forth as she thrashes around the tangled sheets, wailing, "No! Not my..."

Leaving the light off, I kneel at her bedside and rub her upper arm to wake her gently. "Willa. Hey. Wake up, sweetheart."

She jolts upright with a soul-shaking gasp, slowly taking in her dark bedroom. I squeeze her shoulder to make her aware of my presence, and she jumps.

"Hey"—I say, holding up my hands—"it's Trev. It's okay. You were having a nightmare."

"I know that!" she snaps. The scrunch in her forehead melts, and she covers her face with her hands. "*Ugh*, I'm sorry I woke you up."

"I was still awake. Let's get you back to sleep." I reach to replace her comforter, but she stays my hand.

"No." She fixes the hair scarf threatening to slide off her head. "I can't sleep now."

"What do you mean?"

"The first night this happened, I just went right back into it."

"The first night? How long has it been happening?"

She sighs and wrinkles her nose, pulling her comforter off her feet. "Almost two weeks."

"Willa—"

"*I know*," she huffs. "I should have told you. I'm sorry, okay? But they're nightmares, Trevor. Not exactly something you can fix." She swings her legs over the side of the bed and flips on the Tiffany lamp on her nightstand, bathing the room in a stained-glass glow. Her dark purple comforter and sheets are a wadded mess.

"And you're having them every night?"

She nods and rubs her face.

"What do you do when you have them?"

"I usually watch TV until it's time to get up for the day."

"Well, that stops now."

She leans away from me with a glare. "Excuse me?"

"TV is overstimulating. You're making it worse."

"Okay, well, I'm not going back to sleep just to be tortured awake again. What am I supposed to do?"

"Talk to me about it."

"*Ew*," she whispers, swiping her twists to the side so they cascade over her shoulder.

I shift off my knees, crossing my legs as I sit in front of her. "I'm serious. What happens in your dream?"

"I'm minding my business, holding the baby, and then a gale-force wind rips her away."

"*Her*? Did I miss some announcement?"

Her exasperation comes out as a prolonged sigh. "Look, I

don't know. She's a girl in my dreams. All I know is everything's fine until a storm cloud comes and rips her away."

"Okay...and what happens next?"

"I jump for her, but she's just out of reach. And then she's gone, and I wake up like I just did." Willa shudders and wraps her hands around her elbows.

"Do you trust me?"

"Eh..." Her nose scrunches as she looks me up and down.

Chuckling, I point to her pillow. "Lie down and close your eyes."

"...Why?"

Reaching around her, I plump it up, holding my hand out toward the bed. "You'll see."

She shakes her head, muttering under her breath as she lies down, staring at me the entire way.

I fix her bedding and drape it over her. "Close your eyes."

"Who's being bossy now, huh?" She shimmies her shoulders into the pillow, closing her eyes once she settles.

"Okay, so the sky's stormy, the baby gets lifted into the air, you can't reach them—

"Her."

"You can't reach *her*...except there's a bright pink ribbon strapped around her ankle and your wrist, keeping her anchored to you."

"What? That's not what happens..."

"What if you imagine it that way? Try it. Visualize your nightmare right up to the bad part and add in the ribbon."

She takes a few deep breaths, grimacing at first, but soon the tension in her body eases. When she opens her eyes, I can't help but smile at the wonder on her face. "Feel better?" I ask.

"What kind of sorcery was that? I threw in the ribbon, pulled her back to me, and the sun came out. Where did you learn that?"

"Therapy." I smile.

"You too, huh?"

"Yep. I had vivid nightmares for a while after I was adopted, and my parents got us into play therapy. I've kept it up with talk therapy through the years, off and on, whenever I need to go."

With a yawn, Willa nods, rubbing her eyes. I think my job here is done.

"Get some sleep. I'll be out on the couch if you need me." I push my knuckles into the mattress to help me stand, but she grabs my wrist.

"Could you stay with me?"

"Uh, sure. You have an extra blanket?"

"What's wrong with this one?" She waves over her blanket-covered body.

"You want me to sleep in the bed with you?"

"Yeah. Just in case your dream magic wears off and I wake up in a panic again. Plus, the bed is more comfortable than the couch..." She scoots to the other side of the king-sized mattress, flips open the covers, and pulls me down next to her. I lean back to scan her face. The last time we were in a bed together, we couldn't keep our hands off each other. Granted, I'm game, but she's just come around to the idea of us being friends. "It'll be *fine*, Trevor." She sighs. "We're adults. We can share a bed without having sex. And it's not like you can impregnate me...again."

"Watch it, Gem." I chuckle, shaking my head.

"Back at you, Dimples."

Stretching out next to her, I slide my hand behind my head as she plumps the other pillow. *This will be okay... I'm not a caveman.* I can control my urges for one night, no matter how much I want to wrap my arms around her and pull her into my lap. *We're friends.*

As soon as I have the thought, she rolls on top of my chest, nipples brushing against me through the worn fabric of her T-shirt. She reaches for the lamp and clicks it off, and I clench my fist to make sure my fingers don't graze the soft skin of her now exposed waist. I hold my breath, failing to ignore the searing swipe of her fingertips on my hip as she steadies herself. When she lies down, she turns and snuggles into my side. Warm coconut grips my senses as her touch seeps into my bones. She has no idea how close I am to losing my mind.

CHAPTER EIGHTEEN

WILLA

My bedroom is bright when I wake up, which is weird. I never sleep in. Once I blink clarity into focus, Trevor shifts around me. Literally. I'm curled into him, my head tucked under his chin, my arms wrapped around his waist while his encircle me completely. The nightmare started again last night, and I don't know if I reached out first or he did, but the warmth that spread through me as he enveloped me in his arms stopped everything. I woke up just enough to hear his heart beating and settled my head against it, holding on tightly until I drifted back to sleep.

"You up?" Trevor asks, rubbing my back.

I nod against him but make no attempts to move. As annoying as it is to admit, snuggling with him like this feels good. I've never been big on cuddling in past relationships. The men I've dated stayed pretty hands-off unless we were having sex. I'm not against it, as evidenced by the way I'm pressed up against this man in my bed, but it never seemed necessary.

Now that I know he's awake and *still* holding me, my heart thumps wildly. *This is couple behavior.* Too close—too intimate. His fingertips run up and down my spine in soothing passes, while his other hand anchors at my waist. We're welded together where his warm skin meets mine, as if melting into his touch has always been inevitable. It calms my racing thoughts enough for me to stay put, but not enough for me to resist bringing it up. "Is this weird? This is weird, right?"

"Not for me. I'm all for cuddling. Friends can cuddle."

"Yeah, *okay*," I mock, propping on my elbow as I adjust away from him. Not so far that we're no longer snuggled up, but just enough to feel like I've got some sense. Of course it's not weird for him. *Mr. Touchy Feely loves cuddling. Who would have guessed?*

"They can."

"What kind of friends cuddle, besides friends with benefits?"

"Us." He shrugs and sweeps a few twists over my shoulder, just staring at me. I'm waiting for a smile to signal his playfulness, but it takes a beat longer than I'm used to. His eyes peruse my face, mapping a trail of longing that makes the tips of my ears burn. My gaze drifts down to his lips as I recall how incredibly soft they were skirting over my skin. *No, ma'am—not going there.* Blinking rapidly, I will the logic back to my brain. *I shouldn't be staring back at him like this. I shouldn't be lost in his golden eyes flecked with green.* We're not compatible, and these damn hormones are messing with my mind. Clearing my throat, I sit up, his arms falling away. I need to change the subject.

"Can I ask you something?"

"Anything." He smiles. *Finally.*

"You talk about therapy so casually. Telling people doesn't bother you?"

"Nope. I've been going for so long; I can't imagine life without it." He sits up and stretches his back against the head-board. "Everyone needs help sometimes, and I like the unbiased view."

"I've been going for a year but still haven't told anyone."

"It's not anyone's business," he says. No prodding. No advice. Just a nonjudgmental shrug that makes me want to spill my guts.

"The whole reason I started was a little embarrassing. Admitting that I don't have it all together isn't easy for me, so it feels safer to keep it to myself, you know?"

A slight crease settles between his eyes, but he doesn't ask me to clarify. "If someone's going to look down on you for improving your quality of life, they're not someone worth keeping around."

Maybe that's what gets me—his willingness not to pry—because I surprise even myself when I tell him about my ex. "After being cheated on for the third time by the same guy—Carter—I figured it was time for an outside opinion on what my problem is."

"Relatable." He looks down and nods. "If it helps you feel less alone, my ex, Marla, cheated on me too. I've had maintenance appointments every few months for the last several years because of it. Keeps me on track."

I'm speechless. Partly from the way he talks about therapy, like it's an old friend he meets for lunch when they're in town at the same time. But also because—who would cheat on the all-American, always there for you, wouldn't hurt a fly superhuman? Those qualities translate well into a relationship. Why would someone throw that away? And of all the things, why is *this* the one we bond over? I'm tempted to ask what happened, but the way his face has fallen gives me pause. "Well, look at us." I nudge his leg with my foot. "We found something in common."

He chuckles, and by the time he looks back at me, the sullenness marring his face is replaced with a smirk. "Thanks for letting me crash here last night. I'll get out of your hair."

He flips the covers off his legs, and the loss hits me in the chest as if the wind is knocked out of me. The closer he gets to the door, the more my heart races at the thought of him leaving. I bite my tongue with the admonishment that this is not a thing. We spend time together for the baby's sake. That's it. We don't spend the night and snuggle and bond over failed relationships. *Except we just did*. And I enjoyed every second. When he reaches for the doorknob, I can't stop myself. "You could stay...if you wanted to. I have toiletries in the guest bathroom, and we could eat breakfast and—"

"You don't have to convince me to stay, Jim."

I growl. "Okay. New rule: *stop* calling me *Jim*. Wills is fine enough. Even Will. But Jim makes me sound like a basic-ass side character from a sitcom."

Trevor tilts his head, face twisted in confusion. He's quiet as his eyes scan around me, and then he hisses out a laugh. This man slumps against the door, laughing so damn hard he can hardly keep himself upright. I'm pretty sure those are—yep. He's wiping fucking tears from his eyes. How calling me *Jim* is so funny to him, I'll never understand, and this is what I mean. I don't get his humor. We're not compatible.

"Willa..." He wheezes, tipping his head back against the door frame. "I—" Another laugh rips from him, and he covers it with his hand. "Shit, no wonder you're always giving me stink eye." His chest heaves, stifling titters while he struts back to the bed. "Willa, I haven't been calling you *Jim*. I've been calling you *Gem*, like a jewel."

"Gem? Why the hell are you calling me Gem?"

"Gems in the ocean," he says with a bright smile.

"Is that a song or something? I'm confused..."

"A few years ago, after Chase and Kayla's wedding, you told me about the history behind Crystal Beach—how the ocean transformed the glass. It stuck with me. And the more time I spend with you, the more facets you reveal." He reaches down and tweaks my nose, snorting as I jut my head back in surprise. "After that revelation, I'm convinced. You're precious, Gem, and I refuse to believe otherwise." Trevor lets one more chuckle slip before he turns and walks from the room, calling out, "I'll stay for as long as you want me to."

The bathroom door shuts down the hallway, and I collapse on my pillow. For years I've been so irked by him calling me *Jim*, sometimes avoiding him in annoyance. I thought he was doing some juvenile grade school teasing, but never once considered he was saying something else. Something completely cute and sweet. Something that has me biting my lip as butterflies trample all over my reasons not to like him.

WILLA

Coming back to Fort Bender is always bittersweet. Cozy and familiar, but rifling with conflicting memories. Home is where I realized I was more than my textbooks. Where I fell in love with photography. Home is not my parents' house. That's why I'm at Sam's flower shop—phone turned off—instead of suffering through Thanksgiving meal prep.

Forget Me Nots has come a long way from the flower arrangements Samson sold out of the bed of his truck in high school. A large garden window is filled with a fall themed spray underneath the illustrated logo of a singular forget-me-not on the glass. The muted green walls of his updated shop are a stark contrast to the bubblegum pink they used to be when the building was Ye Old Candy Shoppe. He's doing some rebranding, and I offered to take his promo pictures while I'm here. With the amount of support he's given me through the years, I'm honored to.

We met in high school and became fast friends. I was the Type A bookworm tutor, and he was the lanky, misunderstood loner who was unapologetically obsessed with botany. He followed his passion and taught me how to follow mine. He's the only one who saw my love for photography back then. Encouraged me to hone my craft, even if it was just for myself, and helped cover for me when I dropped the accounting club to take photography lessons under the table. He was there when I chose myself and left my strict household. Even when I stayed away from town for all those years, he made it a point to keep in touch. Sam was the only one who showed up to my graduation from TAILA—him and his flowers.

"This place really looks great, Sam." I adjust the camera strap around my neck. "Turn to the left and prop your elbow on the counter." He fiddles with the curly brown man bun at the top of his head, then adjusts the blue flannel under his charcoal vest. His hipster lumberjack aesthetic, full beard included, might seem too rough around the edges for a flower shop owner at first. But one flash of his disarming smile against his brown skin pulls everything together. In a town as small as Fort Bender, everyone already knows who he is. Between the shop and running the town's only Christmas tree farm, Samson's the go-to plant guy in town.

"I really wish you'd let me pay for this," he says, still adjusting his clothes.

"Absolutely not. And if you bring it up again, I'll swap out those dahlias in the background for carnations."

"That's offensive, Will." Wrinkling his nose, he settles against the butcher block counter behind him. "Carnations are the ruffled tuxedo shirt of floristry. They should have gone out of style decades ago." They've been his least favorite flower for as long as I've known him. "Speaking of flowers, how's your Phalaenopsis?"

"*Whooo*?" I ask with a playful rise to my voice.

"Please don't make me say it..."

Laughing, I move the wooden step stool to the center of the room and climb up. "Clittercunt is a dramatic bitch. Too much water, then not enough. And her roots are growing out of the pot. I don't know what the hell she wants anymore."

"Phalaenopsis are the easy orchids, and those are the air roots... Did you even look at the care sheet I sent?"

Nope. "Yep." He doesn't need to know I accidentally drowned her when I got her, and she's lost all her flowers. I think I just need to let her dry out...

"So... How's the fam?" he asks.

I snap a couple of test shots, then step down and move the stool farther back. His tall, burly frame—bulked up since the last time I saw him—is still just a bit high for me to get a good shot. "They're doing what they do best. And that's why I'm here." My tight-lipped grin makes him laugh, giving me the perfect opportunity to take a candid shot. My parents "tried" to be more hands-off a few years ago, which only lasted a couple months before they were back on their overly critical bullshit. They haven't let up since, and coming home is an automatic lecture down high school memory lane.

"You're always welcome to come up to the farm. Dad's already planning to make way too much food. Claire and Maci would love to see you too."

"Hmm," I say, adjusting the focus with a twist of my hand. It's tempting, the thought of joining Sam for Thanksgiving. Escape is exactly what I want right now. I've done it before on holidays, when the scrutiny of my family was too much to handle. Hiding out in the redwoods is always perfect. The sense of peace that washes over me when I think about keeping this big news from my parents and walking away for good is immense. I don't tell them details about my life anyway, and they don't ask. It would be the easiest thing to keep this to myself, but as much as I want to accept his offer, I came into town for one reason. I need to go through with it no matter how much I'm dreading it. "As tempting as that is, I have to tough it out this year."

"What's special about this year?"

Hiding behind the camera, I freeze. I haven't told anyone yet—not even the girls at work. A few people know, sure, but I haven't said the words out loud to anyone except Trevor. It's not like I'm waiting to tell my parents—I don't want to give them that much power. But as soon as I say the words to someone else, it'll feel real. More real than the morning sickness that has petered out the last couple of weeks. As tangible as the ultrasound pictures sitting in my backpack in the corner. Pursing my lips, I lower the camera, letting it hang as I stare at my best friend. Telling Sam might be the comforting embrace I need before ripping off the bandage with my family. Air seeps from my lungs as I clutch my fingers. "I'm—"

A chime over the door sounds, and in strolls Super Dimples... *without his usual smile*? His eyes widen when he sees me, quick steps bringing us eye to eye. Sighing, he squints at the step stool. "You really shouldn't—"

"Yeah, yeah. What are you doing here? Did my mom send you?"

"Nope." The word comes out clipped, but he softens it with, "Ash said you'd probably be here."

Snitch. I roll my eyes and turn back to Sam, who holds his pose at the counter while his eyebrows do their best impression of the wave. "Sam, this is Trevor. He's...we're...I'm pregnant." *That wasn't so bad.* A little messy, but it's done now.

Sam's eyes widen, looking between us. "Can I...?" He hesitates, waiting for the all clear. He's the only one who ever asks for permission to hug me, even though he's the only one who doesn't need to ask. As soon as I nod, I'm eye to eye with him too as he wraps me in a bear hug, unaffected by the camera lens digging into our embrace. "Will! That's amazing—wait, is this a good thing?" He pulls back and searches my face as I shift the lens to the side.

"Yeah. It was unexpected, but still a good thing."

He turns and offers a hand to Trevor. "Hey, man. I think we've met before. Chase and Kayla's wedding?"

"I knew you looked familiar." They shake, and Trevor holds out his hand to help me down from the stool.

"And why didn't you tell me you were seeing someone?" Sam asks. "Last I heard, you were dealing with Carter's sorry ass."

"Because I'm *not* seeing anyone," I say, backing up toward my bag. Sam's eyebrows dance again.

"One too many birthday Lemon Drops and a faulty condom equals baby," Trevor explains.

Sam bursts out a laugh. "That's probably the most on-brand way for you to get pregnant, Will. Let loose *one time*, and now you're in for the ride of your life. How far along are you?"

"A couple days short of twelve weeks." Holding up the pictures from the ultrasound, I sidle up next to him.

"So tiny! I remember when Maci was that small." He traces a finger over the black-and-white images, then pulls me in for a one-armed hug. "Congrats, Will! You'll be the best mom." The warmth spreading through me as I let my friend's excitement fill me up gives me a little hope that the conversation with my parents might go over well too.

"...A BAR?" TREVOR STOPS ABRUPTLY ON THE SIDEWALK, my purple camera backpack slung over his shoulder. "I thought you wanted food."

"I do," I say, pulling open the heavy metal door. "From *Harv's*." When I step inside, the place is dead. *Perfect. No noise.*

"Is it even open?" Trevor says, looking around the deserted room. "It's Thanksgiving."

"Harv's is always open." I take off for a stool at the bar, the familiar stick of my sole to the epoxy floor bringing a smile to my face. Flickering neon beer signs hum against the walls among the red Christmas lights left up year-round. During tourist season, everyone flocks to Patti's Place across the street, leaving Harv's as a quiet oasis for the locals. This dark, dingy dive is my preference any time of year. I drum my fingers on the wooden bar top as Trevor settles on the stool next to me. "It'll be busy tonight, once everyone gets sick of their families."

"So that's why you snuck out this morning? Sick of your family?"

I click my tongue, pointing at him. "Bingo. The less time I spend there, the easier it is on everyone."

"Eh. Not *everyone*..." he says quietly. The concern on his face shoots unease through me, but I glance away when the swinging kitchen doors bang against the wall. Harvey Morales stands with his hands on his hips, bald head gleaming with sweat. Thick gray chest hair tufts out around the stretched neck of his white T-shirt. A salt-and-pepper beard covers his tanned face, and he looks like a gruff pirate with his squinted eye. He stalks toward us with a determined limp, a low growl rumbling from his chest when he settles across the counter from us. His hardened gaze lands on me, then a toothy grin slides across his lips. "Well, well, look what the turkey dragged in...

"It's a cat, Harv," I tease.

"Yeah, yeah..." He plucks a pen from behind his ear and positions his palm like an order pad. "Lucky for you, I popped some cheese sticks in the fryer just now... Interested?"

"Is that even a real question?" I laugh. "How'd you know I was in town?"

"I saw you creep into Sammy's place when I opened this morning. Knew you'd harass me for fried cheese sooner or later." He jots on his hand, then leans against the counter. "How's my favorite former student?"

Trevor juggles a quizzical look between us, and I laugh again. "I used to keep the books for Harv in exchange for photography lessons." My explanation only deepens the furrow between Trevor's eyes, but he says nothing. *Why's he so quiet today?* "My parents nixed photography classes in high school, so I found a way to do it under the table." I shrug and turn back to Harv. "This is Trevor."

"*Oh?*" He lilts, reaching a meaty palm across the bar top to shake Trevor's hand. "A strapping suitor?"

"Just a friend," I assure him.

"Well, *just a friend...*" he says to Trevor. "Can I get you anything?"

"I'm alright, thanks." He flashes a polite grin that doesn't reach his eyes. *Weird.*

"Alright." Harv slides to the drink dispenser, fills a couple of glasses with water, and sets them in front of us. "Gimme a few minutes. And don't you think about pulling out your wallet, Willa. It's on the house." He turns on his heel and pushes through the swinging doors.

"Bad business model!" I call, smiling at his boisterous laugh muffled by the wall. We used to battle over his business losses daily. As I turn toward Trevor to finish explaining how our barter worked in high school, the brooding shadow over his face catches me off guard. "Everything okay?"

His eyes are glued to his fingers as they tap the bar top. "I wouldn't know."

"Wha—are you mad at me or something?"

"Not mad. Frustrated."

"With *me*?" I scoff. Clearly Mom has got her hooks into him if he's already blaming me for ruining today. "What the hell did I do? I haven't seen you all day."

"Exactly. You disappeared, Gem. Turned off your phone and didn't tell anyone where you were."

"I've told you before, you're not my handler."

He grumbles under his breath, dragging his palm down his face, spine rigid. I've never seen him like this. Nodding slowly, his hand settles over his mouth like he's physically stopping himself from saying something rash. After a deep breath, he drops his hand and turns to me, voice calm. "I didn't know if you were sick again. Or hurt. Worse. I've been worried all morning."

Duh. The baby. I swear these hormones are making me stupid, and now I feel like a bitch. Of course he'd be worried about the baby. Having him—anyone—in the picture is still an adjustment, but since we're doing this together, taking him into consideration needs to start immediately. "Hey..." I place my hand on his forearm. "I know I need to be better about keeping you in the loop with the baby. But everything's oka—"

"Not just the baby, Willa. You. I've been worried about *you* all morning."

Oh. "Why?"

"Because you've mentioned how much you hate it here. How horrible it was for you."

Aw, shit. Now I feel like a super bitch. I didn't even think about it when I left this morning. Staying away is how I cope when I come home. No one's ever had a problem with it until now. That the father of my child might be concerned about my well-being never even crossed my mind.

"Hot cheese!" Harv bursts through the doors right as I open my mouth to apologize. Trevor drops his gaze and turns back to the bar as Harv sets the mozzarella sticks down. "It's good seeing you, Willa. The game's back on, so I'll leave you to handle these. Don't be a stranger, okay?"

"No stranger than you." I fake a smile as he squeezes my hand. He disappears into the kitchen, leaving Trevor and I in awkward silence. After several minutes, I whisper, "I'm sorry, Trev." I swing my legs around to face him, waiting until his eyes meet mine to finish. "You're right. I should have told you I was leaving."

"I'm not trying to control what you do or who you're with. Your business is yours alone. But it would be nice to know you're okay."

"Okay. I can do that... I'm just not used to people caring, I guess. But I can do better."

"Thank you." With a smirk, he steals a mozzarella stick. "Now let's see what's so special about these that pissing your mom off on Thanksgiving is worth it."

"Oh God, what did she say now?" I roll my eyes, but giggle at the deepening smile on his face. *There he is.*

"Very colorful language for eight in the morning."

"I'm sure it'll come full circle when I break the news."

"*We.*" He taps my foot with his. "When *we* break the news... Have you thought about when you want to do it?"

I don't *want* to do it at all. But I think having him participate in the conversation will only make things worse. "After dinner tonight. I'm hoping the pie lessens the blow," I tease. "But let me handle it. It'll be best coming from only me."

"Willa..."

"It'll be best that way. Please, just trust me." I can't help the grimace that pinches my face. I'm not even sure I believe myself at this point.

He slips a hand on my shoulder, giving it a little shake. "It'll all be okay."

I sure fucking hope so.

CHAPTER TWENTY

WILLA

That hopeful shit was short-lived. As soon as Trevor and I walked back into my parent's house, Mom was on one. Not with Trevor. *Nooo.* He can do no wrong in my parent's eyes.

Ashlie and Hunter have invited him to a few family gatherings over the years, and my parents are completely taken with him. When I told them Trevor was coming again this year, they didn't even hesitate before asking how they could accommodate his stay. They have no idea he's the other half of their future grandchild.

Mom's problems today are solely with me. First, she took issue with me being gone all morning, grumbling about hours wasted on food prep like she wouldn't have sent me out of the kitchen if I so much as looked at her side dishes. When I tried to appease her, despite my aversion to every single smell coming from the stove, I was in the way. Now I'm selfish for staying out of her way, and she's made sure everyone at this dinner knows it. Her glare cuts across the table anytime I say something. I'm finding it harder to remain neutral with my rage bubbling under the surface.

"Any set date for the wedding?" Dad asks Hunter and Ashlie. His bald head shines under the chandelier lights, dark brown skin wrinkled at the corners of his eyes.

They glance at each other quickly and back to Dad before Hunter clears his throat. "Not yet. We're still talking about it."

"Ashlie, is a long engagement really your style? You'll want to get your venue early to make sure there's enough space for everyone." Mom taps her tiny afro as she looks over her glasses, her amber skin just as vibrant as it's always been. I reach for the mashed potatoes, the only thing I've been able to choke down tonight, and she clears her throat, side-eyeing me. "Don't you think you've had enough? Remember, a moment on the lips, forever on your hips, Willa."

Worry about your own damn hips. Glaring at her scrutiny, I dig the serving spoon deep into the potatoes and plop triple the amount I was originally going for. Will I eat it all? No, but it took me a long time to love my body the way it is. I'm not letting this quick trip back to hell ruin that. Her nostrils flare at my rebellion, but Ashlie quickly chimes in.

"We've only been engaged a few months. I think we're okay to wai—"

"A dress!" Mom says, eyes still fighting with mine. She slowly turns back to Ashlie, shifting into a pleasant look that would give the best supervillain whiplash. "You'll want to start those fittings soon..." This isn't new behavior from her. She likes to insert her ideas and make you think you're crazy if you don't agree. Meanwhile, Dad watches it all quietly, as usual. It's clear who dominates in this household.

"Mama, we're not—"

"And flowers! I bet Samson would love—"

"Mama!" Ashlie slams her knife and fork down, halting Mom's diatribe. "We're not having a big wedding."

"Nonsense." Mom waves her hand in the air and takes a sip of her water. "Don't be selfish. We have a lot of family who will be so disappointed if they aren't invited."

"I guess they can be disappointed from the courthouse parking lot then," Ashlie mumbles down at her plate, picking up her fork. Hunter chokes on his drink next to her.

Mom's icy glare flashes on Ashlie so quickly, my older sister protective instinct takes over. I'm tired and grumpy, and watching Ash struggle to be heard makes something in me snap. "So, I'm pregnant."

Hunter chokes again, Ashlie drops her utensils on her plate, and all eyes are on me as I shovel mashed potatoes in my mouth. I chance a look at Trevor, who's gaping at me.

Dad puts a hand on Mom's shoulder, but she pushes it away as she stands. "A word, Wilhelmina." She takes calculated steps toward the study, and I indulge in one more bite of potatoes before wiping my mouth with a napkin and throwing it over my plate. When I stand, Dad follows me, creating an intimidation sandwich. Ready or not, this is happening.

As soon as he closes the door, Mom starts in on me. "How could you be so irresponsible, Willa? And lying to us all day about it. This is art school all over again."

The viridian glow from the banker's lamp on the desk tints her skin like the wicked witch she is. Jumping to all those conclusions must be exhausting. I perch on the arm of the leather wing-back chair by the door, staring past her at the jacquard curtains like I did when I was seventeen. My arms settle across my chest as I armor up. *Déjà vu has nothing on this.*

Dad paces the room, not saying a goddamn thing about her tirade. *Fucking typical.*

"What were you possibly thinking?" Her shrill voice puts my glare back on her. "Why do you insist on throwing your potential down the drain?"

"Why are you talking to me like I'm a child who—"

"Because you're acting like one!" Mom snaps. "Don't expect us to pay for any of this, Wilhelmina. You're grown. Now act like it." She marches up to me and sticks her finger in my face. "Your little outburst ruined Thanksgiving dinner. You *will* go out there and apologize to everyone at the table."

She won't shut up long enough for me to explain this was all unplanned. That all precautions were taken. Hell, I haven't even said who the father is. I'm one more assumption away from storming out of here and never coming back.

"I know I'm grown. It's *you* who seems to forget. Most people would be elated to learn their daughter is pregnant with their first grandchild. But not you. *Oh, nooo.* You use it as a way to prove some point and lecture me over a choice I made fifteen years ago."

"But how can you support a baby with an unpredictable salary?" Dad's voice is a soft contrast to Mom's.

"My studio is thriving. Nothing about it is unpredictable. You'd know that if you pulled your head out of Mom's ass and opened your goddamn eyes." I spit the words out, which makes Mom take a step back despite the scalding burn in her gaze. The rage I've been pushing down roils over the surface as I come to realize there's no other way this would have played out. I didn't follow their prescription for life, and for that reason, I'll always be a failure in their eyes.

CHAPTER TWENTY-ONE

TREVOR

"Is it Carter's?" Robert Willis asks.

"Of course not! She wouldn't dare do something like this with someone who has a good head on their shoulders," Jackie answers.

Their muffled voices amplify behind the wooden door, loud enough that Hunter, Ashlie, and I hear them from the brown floral couch in the living room.

"I should go in there..." I shift to stand, but Hunter's arm stops me.

"Naw, bruh." He shakes his head emphatically. "I don't think that'll help right now."

Ashlie shivers on his lap and turns to me with a grimace on her face. "Yeah. You might want to wait. This conversation is long overdue."

We shift our attention back to the study, and everything inside of me is screaming to go in there and rescue Willa. Even though she asked me to let her handle it, this doesn't feel right. She's dealing with her parents alone, getting attacked about things that have nothing to do with being pregnant. It all feels so wrong, and I'm letting it happen. I try to stand again, but this time, Ashlie's the one to stop me.

"Just one more minute, Trev. This isn't about the baby," she says.

"We're not helping you," Jackie booms. "You made your bed; now lie in it."

"I didn't ask you to! I don't need your help, and I damn sure don't want anything from you. I'm done." Willa rips the door open and storms right out of the house without so much as a glance behind her.

Before anyone can stop me, I run after her, grabbing my coat off the hook by the door and racing down the sidewalk. The chilly air shocks my system as I rush down the pavement. *I should have gone in there*. I should have followed them into the room and taken responsibility for the situation we're in. Less than twelve weeks, and I've already let her down.

Willa's walking fast. It takes me several jogged steps to catch up with her as the wind whips her twists behind her.

"Willa, wait."

She doesn't, and I can't blame her.

"I'm fine, Trevor," she snips over her shoulder. "Go back inside."

"I'm not doing that..." Falling in step with her, we round the corner at the end of the block. We cross the street and enter a large field. The sun has been down for at least an hour, the frigid wind curling around us as I try to keep from shivering inside my sweater. "It's freezing out here."

"So put your coat on and *go inside*." She marches through the damp grass, straight for the playground ahead of us.

"This isn't for me, Gem." I slide my coat over her shoulders, and for the first time since I caught up to her, Willa looks at me. From any other person, I'd expect a tear-streaked face, but the only sign of wayward emotion is the flicker of hurt in her eyes before she takes a deep breath. She slides her arms into the sleeves and ambles over to the swing set, holding out the other swing for me once she sits. We sway back and forth silently for minutes that seem to stretch into hours. I want to apologize. *Need* to. But I don't know that breaking the silence is what *she* needs right now. As much as I like to talk things out, I'm learning she needs time to process. For now, I hope my presence is a sufficient peace offering.

Shifting my eyes to her periodically, I check the progress of the waning scowl on her face. She twists in her swing, the metallic clink chipping away at the tension each time the chains cross above her head. Finally, she sighs. "I used to spend so much time on this swing after fights with my parents." She chuffs bitterly. "I'd sit here and imagine running away—starting a new life—until one day, I finally did. I guess old habits die hard."

"Willa, I'm—I should have been in there with you. I'm so sorry."

"You being in there wouldn't have mattered. It probably would have made it worse. Don't worry about it." Her eyes lift to mine, but there's no anger. The remnants of hurt have disappeared too. *Apathy*. Considering what just happened, my heart breaks for her.

"It matters to me..."

She shrugs, sliding her feet along the rubber playground tiles as the chains on her swing straighten out. "They said almost the exact same things when I told them I was going to art school. I've spent all these years trying to prove to them and myself that I could make it on my own. Gave up so many frivolous rites of passage in college to get where I am today. No parties. No breaks. Very few friends. Still, no matter how much I achieve, they shit on it." Willa turns to look at me head-on. "Do you know what that feels like? Trying to be seen by your own parents? Killing yourself to earn an ounce of support from them?"

I can't say I know what that feels like. Not really. My parents are the most supportive people around, and my memories from before I was adopted are fuzzy, at best. As she searches my eyes with what feels like longing for a kindred spirit, I want so badly to give her the support she deserves. I failed her back there, and after tonight, it's clear to me she doesn't believe she has anyone in her corner. I want her to know she's not alone. "Come home with me," I say, side-stepping her question.

"What?" Her eyebrows dip, and she stops fidgeting in the swing.

"For Christmas. Come home with me. Meet my family. Let me show you there are people out there who will support you."

"They don't even know me..."

I shrug. "Doesn't matter. You're carrying a part of me. That'll be enough for them."

"Aren't you from Iowa or something?"

"Nebraska"—I chuckle—"but same difference. They'll love to have you, especially after we share the news."

"I don't know, Trev. That sounds eerily similar to *meeting the parents*." She squints at me, but a playful smile creeps across her lips.

"Is that a 'yes'?" I ask, waggling my eyebrows. Laughing, she rolls her eyes, which I'm learning is her tell before giving in. "Yeah?"

Chewing on the inside of her lip, she nods. I can't deny the elation spreading through my chest at the thought of bringing Willa home.

"I'M NOT GOING BACK IN THERE." WILLA SHAKES HER head as we near the walkway to her parents' house. "Ashlie can bring my stuff out. But I'm not—"

"It's already handled." Slipping my phone from my pocket, I shoot off a text to Ashlie and Hunter. While we sat out on the swings, I had them pack up our bags and book the next flight back to LA. I'd already planned on flying back with everyone to make Willa's twelve-week appointment on Monday. A few extra days there is worth it just to get her out of here tonight.

"What do you mean *handled*?"

"I mean, you and I are flying back to LA tonight, and after I go in there and have a word with your parents, I doubt they'll want me to stay anyway."

Ashlie comes out then, rolling Willa's suitcase and her own. I start toward the door, but Willa grabs my wrist.

"Trevor, you really don't need to say anything."

"Yep. I do. I should have said it an hour ago." Squeezing her shoulder, I give a reassuring smile. "It'll only take a second, then we can leave." I don't wait for her response before I head up the porch and into the house.

Hunter meets me in the foyer, holding my bag and his. "You're leaving?" I ask.

"Hell, yeah. Bruh, there's no way we're staying after that shit show. I hate it here." He hands me my bag, and I stick it on the floor next to the door, ignoring the confused look on his face. "You good?"

"Yep, just need to handle something." I take a step toward the kitchen.

"You need backup?"

"Nah, I got it."

I've never felt as determined as I do now, walking through the first floor of the Willis house, following the sounds of dishes clanking in the kitchen. The shaggy brown carpet quiets my foot-steps so I unintentionally surprise Rob and Jackie when I step onto the vinyl floor. I clear my throat, and they both start.

"Oh! Trevor, you scared the living daylights out of me," Jackie says. She dries her hands and holds her arms out to me, as if hugging it out can make up for anything. The thought of her touching me makes my skin crawl. "I apologize for my daughter's tantrum at the dinner table. Wilhelmina is—"

"—Carrying my child," I finish for her. The pleasant smiles drop from their faces. Robert and Jackeline have always welcomed me with open arms. I've never had reason to think they weren't decent people, until tonight. And now, I have to remind myself to breathe deeply, trying to hold on to a modicum of self-control while watching an array of emotions contort their faces.

"*Y-you*?" Robert's voice matches the surprise creasing his face

Nodding, I cross my arms over my chest, removing all the friendliness from my voice. "And to address your concerns, Willa won't need your help with a damn thing. She's resilient and strong, and the most brilliant person I've ever met. She has every-thing covered, and I have *her* covered." Stepping forward with rage settling into my jaw, I juggle my measured stare between them until I'm sure my message is received loud and clear. *This won't happen again.* "Despite the mediocre examples she obvi-ously had in you two, she'll be an amazing mom. So you can go ahead and keep those projections about your own parenting to yourselves. We're good on that. Wouldn't want to stress the baby, now would you?" An arrogant smile slides across my lips as I wait for them to fill the silence swallowing up the kitchen. They don't. "Thanks for having me. We have a flight to catch." I turn on my heel, and I'm met with a gaping, wide-eyed Willa. Her expression remains as I walk toward her and slip my hand around hers. "Ready?" I ask.

She nods, turns her back on her parents, and after I grab my bag, we head outside to the waiting rental in the driveway. Before climbing into the car, she stops me with a hand on my chest.

"You didn't have to say all that... Thank you." Her eyes give just enough vulnerability to seize my heart. *Has no one ever fought for her*? If she doesn't think I'd do that ten times over, she's dead wrong.

I pull her into a hug, expecting her usual stiffened reaction, but she surprises me by fully wrapping her arms around my waist. Burying my face in her hair, I kiss the top of her head. "I meant every word, Willa. I want you to know that."

WILLA

This whole peeing every thirty minutes is pissing me off. I've barely made it through each holiday mini-session before beelining to the bathroom. I swear I've run back there ten times today. Yet, here I am, sipping water at my desk because I've never been this damn thirsty in my life.

"Hey, Willa!" Cara strolls through the door with a smile and a newly dyed lavender bob framing her face. My junior photographer is taking over the rest of the holiday minis today so I can get to my twelve-week appointment. She just doesn't know that's the reason.

I still haven't told anyone at work about being pregnant, and luckily, my assistant Emily is too much of a space cadet to notice my frequent breaks. At first, I didn't want to jinx anything, knowing how iffy the first trimester can be. But after my parent's reaction last week, I don't have any interest in sharing baby news with anyone else.

"Hey!" I minimize the seven mommy blogs on my computer screen as she passes by. I've channeled my anger from Thanksgiving into researching how to travel through Europe with an infant in tow. There are a few bloggers who've done it, and it seems doable for me with some adjustments. Excitement sparks in my chest, my teeth stifling the smile threatening my lips. *I don't have to give up Europe. I can make this work.*

"Who's coming in today?" Cara asks, her hip leaning against the edge of my desk. I stand to show her today's setup.

"The Barlow family is first. They requested candy canes and snowmen, which I've already laid out." I gesture toward the snowy backdrop hanging on the wall.

"Ooh, the kids will love that!"

"My thoughts exactly." The little Barlow twins are going to lose it over the tiny snowman stuffies I found. "Emily confirmed the pet deposit went through for Mrs. Albert, so we should be all set there. Just remember, her dog tries to eat everything."

"Got it. Thanks for trusting me with this on my own, Willa. I really appreciate it."

"You've come so far this year." Squeezing her arm, I give her a reassuring smile, mentally sending her all the good luck I can. "You'll do great. We'll work together on edits later this week." These will be her first solo sessions, and even though it's only two, I remember how nerve-racking it can be. That's why I haven't told her this is a trial run for when I leave on my trip.

Settling back at my desk, I dig into the bag of peanut butter crackers I've been thinking about since the Delta family walked out ten minutes ago. I want to get some Christmas card sneak peeks sent off before I head out, but as soon as I wake up my computer, my phone buzzes.

TREVOR

You sure I can't pick you up?

ME

I'm just down the street. I'll be fine.

TREVOR

Okay, but dinner's on me…

> Oh, and don't be surprised when you come
> home to a clean kitchen 😊

I roll my eyes as I set down my phone, but the smile sliding across my lips is undeniable. He *would* clean my kitchen, even after I told him to leave the mess for me as I rushed out to work this morning. We got back from Bender a few days ago, and Trevor's stayed with me all weekend, taking a personal day so he can be at my appointment this afternoon. After seeing him stick up for me to my parents—hearing his confidence in my abilities to be a mother—I have to acknowledge how nice it is to have someone on my side. To feel protected for once. Not to mention every horny molecule that surged through my body at his deep, assertive baritone. I still have to fan myself when I think about it. But that's definitely just the hormones speaking. I looked it up to be sure.

"How's my favorite patient?" Dr. Quentin asks, sliding her rolling stool in front of the exam chair. "Still feeling yucky?"

"It's tapered off, as long as I eat every forty-five minutes."

"Good. Good. Make sure you're eating lots of fresh produce along with your cravings. Any questions for me?" She looks from me to Trevor and back. When I shake my head, he scoffs.

"She's been having nightmares and can't get back to sleep after." He glances at me, smirking at my side-eye.

"See! I knew I liked you, Trevor. Keeping our girl honest." She smiles at him before fixing her eyes on me. "Vivid dreaming, nightmares, even sex dreams—they're all normal. Your body's going through a lot of stress right now. Hormones are all over the place. It should taper off as the pregnancy progresses. In the meantime, try to minimize stress during waking hours. Rest when you're tired, less screen time in the evening, daily walking. Oh, and sex."

"Uhhh..." I swear my gulp is louder than the snickering happening behind me. I don't dare look back at Trevor.

"Yep. Well, orgasms, specifically. You don't have to have intercourse, but any of those things should help with stress." She smiles and turns around on her stool to open the cupboard behind her. "Now, let's check on that baby. Let me grab the Doppler." My heart thumps wildly. I can't decide if this is nerves about the baby or the thought of having doctor-prescribed sex with the man I've been cuddling in my bed the last several nights.

She smears the warmed gel over my belly with the fetal Doppler wand. "We're just going to see if we can hear the heartbeat. It's early, so I don't want you to worry if we can't pick it up. I'll double-check everything with another ultrasound if it comes to that."

Holding my breath, I nod quickly, suddenly terrified we won't hear anything. Just as soon as I tense, Trevor's warm breath fans over my ear. "You gotta breathe, Gem."

The air stays trapped in my throat anyway. This is the most stressful thing I've ever experienced, waiting to see if those ever-persistent sound waves will pick up the tiniest heartbeat.

Dr. Quentin smooths the wand around my belly. "Oh, that's loud!" She cranks the dial down on the machine and flashes a smile. "That one's yours. Let's just move it...yep! There it is. That's your little nugget!"

My eyes widen at the rapid pulsing coming from the speaker. It's so fast, as if the little one is sprinting in a marathon inside me. *There's an actual baby in there.* I turn to a slack-jawed Trevor with tears in my eyes, his gaze plastered to the machine.

Smiling, she reaches for a towel to clean the wand. "It's amazing, isn't it? Hard to believe that little chaos maker is in there and you can't even feel them. Let's get you cleaned up. I'll see you back in four weeks." She wipes the gel off my stomach as calm as a summer's day, tossing the towel in a basket casually, as if she didn't just witness my entire world changing. With one repetitive whoosh, that tiny nugget has carved out the center of my heart and nestled in tightly. I'll do everything in my power to ensure safety. I'm going to be a mom. A damn good one too.

CHAPTER TWENTY-THREE

WILLA

"That was surreal." Trevor shakes his head as we walk through the parking garage, his hand secured to my lower back.

"Amazing." The smile hasn't left my face since we heard the heartbeat. "Now the little nugget wants chicken nuggets," I say through a yawn. "And a nap, apparently."

"How about you go home and relax? I'll pick up dinner."

"I can just pick up nuggets on my way, Trev."

"True. But you're tired and need to rest and *de-stress*..." His eyebrows dance playfully. "...For the little nugget in there..."

"Okay, fine. You can bring me dinner. But I want them from Mindee's. And it's *Deserted Desire* night."

"Is that some kind of pregnancy foreplay?"

"Wh—no! It's a show." I push his shoulder, and he flashes that dimply smile.

"Hey, you heard the doctor." He laughs, holding up defensive hands like foreplay is a perfectly normal conclusion to come to right now. "It sounds like the kind of show you find on very specific websites... What kind of shows are you into, Willa?"

"The reality dating kind of show, *Trevor*. We'll eat, watch a show, and go to bed."

"*Bed*?" He wiggles his eyebrows again.

My ears burn at his implication. "*To sleep*. That's all." It's been a task, admitting to myself that sharing a bed with him satisfies the touch-starved version of me I've ignored for years. The part that pretended she was okay with purely physical relationships without the intimacy. Cuddling in bed with anyone else has always felt forced and unnecessary, a notion upheld by the men I dated. With Trevor here the last few days, I reach for him at the first sign of my recurring nightmare without hesitation. I'm relying on his comfort in a way that scares me if I think about it for too long.

"I dunno... Kinda sounds like a *date*, Gem," he teases, opening my door. This conversation is couple behavior, and I'm not sure how to feel about that. I slide behind the wheel and flip him off, which only makes his smile grow with his laughter. Grabbing my wrist, he dips his head to kiss my middle finger. The feeling of his lips on my skin sends heat spreading up my neck in a rapid wave. He must hear my breath hitch because he winks before giving my hand back. "I'll meet you at your place."

I spend the entire drive painfully aware of the tingling spot on my finger where Trevor kissed it. *This is so stupid*. I know he was just messing around—but his wink replays in my mind, and I almost miss my damn exit. *What the hell is wrong with me?*

It's not until I'm under the shower stream trying to convince myself I don't need to slip the shower head wand between my legs that I realize what's going on here. I'm pregnant, horny, and have a hot man giving me his undivided attention all day, then holding me in bed all night. In a huff, I turn off the water and squeeze out my washcloth, leaving the shower head in its holder out of spite. *This is all just hormones*. The doctor even confirmed my hormones are all over the place. I repeat the mantra as I reach for my body oil and drip the coconut scent over my arms and legs. *Just hormones*. Slipping into my lavender satin pajama set, I repeat it still. *Hormones*. That's the perfectly logical reason for why I can't stop myself from remembering the way his big, strong hands held me over his hips while I—

Three quick taps at my front door snap my horny ass out of it. I scurry down the hallway, and I'm all but recovered by the time I turn the knob. Until I open the door and get an eyeful of him holding the chicken nuggets I've been craving since my appointment. *Dinner and a motherfucking snack.* For a split second, I don't know which one I want to reach for first as we stare at each other over the threshold. But then Trevor tilts his head and opens his mouth to speak, and I remember I only have a claim on the food.

"You okay?" His eyebrows dip over the confusion in his hazel eyes.

"Yep." I smile and drop my gaze to my toes as I step aside to let him in. "Just tired."

"Well, let's get you fed so you can sleep." He leaves his shoes at the door and strolls right into my kitchen to wash his hands. I'm stunned as he pulls out plates and bottles of water, like he owns the place. I open my mouth to tell him off, but get distracted by the way his jeans stretch over his ass and lick my lips instead.

"Willa?"

"Hmm?" I blink at him. Not only have I missed whatever he just said, but I've been caught ogling the hell out of him while I stand at the open door.

"Did you want water?"

"Yeah," I squeak, resisting the urge to fan my face. Nudging the door closed with my hip, I try to gain my composure. I make a beeline for the couch, settling under my blanket once I get there. When Trevor comes around the sofa with the food, I pull my feet onto the cushion to give him better access to the coffee table. One plate is piled high with nuggets, while the other has small containers of every dipping sauce Mindee's offers. "I don't think you got enough sauce there, Trev..."

He chuckles and turns back for the water bottles in the kitchen. "I didn't know what you or little nugget liked. Getting one of everything seemed like the safest choice." He hands me a bottle, and the gurgle from my stomach is so loud his eyes widen with amusement. Grabbing the entire plate of nuggets, he puts it in my lap with a flourish. "Oh, and this." A small cup lands on the plate with the other condiments. Stealing a nugget, he sits next to me on the couch.

"Applesauce? What am I supposed to do with that?"

"People generally eat it..."

I sigh, side-eyeing him. "I *meant*, why is it next to my honey mustard?"

"This was the only way I ate them as a kid. Try it, Gem. You might like it." He grabs another nugget from my lap, dunks it into the applesauce, and brings it to my lips with a playful expression. I wrinkle my nose. *He's not serious...* "You scared?"

"No," I scoff. The look on his face makes me want to accept the challenge just to show him I'm not intimidated by him or his weird food combinations. I lean forward and take a bite, holding his gaze the entire time, stifling a moan when his eyes dart quickly to the finger brushing my lips. They settle back on mine, the subtle ring of green drawing me in like a moth to an intoxicating hazel flame. My urge to lay him out right here threatens to override the logic quickly slipping from my grasp. The food combo isn't bad; I can see why someone would like it. But this eye contact is dangerous, and neither of us has looked away yet. "It's good, yeah?" His husky tone sends a shiver through me.

Even after all my self-imposed warnings tonight, I nod as I lean forward for another bite, closing my lips over the tips of his finger and thumb. What harm would it do to give in and have a repeat of that night in San Diego? He's fine as hell, and I'm *already* pregnant. My body is screaming at me to flip this plate of food and climb on his lap. I'm ready to do it, too, right as he clears his throat and sits back against the couch arm.

He hands me the remote, stealing another nugget in his retreat. "Now, for the dirty movie portion of the night."

"*Ugh*, it's a show!"

"Whatever you need to tell yourself," he jokes, sliding his hand over my blanketed foot. And then he leaves it there, making lazy passes over my toes through the first thirty-minute episode. When we start the second, he tugs my legs onto his lap with no protests from me. Even with the blanket as a barrier, his touch seeps through to my skin. I give in to his warmth, and after a few yawns, I don't remember seeing the previews for next week.

CHAPTER TWENTY-FOUR

TREVOR

Willa groans next to me, waking me enough to peek blurry eyes over to the alarm clock on the nightstand. I carried her to bed after we fell asleep on the couch a few hours ago. It's about time for the nightmare, so I tuck her into my side, rubbing her back to soothe her. She moans again and plants one leg over mine, wedging my knee between her thighs. I try to adjust to a friendlier position, despite the twitching in my boxers. While I really don't mind having her up close like this, I know she doesn't feel the same way...when she's awake. She clamps her legs tighter, but it takes another moan and gentle hip rocking before my dick springs into action. I realize what's happening a split second later.

"Willa," I whisper, trying to wake her.

"Mmm, that feels so good." Her breathing turns ragged the longer we lie like this.

"Willa, you gotta wake up." I look down at her face. Her lower lip sits trapped between her teeth, and all it takes is a little giggle from her before I'm doing some moaning of my own. This is torturous. As much as I enjoy being used as her personal sex pole, I have to get out of here.

"Trev, you're so good to me," she whispers, rubbing against

my knee with a languid rhythm that adds to my internal battle. She's not just having a wet dream on me; she's having a wet dream *about* me. How am I not supposed to be turned on by that?

Still, I want her to want me while she's conscious. Peeling her arms off me, I begrudgingly pluck my thigh from between hers. I kneel on the floor next to the bed and shake her again.

Willa wakes mid-moan, blinking a few times before seeing my face. "*Oh. My. God.*"

"Hey, it's okay…"

Shooting out of bed, she scrambles to the other side of the room. "*Ohmygod!*"

I stand and take a step toward her. "Willa, it's oka—"

"No! *No!*" She braces the air with her palms. "Y-you stay right there!" Skirting around the edge of her darkened bedroom, she slinks toward the connected bathroom. "I'm—I have to go." The door closes, and I hear the faintest protest on the other side. Everything happened in such a whirlwind, I'm not sure what I'm supposed to do next. The only thing I know is that it would be an absolutely terrible idea to climb back into that bed with the semi I'm sporting. I grab my phone and charger, shaking my head all the way to the couch. With only a few hours before I need to get up for my flight, I highly doubt I'll be able to sleep—especially after that interaction.

After the sun comes up, I'm finishing a cup of coffee, staring at the struggling plant in the kitchen window. It looks like it's *supposed* to have flowers, but all that's there are wilted leaves and squishy roots. From the corner of my eye, I watch Willa tiptoe down the hallway, fully dressed. She takes one look at me, hangs her head, and shuffles across the hardwood. Wordlessly, I slide her full travel mug across the counter. Her eyes slowly make their way to mine, and I jut my tongue into my cheek, trying not to laugh.

"I'm completely mortified," she groans, covering her face.

"Don't be. It happens to the best of us."

"Yeah, *okay*," she scoffs.

"Did it help with your stress, at least?" If I press my tongue any harder, I'll leave a bruise. She glares at the snort I can't hold in anymore.

"You're really enjoying this, aren't you?"

"I am," I say, walking my mug to the dishwasher. When I turn around, she's leaning against the counter, her face set in a scowl, arms crossed tightly in a way that would have scared me off before. Right now, though, the only thing I'm worried about is the utter need sparking inside me. I want her so fucking bad, and according to somewhere deep down in her psyche, she wants me too.

Placing my hands on either side of the countertop behind her, I cage her in. Her quickened breath fans over my face, eyes fluttering when I lean closer. Licking my lips wasn't a planned thing —but she wets hers in response—and I can't help but smirk at her reacting to me in this way. Can't get her moaning my name out of my mind either. Knowing I might have the slightest spot in hers has me firing on all cylinders. "This has been fun...but last night was better," I whisper, dipping my head so we're eye level. The suppressed gurgling from her throat when I wink at her is satisfaction enough. I grab my keys from the counter behind her and smile, our lips a whisper apart. "I have to catch my flight, Gem. Be back on Friday."

She squeaks in response, frozen in place as I step away. I take one last look over my shoulder, grab my bags, and head out the door. As I trek across the courtyard, she's the only thing on my mind.

I HEAD STRAIGHT INTO WORK AFTER LANDING IN SAN Francisco, unlocking the door to my office right as the clock strikes nine. Tucking my bags in the corner, I boot up my computer to see what kind of mess my associates have gotten themselves into over the holiday. Skirting over the seasonal newsletter from corporate and ignoring the email from Marla at the top of my inbox isn't my best move, but with it being a Tuesday, I have less time to catch up on work this week. I'll read all that nonsense after I've worked through my review pile.

I'm elbow deep in partially completed sales proposals, ready to pull my entire team from the field for a week of clerical handholding when my phone lights up.

WILLA

Thanks for cleaning up.

ME

Tell me, did I clean up in your dream too? Is that a thing for you?

WILLA

Don't push it, Eagle Scout.

ME

My bad, JIM.

WILLA

You're never gonna let me live that one down, are you?

ME

You started it 😊

Hey, what's that plant in your kitchen?

WILLA

An orchid Sam sent for my birthday. Her name's Clittercunt, and she's a petty bitch. Pretty sure she gave up the ghost.

"Look at you, grinning like a fool." Chase leans against the doorframe, hands in his pockets, smiling wide. "So, I take it things with Willa are going well?"

I chuckle. "I guess you could say that. We're more friends than we were before."

"Let me get this straight. You're having weekend sleepovers with the woman you've been pining over for years, and you're just friends?" His head tilts as he walks to my desk. "You're not trying to take things further?"

"It's kind of hard to do that when she's busy growing fingers and toes."

"But you want more?"

I nod. "The more time I spend with her, the harder it is for me to catch flights back here."

"So don't."

I blink at him, not fully grasping what he means.

"Trev, why fly back here every week when you can transfer to the LA office?"

"Because this is my home base. We make a good team."

"Team aside, you've outgrown this place, man." He nudges my shoulder. "What were you going to do once the baby comes?"

"I...haven't thought that far ahead yet, I guess."

"Look, you're one of my best friends, and we'll miss you around here, but you have bigger and better things waiting for you on the horizon. What are you doing?"

I look back to my computer, seeing the slog of work in my inbox for what it is: a distraction. This place, this city, it's not where I need to be anymore. Not where I *want* to be, and honestly, I felt the call for something else long before Willa and the baby. This is where I live, but it's not home. "You make some good points. But how are you going to distract me from work if I'm all the way in LA?"

"I'm sure I'll find a way." He laughs, checking his watch. "Speaking of work, I have to go razz my team. They're so bad at these proposals."

"*So bad.*" I shake my head. "It wasn't even this bad our first year. You sure you wanna push me to LA right now?"

Chase laughs and knocks my fist with his. "They'll get there.

They just need a little more training. Now stop deflecting and go start your transfer paperwork with HR."

"Oh, hey. How's Kayla?"

"She's good. The babies are great. HR, man. Go, before you talk yourself out of it." He stands there, staring with anticipation until I get out of my office chair, then follows me out of the room.

CHAPTER TWENTY-FIVE

WILLA

Now that my embarrassment from grinding all over Trevor in my sleep has mostly worn off, I have a new dilemma. I miss him. He's only been in San Francisco for three days, a shorter work week than usual, and I keep checking my phone for a message saying he's landed back here in LA.

It's Friday, but I've had no nightmares this week, or sex dreams, for that matter. Snuggling up to the pillow that still smells like Trevor is great and all, but it's a poor substitute for having the real thing. I like the coziness that settles into me when I'm wrapped in his arms at night, and the gentle caresses he sweeps across my spine. The brief, incidental touches he leaves on the small of my back while we're out, and the mindless way his hand strokes my foot when we're lounging on the couch. They both take up significant real estate in my mind lately. Hell, even his music tastes are growing on me. Never thought I'd come to this conclusion, but I'm pretty sure I have a crush on the father of my child. A minuscule, hormone-induced crush. Heavy on the hormones.

"So, uh, we need to talk about something..." Trevor sets his empty bowl on the coffee table, fork clanging around the red remnants of the pasta sauce clinging to the sides.

I blow out a breath and sit cross-legged on the couch cushion, wondering what took him so long to bring up the other night. Since it's my fault, really, it's probably better if I rip open the wound. "Yeah... I'm sorry I humped your leg, Trev."

He sputters out a laugh and throws his head back, shaking it like I caught him off guard. "Not that, Gem. *Never* apologize for *that*." Grinning, he reaches over and pulls my feet into his lap. "No, I need to talk to you about work."

"Is everything okay? I told you not to take so much time off—"

"I put in a transfer to EdTechU's LA office."

"Oh." An entire fleet of butterflies releases in my body.

"Yeah. I just figured it makes sense, especially the farther along you get. Even though we haven't talked about what to do after, it's better for me to make the move now rather than later."

I'm floating with the lightness that's burst in my chest. *Trevor's moving down here to be with me.* Okay, not me, specifically. He's moving for the baby, but my body reacts just the same. The thought of seeing him every day has excitement coursing through me like it's Christmas morning.

"The request takes a few weeks to process, so I'll still need to head up to San Francisco periodically, but I should be all set by the end of January. Would it be okay with you if I crashed here until I find an apartment?"

"You can just stay here." I don't even have a second thought before the words fly out of my mouth.

"Gem, no. You like your space. I'll find my own place."

"I like you in my space." Another thought bypasses my filter, and he stills, eyebrows sky high. "I *mean*, I don't mind you being here. It could be a good trial run before the baby comes so we're not adjusting to each other in addition to a newborn." His head falls into a skeptical tilt, but he says nothing. "...Is that—does that work for you?"

Nodding slowly, the pinched lines on his forehead relax when I give him a smile. "You're sure?"

"Yeah. I've been thinking about it for a few days now. We can go make a key tomorrow."

He nods again, watching me like I'm going to change my mind and kick him out at any second. When I don't, he gives me that cute, dimpled smile. "Hey, Willa?"

"Yeah?"

"Thanks for dinner. Let me clean up."

The somersault in my belly makes me blush as I watch him gather the dishes and head to the kitchen. If I was crushing before, this is an all-out rapture.

CHAPTER TWENTY-SIX

WILLA

"No boy bands today, huh?" I ask as we pull out of my neighborhood. Trevor's picked my favorite throwback R&B station.

"I noticed you had this on at the studio a couple weeks ago. Figured it was a safe choice," he says.

"You...did?"

"Yep." He turns to check his blind spot. "I notice lots of things, Gem."

"Like what else?"

"*Like...*" His eyes flick to the rearview mirror. "You didn't say anything when I cleaned up last night."

"That's because it's a waste of breath. You'll just do it anyway."

"Look at you, finally catching on..." He flashes a smile. "You don't freeze when I touch you anymore, either."

"When did I do that?"

"Every time, usually. And you smile at me, even if I haven't tried to make you laugh."

Oh, so he's just calling me out now? "Okay...and what does this mean, *All-Knowing Trev?*"

"Oh yeah, you call me Trev now too... Admit it, Willa. We're friends."

I laugh. "Yes, *Trevor*, we're friends. Happy now?"

"Mostly." He smirks, angling the car into a parking spot.

Havenwood Shopping Center is set up like an outlet mall, with larger department stores surrounding the interior chain shops and food court. The Sunday morning crowd is already bustling, carrying Christmas packages and large bags filled with goodies. I'm not looking forward to barreling through overzealous shoppers today, but it snows in Nebraska. A heavy coat and winter maternity clothes for our time in Heritage are a necessity. I shoot a text off to Ashlie and Hunter, who are meeting us here. Before I can reach for the handle, Trevor's already opening my door. My instinct to roll my eyes fizzles when they meet his sexy smile, and I suck my lip between my teeth. He offers his hand, and once I'm out of the car, disappointment hits from the loss of his fingers around mine. *This is ridiculous.*

"Hey, girl!" Ashlie waves when we enter the food court, untangling herself from Hunter's arms and bouncing toward us. Hunter nods in our direction. Ashlie checks me with her hip and slips her arm around my back. "Let's get started before you change your mind and decide to go home."

Wordlessly, Trevor digs in his back pocket for his wallet, prompting me to shake my head. "Absolutely not. I draw the line at you paying for my clothes." He stares right at me, smirking while he pulls out his credit card anyway and hands it to Ashlie, triggering the eye roll that fizzled in the parking lot. "I can buy my own clothes, Trev."

"Oh, I know you *can*. But you're not gonna." He turns to Ashlie like they preplanned for this to happen. "Make sure she gets everything she wants, even if she puts it back."

"This isn't my first rodeo, Trev. I'll hook your girl up."

Trevor leans in to whisper in my ear. "Remember the bookstore? Don't think I won't buy everything on the racks if I find out you put something back that you really want." Heat fills my cheeks, and I shudder as his breath tickles my neck. The goose-bumps rising at his satisfied chuckle almost make me come undone in this very public space.

Hunter claps his hands together. "Okay, you two, save your power struggle kink for the bedroom. I want to play around with that new Starbar notepad before the store gets crazy."

Trevor laughs and squeezes my shoulder as he steps away. Before they turn the corner into the shopping center, he calls over his shoulder, "I better see bags, Willa."

"Ooh, girl. I might lose the bet. He's done for." Ashlie fans herself with Trevor's credit card before slipping it in the pocket of her jeans.

"What bet?"

"The one Hunter and I have on how long it'll take you two to boink again. I say you'll hold out until New Year's. Hunt thinks you'll cave by Christmas."

"Please don't make bets on me 'boinking' anyone."

"Oh, I forget we have Ms. Academia over here." Ashlie straightens out her shoulders and takes on a deep voice. "Our wager, Professor Wilhelmina, is a conjecture of the initiation of coitus between you and Mr. Jones."

"I'm ready to go home now." I take a step toward the door, and she pulls me back, cackling as she tugs me farther into the mall. "Why are you betting against me? As my sister, aren't you supposed to be on my side?"

"Girl, I *am*. He's good to you, Wills. Good *for* you. Better than anyone else you've ever been with, and it's clear as day he's gone for you. You just need to get out of your head and let him sweep you off your feet."

"Sounds horrible," I mumble, trying to slam the lid on the feelings blossoming inside me. I've never been swept off my feet and had it stick. In my experience, feet sweeping is always accom-panied with whiplash whenever the guy gets comfortable. Maybe not right away, but it happens eventually.

"Come on. This card is burning a hole in my pocket." Ashlie

loops her arm in mine as we round the corner, smiling like the ray of sunshine she is. My nightmare of a man-sponsored shopping spree is a dream come true for her.

After making me try on way too many winter coats, Ashlie convinces me to go for the lilac puffer jacket with faux fur lining the hood. It's my favorite color, so I was drawn to it when we first entered Parka Emporium. But one look at the price tag had me charging for the clearance rack. The thought of spending that much money on something I'll only wear for a week churns my stomach, especially when I'm not paying for it myself. Since my sister's loyalties clearly lie with the cardholder, she threatened to call Trevor if I didn't at least try it on. Once I did, and she pointed out the smile on my face, I agreed it looked good. She wouldn't even let me get it back on the hanger before she marched to the cash register with it.

Now that we're in Mama Maternity, Ashlie leans a hip against the wall while looking at me through the mirror. "Wills, you can't hate everything you've tried on. And I know my little nibling is getting hungry. What's the problem?"

I cringe at her through the mirror. "The problem is you calling my kid a *nibling*." Sighing, I pull at the empire waisted tunic with a frown. It's a cute top, but the more things we pull off the racks, the worse my attitude gets. I need new clothes. My jeans are already too tight to be comfortable, and I know it's only going to get worse from here on out. Maternity clothes are a basic necessity, but Trevor's insistence on buying them for me is a major mental block. I sit on the wooden bench next to my dressing room and slump against the wall. "I don't know. It's all of this, I guess. The clothes. The credit card. Trevor giving me whatever I ask for."

"You're worried this is a Carter repeat?"

I puff out a breath and nod. My ex would drag me to this mall and force me to buy clothes he deemed fitting for the girlfriend of an up-and-coming hotshot lawyer. Clothes that I didn't get a say in because he was footing the bill. Clothes I wouldn't have been caught dead in before, and that I've stayed away from since. He was controlling, with a temper he hid behind expensive three-piece suits.

"Willa, Carter was a polished turd at best, and a piece of shit at his worst. I can see why today might give you pause, but Trevor's not trying to control you. He's trying to support you. You don't see the difference?"

I shrug, letting out a heavy sigh. "It's the whole surprise aspect. Neither of you told me about this secret plan today, and I'm in my head about it."

"Explain please?"

"Really?" I roll my eyes.

"Yes, really." She sits next to me on the bench, turning to face me. "I'm having a hard time understanding how a surprise shopping spree equates to Trevor being the next Carter, so help me out."

I guess she doesn't really know this, since I kept the complicated aspects of my last relationship from everyone except Sam. There's no way she could understand how I felt like a hostage trapped behind a glimmering facade that no one seemed to question. I shrunk inside myself until I was unrecognizable, letting Carter rule almost every aspect of my life, save for my business. It sounds dumb as hell, but the bastard was a familiar replacement for how I grew up—controlling, intrusive, callous. "Carter would surprise me like this, pulling out special collections of expensive clothes he wanted to see me in, going into a rampage about my being ungrateful if I didn't like something. I know it's not the same, but it feels too similar, and I can't shake it."

"Wills, I had no idea."

"That's because I didn't want you to know. I didn't want *anyone* to know. It's embarrassing I fell for any of it."

"Girl, if I knew, I wouldn't have suggested this to Trevor."

My mouth falls open right as a pang of guilt hits me. "This was your idea?"

"Yeah." She flashes a quick smile. "I like seeing you being

pampered for once. When I suggested it to him, he was giddy at the thought of spoiling you." Her hand slips over mine, and she gives a reassuring squeeze. "I thought it would be a good thing, but we can put all of this back."

"I—oh." I blink several times, trying to integrate this new information into my assumption-induced attitude. Trevor and Ash were trying to help me feel special, and I turned it into a Carter memorial. *What is my fucking problem?* Ashlie squeezes my hand again, then walks into my dressing room. *Am I really trippin' over some clothes? Vulnerability from all of this support? Or is it that I feel my heart softening to someone when I swore I'd never let that happen again?* She comes back a few minutes later with the stack of clothes neatly placed back on the hangers, and the truth hits me hard. *Maybe it's all of it...*

"Ash, it's okay. I'll get the clothes."

"Are you sure? I don't want you to feel pressured. I'll deal with Trev—"

"I'm sure. You're right. This isn't even close to the same thing."

Relief relaxes the dent between her eyebrows as she comes toward me. "Okay. Let's pay and get a snack while we wait for the guys. If I'm hungry, I know you've got to be starving."

"Starving was thirty minutes ago," I tease, climbing to my feet. She turns toward the register, but I catch her elbow. "Hey, Ash?"

"What's up?" The worried shadow falls back over her face as she searches mine.

"Thank you for thinking of me..."

Her bottom lip wobbles as a soft smile appears, and she pulls me in for a hug. This damn baby must be making me soft because I hug her back. "I just like seeing you happy, okay?" she warbles. "No thanks necessary."

With bags in hand, we head to the food court for soft pretzels with mustard, one of our only bonding points when we were younger. I've just polished mine off when something grazes my shoulder. Like he was summoned from the depths of hell, the dark brown eyes of a suit-wearing demon with platinum blond hair appears. *Carter-fucking-Zane.* Seriously, who wears a suit to the mall on a Sunday?

"Wow, sweetheart, it's been too long." His blinding white smile doesn't reach his eyes, and I have to tell myself not to look away. He's sizing me up, seeing how much of a hold he still has on me. I can say with absolute certainty, he has none.

I drop my shoulder and his hand falls slightly before he recovers by putting it on the back of my chair. "Not long enough," I reply with a scowl.

"Ashlie," he taunts, keeping his eyes on me.

"Asshole," she fires back, tapping on her phone.

"Well, aren't you lovely? It must run in the family... You been getting my messages?"

"What messages?" I ask in a level tone.

"Oh, you know which messages I'm talking about, Willa. The ones you refuse to answer." With a finger covered in fake tanner, he sweeps a twist over my shoulder. Ashlie promptly pulls me toward her with a scoff. His eyes flick to her, but just as soon, they're making a sweeping assessment up and down my body. If I could crawl out of my skin, I would. "We really should catch up..."

"Catch me in hell." My hands curl into fists on the table while I seethe at how close he is. "And keep your hands off of me."

He tuts. "I *do* miss that mouth, beautiful. You remember how great we used to be together?" Brushing another twist over my shoulder, his fingers skirt across my neck, and I see red. I fling his hand away, about to spring into his face, when Trevor steps in between us. Scooting my chair back, I make room for whatever is about to happen.

"She told you to keep your hands to yourself." Trevor's voice is low and gruff, a stark difference from the jovial tone I'm used to hearing from him. He positions himself in front of me completely. "If you want to keep them, I suggest you listen."

Carter tries to step back but bumps right into Hunter, whose hard scowl is withering. "And you are?"

"Trevor. You?"

"Carter Zane. Attorney at Johnson and Associates."

"And that's working out well for you?"

"I'd say so, considering I just made partner."

Hunter scoffs, but I can't see anything around Trevor's rigid back.

"I suggest you leave these ladies alone before your partners get a complaint of sexual harassment against you." Trevor squares his shoulders, that deep vibrato in his voice doing things to my insides. The sound alone sends shivers up my spine in a "take me home right now" kind of way.

"Oh? And what proof do you have?"

"He has none, but I sure do." Ashlie nods toward her phone. "Evidence of textual *and* sexual harassment. And if you mess with her again, I'll blast this shit everywhere. Smile and wave, Carter Zane." Trevor steps to the side, and I catch the flash of fear in Carter's eyes before he reels it back in. I smirk at the glare he sends me, holding his gaze until he clears his throat and looks around the room.

"You take care of yourself, sweetheart." He raps his knuckles on the table, then straightens his pretentious suit jacket and walks away.

The muscle in Trevor's jaw flutters wildly, nostrils flared while his eyes stay fixed on the door. It's not until Carter exits to the parking lot that he squats next to my chair. The hard lines on his face melt into concern when his eyes meet mine. "You okay, Gem?"

"Yeah, I'm good." I'm more than good, really. Twice now, he's stepped up to someone in my defense. Both times, it's left me with this undeniable urge to latch on to him and never let go. *Maybe I should stop fighting it.*

CHAPTER TWENTY-SEVEN

TREVOR

"Thank you," Willa says as I buckle my seatbelt.

"I'm sorry we didn't get there sooner." When I saw Carter touch Willa, play with her hair, it took everything in me not to clock him. Rage boiled through my veins as soon as she bristled at his touch—the clearest sign that I've got it bad for her. I was ready to hit first and deal with the consequences later, if it came to that, and I'm not ashamed to admit it. "Do you want to talk about it?"

She takes a deep breath and nods. "Yeah, but could you start driving? It'll be easier for me to tell you everything if you're not looking at me."

I start the car and back out of the parking space, but she doesn't speak until we reach the street. Gripping the steering wheel tightly, I try to focus on the road, still pissed over seeing her reaction to that motherfucker.

"Carter was sweet and generous, until he wasn't. It was day and night. One morning, he woke up as Prince Charming, but by the time the clock struck midnight, he'd turned into a dragon. He latched onto my insecurities and exploited them any time we went out in public. Tried to control what I wore by buying extravagant clothes and guilting me when I didn't wear them. And my sensitivity to noise"—she shakes her head—"whenever I did something he didn't like, he'd lie in wait, then torture me with sleep deprivation by blasting all the TVs and stereos at three in the morning. I've always had sensory issues, but that has made it infinitely worse the last few years. Then the switch would flip, and he'd try smoothing things over by calling me *sweetheart* and *beautiful*. Hearing them now still leaves a bad taste in my mouth."

Shit. This is why she hates the pet names? I thought it was a *me* thing, not the result of a traumatic relationship. Glancing at her, I note the tight clutch she has on her fingers while she wrings her hands together. I just want to reach over and slide my hand around hers, raise it to my lips, and kiss away all the pain she's reliving right now.

"It took him slapping me across the face for me to find my common sense."

"He put his hands on you?" My voice comes out low while fifty-seven ways to torture Carter and hide the body cycle through my head. "When?"

"Only once. A couple of years ago, right before Chase and Kayla's wedding...but I handled it."

"What do you mean, you handled it?"

"I mean, I smashed him over the head with a table lamp." She lets out a humorless chuff. "He had me by the neck, pinned down on the couch after I 'embarrassed' him at one of his firm's events. I couldn't get him off. When he slapped me, the closest thing I could reach was the table lamp next to my head. Once he fell to the floor, I left and never looked back. That's when I figured therapy was a good idea. Still took me a year to start, though."

"Shit." I drag a hand down my face. "Did you file a police report?"

"So he could twist it all around and claim I was the aggressor? He works for one of the best domestic violence law firms in the country. Even if I reported, he's got the cops in his pocket. Besides, he's too concerned with his image to admit he'd been bested by a woman. He won't do anything."

"How can you know that? Guys like him don't just give up."

"Because he's too chickenshit to escalate it. He already knows where I live, where I work, and the only thing he does is text every few—"

"He's *messaging* you? That's stalking, Willa!"

"Yeah, I know." She purses her lips, her gaze dropping to her hands. "The police won't do anything unless he escalates...which he won't. He just wants to get under my skin."

I'm trying to hold it together. Keep the words she's saying separate from the fuzzy memories trapped in my mind. But the screaming in my head grows around the resounding crash of bottles smashing against walls, finally silenced by crooning '90s music covering my ears. As soon as I realize my heart is pounding, I reach for the radio dial, turning right to the throwback station.

We pull into Willa's parking lot, and as soon as I park, I turn to her. "Thank you for telling me. It means everything that you felt safe enough to share it with me, and I..." I take a deep breath and reach for her hand, knowing I'm about to toe the friendship line. "Willa, I'll spend every day making sure you know you're a priority. Every single day, Gem. I promise you."

Tears well in her eyes, but she blinks them away. I give her fingers a squeeze, my heart leaping in my chest when she slides her other hand over mine. "Let's get inside, Trev. You have a flight to catch."

AFTER A QUICK SWEEP OF HER HOUSE, MAKING SURE I have everything in my bag, I meet Willa in the kitchen to say goodbye for the week. "Okay, I'll meet you at the terminal on Wednesday. Do you need anything before I go?"

"Nope, I think I'm good."

"Okay. Oh...uh, I forgot about this." Sliding my hand in my

pocket, I pull out the small velvet bag from Zim's Jewelry and curl my fingers around it, second-guessing this move. "This probably isn't the best timing, seeing as you just told me about your controlling ex." When we passed the jewelry store window, I felt confident about giving this to her, imagining a shy smile spreading across her face. The one that happens whenever I do something that surprises her. But after our drive back to her house, I'm not so sure.

A furrow creases her forehead as she glances at the bag. "What is it?"

"If you hate it, or you don't want to wear it, I understand. I can take it back or—"

"Just show me."

"Uh..." I slip the golden necklace from the bag and place the dainty camera charm in my upturned palm. "I just, um...I saw it and thought of you. But don't feel like you have to—"

Willa's lips silence my fumbling words. The soft pressure is both timid and brazen, uncertain and sure, intoxicating and centering. Her hand cradles my face, the gentle graze of her fingers down my cheek scorching every rational thought I have. Clutching the necklace, I pull her in tightly, grasping her hip as the need to feel her closer floods over me. Her kiss could occupy every second of my day, and I'd still beg her for more. I sweep my tongue across the seam of her lips, pleading for even the smallest taste. When she greets me with hers, the strike of a thousand matches ignites a path straight to my sanity. She backs me up against the counter just as the alert for my flight chirps on my phone, causing her to scramble backward with a gasp.

"*Oh. My. God.*" She slaps a hand over her mouth, shaking her head quickly while she retreats.

"Willa." I drop the necklace on the counter and take a step forward.

"*No!*" she yells, wide-eyed, her palms bracing the air in front of her. It stops me in my tracks. "Stay right there. I—I don't... Oh my God. It was the hormones..."

"It's okay, Gem."

"No, it's *not*. I just kissed you!" Her back hits the fridge with a thud. "I'm not supposed to *like* you..." she whines through her grimace, bouncing on her feet in a mini tantrum. Watching this realization spread through her is the cutest damn thing I've ever seen. *She likes me.* Her hand scrubs across her forehead, as if trying to wipe away the very moment I'll never forget. "It's been a long day and I'm...hungry? Yeah. I'm hungry and need to eat."

"Okay, so let me get you something to eat."

"No!" She gasps, her eyes roving the floor frantically. "No. I'll get it after you're gone. You go. Catch your flight. I'm fine... Maybe I'm tired?" It sounds like she's trying to convince herself at this point. "Yeah. I'm tired, and I just need a nap. A *long* nap." She sidesteps out of the kitchen and backs down the hallway. "So I'll go take a nap and you g-go to the airport and...and get on the plane." The words stutter out of her as she turns on her heel and scurries to her room.

The door clicks shut, and I scratch my prickling scalp, frozen to my spot in the kitchen. I'm stuck on how adorable she is when she gets flustered, how she bit her lip as she battled her logic with her undeniable desire...the way her voice went up an octave while she stumbled on her words. My mind reels at the kiss we just shared and what it means. Not our first kiss, but possibly just as memorable. One I'm aching to repeat. She's in her room freaking out about kissing me, while I'm out here trying to figure out how to get her to do it again. The reminder on my phone rings out, signaling five minutes before I absolutely have to get in my car. That gives me enough time to fix her a snack. I grab the mini cooler, load it up with some of her favorites, refill her water tumbler, and head down the hallway.

I knock, and when she doesn't answer, I slip into the room quietly in case she really did fall asleep that fast. Willa's sitting in the middle of the mattress, hugging her knees with a wide-eyed stare. Giving her a smile, I step slowly, as if we're in a nature documentary and she's about to flee from the watering hole. I set the cooler on the floor next to her bed and slide the tumbler on her nightstand. She watches me, tucking her chin between her knees, saying nothing. "I packed you some snacks in case you get hungry after your nap, and slipped in some of those cookies you like, just because. Your water's fresh with lots of ice. And here's your phone."

"I need you to stop being nice to me," she whispers.

I smile. "No."

"*Please*?" Her voice cracks with her pleading.

The edge of the mattress sinks as I take a seat. As much as she looks like she wants to run away right now, she stays put. "Why?" I ask.

"Because when you're nice to me, it blurs all the boundary lines in my head. And I do unhinged things like kiss you."

I bite my cheek to stifle the smile threatening to break free at her confession. Everything within me is screaming to pull her closer. "I wouldn't call you kissing me 'unhinged.'"

"Yeah, *okay*," she scoffs, glancing down at her lap. "What would you call it, then?"

"Inevitable," I whisper, leaning in. Peering into her brown eyes, clocking her avoidance for what it is, I can't resist any longer. I grab the back of her neck and pull her to me, meeting her quivering lips with a kiss full of all the pent-up desire coursing through me. She moans, and I urge her closer, tangling lips and tongues with a shared fervor I'd love to get used to. Willa is everything I want. She's starting to feel like an outright need the more time we spend together. I'm drifting deeper into her orbit, and I hope gravity never finds me.

My damn phone goes off yet again. Pulling back, I look into her eyes, hoping to convey every ounce of what I feel for her right now. "And another thing..." I place a lighter, lingering kiss on her lips as a response, then leave another on her forehead, and when I stand, I drop a third on the top of her head. "I have to catch my flight, but I'll check on you when I land, yeah?"

Her eyes flutter closed as she nods, and I contemplate

canceling everything. Calling in sick for the next two days just to stay here and take my fill of Willa's lips would be more than worth it. I quickly weigh it all out in my head but ultimately decide letting this simmer for a few days is probably for the best. I know how I feel about her, know what I want. Now I need to give her the space to make up her mind about me.

CHAPTER TWENTY-EIGHT
WILLA

The escalator crests the second floor of the flight terminal while I nervously slide the small gold camera charm back and forth on the chain around my neck. I hook my other thumb under the strap of my camera backpack, ready to start the trek through the crowd. You wouldn't think Wednesday would be a busy day at the airport, but with Christmas this week, I guess it makes sense. Trevor flew in from San Francisco, so he's meeting me at the gate. I don't know what to expect when I see him. It's been a couple of days since I kissed him—since he kissed me back—but neither of us has brought it up over text. I'm not sure where this leaves us. I know I haven't been able to get him off my mind, but he might instantly regret everything the moment he lays his eyes on me. There's no telling how this will go.

When I reach the top, the brightest smile flanked by infuriatingly cute dimples is waiting. He's standing with his hands in the pockets of his jeans, his computer bag slung across his body. His olive-green quarter zip sweater complements his auburn hair and brown skin in a way that emphasizes his radiating warmth. He reaches up to smooth a hand down his fade, and my knees threaten to buckle. Looks aside, Trevor's the whole package. I've never let myself appreciate it before now.

"Hey, Gem." He wraps me in a hug and kisses the top of my head. Giddiness flutters inside of me at the deep baritone of his voice calling me *Gem*. Lightheaded, my body fuses to his, and I fall into the immense safety I feel whenever I'm tucked under his arm. Suddenly, he goes rigid, and every doubt I had on the escalator washes over me.

"Can I still call you that?" he whispers in my ear. "*Gem*?"

The giggle that bubbles from my throat at my surprise prompts him to step back and search my face with furrowed brows. He's worried about using the nickname that just had me swooning? "Yeah, Trev. You can still call me *Gem*."

The smile stretches back on his face. "Good. I think I'd have a hard time stopping that one. It's just your name at this point. You hungry?"

I smile and shake my head. "I already ate. I *am* ready to sit down, though."

"Well, let's go then." He slides my backpack off and slings a strap over his shoulder. We venture into the crowd toward the gate, my anxiety kicking up a notch. The noise and bodies bumping into me sets my teeth on edge. Right when I'm about to move to the outskirts of the walkway, Trevor slips his hand around mine, giving a squeeze that immediately sets me at ease. He's not acting any differently than he has been. Maybe this is a good sign the kiss didn't ruin everything. This hand-holding thing is new though. "Almost there," he says, and when he flashes that smile, I don't have a care in the world. He could lead me right into the loudest chaos, and I'd only hear his calming timbre.

It's only a twenty-minute wait before boarding the nonstop flight to Nebraska. We're riding in first class, our seats the only ones in our row, and once we've settled, the panic I've been pushing down for weeks takes over. I'm meeting Trevor's entire family tonight. We haven't even discussed what's going on with us, and we're about to drop a pregnancy bombshell on them, dealing with whatever the resulting fallout is for the rest of the week. Every single aspect of this trip is new territory for me. I've never met a man's parents before, so I've certainly never told anyone I'm pregnant with their grandchild seconds later.

"Breathe." Trevor's smiling at me when I meet his gaze. "You know you do this thing with your hands when you're nervous?"

I look down at the intense clutch I have on my fingers and pull them apart, shaking them out for good measure. "I...yeah. Since I was a kid. Used to rub the skin raw."

"Here, let me help." He reaches over, wrapping his hand around mine and settling them on the fixed armrest between us. That same calming effect washes over me, and I can't deny what's happening. Trevor's becoming a silent comfort. A subtle demand I can't outrun anymore. "Better?"

I take a deep breath and smile back. "Yeah, but can we talk about the other day, just to get it out of the way?"

He quirks a brow. "What about it?"

"Well, I kissed you, and then you kissed me, and we haven't talked about it..."

Trevor smirks, hooking a finger under my chin as he leans in. "You want me to kiss you again, don't you?" he whispers.

Hell yes. The feeling of his lips on mine has been a dominant scene in the couple of wet dreams I've had since Sunday. I nod, and his eyes flicker with craving as they travel down to my mouth, taking their sweet time finding their way back to mine. Whatever's brewing between us feels inappropriate for the front of a bustling airplane. "I think so."

"Scale of one to ten?"

Ten. But I don't want to seem too eager. "Uh, maybe an eight," I say, unable to stop my teeth from sinking into my bottom lip.

His thumb trails over my chin, pulling down slightly until it releases my trapped lip. "Kissing you has been the only thing on my mind since I *stopped* kissing you. Let me know when it gets to ten..."

"W-what?"

"I *said*"—he inches closer—"I won't kiss you again until I

know you want it as much as I do." His deep rasp skitters over me as his nose grazes mine, our eyes bolted together. I'm trapped. All it would take is a few centimeters to get us to our destination. "Not until you're aching for it so much"—he wets his lips—"you can't think of anything else..." I've made up my mind to close the gap right as the speaker crackles above our head. The jarring static pulls us apart, with the flight attendant who settles in the aisle next to us keeping us from diving back in. Trevor doesn't let go of my hand, though. Sweeping his thumb over mine, he leaves tingling streaks across my skin as we listen to the introduction from the cockpit.

"Do you have a picture of your family on your phone?" I squeak out. The proud smirk on his face doesn't help the pounding in my chest.

"Yep... Is that what you're nervous about? Meeting my family?"

Nodding, I drop my eyes to my lap. "I think it might calm my nerves if I can put faces to their names."

"They're gonna love you." He squeezes my hand.

"You keep saying that. Picture?"

As he leans in, the smell of his citrus and clove cologne wraps me in a cozy cocoon as he digs for his phone. He pulls up a picture taken from Christmastime last year. "Okay, so these are my parents, Asa and Adele." He points to a short Black man wearing glasses and a slender Black woman with a silk press brushing her shoulders. "Then there's Lainey and Eli. Both students at Omaha University. We call them the twins."

"Twins run in your family?"

"Adopted, remember?" He blows out a chuckled breath. "But still, no. It's a long story."

"It's a long flight."

"True... Okay, so about ten years after we were adopted, my parents were contacted by a social worker. My bio mom had just given birth again and gave up her rights immediately. Despite being six months pregnant with Lainey, my parents jumped at the chance to start the adoption process. They're only three months apart, thus twins."

"Pseudo-twins. Got it."

"This is Maya and her husband, Ben." He points to a tall woman with light brown skin covered in freckles. Her tight auburn curls fan around her face and down her back. Standing next to her is a lanky Asian man with short black hair who has a protective grip on a toddler. Trevor circles around the two little girls hugging in front of them, one redhead, one brunette. "I guarantee Harper and Hazel—the actual twins—and baby Holland will be running all over the ranch this year."

His voice tinkles with pure adoration as he shows off his older sister's family. The smile on his face when I peek up at him pulls at my heart. For all of this being unplanned, I couldn't have accidentally picked a better person to experience this pregnancy with.

"How else can I help calm your nerves?" His thumb continues those slow swipes over my skin. It's entrancing. I've never felt tranquility like this with any man before. *With anyone, really...*

I'm surprised by a yawn. Growing an entire person from scratch is the most exhausting thing, and it's catching up with me. All I want to do is snuggle into the heat radiating off his body and sleep for the rest of the flight. It's irrational, considering first class gives me plenty of room to stretch out. This wide-ass armrest is in the way too, but he's warm and smells so damn good, I just want to lean my head on his shoulder.

"Come here, Gem." Trevor untangles our fingers and tucks me under his arm.

Another yawn slips, and I shake my head. "I can just lean against the window."

"And let this perfectly good-looking Willa pillow go to waste?" He waves a hand over his body like he's on display. "Come on. You can sleep, and I can cuddle without you rolling your eyes at me."

I roll my eyes despite the edges of my mouth turning up, and adjust in the seat, rotating on my hip to rest against him. A third yawn has me nestling my head into his chest. As his quickened heartbeat slows, I snuggle into him. His hand stroking my upper arm is a serenity song, sending calming surges through me that lull me into a restful sleep.

BY THE TIME WE GET TO HERITAGE, STARS ARE twinkling in the dusky periwinkle sky. Snow blankets every surface as we drive down Main Street, the warm glow from shop lights rivaling a holiday winter portrait. I wish it was light enough for me to snap a picture, just to remember how magical it all looks.

Trevor's signature music croons quietly through the radio, and I realize I'm humming along with the catchy song. When I notice my hand tapping my leg to the beat, I curl my fingers, staring out the window to hide the grin tugging my lips. *Okay, maybe I like Trevor's music too.*

"I see you dancing over there. Admit it, my music's pretty good."

"Yeah, maybe twenty-five years ago," I tease. A few flurries drift past the window as he slows the rental at a stoplight, right next to a single-story brick building that spans the entire block in front of us. "Is that where you went to high school?"

"And middle school." He blows out a breath, accelerating slowly as he turns the opposite direction. His fingers drumming on the steering wheel pull my attention away from the window. Hard lines mar his face, and I have the surprising urge to smooth my fingers over each and every one until he looks at peace again. I dig my fingernails into my palms instead. "I'll show you around town later this week," he says. "We'll be at the ranch in about twenty minutes."

The SUV shudders over the gravel as we turn onto a dirt road. I grip the door handle to keep from jostling, clutching at the queasiness in my stomach with my other hand. The baby revolted over the food on the plane. The smell was just...not happening. And the few snacks I packed in my backpack were gone about an hour ago. I breathe through a fresh wave of nausea. We're supposed to be joining Trevor's family for dinner, so food is on the horizon.

The dense forest gives way to tall trees lining a lengthy, paved drive. Victorian-style lampposts flank every fourth one. My mouth drops when we pass under the giant arched entrance gate inscribed with Heritage Ranch Homestead, my gaze fixed on the stately mansion just beyond it. There's enough light for me to see the surface area the house takes up, and the closer we get, the wider my eyes grow.

I turn my expression to Trevor, who smirks as he shuts off the car. "So...this is the house."

"That's no damn house. You grew up here?"

"Yep. The Jones family were some of the first Black homesteaders here in Heritage. Dad's ancestors were one of a few Black families who stayed amid harsh farming conditions, while others left for Omaha. Heritage Homestead started small, but we've expanded on the land. And it's grown to be one of the most successful ranches in the area."

"How successful?" I ask, still staring at the mansion.

He laughs. "Successful enough."

"Trevor..."

"*Willa*..." he mocks back, smiling as he reaches for my hand. "Don't freak out. It's not a big deal."

"Says the one who grew up in a motherfucking mansion! What the hell, Trev? You didn't think this was information worth sharing when I asked about your family?"

"I didn't think it would matter."

"It doesn't *matter*. I just don't want to be caught off guard when I'm trying to impress your family."

Cocking his head, he bites the smile on his lips. I can't believe I'm falling for those dimples right now. "You want to impress my family?"

"Of course I do. I've never done this before. I don't want them to hate me."

"That's not possible, Gem."

"How do you know?"

"Because there's nothing to hate." The genuine confusion in his eyes makes me swallow my rebuttal. I don't think this man has a hating bone in his body. "Besides, you should be more worried about all the hugging."

"*What* hugging?"

With a smirk, he gets out of the car.

"Trevor," I shriek as he walks around the rental. "What hugging?" There must be a distasteful look on my face because I'm met with a tickled laugh when he opens my door.

"Mom, especially. Oh, Lainey too."

"You know I'm not a hugger..."

Shrugging, he offers me his hand. "You're gonna get loved on this week, Willa. Consider this your warning." He holds on tight, pulling me in close as we walk toward the estate.

CHAPTER TWENTY-NINE

TREVOR

We don't even make it to the door before Eli flings it open and leans against the frame, dark brown skin illuminated by the porch light. He rubs a hand over his short afro, the sleeves of his blue Omaha University hoodie bunched around his elbows. One look at Willa's hand in mine, and he breaks out in a wide grin. "A friend, huh? You know you're not foolin' anyone, right? You're engaged or eloped or somethin'."

I drop Willa's hand and pull him into a hug. "Keep it up and you'll be the one to tell Mom why I hopped back in the car."

"You'll be back for graduation next year anyway. She'll live." Eli laughs and claps me around the back. "Missed you, bro. Who's your *friend*?"

Reaching for Willa's hand again, I tug her closer, flashing a smile when her eyes widen with nerves. "Willa, this is li'l doofus. Eli, Willa."

"It's nice to meet you, Willa." He shakes her hand but hangs on as he calls over his shoulder, "Ma, Tre knocked someone up!"

Willa snatches her hand back and turns wide eyes on me. "You already told him?"

I sigh, scratching my head. "Nope."

Eli's eyes dart between us as realization dawns on him. "Oh shit, Tre... You really did?"

"Will you move so we can come inside?" I say through gritted teeth, shooting a narrowed glare that makes him step back. I nudge Willa ahead of me and help her shrug off her puffy coat as she marvels at the large wagon wheel chandelier above us.

"*Tre*?" she whispers, quirking her brow.

"You're not the only one with nicknames." Stepping around her, I hang her coat on the clawfoot rack in the entryway. My wet boots squeak against the maple hardwood as I step out of them and set them in the tray by the door. Willa follows suit, leaving hers next to mine. The door closes behind us as Eli tuts playfully.

"E, don't start," I warn.

"I didn't say any—"

"Very funny, Elijah." Mom's voice reaches us before she rounds the corner. She smiles when she sees me, settling her readers on the top of her head to pull her pressed black hair out of her face. "Trevor knows better than that."

She's so short, I have to stoop so she can wrap her bangle-clad arms around my neck. Her long cardigan billows around our ankles, warm vanilla perfume welcoming me home like it did when I was a child. "Hey, Ma."

She rocks us side to side. "*Oooh*, I've missed my Trevor hugs. Once a year is not enough!" Leaning back, she pats my cheeks with a watery smile. "Now introduce me to your friend over here."

"It's nice to meet you, Mrs. Jones," Willa says with an outstretched hand.

"Beauty *and* manners? Maybe you can teach my boys a thing or two. Lord knows they don't listen to me." She secures Willa's hand between hers, patting it softly.

"This is Willa. Gem, this is my mom."

"*Oh*? A friend with a special name?" Mom pins me with a knowing look, then smiles at Willa, dropping her hand to wave us toward the kitchen. "Well, dinner's already on the table."

"Uh, could I talk to everyone first?" I ask.

Looking between us, lips pursed perceptively, she calls over her shoulder, "Trevor requests a family meeting!"

Skittering footsteps fall behind us as I lead Willa into the family lounge. This room is reserved for game nights and family meetings, two of the most intense gatherings we ever hold. The recessed lighting in the white coffered ceiling feels like a hundred spotlights when I flip them on. I have no reason to be nervous, but this is the biggest news I've ever shared. Willa settles on the powder blue loveseat, and I perch next to her on the arm of the sofa. She rolls her lips together, grabbing at her fingers the way she did on the plane. Her parents didn't take this news well at all. I get why she thinks mine will react the same way. They won't. Might tease me about bringing home a surprise baby, but they'll be excited about this.

"Hey," I whisper in her ear. "There's nothing to worry about. Do you want to hold my hand?" Willa stills her fingers, then quickly reaches for mine. I give a little squeeze right as Dad walks in the room.

"So what? You get back in town and think you can tell us what to do?" Dad's wide smile as he shakes his balding head completely invalidates the sarcasm. He strolls across the room and playfully puts me in a headlock, rubbing his knuckles into my scalp. "Glad you're back, son." Turning to Willa, he sticks out a hand. "Asa Jones. I'm sorry you have to deal with this knucklehead."

She laughs and drops my hand to shake his. "Nice to meet you."

"Uncle Tre!" Harper and Hazel barrel through the room, almost knocking me over with a tackle. Their twin unison act is really coming along too. My sister Lainey files in with a not-so-little baby Holland on her hip, both wearing hooded pink dinosaur onesies.

"Uh-oh... I think you two are taller than I am by now," I say to my nieces. "You get into the cattle feed again?"

"Ew!" The girls shriek, making faces with their tongues out.

I glance around the room for my older sister. "Where's Maya?"

"I'm right here," Maya says from behind me, closing the patio door and leaning a broom against the wall. "That damn cat got stuck in the tree again."

Sprinkles, our mostly blind Tabby, used to be a barn cat. But once she started going blind, mom moved her inside the house for safety. She tries to live that outdoor cat life whenever she can slip outside, where she usually ends up stuck in a tree. Maya peels the twins off my legs, directing them to the tiny rocking chairs Dad made for them last year. Then she crushes me with a hug, suffocating me with her auburn curls. "Hey, T."

"Missed you, My." I hold her close, letting out a breath. *Now it feels like home.* For as long as I can remember, Maya's had a soothing presence. She's seven years older, and since we've been through a lot together, she's always been a main source of comfort. Keeping everything from her has been wearing on me.

"Maybe if you came home more often, you wouldn't miss me so much." She drives a soft punch into my stomach.

"Where's Ben?" I ask.

"He got called in, so he'll be here after his shift. Now what's with the family meeting, and why haven't you introduced me to the pretty woman sitting next to you?" She steps around me and smiles at Willa. "Excuse him. He was technically raised in a barn."

"This is Willa," I say. "That's what the meeting's about..." I clear my throat, and everyone takes it for the beacon it is, turning to look at me. "Willa and I are—"

"Engaged!" Lainey calls out.

"Married!" Eli joins in with a smirk.

"Will you two shut up? Let him talk!" Maya glares at both of them. "Go on, T."

My parents sit in their armchairs next to the fireplace, eyes twinkling as they watch us.

"Uh, we're having a baby."

"Oh!" Mom squeals, jumping out of her seat. Her hands flap vigorously as she bounces across the room, tears welling in her eyes. She stops in front of us, unable to decide who she should hug first. "Trevor. Anthony. Jones. This better not be a joke!"

"See, I told you she'd do the Jazz Hands," Maya slips in.

"This is great news," Dad says. "But don't get it twisted, son. Willa's doing all the work here. All you did was wield your willy."

"Pops..." I slap a hand over my eyes, hiding the cringe on my face as I groan my amusement.

"You grew up on a farm, Tre. I taught you about the birds and bees myself. You know what sticking your will—"

"Dad!" Maya shifts an icy look across the room, nodding toward the girls.

"Ooh, I love birdies!" Harper's dark brown ringlets bounce as she shakes excited fists in a little happy dance.

"Mommy, what's a willy?" Hazel asks, her rust-colored corkscrews falling over her eyes as she stares down Maya.

"It's a penis, Haze," Maya answers without hesitation. Correct terms are the only way to go when you have two medical professionals as parents.

"Gramps, that's a private part! You're only supposed to worry about your own private parts!" Hazel wags her finger at Dad.

"You hear that, Tre?" Dad laughs. "You're supposed to worry about your own private parts."

"Oh, all of you hush. I'm gonna be a nana again!" Mom goes for me first, squeezing so tightly, I'm sure she'll leave marks. Then she sits next to Willa and pulls her into a side hug. "Tell me everything."

Willa flashes wide eyes at me, but the smile on her face is one of amusement instead of panic. "We have all week, Ma. Willa needs to eat."

"Oh! Of course. Everyone, food's on the table." She pats Willa's leg and flits to the dining room.

After everyone else files out behind her, I slip my hand back around Willa's. "You okay?"

"Yeah." She nods and glances toward the sound of scraping chairs against the floor. "They're fun."

"They're loud and nosy. I'm probably the quietest one."

"That's saying something." She knocks into me with her shoulder and smiles. "I'm good, Trev. This is good."

"Okay. But you tell me if it's too much, and I'll get you settled in the bedroom." Standing from the sofa arm, I pull her up from the cushion, our fingers entwined.

We stand there, face-to-face, staring at each other like a crowded dinner table isn't waiting for us. The longer we stay like this, the more aware I am of how tall she is. Everyone's short when you're 6'3". But not her. I don't even need to bend my knees to reach her lips. *She's perfectly kissable.*

I've spent the entire day on the outskirts of her force field, just wanting to dive over the border and head straight for what I want. Maybe it's seeing her here in my childhood home, or maybe it's how my family embraced the news. But my mind is jumping to what life will be like when we visit next year, and the year after that. We're not even close to being in a relationship, but as we share this moment, there's no one else I can see myself bringing home. Willa's all I can imagine.

CHAPTER THIRTY
WILLA

Last night's home-cooked soul food meal was the kind of welcome I needed to squash my nerves. Crispy oven fried chicken, collard greens, and more side dishes than I was able to taste—I wish I'd had room for seconds. Fetuses are party poopers, though, and my little nugget rendered me exhausted in the middle of the Trevor roasting session after dinner. I excused myself to bed, and he helped me settle into his old room before dipping back out to catch up with his family.

This bed is so damn comfortable, I'd be tempted to snuggle back into Trevor if he were next to me. Sitting up, I take in the suitcases casting shadows in the corner beside the bay window. Early dawn peeks around the edges of the curtains as my eyes sweep the darkened room. The connected bathroom door is wide open, with no sounds coming from there either. *Did he sleep somewhere else?*

Unexpected disappointment shoots through me at the thought, and I'm not sure how to feel about that. *Get a fucking grip, Willa.* Why would he climb into a bed next to me under his parents' roof? We're not together. *Do I want to be?* Hell if I know. I do have to pee, though, and the longer I sit here, the more urgently I need to go. Swinging my legs over the side of the bed, I hop down from the mattress and land right on the back of Trevor's thighs. I yelp, jumping away with a hand to my chest.

"*Owww.*" Trevor's muffled groan sounds from the stack of pillows he's buried his face into on the floor. The hard muscles on his shirtless back flex as he turns his head to me, black durag tied tightly.

"*Ugh*, you scared the hell out of me, Trevor! What are you doing on the goddamn floor?"

"I was sleeping until you decided I'd do better as a stepping stool."

His sleepy rasp goes right to my clit. *Oh, God, now I'm thinking about his tongue.* I release a breath, crossing my thighs to play it off. "Again, *why* are you on the floor?"

He peeks an eye open with a yawn. "You were knocked out when I got back in, and I didn't want to wake you. Plus, the kissing thing."

"Kissing thing?"

Propping up on an elbow, he scrubs a hand down his face. "Yeah. You know, when two people smash their lips together..."

Ass.

"I know what kissing is. But how does that amount to you sleeping on the floor?"

"Honestly, since we're in this blurry boundary limbo, I didn't know if you'd want me in the bed."

"...Blurry?"

"Yeah, like you said, you kissed me, I kissed you back, and we haven't actually talked about it." He shrugs. "I figured the floor was a safer option in the middle of the night." There's enough light for me to see the flicker of uncertainty in his eyes before they drop to the floor, and it catches me off guard. He's always so sure of himself. This stripped-down vulnerability tugs at the edges of my heart.

"I want you in the bed." My quiet voice fills the space between us as I keep my gaze on his face. Being unguarded around him is still an adjustment, but I want him to know I'm just as nervous as he is right now. Blurred lines and all, he should know I feel the tides changing, and I'm open to wading in the water with him. When his eyes find mine, I smile, he smiles, and the butterflies dance on my bladder, reminding me why I got up. "I have to pee."

He chuckles, and the last thing I see is him tossing a pillow on the bed before I close the bathroom door.

When I'm done, Trevor's propped up against the headboard, head tipped to the ceiling. His attention snaps to me when the door creaks, his smile filling me with jitters. I'm giddier than a motherfucker as I step lightly across the cold hardwood floor and slide in next to him. It's almost seven o'clock. I'm sure farm life has already started for the day, but I could fall back asleep for a few hours. Pulling the fluffy bedspread around my waist, I smooth it out with my hands, feeling Trevor's eyes on me while the nervous fluttering inside rages on. *I'm a grown-ass woman, and I can't find the gumption to look this man in the eye right now?* Flattening the fabric under my fingers again, I take a deep breath.

"Gem, come here. I need to tell you something." He slides an arm around my back, gripping my hip with his hand and pulling me closer. With a gasp at the suave audacity, I look into his eyes, and I'm locked in. He reaches a thumb to my cheek, grazing lightly on its way down to my chin. The desire in his stare sends a torrent to my core. I can't blame any of this on my hormones anymore. I'm melting like a popsicle in his arms, and all he's done is call me *Gem*.

"Why are you looking at me like that?" I ask innocently. Sure, I want him to lay me out on this bed and have his way with me, but I also have the striking need to hear him say he wants me just as badly. I want him to say the words, knowing full well they'll be the end of me.

"I've always looked at you like this, Willa..." He rests his forehead on mine. "Always." Just as I lean into him, his phone buzzes on the table across the room. He closes his eyes and lets out a frustrated groan. "That's probably my cockblock younger brother. I said I'd help him and Dad with the fence at the far end of the ranch this morning. It should only take an hour or two. You can come with if you want to sit and watch us work. Or you can stay at the house with Mom and my sisters. Or relax. The house is so big, it stays pretty quiet up here."

"Oh." Disappointment cascades over the warm fuzzies, and I drop my eyes. "Okay. I can stay here. I think your mom wanted to spend time together anyway, so this is kind of perfect."

"You sure?"

"Yeah. Of course." I try to keep a level voice and get a handle on my dejection. "I'll be fine."

He doesn't move, though, instead leaning down to my ear. "If I thought I could control myself, I'd guide you onto my lap right now." His hold tightens on my hip, my breath catching as I register his words. "I want to do so much more than kiss you, Willa, and I plan to take my time when I do."

He smirks at my sharp inhale, his eyes trailing down my body and back. His phone buzzes again, and the groan that rumbles in his chest has me crossing my thighs and giggling.

"You go ahead and use this shower. I'll use the one down the hall." Trevor presses a kiss to my temple and hurries to check his phone before digging in his suitcase. I watch him the entire way, my heart pounding at the sight of his sweatpants sitting low on his waist, hugging him in all the right places. He's innocently gathering his clothes, but the tattoos down his arm as he flexes have me in a trance. He smirks faintly when he glances over his shoulder, and I bite my lip. "What?" he asks.

"I..." My eyes dip to my wrestling hands. I want to tell him I'll miss him, but that feels way too intense when everything's hanging in the balance between us. "I, um, hope you have fun," I say slowly, adding an awkward scrunch to my nose.

Trevor sets his things on the edge of the bed, untangles my fingers, and dips until we're eye level. "I'll miss you too." My neck flames at his dimpled smile, and then he winks, lighting up the rest of me. "Breakfast is usually on the table by eight-thirty." A quick peck on my forehead, then he grabs his things and closes the door behind him. I finally take a breath. *Silence.* This is the type of stillness I crave every single day, but as soon as he leaves, the quiet is sonorous. Never in a million years did I think I'd say this, but I'm fucking jonesing for Trevor Jones.

"Good morning, Willa! Do you have any allergies?" Mrs. Jones—Adele—asks as I slink into the open concept kitchen. Sunlight reflects the fresh blanket of snow, illuminating the room through the wall of casement windows. Her dark hair is piled on top of her head, secured with a claw clip, and her long navy cardigan sweeps the ground. The bangles on her wrists clink as she flips the food with a spatula. Whatever she's cooking smells perfect. If dinner was any indication, I'll love what's she's making this morning too. "We're having blueberry pancakes."

"No allergies. I'll eat anything." I smile, holding my stomach as it rumbles. "Do you mind if I grab some fruit?"

"Honey, you're family. Grab anything you'd like." She puts a hand on her hip and points the spatula at me. "You better feed my grandbaby."

Laughing, I pick out a banana right as Maya and her daughters come in. All three girls are dressed in matching blue sweater sets sparkling with sequined snowflakes, while Maya sports a black ribbed turtleneck and leggings. I choose the same chair at the honey-brown and white farmhouse table I sat in last night, hoping I'm not taking someone's seat.

"Good morning!" the twins—Harper and Hazel—say in unison. I smile at Maya's eye roll as she straps a babbling Holland in her highchair. At the dinner table, the girls explained how much they've been practicing talking at the same time, just to be able to trick their teachers at school. But they're four, and still don't fully understand that they're fraternal. Harper's dark brown ringlets bounce as she flits across the kitchen to give Adele a hug, while Hazel's cinnamon corkscrews dance as she wiggles into her chair.

"Ooh, good. I was hoping breakfast would be early today. I have to get to the theater for practice." Lainey's jet-black blowout lays French braided down her back.

"Are you in a show?" I ask.

"Yeah"—she buttons her green peacoat over her jumper—"the Christmas Spectacular is tonight, and they called for an early morning dress rehearsal. It's a revue of all the holiday clichés. You're coming with everyone, right?"

"Oh, I don't want to intrude on any family traditions."

Maya slides into the chair next to me and pulls the highchair beside her on the other side. Her auburn curls cascade from a high ponytail, freckles covering every inch of visible skin. "Willa, you're family, and you're coming. Whether. You. Like. It. Or. Not." She pokes my shoulder with a smile, punctuating her last words.

"Well, I'm excited to come then." That's twice in less than ten minutes I've been told I'm part of the family. They've been more than accommodating. Everyone's extremely friendly, but my cognitive dissonance surrounding family is working overtime. I can't get the feeling of impending implosion out of my head.

"Yay! You'll love it!" Lainey squeezes my shoulder as she passes behind me and sits in the chair on my other side. "So tell me, what's LA like?"

"Busy." I laugh. "Loud and busy, but there's lots to do."

"I've always wanted to go to a musical out there. Tre took me to one in San Francisco a couple years ago, which was awesome, but LA just seems bigger and better."

"Where's T, anyway?" Maya asks to no one in particular.

"The boys went into town for supplies to fix the southern perimeter." Adele slips a steaming platter of pancakes on the table, glancing at the sound of a door closing. "The calves keep wandering over to Elizabeth's training stables. She's been giving

Eli an earful—I *know* you're not wearing a hat in my house, Trevor."

"Uncle Tre!" Harper and Hazel bolt from their seats, taking hold of each of Trevor's legs as he slips a black, snow-covered cowboy hat off his head.

"Who's Uncle Tre?" he teases, lowering his neck gaiter and beaming down at them, then smiling at me as if I'm the only other person in the room. He makes a show of hauling the twins across the floor while they giggle and squeal, trying to hang on as his boots shuffle across the hardwood. His dark brown sherpa-lined coat is unzipped, exposing a gray US Coast Guard hoodie underneath. *Where has this damn cowboy been hiding?* Shit. Now I'm having dirty thoughts of him, me, and that hat at the break-fast table.

Bringing the twins right up to my chair, he places a hand on the back of it. "I just wanted to make sure you're okay. We're about to head south, and I—"

"Yes, T. *She's fine.*" Maya rolls her eyes. "You think we're gonna vaporize her?"

"More like talk her to death," he says.

"Is he always like this?" Lainey asks me.

I nod, squinting playfully at him. "Usually, it's worse."

"Hey! I came home this year and everything. Be nice to me," he says to his sisters. He squeezes my shoulder, leaving his hand there for a few lingering seconds.

"We won't lose her, Trevor. Might even feed her while you're gone," Adele teases.

His head shakes in exasperation, but the smile remains on his face. "Okay, I'm going. I'll have my phone, so if any—"

"We got it!"

"Boy, get out of my kitchen!"

"Chill, bro."

All three voices ring out at the same time, and I don't even try to hide the giggle bubbling from my throat.

"Look, I know how to take care of her better than anyone

here. I will personally make sure she only rides one horse," Maya says.

"Ooh, that sounds fun!" I say with a teasing smile. "Baby's first horseback ride."

He sucks his teeth, shaking his head at the collective laughter from his mom and sisters. "Yeah. You'll fit right in here, Gem." Trevor presses a kiss on the top of my head and stoops to peel the nieces off his ankles. He grabs a pancake from the table, smiles at the protest from his mom, and leaves the way he came.

"Aw, he calls you *Gem*? That's so sweet!" Lainey makes a puppy dog face, complete with a puffed out lower lip. "It's nice to see him so happy."

"He's not usually like this?"

Maya snorts. "We wouldn't know. He's never brought anyone home before. Looks like you're doing a great job keeping him on his toes though."

Luckily, the room is so busy no one seems to notice how speechless I am. *Never*? Trevor's *never* brought anyone home before now? I'm the first one? How is that even possible?

Lainey scarfs down her breakfast and is out the door before I've added blueberry syrup to my pancakes. Adele finishes up at the stove and joins us at the table, sitting directly across from me, right in between Hazel and Harper. "Alright girls, it's just us today. We got a fresh blanket of snow last night, so I'm thinking it's a snowman day."

Harper dances in her seat, hyped up by Hazel's cheering, accented by little Holland giving her best attempt at saying *snowman*. Maya nudges me with her elbow. "Perfect. She can tire them out while we stay warm and cozy in here. Do you like cross-stitch?"

"I've never done it before." I shrug. "Photography's my go-to hobby, but I'll try it."

Her eyes flash with amusement. "I'm not the best, but it keeps my fingers nimble for surgery. We can both ride the struggle bus today."

We finish up in the kitchen, and Adele takes the girls outside, leaving me and Maya to *craft the day away*, as she put it. I wait in the family room, admiring the thick, white beams checkered across the ceiling as the matching carved column fireplace crackles on the far wall. From here, we can watch the girls and Adele playing in the snow through the picture window. My feet sink into the plush beige carpet as I settle on one couch with a sigh. *It's so peaceful here.* My phone buzzes.

TREVOR

Ready for a nap yet?

ME

It's only been an hour.

TREVOR

This fence is gonna take a lot longer than I was led to believe. Say the word, and I'll come back.

ME

I'm fine, Tre. About to hang out with Maya

*Trev

TREVOR

You can call me Tre if you wanna, since we're about to be family.

ME

According to everyone here, I already am.

TREVOR

Must be true then ☺

"Okay, we have lots of choices here. Mom's hobby is collecting craft supplies so we have everything from 'beginner' to 'what the hell was she thinking buying this professional pattern?'"

"Definitely beginner. Between pregnancy brain and pregnancy clumsiness, I don't want to press my luck while wielding a needle."

"Isn't the brain fog the *worst*?" Maya laughs as she digs through a blue plastic tote.

"It's so bad. I used to be smart, and now I find my car keys in the microwave."

"When I was pregnant with the twins, my husband Ben would follow behind, replacing anything I put in the wrong place. He's on call at the hospital for the holiday, but he should be here tonight for Lainey's show." She smiles, her gaze falling into one of professionalism. "How are you feeling otherwise? Any complications?"

"Nope. Nothing besides the morning sickness, but that's kind of died off too."

"That's good news. I was on bedrest for both of my pregnancies. My cervix just did *not* like holding them in there. Plus the whole 'advanced maternal age' aspect."

I shudder at the thought. "I'd go crazy if I was forced to be in bed all day. How did you make it?"

"Cross-stitch." She laughs and digs in the box, coming out with beginner and intermediate patterns. "And yet, I somehow didn't master it." Maya hands mine over and plops on the opposite end of the couch, pulling her legs up on the cushion. We take a few minutes of silence to read the instructions and sort the multicolored floss. I'm stretching my canvas over the plastic frame when Maya's phone buzzes by her feet. She snorts. "Trevor told me to make sure you're drinking enough water, like I don't take care of pregnant women for a living."

"Has he always been so attentive?"

"Yep." Her nose wrinkles. "He was a super shy kid and needed to observe every situation before joining in. In foster care, he would watch everything from the corner, no matter where we were. The shyness melted away once we got stable here, but his protectiveness only got worse, as you've seen." Her giggle reveals the slight impression of dimples on her cheeks. They're not as deep, but I can see the resemblance to her brother. Well, to

Trevor. Eli, on the other hand, looks completely different with his dark brown skin and black hair.

"Can I ask...you and Trevor look so much alike, but Eli..." My voice trails as I realize how personal this conversation is. Not everyone likes talking about their family business like this.

Her smile melts my worry. "Yeah, so T and I have the same bio mom and dad, and we take after our dad. Eli has a different dad, but he takes after our birth mom."

"So your dad had the auburn hair too?"

"Yep. A Black man with red hair and freckles. Minus all the freckles that I got, T looks just like him, which was a big part of the problem..."

Nodding, I slide my gaze to the embroidery hoop in my hand. I don't have the slightest clue what she means, but we're crossing into some private history I have no business asking about until the information is offered up to me.

"He hasn't talked about all of that much, has he?"

"I know the basics, but we don't have to get into it. It's personal."

"Girl, you're family now. You're carrying a part of him. These are things you should know, if just to be able to pass the information on to your child."

Family. The way Maya sets down her cross-stitch and puts all her attention on me makes me feel like they all might just be serious. *I'm family.* I haven't felt awkward once since arriving yesterday. If anything, they've been a little too open at times. *Like you'd expect from family.* These strangers have opened up their home and hearts so easily, but it doesn't feel strange. I'm more at home here, in one day, than I've ever been in my parents' house.

"You've seen his nervous habit, right?" Maya asks.

"Um..."

"The love songs?"

"Oh." I laugh. "Yeah, he doesn't do it as much anymore, but it was all the love ballads every time I got in his car for the first few weeks of the pregnancy."

"Yeah, he was overwhelmed. He's been listening to them to calm his nerves since he was little. And I've learned enough about you to know you're not going to ask why, so I'll just tell you." Her eyes narrow as she wags a finger at me playfully. "Whenever our birth parents would fight, I'd grab headphones and my portable cassette player, crank it loud, and put Trevor in the closet so he didn't have to see or hear any of it. The only cassettes I had were '90s R&B and boy bands. We've worked through a ton of shit, but that habit of his is one soothing technique he's held on to. I'm the one that gave it to him."

My mouth drops. *I'm such a bitch.* "Oh my God. I've been teasing the hell out of him. If I had known..."

"Hey, don't feel guilty about not knowing." She smiles, placing her hand on my knee. "We've both been through extensive therapy, and he's a good sport about it now. He accepts it as a part of his self-regulation toolbox." After a squeeze, she sits back against the arm of the sofa, getting right into her stitching. "Now, I don't know how long Nana can keep those girls outside, so let's get started."

How can I focus on making tiny *x*'s in the fabric now? My mind is busy replaying every single time I got into Trevor's car and rolled my eyes at his music choices. How many times did he hide his overwhelm, all because I was being mean as hell?

CHAPTER THIRTY-ONE
TREVOR

"Let me grab my camera." Willa's burgundy and white sweater dress brushes my hand as she slides past me and hurries up the stairs. It's Christmas Eve, and I want to show her all the decorations and lights downtown, just the two of us.

I hadn't planned on spending the entire day away yesterday, but Dad and Eli tricked me. The damn fence was busted beyond repair, requiring us to dig new posts into the frozen ground and replace the barbed wire. Dad and Eli used the six hours to interrogate me about everything from work, to Willa, to asking in-depth questions about how I plan to provide for the baby. They even packed lunch, unbeknownst to me, and grilled me in the truck for an hour while they took their sweet time eating. By the time we got back to the house, it was just long enough to shower and eat an early dinner before heading out to the Christmas Spectacular. Needless to say, Willa and I were both exhausted by the time we laid down for the night.

I grab Willa's coat and wait for her by the door, eager to take a little breather from my intrusive family. They adore her, and their excitement abounds, but *I* need the break. Every year, I seem to forget how much I enjoy my solitude until I don't have any during my Christmas trip.

"Okay. Ready." Willa smiles, reaching for her coat.

"You two will be back for the movie, right?" Mom asks, peeking around the corner.

"Yep. Wouldn't miss it, Ma. Already set an alarm."

"Good. You kids have fun!" She slips back into the kitchen, where the sound of dinner dishes fills the air.

We make it to the car, the sun painting pink across the cloudless sky as it sets. I crank the heat up high, and Willa blows puffs of air in the residual cold, giggling at the vapor. These past few days have been the most relaxed I've ever seen her. She's downright giddy. "So you're a cold weather lady, huh?"

"I guess I am. It's just so peaceful out here, and all the acreage makes it seem even quieter. I love it."

"The sound waves are sufficient in Nebraska?" I tease.

"Yeah. And the fact that we're so far from town. The stars are brighter, the air feels cleaner, and the noises here are soothing instead of grating."

"So when I bring you back next year, you won't fight me on it?"

"Next year?" She raises her eyebrows playfully.

"I'm pretty sure my family will disown me if I don't bring you home from now on."

"I guess you'd better, then..."

"I guess I will, then." Lacing our fingers, I give hers a squeeze before letting go to put the car in drive. Willa reaches for my hand again, and we settle on the armrest.

Driving back through downtown, I feel lighter than I did when we arrived. This place still holds some painful memories for me, but watching Willa's wide-eyed joy as we pass by snow-covered parks and trees alight with all sorts of LEDs is worth it. Her smile strikes a spark inside me, illuminating so brightly it forces the harrowing memories into the shadows. I park in front of the library, and as we stroll down Main, my ghosts seem to be chased away by the sound of her laughter. Her excitement makes it easier to ignore my history a couple of blocks away. For the first time in a long time, I'm alright being here.

Camera bolted to her face, Willa crouches, bends, and climbs just to get her shot. Her unbridled passion is mesmerizing. I try to stifle the dopey smile on my face every time she looks at me, but it's useless. This woman is becoming someone special to me, and not just because she's carrying my child. The person she is, her intelligence, the soft empathy she holds—my heart is well on its way to making room for her. An oasis. A spot that's solely hers. *What would a life with Willa look like*? One where she opens up completely—lets me care for the most sensitive parts of her. A life where we're together, in all ways, for all time.

"Trev?"

"Yep. Yeah?"

She cocks her head, eyebrows cinched as she assesses me. "I was asking why you don't like it here. Heritage is beautiful."

"Ah, yeah. The scenery is great. I guess I just outgrew the place, you know? I needed more than it could offer, and with my early history here, it never really felt like a good place for me, anyway."

"Maya told me a little about your life before adoption."

I nod and take a deep breath. I've never had the urge to share this part of myself before, but I feel like she'll keep it safe. "Can I show you something?"

As soon as she nods, I take her hand and lead her down the rest of the block. Then we turn opposite town square to cross the street.

"Where are we going? We have to get back for the movie." She picks up speed as we hurry down the sidewalk.

"It'll only take a minute." My determined steps move in time with my pounding heart, setting the cadence for this traumatic detour. The red-brick buildings give way to trees after another block. I finally stop at a rundown apartment complex behind the Quick Mart, right across the street from the conjoined middle and high school. The streetlight casts a nefarious glow on the decrepit building. "This is where they found us."

"Wha—" Willa sweeps her eyes back and forth, over broken windows and boarded-up doors. "Where *who* found *who*?"

"This is where I grew up." Dropping her hand, I stuff mine in my coat pocket. I've never told this to anyone outside of therapy, let alone shown anyone. But right now, it feels safe to hand this fragile memory to her. "The night we went into the system, the police found Maya and I huddled together in a closet after a full night of our bio parents drinking and fighting. She was ten, I was three. I don't know how long we were in there, and don't remember a lot, but when they helped us, the apartment was unrecognizable." Fragmented images flash in my mind, but I push past the dread settling in my gut. *I want her to know.* "I just remember glass crunching under my slippers and a lot of blood. *So much blood.*"

She touches my arm lightly, and I start. "Whose?"

"Bio dad's mostly. My birth mom stabbed him in the leg with a mirror shard after getting tossed around all day."

"And he…?"

"Nope. The bastard's still alive and kickin'. Nebraska State Pen, last I heard."

"And your mom?"

"Oh, she's in prison too. She got out when I was a teenager, long enough to get pregnant with Eli, and got herself locked up again. They were both young and had a lot of issues. Had no business having a kid, let alone two."

Willa slips her hand into my pocket, her fingers curling around mine. My deep inhale does nothing to rid myself of the memories, not with the menacing building in front of me. Dropping my eyes to the ground, I take another shaky breath. The sound of the glass crunching under my feet was so distinct; I've never been able to forget.

I glance back at Willa, but she's looking past me, toward the schools across the street. The sympathy on her face hardens into realization. "You had to walk past this place every day," she says.

I nod. "Couldn't forget it if I wanted to. I could see my worst day through my English classroom window for a solid five years."

"No wonder you hate it here. I'd hate it too," she says softly, and the change in her tone has me searching her face. She swings her camera behind her and pulls me into a hug. Her palms smooth over my back, easing the tension settled there. "Thank you for bringing me here, Trevor."

I hold her tightly, closing my eyes to stop the visual assault that comes from looking at this building. Willa's touch is a balm, each pass of her hands soothing the deep fissures etched into my psyche. I had no hesitation about showing this messy part of myself to her. As we embrace in the rundown parking lot, I have no second thoughts. Willa can have all of me.

Barn Movie Night has always been one of the best family traditions. Gathering all of my favorite people around the space heater. The projector playing a Christmas classic on the wall. Snow falling just beyond the barn doors. What's not to love? Having Willa snuggled next to me, a blanket draped over our shoulders, is icing on the cake this year.

"Do you need anything? Snacks? Water?" I ask her.

She shakes her head and wiggles her fingers in between mine. "Just this." Her smile knocks the wind out of me. Something in these past few days has shifted with Willa, and even though I don't want to rush anything, my mind reels at the possibilities. Everyone else laughs at the movie, but I'm fixated on the gentle caress of her thumb, the heat exchanged between her skin and mine, and the way my stomach flutters at her giggle. My family has kept us so busy, I haven't been able to get a repeat of that kiss. The demand to get her alone screams inside my head. I'm about to suggest a walk when her phone vibrates.

"It's Ash. I'll be right back." She drops my hand, and it feels like she disconnected a power source.

"Here." I stand with her, wrapping the striped wool around her. "Take the blanket."

She rolls her eyes, that same smile from earlier sucking all the air from my lungs.

"We'll go in with you. The girls are spent," Maya says, holding Holland over her shoulder. Ben balances the twins on each of his as he follows behind. I watch until they turn out of the barn, a beat too long based on the handful of popcorn Eli throws at me.

"Boo, you giant! Down in front!"

Flipping him off, I move to the side to lean against the wall. I check the time every few minutes, and at fifteen, decide to go after her. When I walk outside, I hear her laugh traveling across the glistening snow, the sound tunneling through me, cataloging into that affectionate place in my heart. The glow from her phone lights up her face as she leans against the horse corral. I stick my hands in my pockets, the wind whipping around me. The slow crunch of my footsteps seems to echo in the wide-open field, and she looks up at my approach.

"Hey, Ash, I have to go."

"*What*? You can't just leave me hanging! Stay strong. Hold out until New Year's. I have designer shoes hanging in the balance," Ashlie screeches through the speaker.

"I'll call you tomorrow to wish you guys a Merry Christmas."

"Wills, don't you dare hang up on m—"

Willa shakes her head, ending the call. "She's been asking if she lost the bet since we got here."

I make the last few steps to her, stopping only when the toes of my boots nudge hers. "And what did you tell her?"

Her rapid breathing curls into tiny frozen clouds, setting me ablaze. "That we haven't even kissed...again," she whispers. When she bites her lip, my attention flies to her mouth. It's all I can do to drag my eyes back to hers. She watches me through her lashes, and I almost come undone. "Is that okay?"

"Sure, Gem." Laughter floats from the barn, snapping me out of my stupor, and we giggle nervously. "They love you, ya know? My family, they're crazy about you."

Willa smiles, her gaze falling as she pretends to adjust the blanket around her shoulders. "You were right. They're pretty great."

"Willa?" I grab the edges of the blanket and tug her forward, holding her against me until her eyes meet mine. Leaning in close enough to feel the warmth puffing from her parted lips, I whisper, "Scale of one to ten—"

"Eleven, Trev."

"Call me Tre," I mumble, before taking the smallest taste of her. Another, and I can't hold myself back, diving hard against her mouth.

She matches the force of my kiss, sucking my lower lip with a sensual tug. Shooting stars sail behind my eyelids as she trails electric fingertips down my sides. Her lips are softer than I remember, but just as brazen, and just as sure. I pull her in at the waist, knowing damn well it's not close enough, and lavish her with all the dreamed kisses I've collected in my head. She snakes her hands around my neck, crushing my mouth with hers before trapping my lip between her teeth. *Carry her into the house. Screw the consequences.*

The screen door bangs, driving a reality crushing wedge between us as we jump apart.

"Ope! Don't mind me." Maya waves a broom in the air while stomping across the patio. "Just gotta get that damn cat. Carry on." We watch as she disappears around the corner, but her grumbling carries across the wind.

I turn back to Willa, whose eyes are scanning the ground with a light smile playing at her lips. "You okay?" I ask. "That was..."

"Intense. Yeah." She smiles up at me. "Um, I think I'm going to turn in."

"Dammit, Sprinkles! Get your ass in the house!" Maya's voice echoes, pulling away our attention again.

"Let me walk you," I say eagerly.

"No, no. You go finish the movie with your family. I'm tired, and I need to think." She takes a deep breath and glances at the house.

"Okay, well, consider this too." Hooking a finger under her chin, I tilt her face up for another kiss. "And this." Her lips eagerly meet mine in a slow embrace. "And this." I leave her with another that takes all of my self-control to pull away from, with the sweet tug of her lips. "*I'm* crazy about you, Willa."

A sigh squeaks out of her, and she nods quickly, tightening the blanket around her shoulders. "I think I'm crazy about you too," she whispers. Stepping away slowly, she ambles across the snow toward the house. Sprinkles darts between her legs when she opens the door, and she pauses, throwing a sultry look back at me. *Go after her, dummy.*

"I hate that cat." Maya trudges toward me through the snow, broom in hand. "Did I ruin the moment? Where's Willa?"

"Thinking..." I say, scratching the back of my head.

"She's great, T."

"She's amazing..."

"You're in love with her?"

I chuckle quietly. "Not yet."

"Yeah, but you will be." She pokes my arm with the broom handle.

"Without a doubt."

"So why are you out here talking to me instead of in there with her?"

"I'm giving her space to think."

Maya nods, laughing. "From what I've learned about her, you two are the same in that way. She processes her thoughts internally, just like you do." She lands a soft punch on my arm. "Just don't get so caught up inside your heads that it gets in the way of the important stuff, T."

The broom leaves streaks in the snow as she drags it behind her, making her way into the house. I begrudgingly turn back to the barn. No matter how much I want to chase after her, Willa needs to make the next move.

CHAPTER THIRTY-TWO

WILLA

I lied. It's been an hour, and there's not a tired bone in my body. Not while Trevor's kiss replays in my mind like it's my new favorite love ballad. *He's crazy about me*? The way I latched onto him while we kissed, it's blaringly obvious I'm falling for him too. I wring my hands, ruminating on the week and what it all means for me. For him. *For us*. Is there even an us? *Do I want there to be*?

He shared things with me tonight that I never would have guessed he went through. Things that tie my stomach in knots when I think about that sweet man experiencing anything other than the peace and protection he so freely gives. I only ever want to imagine him surrounded by the loving family he has now, not as a terrified child dealing with the aftermath of the unthinkable. And yet, he shared it with *me*. He thinks so highly of me that I'm the first woman he's ever brought home to see that side of him. He let me into the most vulnerable parts of his life, and I'm scared as hell I won't meet his expectations.

Trevor's a forever. The kind of man you settle down with when you're sure of what you want, and not a minute before. I haven't looked that far ahead with anyone. It never really seemed to matter. *Before now*. It's scary to admit that I can see it—see *him*

—as I look to the future. Us, and whoever this little one grows up to be.

I freeze as the door creaks open. Trevor pushes it closed behind him, making no attempts to come closer. "…You alright, Gem?"

"Yeah, just…" Nerves bubble out of me in light laughter, my confliction becoming crystal clear. Glancing at my clutched fingers, I shake out my hands. One deep breath for courage helps me quickly make up the rest of my mind. "*Stressed.* I'm just stressed." I bite my lip, letting my eyes trail up his long legs, his chiseled torso, his strong arms, until they reach his burning gaze.

His eyes stay locked to mine as he walks toward me, my pounding heart echoing with each of his steps. "Stressed, huh?"

I nod.

"And you, uh, want some help with your…*stress*?" His voice deepens into a husky rumble, leaving me throbbing between the legs and panting shamelessly.

I nod again.

Trevor drops to his knees in front of me, wedging himself between my legs. He reaches up and grips my chin, tracing my bottom lip with his thumb. Air staccatos out of me, and his eyes darken. "I want your words, Willa."

"Y-yes," I squeak out, eyes fluttering as his touch sears into me. "I want you to help me with my stress."

His other hand skirts up my thigh, only stopping once he gets to my waist. With one swift tug, he pulls me forward, my dress rolling up to my hips as he brings my ass to the edge of the bed. Our lips are a whisper away. "You remember what I need from you?"

I nod, and he quirks an eyebrow. "Please, Tre," I whisper against him.

A growl vibrates from his chest as he pulls my dress over my head. "There's my pretty girl." His mouth meets mine, our tongues greeting in a feverish dance. As soon as my head lands on the mattress, his lips tease down my chin and suction to my neck, leaving a trail of goosebumps in their wake. He unclasps my bra and flings it across the room. I reach for the back of his head to guide him down to where I want him, but he pins my wrists to the bed. "Nope. I'm in control this time." His deepened voice sends shudders through me.

The slow flick of his tongue over my nipple makes me moan, the warm strokes sending pleasure straight down to my toes until they curl. He loosens his grip, and my body trembles when his breath fans over me. I claw at his shoulders with a gasp as he tugs my nipple with his teeth, soothing the sting with a slow draw. My hips buck impatiently while he kisses a trail down to my navel. "Look at you..." He tuts. "You just can't help yourself, can you?"

Damn sure can't. I'm losing my mind a little more with every kiss he etches me with. I need him to mark every inch of me.

He works off my leggings, and they fly across the room too. "You ever wear panties, Willa? Damn."

"Not if I can help it." I pant. Inch-by-fucking-inch, he traces his tongue down my body, focusing everywhere except where I want him.

"Spread for me," he mumbles against my skin. I can't splay my legs fast enough. "Tsk, so impatient. I told you. I'm taking my time." Kissing the inside of my thigh, he slides a knuckle through my slit, fucking growling as it glides through the slickness. "I want to memorize every inch of your body."

I gasp as he swirls my clit. My hips roll, seeking him for entry. "The stress, Tre. *Please.*"

He snickers, making another slow pass with his finger, and then he's devouring me. I buck against him, moaning and begging him to never stop. There's not a chance in hell I'm lasting more than a few minutes with him like this. Once he reaches a hand up and rubs his thumb across my nipple, it's over for me. I'm gone, blissed out in a vortex of warm static. I scratch the back of his head, pressing his face to my pussy while he hungrily laps me up.

"Fuck, I've *missed* you, beautiful," he mumbles, his tongue rolling leisurely as if he's settling in for a conference call with my clit. "Taste just like I remember, sweetheart."

"A-are you talking to my puss—?"

"Shh, it's been a long time," he mumbles. "Let me enjoy this reunion."

My eye roll takes a blurry excursion to the back of my head when his finger curls inside me. Everything's black, then flashes of color twinkle like Christmas lights behind my eyelids. I levitate as I cry out, my back arching when my orgasm surges through me in waves. "You're all mine, aren't you?" This man just sucked me into a stupor, but that question may send me to Elysium. I collapse on the bed, chest heaving, thoughts jumbled while Trevor slowly kisses my pulsing clit like he can't get enough of me.

I've never felt this before, the utter desire emanating from someone I'm with. Tears slip down toward my hairline when I realize I didn't have a visceral reaction to him calling me *sweetheart* and *beautiful*. I wipe them, but not quickly enough to escape Trevor's attention. "Willa?" He slides onto the bed next to me. I don't dare open my eyes, knowing I'll lose it if the look on his face matches the worry in his voice. "Hey, let me in... Was this too much?"

"No. Not too much." I swipe at my cheeks and blow out a breath, trying to organize my words before I turn to face him. When I open my eyes, his own track a nervous course over my face. "It was perfect. *You* were perfect. It's just..." Another tear slips, and he's quick to wipe it away. "The pet names. For the first time, I didn't hate it. And the only reason I'm crying about it is because I'm pregnant."

His soft smile wraps around me, clearing the haze in my head until all I see is him. "Willa, let me redefine those words for you. I'll mold them into something pristine and new, something to remind you how wondrous you are. No matter how long it takes, I'll transform every meager memory of those words until all you've ever known is my voice using them in adoration. Until they only ever meant you."

I'm speechless. Trevor holds my cheek in his hand, having no idea he juggles my heart at the same time. When he presses a kiss on my lips, it's the most familiar feeling. *Home.*

"Will you let me do that for you, sweetheart?" He drops his forehead to mine. "Allow me to care for you?"

Despite the fresh tears welling in my eyes, I smile. "I will."

Trevor smirks as he sits, surprising me with a gentle hand on my belly. "You're starting to show, beautiful. Have you noticed?"

"Yeah. A few days ago."

He leans down and places the sweetest kiss on my stomach. "I can't wait to meet you," he whispers to the baby. My insides melt into flutters.

Helping me off the bed, he drops another kiss on my lips, the taste of me on his tongue getting me going again. All I can think about is his dick.

"You go ahead and take the shower first."

"I don't know if that's a good idea..." I say. His eyebrows dip while he waits for me to finish. "I just...feel the *stress* building again."

"Oh, really?"

I trail my fingers down his chest as I step past him toward the bathroom, taking slow strides. *"So much stress,* Tre."

He chuckles, but when I turn back, his eyes are an inferno. "You're trouble."

"Not trouble... *Stressed.* But I guess I can manage on my own if you're tire—"

Trevor whips his shirt over his head as he breezes into the bathroom, walking right to the frosted shower door and flipping on the water. "You want me to get a condom?"

"What are you gonna do? Get me pregnant?"

"Good point. Uh, there hasn't been anyone since you... I'm all clear, and I—"

"You always talk so much?" I tease.

Quirking an eyebrow, he checks his watch, then unbuckles it as his foot taps on the floor. "I'm waiting on *you.*"

I scoff, grabbing my silk scrunchie from the counter and securing my hair on the top of my head. My eyes wander over the small patch of curly hair at the center of his chest. "I'm coming."

"Not yet"—he grabs my waist—"but you will." Hauling me to him, he silences my surprise with a plunging kiss.

I moan, my fingers fumbling with the button on his jeans. They fall to his ankles, and I dip my hand into his tented boxers, freeing his hard length. His lips leave mine with a groan, eyes dropping to my hands, stacked and wrapped around his thick, rigid dick, the crown just visible. It twitches when I swipe the precum leaking from his tip and fix my eyes on his, slowly licking his brackish taste from my thumb. "Shit, Gem..." His breath stutters, and I drop to my knees with a smile.

"You were saying?" I rock back on my legs, settling into the bathroom rug.

"Fuck if I know," he mumbles, eyes rolling back when I massage his balls. Watching this big, strong man fall apart from my touch is sexy as hell. I suck him into my mouth, and he places his hands on my shoulders, his hips swaying with each sloppy glide of my tongue. I'm dripping just from the sounds hissing out of him. He meets my gaze and caresses my chin. "You see what that pretty mouth does to me?"

I fucking shatter, dropping a hand between my legs while taking as much of him in my mouth as I can. His hips pivot, driving his length to the back of my throat while I strum my clit furiously. Moaning around him, I take him deeper, even as pleasurable tears stream down my face. "That's it," he grunts. "Make yourself come while you're choking on this dick." *Good God.* I could get off on his words alone. My orgasm ricochets through me, and he slides from my lips, watching me with pure lust in his eyes as he slowly strokes himself. He waits until I catch my breath, smirking devilishly. "Up, Gem. In the shower. Hands on the wall." His eyes linger on the wet spot I left on the rug, then he follows me through the shower door.

He pulls me against him, his hardness pressing into my ass

cheek as he weaves his fingers with mine. "Don't get my hair wet," I sass over my shoulder.

"No need." Nipping my ear, he slides our hands against the wet tile. "You're already soaking." He angles the shower stream away from my face, and I shudder when he drops a tender kiss on my shoulder. Gently, he bends me at the waist. "Spread your legs, sweetheart. Let me show your pussy how much I've missed her."

"Who's the bossy one now?" I mock, despite widening my stance, teasing him with a wiggle of my hips.

"Still you."

One firm smack on my ass steals my breath and my cheekiness. I'll do whatever he asks if it means he'll pound the backtalk out of me. His tip notches at my slit, our moans harmonizing as he eases inside. Curling an arm under my belly, he lifts me on my toes until he's so deep, all I'm able to do is blink the stars away. "Feel that?" He ruts into me, pressing me against the wall, hips canting slowly. "Perfect-fucking-fit."

Leaning my head back, I nod against his shoulder. He fills me so fully, every thrust makes me whimper in delight. "*Shit*," I mumble, each stroke scrambling my coherency. "How do you feel *this* good?"

"Because I learn from my mistakes, Willa. I'm not letting you go this time." His fingers brush my nipples, rolling and tugging until my hips sway with his. "*Fuck*," he groans, his forehead falling into the crook of my neck as he thrusts faster. "You have no idea what you do to me, do you? How many nights I've imagined being with you again?" He kisses my shoulder, his hand sliding down to my sensitive bud. "I'd fuck you fast and rough until your legs give out, but I'm clinging to my last shred of dignity just to savor how good it feels to be buried inside you."

My pussy clenches at the thought of him having his way with me, and he growls in response. I'm not above begging, but he pinches my clit, and I cry out before I can even try.

"Goddamn," he grunts, hips stuttering while he catches his breath. "You tryna kill me, greedy girl?"

"I'm tryna *fuck*," I pant, pulling him down to my lips, sloppily showing him exactly how greedy I am. I need him touching me everywhere, inside and out, and I'm too damn horny for the pretense. His steady cadence on my clit, dick rubbing my g-spot into oblivion, has my head spinning in ways I've only ever managed to accomplish on my own before. Gasping, I pull away, slapping my hands on the slick shower wall to brace myself. He adjusts behind me, tugging my hips back as he goes.

"Bet." Gripping my waist, he slams into me, and the change in position blurs my vision.

My body tenses in waves, one part losing control as the next gears up for sweet release. "Right. Fucking. There," I whine, punctuated by each slap of our skin. Throwing my ass back, I drive him deeper until I damn near feel him in my throat.

"Look at you taking this dick, baby." His labored breath gives him away as his hips jerk wildly. "Shit, I'mma nut if you keep *fuuu—*" He slumps over me as he fills me up, somehow finding the energy to grace my clit with attention. In firm, quick circles, he brings me right back to the edge, his hardness still pulsing inside me. "Your turn," he rasps, and I fall apart, screaming his name as I'm reminded of just how much fun we had in San Diego.

CHAPTER THIRTY-THREE

TREVOR

Jones family Christmas was a success. I'm biased, but I'm positive I got the best gift of all. Willa and I were absolutely nauseating today, touching and kissing every chance we could. She snuggles into my side as we lie in bed, trying to keep our eyes open while talking in the dark. We have an early flight tomorrow, but I can't get enough of this. Of *her*. It's more amazing than I could have ever imagined.

"Why does everyone call you something different?" she asks.

"What do you mean?"

"Trev, Tre, T..."

"Ah, yeah. So Maya's the only one who calls me T. She's always called me that. Kind of aggressive about her claim on it. Tre is for the family..."—I kiss the top of her head—"and you. Trev is what friends have always latched onto."

"Your mom's the only one who calls you Trevor."

I smile. She *would* notice that. "The day my parents brought us home, Mom found me in here, sitting in the window seat next to the trash bags that held all my belongings. Unpacking felt like a bad omen to my five-year-old mind, and when I told her I didn't want to, she told me, "Your room—your decision.""

"That explains your naked apartment," she teases.

"Probably. She gave me autonomy. I'd never had that before. Then she asked what I'd like her to call me, and that was the first time anyone had. Even social workers called me Trev. I think they meant to lessen the blow of my unstable reality, but I was too scared to speak up back then. When Mom asked, when she gifted me that choice, it finally felt like what I wanted mattered. So I chose my full name, and that's what she's always called me."

"Your mom's amazing."

"She's the best."

Willa presses a kiss to my lips and snuggles back into my side. "Thank you for bringing me here...you were right."

"Hold up. I was *what*?"

She giggles, burying her face in my chest. "You heard me." Her phone goes off on the nightstand, and her adorable giggle when she rolls over and reads the text makes me drop a kiss on her shoulder. She turns back toward me to show Ashlie's message about the bet. "I should tell her she lost so she leaves me alone."

"Mm, I have a better idea," I say, pulling her back to me and nuzzling her neck. "You could tell her she lost four times over."

"Four, huh?"

"Mm-hmm, just really rub it in her face."

"Uh-huh, and when was this fourth time? I count one on the bed and two in the shower last night. That's three..."

"Four is pending." Shifting, I arch over her body, her head in between my hands. "I have one last Christmas present for you." I kiss a line from her lips to her cheek, smiling at the shiver that ripples through her. She moans, digging her fingers into my shoulders when my tongue grazes the shell of her ear. I'm halfway to busting, just enjoying the warm coconut scent on her skin. I can't get enough of her, and I'm not complaining about this pregnancy libido anytime soon. She's all over me too.

"If it's my gift"—she says with a roll of her hips—"shouldn't *I* decide how I want to open it?"

"Sure." I nibble her earlobe, barely containing myself when

she whimpers her need. "Tell me what you want, sweetheart," I whisper.

"I want to sit on your face while you tongue fuck my pussy like a good boy." She wraps a leg around my waist. "Want to ride you until my name is a prayer on your lips." Her nails dig into my shoulders, and I shudder. "Fill me so deep, we can't tell where I end and you begin."

Fuck me. My brain lags as all my common sense rushes to my dick, and I stupidly stutter, "S-sit on my face?"

Her lips ghost mine with a seductive smile. "You can take it."

Pulling down my sweatpants quicker than a bat out of hell, I roll onto my back, ignoring her giggles at my eagerness. "You keep talking to me like that and I'm not gonna last."

"You'll come when I say, and not a second before."

"Better watch it. You're gonna get yourself in trouble."

"*Oh no...*" Her sarcasm is accented with another giggle. "*Orgasms.*" She pulls her pajama shirt over her head, then shimmies out of her pants. Shifting to her knees, she grabs the headboard, and I settle underneath her and dive in. The taste of her throws me into warp speed, licking and sucking like my life depends on it. It just might. Her sweet whimpers fuel my hardening dick as her hips gyrate, pussy gliding all over my tongue. Gripping her thick thighs, I pin her to my face while I feast. "Shit, Tre. Don't fucking stop."

Not a chance in hell. I could fucking live here. I'll do this every damn night if she'll let me. Her thighs become my new favorite earmuffs while she trembles through her release, wailing my name into the darkness. I tease her clit with playful nibbles as she catches her breath, her euphoric giggles lighting me up each time a quiver zaps through her. She clings to the headboard to hide from my tongue. "Gimme." I chuckle, craning my neck to reach her. "I'm not done."

"Neither am I," Willa says breathlessly, swinging her leg over my head. Rivaling the speed of light, she settles around my hips and leans down for a kiss. She lifts slightly before sliding right onto my dick, already so wet I know I won't last long. "Feel that?" she croons. "I'm dripping for you."

Goddamn, this woman... I take it back. *This* is the best Christmas present I've ever received, this dirty talking goddess telling me how much I turn her on. *I'm not gonna make it.* She finds her rhythm, eyes locked on mine as her breathing grows shallow. Her fingernails rake over my chest, and a moment of pure bliss causes my eyes to fall closed. Warm breath in my ear sends me into a spiral as she whispers, "Watch me. I want you to see how you make me feel, handsome. I'm yours, Trevor."

Fuck me—*twice.*

My eyes fly open. Do I focus on the filthy poetry falling from her plump lips or the stark sense of protectiveness crowding out all logical thought when she says she's mine? I'm captivated by her bobbing up and down as she rides out her pleasure, my eyes focused on the perfect jiggle of her breasts while she grinds on top of me. *I'll do anything to protect her.* "Fuck, Willa. You're incredible."

She moans as she plays with her nipples, and just like the first time, I'm mesmerized, unable to keep my hands from caressing her hips. This sexy woman is all mine now, and I'm the luckiest man alive. The first time, Willa looked like a queen on a throne, but right now, hearing her give herself to me, there's no doubt. She's *my* queen on *her* throne. No one else can compete, and no one ever will. I'm completely under her spell.

My eyes flutter when a tidal wave crashes over me, heat twisting in my spine as the waves bury me alive. I grip her hips, pumping into her while I spiral into the void, my senses scattering through the abyss. She falls apart around me and collapses on my chest with a sated sigh. "Hands down"—I pant against her hair—"that was the best gift I've ever received."

She nods and yawns, snuggling into my chest like she intends to fall asleep like this, with me still inside of her. "I thought this was *my* present."

I kiss her shoulder and shift her off my lap, our release dribbling on my leg as I slide away. "Let me clean you up, beautiful. I made a mess of you." I click on the bathroom light, reach for a washcloth, and wet it under warm water, whistling without a care in the world. Willa's still blissed out on the bed when I make it back, and I can't help the smile on my face. It's as if I've been split into two, then fused back together with her at the center. She's awake, barely, and her unguarded smirk is the most beautiful thing I've ever seen. *I'm the reason for that smile.*

Dropping a kiss on Willa's knee, I part her legs, and my hand stills mid-wipe. She props on her elbows, saying something I can't hear over the pulse in my ears. I'm stuck focusing on the one thing you shouldn't see during pregnancy. Not unless something's really wrong.

Blood. A lot of blood. *So much blood.*

"Trevor!" Her fingers on my face snap me out of my freeze response. "You're scaring me. Wha—" She sees the stained cloth in my hand and her eyes snap to her legs. The color drains from her face, jolting me into action. I pick her up and carry her straight to the shower, setting her down gently before turning on my heel. She grabs my arm, spinning me back to her. "W-where are you going?"

"I'm getting Maya."

"Tre."

"I know." I tip my forehead to hers. "I'm scared too. Just let me get Maya. She'll know what to do."

She nods, eyes wide, blinking back tears. I kiss the wetness from her cheeks, placing another on her lips before reaching around her and turning on the water. Rushing around the bedroom, I jump into my clothes as I call Maya, hoping she'll see it by the time I get across the house. Thank God she and Ben decided to stay an extra night before going back home. The phone rings for what feels like forever as I rush out of the room, cussing under my breath.

I round the corner to the east wing, and Maya's already halfway down the hallway. One look at my face has her rushing toward me. "I saw your call and ran. What's wrong?" she asks, throwing her curly hair into a knot on top of her head.

I grimace. Telling my sister I just had mind-blowing sex and possibly wrecked the chance at my dreams coming true are two things I never thought I'd have to do. "She's bleeding."

"What happened?"

"We, uh..."

"My God, T, I know what grown people do at night. Were you having sex?"

"Yeah."

"Okay, and how much blood?"

"A lot."

We rush back to the west wing, and Maya stops in a storage closet for some pads. When we get back to my room, she walks right into the bathroom while I head for Willa's suitcase.

"Willa, honey, it's Maya. How you feelin'?"

"Um, I don't...there's so much. It won't stop."

"Breathe for me, alright? Is it okay if I take a peek in the shower, just to see how much bleeding there is?"

"Please."

I slip Willa's clothes on the bathroom vanity, and my adrenaline takes me straight to the bed to strip it down.

"Okay, honey, I'm going to help you get onto the toilet. Trevor brought you some clothes."

"I'll make a mess all over the floor."

"Don't you worry about that right now. Let's just focus on you."

Each word lands like a boulder in my stomach, and my fingers tremble as I struggle to release the sheet from the corners of the bed. I trip over the bedspread crumpled on the floor and crash my leg into the nightstand, sending a pitcher of water flying. "Shit." *This is your fault. All of it.* I stoop to gather the shards of glass, dropping them in the garbage bin in the corner, and stay there, eyes sweeping over the chaos in the room. *You did this. None of this would be happening if you weren't here.*

I've been in therapy long enough to realize the words screaming through my mind right now don't belong to me. I recognize my birth father's voice, but rational thought never mixes well with panic. Maya steps out of the bathroom, and when she sees me in the corner, her face morphs into the protective older sister who always kept me safe in the closet.

"I'm gonna grab my things and head to the clinic. I need you to bring her as soon as she's done getting dressed. We'll get her all checked out." Maya puts a hand on my arm, and I try to swallow past the thick lump in my throat. "T, it's not your fault."

"Okay."

She gives my arm a squeeze and pulls me toward the bed. I stare at the glow seeping from under the bathroom door, a spotlight illuminating the trail of crimson on the floor. Maya stops me when I turn to grab the discarded washcloth from the pile of bedsheets. "Clean later, T. She needs you right now. You can fall apart after we know what's going on." She waves in front of my face. "Look at me, Trevor." I slide my eyes to hers, but can't really say that I see them, not as clearly as the memory replaying in my mind. *A lamp crashing into the wall above my head. A trickle of blood dripping down my face to the carpet. A deep, berating voice doling out blame.* Maya snaps her fingers in front of me. "You didn't do anything wrong. This isn't your fault. Tell me you hear me."

"I hear you." My voice sounds miles away, and she snaps in my face one more time before I'm able to shake it off. "I hear you, My. We'll meet you at the clinic."

Once I get Willa to the car, I crank up the heat and grab the ice scraper. The stifling cold clears my head enough for logic to peek through. *Panicking won't help right now. Get Willa to the clinic. We won't know anything until that happens. The roads are icy, and I need to get her there in one piece. Keep it together.*

Sliding back into the car, I pause at the music filtering through the speakers. While I calmed myself outside, Willa synced up my comfort playlist. Despite wringing her hands together, she has a serene look on her face. I want to pull her to me. Wrap my hand around hers to still her fingers. I want to protect her from this, but how do you protect someone from the very thing you caused? *Everything was fine until you showed up.* The grating voice swallows up my instinct, and I pull my hand in a fist to keep from hurting Willa any more than I already have. We let the '90s ballads fill in around us, and keep quiet the entire drive downtown.

CHAPTER THIRTY-FOUR

WILLA

"Has the flow slowed down?" Maya asks as I step into the exam room from the bathroom. I only have the energy to nod and climb on the exam table. "Okay, let's see what's going on." She smooths the cool gel over my stomach, and I tense, grimacing at the sensation. She wrinkles her nose. "Sorry. You were at the door before I could flip the warmer on."

My eyes sweep over the colorful pregnancy and anatomy posters on the wall, each one increasing my anxiety for what we're about to see. *Why me? Why now?* The room is painted a buttery yellow, which somehow makes this all so much worse. Closing my eyes, I focus on the scratchy pad in my underwear that's been rubbing against me in all the wrong places since I put it on. The initial gushing slowed before we left the house, so it's chafing everywhere. I haven't used one of these since I was a teenager. Now I remember every sweaty reason why I changed to a menstrual cup as soon as I could.

"Any cramping?" Maya asks, waving the wand around.

"Not really." I glance over my shoulder at Trevor, who watches from the corner with a hand over his mouth. The way he's staring at the monitor, it's like I'm not even here.

"And you're sixteen weeks?"

"A little over."

"How was your sixteen-week appointment?"

"We had to push it back a week because of the holiday."

"Did you have a scan at twelve weeks?"

"No. My doctor picked up the heartbeat through the Doppler and said we didn't need an ultrasound."

Maya smiles and shrugs. "Different strokes. That's perfectly normal, by the way. Some refuse to do anything more than the anatomy scan at twenty weeks." She points at the screen, and I hear a couple of steps shuffle behind me. When I look, Trevor's close enough I can see the worry in his eyes, but too far to give me the reassuring touches I'm used to. "The heartbeat looks nice and strong." Pointing again, she circles around a dark area on the screen. "This is likely what the problem is." She clicks some measurements with the mouse and slides her chair back to grab a flip chart from the desk behind her, turning pages as she scoots back. "So the chorionic membrane is the outermost part of the amniotic sac. It lines the uterus." Holding up an illustration of a fetus in utero, her finger traces over the parts she labels. She points back to the screen, connecting the illustration to what's going on inside me. "We're not really sure why it happens, but sometimes, blood forms between the chorion and the uterine wall, creating a blood clot. It's called a subchorionic hematoma, and this one is in the midrange of what I've seen. Your doctor would have likely seen it if you'd had a twelve-week scan, but it's just something that can happen during pregnancy." Her eyes shift behind me, and she exchanges a look with her brother. "No one's fault."

"So what do we do?" I jump at Trevor's voice. He's barely said two words since throwing me in the shower, and despite my worry, I can't even begin to imagine how he's handling any of this.

"Well, nothing. The fact that the bleeding has slowed is good. Get in to your OBGYN as soon as you get back for her guidance of care. But generally, we suggest at least a partial bedrest and complete pelvic rest. I'm okay with you flying back home today, but minimize walking. Don't insert anything: pads only. And breathe." She smiles and winks at me. "Breathing is good for the baby."

"Bed rest? I can't go on bed rest. I run a business. I have to be able to work."

"Again, check with your doctor. But I imagine that's what she'll recommend with one this size, at least until the bleeding stops completely."

"And how long could *that* take?" My voice rises as it slips through the tightening of my throat. I've had my independence stripped from me before, and it was hell making my way back from it. *I can't go through that again.*

"Willa…" Trevor says, but I don't look at him. Screw him and his disapproval right now. He's not the one who has to stop working.

"It could be a couple days or a few weeks. Each one I've seen acts differently. I know the thought of bed rest isn't an easy one, but it may be the best thing for you and baby." Maya turns to Trevor. "What time do you leave for your flight?"

He clears his throat. "We need to leave by five."

Maya glances at the clock on the wall. "Six hours. Let's get you two home so you can get a little sleep before then, yeah?" She clicks a few more things into her computer, and the ultrasound machine spits out some black-and-white photos, which she hands to me. "I know you'll have a scan in a few days, but I always loved getting pictures."

I take them, unable to return her smile, and she wipes the gel from my stomach. Trevor offers his hand as I swing my legs off the table. But as soon as my feet hit the floor, he drops it. Sure, he reaches for my coat instead, but the standoffish energy radiating from him puts a cold spin on the gesture.

As we drive back to the ranch, the same playlist I cued up before plays through the speakers. I shift worried glances at Trevor every few minutes as I slide my camera charm back and forth across the chain. His eyes never leave the road. Streaks of light filter in and out of the car from streetlamps, giving just enough visibility for me to see his grip tighten on the steering wheel. The sepia skin on his knuckles is pulled taught, spine ramrod straight. I place a hand on his forearm, and he goes rigid, making all the newfound hopes I let myself imagine hours ago turn to stone and crumble.

CHAPTER THIRTY-FIVE

TREVOR

"Absolutely not," Willa huffs. I'm having a hard time meeting her stare, making it as far as the crossed arms she slams into place. I'm beating myself up enough for putting her through this. If I look in her eyes and see resentment, it will absolutely break me.

I sigh and drag a hand down my face. "Just get in the wheelchair, Willa."

"Maya said minimal walking is fine. I can walk."

Hitching her purple backpack up on my shoulders, I release another sigh. I'm fucking tired as hell, and really don't have the energy to argue this out in the middle of the airport. "Sit down, or I'll carry you through the terminal. Your choice." I look at her then, and the hardness in her eyes turns to surprise before she blinks it away and plops into the wheelchair.

"You're ridiculous, Trevor."

"Back atcha, Willa," I grumble, taking the handles and wheeling her down the corridor. I check my watch as we join the throng of travelers, everyone in a frenzy to reach their destinations before the workweek starts tomorrow. "Are you hungry?"

"No," she snaps.

She's been in the sourest mood since we left the ranch. After all I've put her through, I don't blame her. What could I even say? Everything was perfect before I suggested one last tryst. If I could take back the last twenty-four hours just to avoid hurting her and the baby, I'd do it in a heartbeat. *You fucked everything up.* Blinking against the images in my head, I bite the retort on my tongue, despite knowing it'll only make whatever is happening right now worse.

"What about when I have to pee? You gonna wheel me in the bathroom and post up outside the stall?" Willa's independent streak is back with a vengeance, as if she didn't just see the blood clot threatening our child's life. Everything out of her mouth has been a direct challenge to my trying to help her.

"If I have to." I stop at the small food court and glance ahead to see how far away our gate is. We still have time before boarding, so I'll grab her some food and she can decide whether she wants to eat while we wait.

"I said I'm not hungry..." Willa looks over her shoulder and tracks me as I walk around to face her. She's been trying to bait me into arguments all morning, and when I don't respond, she rolls her eyes and mumbles obscenities under her breath. Arguing with her is the last thing I want. I hate seeing her upset, and fighting with her will give her even more cause to hate me. *You're the reason...*

Leaving her and her attitude at a table, my frustration puffs from my lips as I walk to the register. We haven't eaten since leaving the ranch a few hours ago. Despite her denial, I know she's hungry, and likely even more exhausted than I am. Her body's the one going through all of this. I just want to pull her into a hug, but the hard set to her jaw as I hand her the foil-wrapped breakfast burrito is enough of a spiky warning to remind me this is all my fault. Her glare is as withering as it used to be, as if the past week meant nothing to her. She doesn't want me to touch her. *You never should have happened.* We eat without a word, and even though the terminal is bustling with travelers, her silence echoes through me, amplifying the berating in my head.

Once we get to the seats at our gate, I take a deep breath and blow it out slowly, tipping my head back as if doing so will silence the droning in my mind. *This is your fault, Trevor. You're the reason everything's fucked.*

"Thank you..." Willa's softened voice snaps my head back up. She stares at her lap. "I *was* hungry, and it helped."

"Sure thing."

Adjusting in the chair, she turns toward me. "I really can walk. I'll have to do it when we land in LA, anyway."

"Nope. You won't. I'm coming to LA with you."

"Why?" The edge is back in her voice, like I just told her I'm taking away her driving privileges. "It's Sunday. You go home on Sundays."

"Maya got through to your doctor on the emergency line. Dr. Quentin's meeting us early tomorrow morning for an urgent appointment."

"Us? Don't you work tomorrow?"

"Took an extra personal day."

"You can't keep doing that! I can go to this appointment on my own, Trevor. It's not a big dea—"

"No, Willa. You're not going alone."

"But—"

"Cope!" I stand and walk toward the large wall of windows, growling out my frustration as I go. Her fighting me on this right now rubs me the wrong way. I just need a minute to fucking breathe. *Why can't she get this through her head? After everything we've been through, she still questions my dedication to be there for her?*

Because she doesn't want you, idiot.

I know she blames me for this. How could she not? Hell, I blame myself. Everything was fine until I touched her. It was all perfect until me.

CHAPTER THIRTY-SIX

WILLA

I walk out to the living room to find Trevor, laptop open on his chest, knocked out on my couch. Nausea rises in my throat from the freshly punched feeling in my gut. *He'd rather suffer on the sofa than sleep next to me?* When I went to bed last night, he claimed he had a few more things to finish for work. It's clear now that it was an excuse to create more distance.

Turning on my heel, I stomp back to my room to get ready for my appointment. This bleeding thing is stressful as hell, and he doesn't seem affected by it. He won't even talk about it with me. He'll barely talk to me *at all*, and that confuses me because Trevor never shuts the hell up. I don't have the energy to deal with the emotional whiplash right now. If he's pulling away, so am I. I'm not going back down the gentleman-to-asshole pipeline, no matter if he *is* the father of my child.

By the time I come back out to the kitchen, Trevor has showered, and he's fiddling with the orchid in the kitchen window. *He'd rather fondle a dead plant than touch me? Fucking figures.*

A small plate of eggs and toast is waiting for me on the counter. "You should eat. We need to leave soon." He steps back as I approach, like I'm covered in radioactive waste. It pisses me all the way off. How do you go from begging to be my own personal sex chair to not being able to breathe the same air as me in the span of forty-eight hours? I'm tempted to leave the plate where it is, but now the baby wants eggs and toast. *Traitor.*

As soon as we get in the rental car, the love ballad filtering through the speakers adds to my visceral vexation. The farther we drive, the more the boy bands bother me. Each flowery verse crushes my chest like a passive aggressive reminder of what happened between us in Nebraska. He tossed it all out of the window so quickly, I'm infuriated with myself for letting him get close enough to do so.

After twenty minutes, it's hard to ignore the music. The correct combination of lyrics lands in my heart, cracking open an entryway for sympathy that hits me hard enough to second-guess myself. *He listens to this when he's overwhelmed.* We're dealing with something intense and scary, and instead of clinging to each other, we both scurried to our maladaptive coping caves. He may very well be just as scared as I am. As much as I don't want to be the first one to yield, I might have to be.

"Thanks for breakfast," I say, hoping the small white flag will ease some tension.

"Yep." He doesn't even look at me. Not so much as a twitch in his neck. Trevor's eyes stay fixed on the road, even as he leans forward to turn up the music, and it's like he slammed a door in my face.

Fuck you too, then.

CHAPTER THIRTY-SEVEN

WILLA

Dr. Quentin confirmed everything yesterday. A midrange "SCH" as she called it, with orders to take it easy until my sixteen-week appointment in a couple of days. She'll recheck everything then, hoping it's shrunk.

The percentages for complications are terrifying, no matter how small they are. But after researching for most of the last twenty-four hours, I'm feeling a little more acceptance about my new condition. While I'm still worried, Dr. Q seemed hopeful that it could resolve on its own. By the time I woke up this morning, the bleeding had slowed to spotting, giving me the confidence to get some editing done in the studio. The doctor said to stay off my feet as much as possible, but didn't say anything about not coming to work. I let the technicality propel me right into the studio this morning, staying seated for most of the day.

Trevor left for San Francisco last night, after begrudgingly making me food and tucking me into bed. I couldn't ignore the way he avoided touching me though. How could I? We went from being all over each other on Christmas Day to him barely looking me in the eye. Even as he tucked me into bed, the familiar warmth in his care was gone. He was doing everything the same as he always had, but it didn't feel right. Sweet, generous Trevor turned cold and distant in the blink of an eye. *Just like Carter.*

I try to shake away the thought and focus back on the Jorgensen portraits in front of me, but it slowly creeps back in. As much as I'd like to think it isn't the case, the similarities are messing with my mind. Trevor was well on his way to becoming my person, and as soon as I let him claim me as his, he flipped the script. When a major crisis hit, he closed himself off. How can I rely on someone who does that?

"Okay, Boss Lady...what's going on?" Emily sidles up to my desk. Cara and Monique are out for lunch between appointments.

"What do you mean?" I mumble distractedly.

"I mean, you haven't left that chair all day. You've been scooting it around the room like you're glued to it, and it's starting to freak us all out."

I guess now would be a good time to tell the girls at work about the baby and the complication. They'll need to know what to do in case something happens. I should prepare them for working with a guest photographer when I need to take maternity leave anyway. "I'm—"

"What the hell, Willa!" The boom of Trevor's voice makes me flinch as he storms through the door, indignation burning in his eyes. I've never seen his face turned up in anger like this, and certainly never directed at me.

"What are you doing here? My appointment's not for two days."

"I could ask you the same damn thing." He stands by the door, huffing like a dragon, just glaring at me. "What are you *thinking*?"

"What's going on?" Emily looks between the two of us like a deer caught between rifles.

"The doctor told me to take it easy, and I have been. I've been sitting down all day." My voice falters at the end, and I purse my lips. *I sound fucking ridiculous.*

"She meant *at home*, Willa! Are you shitting me right now? I drove all damn night to take care of you this morning. Imagine my goddamn panic when I walk into your house and you're nowhere to be found."

Our eyes locked in battle, I almost forget Emily's in the room until she asks, "Willa, wha—"

"I'm preg—"

"She's pregnant!"

We both shout at her. If the message alone isn't surprising, the sheer volume may be the reason her eyes are bugging out of her head. I'm so keyed up, noise is the least of my worries.

Trevor takes a deep breath and squeezes his eyes shut like he's trying to force the anger from his body. He's pissed; that's clear as day. But even with the shouting match, I don't feel unsafe. "Get in the truck, Willa."

"My car's outside, so no."

"I'll get your car later, just go get in the truck."

I turn to my computer screen with a roll of my eyes. "No."

A strangled gurgle emanates from his throat, his fists clenching at his sides. "Don't make me carry you..."

"Because *that's* going to help with the bleeding," I chide. "I'm not a fucking hostage, Trevor. Your caveman threats don't scare me."

"You're bleeding?" Emily gasps, her voice barely registering in my ears.

"You can't just threaten to carry me whenever I don't do as you say."

"Try me," he says with a tick in his jaw. "Get in the goddamn truck, Willa."

Lips pursed, I lean back in my chair, arms crossed tightly for effect. A moment of vulnerability flickers in his eyes, so brief that I wonder if I imagined it, before he sets his jaw back into that hard clench. It's just enough to make my tenacity waver. When Trevor takes a determined step toward me, I throw up my hands.

"Fine. Whatever. Give me five minutes to pack up. I'll meet you in the truck."

"Nope. I'll wait by the door."

"You think I'm going to escape out the bathroom window or something?"

"I wouldn't put it past you. Five minutes, and I'm dragging you out of here whether you're ready or not." He shuffles off to the front desk, and my middle finger follows his retreating form, rage burning in my chest.

"Congrats, Boss Lady..." Emily stands next to me, anxiously bouncing on her toes. Her nervous laughter irks my entire being right now.

"Thanks," I murmur, selecting the RAW files to back up to the external hard drive. "Monique and Cara should be back from lunch soon. I'm sure you'll fill them in. I'll call everyone with a game plan when I have one."

"Got it." Emily slips her sleeves over her knuckles, her shoulders scrunched up to her ears. "He's right, you know. You really should be home. My sister had a rough pregnancy too. You don't wanna mess around with bleeding."

"I know." I sigh, glancing at the giant dummy checking his watch by the front door. Trevor thinks he can give me the cold shoulder for two days and storm into *my* studio with demands? I don't care how right he is, I'm the one in control of my time. I take an extra two minutes for petty's sake, grab my things, and walk right out the door.

His silver SUV is parked front and center, and I tap my foot on the blacktop while I wait. He keeps the doors locked until he's next to me, reaching for the handle. Once it's open, he steps back, folding his arms to avoid touching me. The move is like gasoline to the flames. "I can open my own damn door, Trevor," I snap. He sucks his teeth, waiting for me to buckle up, and then closes my door without a word. Everything's the same as it has been, but it all feels wrong.

We don't even make it a block down the street before he starts in on me. "I'm getting real sick of your attitude when all I'm trying to do is help, Willa." I lean forward and turn up the radio to ignore him. Childish? Yes. But he fucking started it. He turns the radio back down, and I'm tempted to reach for the dial again. Tit for tat. "Oh, so now you have nothing to say?" he asks.

I crush my lips between my teeth to keep my rebuttal to myself, turning my body to the window like the view is my favorite movie.

"You heard Dr. Quentin. You're supposed to avoid stress, Willa."

"Okay, well you're the one stressing me out right now, *Trevor.*"

"Me?" He chuckles without an ounce of humor behind it. "How am I stressing you out?"

"You're yelling at me!"

"I'm not yelling at you; I'm yelling at the situation!"

"It's the same damn thing! I get it, okay? You're mad at me. Message received." My voice cracks, and the wall of tension inside breaks, opening up the floodgates. I swipe at my face.

"I'm not—" Trevor sighs and checks over his shoulder before changing lanes. "What are you talking about? Why would I be mad at you?"

"How the hell should I know? You haven't touched me since we left Nebraska, and after all the things you said you wanted, I'm just really fucking confused. And scared. And tired. I had the nightmare last night—*twice*—and couldn't get back to sleep, but I couldn't even talk to you about it because everything's changed." The words fall out of me in a jumbled mess.

"Shit. Willa—"

"And you haven't called me 'Gem,' Trevor. You like dead plants more than me, and you keep calling me *Willa*!" When his eyes meet mine, I wail, burying my face in my hands. It sounds so irrational, but I don't even consider whether all of this nonsense is hormone-induced because it really doesn't matter. Everything I said is true. We need to talk about it, as messy as it gets.

The car slows, and I feel it drift to the side of the road. My embarrassment keeps my head in my hands, and even though the music still plays, I hear the driver's side door open and close. After a few seconds, my door opens too. My seatbelt, the only thing keeping me upright, goes slack, and my slumping body is caught by an orange, clove wall of warmth. Trevor's arms wrap around me, his palms making slow passes over my back.

"I'm not mad at you, Willa. I'm mad at myself."

"For what?" I sniffle. "You didn't do anything."

"I hurt you, Gem. You're fucking bleeding because of me, and I didn't think you wanted me to touch you after that."

Gem. I never thought those three letters meant so much until now, like the sun peeking out from the storm clouds. And then I hear the rest of his sentence and pull back, confused. "You didn't hurt me..."

"You were just fine before we..." He looks down.

"Tre, both Maya and Dr. Q said this complication isn't anyone's fault. It just happens."

"Yeah, I know." He tips his forehead to mine with a sigh, his knuckles gliding over my upper arms. "This is my own shit, and I'm sorry I pulled you into it. I got inside my head... Shut you out, thinking that's what you wanted, when I should have just talked to you." He flicks his worry-filled eyes to mine and back down, and my heart breaks. Whatever it is has been eating him up inside.

"Can you tell me what shit you're talking about?"

He nods. "I will, but we need to get you home first. Please? I'll tell you anything you want to know when we get home."

I expect him to pull away and get behind the wheel, but he doesn't move. His face is pulled in tight, eyes still down as if he's trying to figure out what to say next. He looks so worried, so *tired*, and I want to grab it all from him and throw it out the window. *This isn't him.* Taking his face in my hands, I caress his cheeks with my thumbs until he looks up at me with wet eyes. "I'm sorry for shutting you out, for the yelling. I let you down after I told you I'd always be there for you, and I'll never let it happen again."

"I believe you." When I lay a soft kiss on his lips, he clutches my arms as if he's found a life preserver after days lost at sea. He kisses me back so earnestly; I have full confidence this was a one-time lapse in judgment. Trevor's not this person. I know better than anyone what it's like to get caught up in your own shit. "I'm sorry for going into work. I think I was trying to convince myself I'm still in control of this pregnancy. It was stupid..."

"I'm just glad you're okay," he whispers, finding my lips again. After a slow, repairing kiss, Trevor nuzzles my nose, returning my smile with a small one of his own. God, I've missed those dimples. I never realized how much I love his smile before now. Seeing it for the first time in days sets everything right in the world again. When he gets back behind the wheel, the first thing he reaches for is my hand. We still don't say much, but this feels different. *This feels like it should.*

With the tension between us earlier, I didn't notice the mountain of items smashed into the back of his SUV. "Tre?"

"Yeah, Gem?"

Gem. I melt inside, and it distracts me for a second. When I squeeze his hand, he sends me a smile. "What's all this stuff in the back?"

"Uh, it's my belongings."

"So, you flew home last night, packed up your place, and drove all the way back here?"

"Yep. I need to be here. For you and the baby."

"What about your lease? Your furniture?"

"I've been paying month-to-month for a while now." He shrugs. "It's all just stuff. Not important."

"Did you even sleep?"

He chuckles. "Not really. I tapped into Coast Guard boot-camp sleep deprivation mode."

"Are you safe to be driving right now?" I eye him skeptically, and he wiggles the steering wheel to mess with me.

"I'm good. And before you lecture me about taking a day off, I got approval to work remotely while I wait for the LA transfer to finalize. EdTechU requires a mandatory three days off to transition my workstation to the remote server. I'm all yours until Friday."

"Good. You can entertain me while I'm stuck in bed," I grumble.

He raises our hands to his lips and kisses my thumb. "I'd love to."

CHAPTER THIRTY-EIGHT
TREVOR

"Straight to bed, Gem," I say, nudging her down the hallway to her bedroom.

"Yeah, yeah. I got it."

"Hey." I press a kiss to Willa's nose. She wrinkles it, but my heart skips a beat at the smile she sends me. "Give me a few minutes, and I'll be right there."

"You don't have to..."

"But I want to tell you all my secrets." I flicker my eyebrows suggestively and head back out the door. Unpacking my truck shouldn't take long, but I need to do something more important first. Leaning against the back hatch, I pull out my phone and open up my therapist's scheduling app. The first telehealth appointment available is tomorrow around lunchtime. I should have set this up before we left Nebraska. Hell, I should have set this up before we *went* to Nebraska, but I was so hopeful I wouldn't need a preventive appointment this year. *Better late than never.*

It only takes twenty minutes for me to get my things inside before I'm sliding in next to Willa. I pull her close immediately, hoping to erase the last two days. They happened—and I need to make up for it—but now that I know she wants me to touch her,

I'm not stopping for anything. Forty-eight hours felt like a life-time without her. She snuggles into me, and I light up inside. "How are you feeling?"

"Bored."

I chuckle and nip at her ear. She's going to be insufferable on bedrest. "I meant the bleeding."

"Oh, it's bored too." She jumps when I tickle her side, and says with a sigh, "It's less than it was. Still spotting."

"Any cramping? Nausea?"

"No, Dr. Jones."

"Don't get sassy. I'm just checking." Nibbling my lip while my hand trails up and down her spine, I need to tell her every-thing—*want* to tell her everything. I'm just worried it'll change how she sees me. "So...I made an appointment with my therapist for tomorrow while I was outside." Our eyes meet, and she moves her hand to my chest, right over my pounding heart. "I should have called her days ago when I noticed I was spiraling. And I feel really bad about—"

"Hey." She palms my cheek. "You're already forgiven. Do what you need to do, but I'm ready to move past it."

I nod, settling into her gaze. "Maya's had to fill me in on a lot of this stuff. I was three, so I don't remember much about home life before we went into foster care. But I do remember my bio dad was always yelling and hitting Mom. Whenever he was mad *and* drunk, he'd home in on me, saying, '*This is your fault. Everything was fine until you showed up. You're the reason we're fucked.*'"

"Oh, Tre..." she says with misty eyes.

I glance away to get through the rest. "That's why Maya started putting me in the closet when he got out of control. If I was out of view, I wasn't a problem. The night we went into foster care, he stepped on one of my toys and lost it on me. Threw a table lamp against the wall above my head and a shard caught me here." I tap the scar in my right eyebrow. "When I started drip-ping blood on the carpet, he came after me, yelling about it being my fault he was gonna lose the rental deposit. His eyes were almost black, like the rage blew out his pupils. I remember that part. It sobered Mom up enough that she locked me *and* Maya in the closet."

"What could a literal toddler have done to him, though?"

I take a deep breath and shrug. "Even back then, he and I looked alike, and he hated it. Our parents had Maya in high school. Both of their families kicked them out. They moved to Heritage for the cheap housing. Maya said it was okay for a little while. She remembers fun and laughter until bio mom got pregnant again. I was the surprise neither of them wanted, and I guess me looking like him was a constant reminder of all his mistakes. He started drinking, lost his job, and couldn't hang on to anything for longer than a couple months after that. She started drinking after I was born, mostly to find common ground with him again. The rest is history."

Willa reaches up and swipes her thumb over the scar in my eyebrow with a pained look on her face. "I hate that you had to go through any of that. You were so little."

"I've mostly worked through my trauma from back then, but those key phrases have always stuck around, no matter what I do. With everything that happened after Christmas, I let it get the best of me. But this, *us*, no matter how new it is or how slow we decide to go, it's important to me to get this right with you. I never want you to feel like you're anything less than perfect, exactly as you are. I don't want to be like him."

"You're not." She smiles softly.

"But I *was*. I have the potential to be..."

"No. You had to face a traumatic moment and shut down. We both did... But you—the man that you are—Tre, you're nothing like him." Sliding her fingers around the back of my neck, she pulls me toward her. Her kiss is soft and sure, and the one I return embodies every apology that's been in my mind since that night. She smiles against my lips. "I mean, you put up with me, for fuck's sake. That has to count for something."

"Willa," I whisper, shaking my head. These self-deprecating

comments she makes about herself being too much kill me. She bites her lip and looks down, but I need her to truly hear me when I say this. Tilting her chin up, I dust another kiss on her lips. "How anyone could ever want to change a thing about you is beyond me. You're the prototype—they broke the mold with you. You're timeless, a masterpiece, and I'm in awe of everything you are." Her eyes glisten behind fluttering lashes, but the growing smile on her face is all the reassurance I need. "I promise you, no more yelling and no more shutting you out."

Willa shakes her head. "No more shutting *each other* out. Communication always. We talk about it, even when we're scared shitless."

"Even then." I smile and nuzzle her nose. "Especially then."

"Then I should tell you something." Willa's eyes widen, and I swear her heart beats straight through all the layers of clothes between us so I feel it against my skin. "I'm scared of what you mean to me, Tre."

The pounding in my chest matches hers. Our entire journey has been a whirlwind thus far, but we're about to go the deepest we've ever gone with each other. "And what do I mean to you, Gem?"

"...Everything," she whispers. Her eyes stay fixed on mine as she shows me the full range of her fear. It's raw and breathtaking, seeping into my chest. A privilege I swear to never take for granted.

"You mean everything to me too, Willa. Everything."

With slow kisses, she brands me as if she's my first and my last. Everyone before her is irrelevant. She's the only one who matters. I urge the message forward, my heart to hers, and her kiss answers the quiet call, laying claim on the secluded places inside my heart.

CHAPTER THIRTY-NINE

WILLA

It took all of my composure to keep from erupting into tears right there in Dr. Quentin's office. Three to four weeks of bedrest to see if the spotting will stop. I have a business to run, and an intern to teach. A fucking New Year's Eve party to suffer through tomorrow. I can't do any of that from my bed.

"Gem?" Trevor asks, face pinched into a frown.

"I'm fine." My fingers are gripped so tightly in my lap, I'm not sure how he wiggles his in between them, but as soon as he intrudes and brings my hand to his lips, a wave of calm washes over me.

"Nah. We're not doing that anymore, remember? Talk to me."

"I'm just pissed that I'll be stuck in bed for a month. And I have to come up with an emergency plan for the studio now." I reach my other hand up to slide my camera charm against the chain, the new habit quickly occupying my fingers. It's more than aggravation. Ever since I found out I was pregnant, a small part of me has held on to the hope that I could somehow make Europe happen. Despite the extreme costs a new baby brings, there's been a small glimmer that I could make it work—even if it's a year from now. But every complication I've had threatens to snuff out that hope, and now that I won't be working for a month, I can barely see the flicker. I underestimated just how taxing all of this would be. Juggling a business, a baby, and a once-in-a-lifetime trip to Europe feels daunting now.

Trevor nods and kisses the back of my hand again, knowing I don't need a solution from him. I'll figure it out; I always do. Him sitting with me while I process this means more than any problem-solving could.

He pulls his SUV up to the cluster mailbox, then sets the pile of mail in my lap as he finds a place to park. Flipping through the junk ads and bank statements gives me a short reprieve from my brooding until my fingers still on the large white envelope at the bottom. I read *U. S. Department of* before the final words are obscured by a stream of blurriness. The car jolts when Trevor parks, and his arms are around me as soon as his seatbelt hits against the window.

There's no hope of stopping this right now. Holding my passport in my hands is the final whisper in the wind to snuff out the one thing I've dreamed about for years. This envelope represents something that remains just out of reach—just out of my ability —as my responsibilities drag me back down to earth. I'm about to be a mom. Babies are little for a while, and as much as I've tried to hold on, there will be no Europe anytime soon. To give the nurturing I never got, I need to shift my priorities. My shoulders tremble while I come to conclusions I've pushed away for weeks.

"Let's get you settled inside, sweetheart." Trevor presses a kiss to my forehead as he grabs the stack of mail, the simple act sending a fresh torrent through me. Even without understanding all this nonsense, his support is a constant. He's the calm in the storm, the beacon of light, and as he leads me into the house, he's every last bit of comfort I need.

Trevor drops the mail on the counter and leads me back to the bedroom. I'm still a bumbling mess when he sets me on the edge of the bed, and even more of a disaster as I watch him pull my favorite pajamas from my dresser. He takes them into my bathroom, and as soon as I hear the shower turn on, I wail. Going from stifling despair at losing my dream to utter admiration as I watch Trevor ignore everything else just to care for me shatters my last remaining walls. I adore this man.

He guides me to the bathroom, wipes my tears with his thumbs, and presses a kiss to my lips. "You relax in the shower. I'll meet you in the room with a snack when you're done." The door closes behind him, and I have no hesitation to do what he says. The way my heart is lit up like a Christmas tree, he could ask me to Hula Hoop, and I'd do it.

After showering, I snuggle under the covers and reach for my computer. No sooner than I have it open, Trevor sets a snack tray down on the nightstand and kicks off his jeans with a smile. "What are you doing?" I ask.

"We're on bedrest, remember?"

I shake my head. "No, *I'm* on bedrest. You have things to do..."

"Don't know what you're talking about..." He slides his oatmeal quarter zip sweater over his head, leaving him in a white undershirt, and steps toward the bed.

"Tre—"

"The only thing I have to do right now is hold my girl until she doesn't feel like the world is ending."

The tips of my ears burn, and I melt down to my toes. "Your girl? Is this middle school?"

"Yep. We go together. Now move over and let me snuggle you."

I set my computer aside, and as soon as he's in the bed, he pulls me to his chest. "You got a passport?" he asks.

"I'm pretty sure mail theft is a federal offense."

He laughs. "I didn't open it. It was right on top. I'd recognize that envelope anywhere." I look up at him with raised brows, and he explains, "I like to travel. Passport paperwork is hard to hide."

"Yeah, well, it can stay right in that envelope for all I care. I can't use it anytime soon."

"Where were you going?"

My shoulder raises with my deep sigh. "I was saving for a trip to Europe before all of this happened."

"Europe's pretty nice."

"You've been?"

"Yeah, all over. My family took a trip to Italy when I graduated high school. I went to Oktoberfest with some Coast Guard buddies when we had port calls in the Netherlands. Then France a few years ago, but I didn't explore much there." He clears his throat. "Where in Europe were you planning on going?"

"All over. I've always had this dream of taking a few months and photographing everything I could—architecture, landscape, the rich art history, food—all of it. I wanted to hit every country I could and just get lost. I was so close too." My eyes burn, and I close them to stave off another downpour.

"Why are you talking in past tense, Gem?"

"Because I can't juggle snapping my way through Europe while holding a newborn on my boob."

"The baby won't be a newborn forever, and you wouldn't have to juggle anything." He kisses the tip of my nose. "I'll be behind you, holding the baby while you take all the pictures you want."

I scoff, but the intensity in his eyes holds me captive.

"Sweetheart, you're not giving up your dream just because we'll have a kid."

"Yeah, that's nice to think about. But babies change things."

His head shakes. "Not this. You deserve to follow your dreams. Your happiness is important to me. I'm not letting you give this up." He strokes my cheek, eyes boring into mine like he's engraving his promise into stone. "This is just the beginning, Willa. The best is yet to come." His lips grace mine, his kiss unlocking every secret combination to my heart, mind, and soul. He pours into me the hope I'm failing to keep a hold of, and I clutch to him for more.

CHAPTER FORTY

TREVOR

"Trevor Jones, you said?" The brunette receptionist at the front desk clacks away on her keyboard, flashing a pleasant smile. EdTechU's main office is all windows, the foyer open and airy with the sun shining through. Glass elevators flank each side of the building, leading up to several different floors. A large navy and yellow logo glows on the wall behind the desk.

"Yes. I'm transferring from San Francisco."

She bobs her head. "Just waiting for my screen to load... Can you believe it's already January?"

Flashing a polite smile, I glance at her name badge. "Time's flying by, Sheila." I got the call last night that I've officially been transferred to the EdTechU LA office, ending my remote work status. I can still work from home here and there, but they want me in the office most days of the week, starting today. Leaving Willa this morning was probably tougher on me than her. It's been a full week of spending almost every waking moment together, learning more about each other, watching all of Willa's favorite movies, and cuddling the nights away. We've created a cozy little nest in her bedroom that I'm already aching to get back to.

"There we go. I have a note here for you to head straight to

HR. Here's a temp pass, and I need you to look at the green dot for your permanent ID photo."

I've barely settled into an easy smile when a flash blinds me. "Thanks, Sheila," I say, sliding the pass off the desk. "Could you remind me where HR is?"

"Top floor. They're the only ones up there. Have a fantastic first day!"

When the elevator settles on the fifth floor, I'm greeted by another receptionist and invited to grab a coffee while I wait. I take a seat on the stiff, cognac colored sofa and drum my fingers on my knees, wondering why I'm even up here. When I got the call last night, everything sounded like a done deal. I'm anxious to get started with my new team.

"Trevor?" A short Latina in a blue EdTechU polo identical to mine stands in the doorway behind the reception desk, hugging a tablet. A friendly smile stretches across her face. I maneuver my way to her, and she sticks out a hand. "I'm Gabriela Sanchez. Come on in."

"Nice to meet you, Gabriela," I say, her long black ponytail swaying as I follow behind her.

"Well, Trevor..." She sets the tablet on her steel executive desk and flips through documents in a folder. The floor-to-ceiling windows behind her overlook a large courtyard, surrounded by three other buildings on the EdTechU campus. "It seems you're a hot commodity around here."

"Pardon?"

"We have two departments fighting over you."

Confusion pinches my face. "I requested a lateral transfer to Malcolm's team..."

"You did. And when I called yesterday, that was my understanding too. But apparently, there's another department who requested you months ago, before you ever sent your transfer. You were auto-filled into the open flex trainer position this morning, and the spot on Malcolm's team was filled by another internal transfer. Nothing's set in stone, of course, but this promotion is yours if you accept it."

"Uh..." No one would have needed to sell me on this a few months ago. It would have been my dream being on the road most days of the week. But now, with so many unknowns surrounding the baby? It couldn't be a worse time.

Gabriela's eyes dart behind me as someone knocks on the open door. "Marla! Maybe you can help us sort all of this out."

I had no idea it was possible for blood to boil and freeze simultaneously, but here I am. Marla-fucking-Rhodes holds my job in her hands, and I have no choice but to face her. I clench my jaw as I turn, hoping my teeth meld together so I don't get an HR violation from losing it on her. When our eyes meet and she steps forward, it takes every muscle in my body to lift my hand and shake hers. My skin crawls. I slide my hand into my pocket immediately, turning back to Gabriela. "So, what's the solution here?" I ask.

Marla clears her throat and cuts in. "The flex team would love to have you, Trevor. After we reviewed your file, it's clear you've essentially been doing the job already. Everyone agreed you'd be a perfect addition."

"With your education and experience in sales, you're in a bit of a niche skill-wise. So this would be a dual role with the official title of *corporate and sales training specialist*. That would, of course, be reflected in a nice salary bump for you too, if that helps your decision," Gabriela adds, sliding a paper from the file folder toward me.

Goddamn. A salary increase of 30 percent would put me into six figures. That alone is enticing as hell. And a dual role would hit a lot of my goals, professionally. But being away most of the week goes against the support I've promised to Willa. And working with the headache beside me every day? I don't know... Never in a million years did I think I'd ever contemplate turning down my dream job. *What if it's my only chance?* "Can I get more details about the onboarding process?" I ask Gabriela.

"Of course you can," Marla cuts in again with a smile. *Why the hell does she keep talking?* I jut my tongue into my lower lip to quell the rage. She tucks a clump of curls behind her ear nervously, then straightens her white blouse. "Um, today would serve as a working interview—just a formality, really. You'd go through a provisional training for the next several weeks, similar to the on-site supervision you were doing in San Francisco. Then you'd ease into short overnight trips while you get your bearings. After that, your flex assignment would be traveling Sunday to Thursday, with actual on-site days being Monday to Wednesday. Since it's a dual role, your assignments would be split between the niches as company needs dictate—but never double duty. And Fridays are in-office days for everyone on the team, so you'll be home for the weekends."

"And my supervisor would be...?"

Gabriela clears her throat. "Your direct supervisor would be the training director, Miles Montego. Marla is over all of the flex trainers, but seeing as you two have a documented relationship history, any decisions concerning you will need to be run through Marla's superior—Miles—and HR."

"Miles got called into an emergency meeting this morning, or else he'd be here instead of me," Marla rambles nervously.

At least there's that. It doesn't stop my seething, but she won't be able to make any rash decisions about my career without getting permission first. That's a good thing. "I'm not in the best position in my life to take on a traveling schedule. Circumstances require me to stick close to LA for now."

Marla's curiosity is written all over her face, but I don't want to give her this glimpse into my personal life. It's none of her damn business. "Well..."she says. "Between training and your provisional period, you'd be close to LA for the next several months anyway. Is that enough time?"

From the way she steps back, steam must shoot from my flared nostrils when I fix my eyes on her. "I'm afraid not."

"Is everything okay?" Her voice is soft, nudging a trip wire containing too many memories. "We can accommodate your schedule for illness or—"

"I have a baby due in June, and my…" I choke on the word *girlfriend*. Willa and I haven't talked about what we are, but she's so much more than that to me. "There's been a complication, and I need to be close."

Marla's face falls. She tugs at her sleeves and mashes her lips together, trying to hide the surprise on her face, and I hate that I know this about her. It gives me a little satisfaction though. *Not so fun to be on the receiving end of surprising news, is it, Marla?*

Gabriela steps from around her desk, no doubt sensing the tension in the air. "Well, congratulations on the baby! How wonderful! I hope the complication is under control."

"Thank you. It's being managed for now, but I need to stay close. And I need to discuss it with—"

"We can keep you close." Marla's voice is rushed, the way it used to be when she would try and sway my decisions when we were together. I hate how I know that too. "What about this? You start with my team today, see how you like it, and take the rest of the week to talk it over at home? We'll see if we can come to an agreement on Friday."

Dipping my chin, I rock back on my heels. If they're willing to work with me, this really sounds like the best of both worlds. "I'll likely have some stipulations to negotiate—paternity leave and staying in-office close to the due date."

"As long as they're not too unreasonable, I'm sure we can work something out. I'll have my assistant set up a provisional contract signing for Friday morning. If all goes well, we'll sign a permanent one in February." Gabriela swipes a few more times on the tablet, then tucks it under her arm.

"Great!" Marla's grin fades when I don't return it, and she fluffs her hair, rubbing her lips together. "Come. I'll introduce you to the team." I follow her out of Gabriela's office. We haven't even reached the elevator before she's babbling about how excited everyone is to be working with me, and all I can think about is getting away from her. "You're going to fit right in—"

"I got it, Marla. What I don't understand is why I was blindsided about the flex decision on my first day in the office." The bite in my voice is undeniable. Based on her tiny hop backward when I push for the door to close, she got the message loud and clear. I want no confusion here. We're nothing more than two employees who happen to know a hell of a lot about each other.

"I-I know it was your dream position years ago. When your name floated across the transfer candidate pool, I thought it was because of our conversation at that training a few months ago, so I sent it to Miles. You're more than qualified for this position, Trevor. I just thought, maybe if I could do this for you—"

"What? That'd I'd be so grateful it would make up for betraying me in the worst way? Come on, Marla. You're smarter than that."

"If I had known—"

"*Stop*." The doors open on the third floor. "It's done now. Just take me to my office, and do me a favor?" I step out and turn to face her.

"W-what?" Her voice catches despite the squaring of her shoulders.

"Stop acting like you know anything about my life now. You don't."

WALKING INTO WILLA'S HOUSE AFTER THE SHIT SHOW at work feels like crawling back to base camp after trying to climb Mount Everest. Because of the mixup between departments, all of my access to the workspace portal was frozen. I couldn't do anything but shadow my teammates while they tried to walk me through the protocols for the department. There are five flex employees, making me the sixth, and I've collaborated with trainers in the LA office for so long I already know everyone on the team. That's probably the only thing I have going for myself at this point. A shitty day mixed with great company. Mostly. Marla's a lot more involved than I would like, but she kept a wide berth after our conversation in the elevator.

The house is quiet when I hang my computer bag by the door and slip off my shoes. I have a brief moment of panic, reminded of the last time I came home and Willa was nowhere to be found. Walking slowly to her bedroom, I find my first reason to smile all day sleeping on my pillow. I drop to my knees and place a hand on her belly, then wake her with a kiss on the forehead and my thumb to her cheek.

Willa stretches her neck as she peeks an eye open. "You're home?" she asks through a yawn. "What time is it?"

"Uh." I check my watch. "Five-thirty. You can go back to sleep. I just wanted to let you know I'm home."

"No, it's okay. I didn't mean to fall asleep." She eases up to sit against the headboard. "How was work?"

"Welp, I got a promotion...maybe."

Willa cocks her head, and I don't miss the twitch in her eyes as they narrow.

"You remember that ex who cheated on me? Well, we work in the same department now, and I hate it." I puff out my cheeks, releasing my breath slowly, trying not to shift my eyes from her intense stare.

"Is this something I should be worried about?" she asks, grabbing her fingers.

I slip my hand over hers and squeeze. "Not a chance in hell."

"Then I'm not worried." She reaches around my neck and pulls me into a kiss that takes all the tension in my body and tosses it out of the room. The slow dart of her tongue between my lips makes everything else disappear, and the gentle give and take whispered between our embrace flips the day on its head. Work is work, but *this* is everything. She pulls away, and I chase her for one more, not ready to crash back down to reality. Smiling, she whispers, "You look stressed out. Go shower. Tell me about the rest after."

I *am* stressed. As much as I don't want to spend another second away from her today, the heat from the shower is exactly what my tense muscles need right now. I make it a quick one and head back to the room. The last of my bad mood melts away when I climb into bed, and she tucks herself into my arms. "How was your day, Gem?"

"You'll be happy to know I stayed in bed except for bathroom breaks and getting food, just like you asked me to."

"*Finally*, she listens..." I tease, leaning my head against the headboard with a smile.

She pokes me in the chest. "You're not getting off that easy. Tell me about your day."

I heave a long sigh and give her the play-by-play. The more I tell her, the more confused she looks.

"You're acting like they made you kick puppies all day. Apart from having to deal with your ex, what's the problem?"

"The problem is, I walked into HR this morning with one job and came out with a tentative promotion."

"A promotion torturing puppies?"

"One that will have me traveling all over the country right around the time the baby's due."

"Okay, but don't you like traveling?" She gives a knowing look as she taps her hand on my chest.

"Yeah, I love it. I've wanted this promotion for years, but not right now. You need me now."

"Sweetheart, take me and the baby out of it."

Did she just call me sweetheart?

My heart's pitter-pattering like my crush just said I was cute. I clear my throat, shaking my head. "I don't want to do that."

"Just humor me. If we weren't a factor, would this promotion still be tentative?"

Sighing, I run a hand over my head. I see what she's doing

here, trying to spin this the exact way I spun Europe for her. Even with Marla's intrusion, I'd have jumped at the chance for this a few months ago.

"If I'm not allowed to give up Europe, you're not allowed to give this up either."

"But—"

"Nope. Take it."

"I'm gonna have them write in some stipulations about distance and—"

"Tell them whatever conditions you need to make you feel comfortable taking the job. We'll adjust and figure it out." She shifts to her knees and holds my face, making me melt into the soft touch of her fingers on my cheeks. "You've worked hard for this. Don't let anyone take it away from you. Not me, not the baby. Especially cheating-ass Marla. You hear me, Trevor Jones? I want your happiness too. Take the promotion." She presses her lips to mine as if she's trying to sign the contract for me through the sheer force of her kiss.

"You called me *sweetheart*." I grin, still giddy inside. "Am I your sweetheart?"

"Between the two of us, your heart is definitely the sweeter one..." She looks up at me through her lashes, wrinkling her nose. "I *guess* since we go together now, I should make this extra corny and tell you I'm sweet on you."

"You gonna wear my letterman jacket and let everyone know we're going steady?" I tease.

Willa's laugh shoots straight into my chest. "Do you have one?"

"Somewhere back home."

"Your Mom loves me. She'd gladly dig it out for your girlfriend."

"You're so much more than that, though."

"So I'm...?"

"Gems in the ocean," I say. Her eyebrows dip, and I chuckle. "After the wedding a couple of years ago, the way you talked about the ocean molding something as simple as glass into precious gems was poetic. I've only ever seen you as something to be admired. Treasured. You're more than a friend, more than a girlfriend. You're my gem, Willa. Just mine."

Her eyes glisten, her lashes fluttering with emotion. "Yours," she whispers, swiping silken fingertips down my jaw. She kisses me again, and if I thought I was branded before, this is transcendental. I'm floating somewhere between reality and euphoria, and her touch sends me straight to the peak of happiness. I'm so gone for her; it wouldn't be possible to find a way back even if I wanted to.

CHAPTER FORTY-ONE

WILLA

I survived. Three weeks stuck in bed was absolute torture, but I defeated bedrest and got the all-clear from Dr. Quentin yesterday. The baby is healthy, the bleeding stopped, and the SCH is gone. When she told me I was cleared to go back to work, I almost did cartwheels around the exam room. No dick for another month though. A small price to pay for getting back into the studio.

My phone rings right as I step out of Framed Orchid for lunch, my heart pounding just seeing Dr. Q's office number on my phone so soon. Right after my twenty-week appointment yesterday, she sent us to the hospital for my scheduled anatomy scan. Trevor and I saw our little nugget wiggling around while they took measurements, but hospital protocol requires a review from my doctor before the gender results are released. They said it would take three to five business days, and they'd call if there were any concerns. I answer with my pulse beating in my ears. *What if something's wrong?* "Hello?"

"Hi, Ms. Willis? This is Nurse Amy from Dr. Quentin's office, calling with your gender results."

"Yes. Hi."

"She didn't want you to have to wait over the weekend. Do

you want us to slip it in an envelope for you to pick up, or would you like to know over the phone?"

"Over the phone is good." I say breathlessly.

"Okay. I'll count to three. One. Two. Three—"

The nurse's words wash over me as she reads the results, and my body seems to float with all the possibilities this little life inside of me could become. I start my car and whip out of the parking lot, abandoning all thoughts of lunch. Before I realize where I'm headed, I'm already halfway to the EdTechU offices. As soon as the phone line went dead, my first instinct was to share the happy news with Trevor—in person. When I pull into the multi-building campus, a niggle of doubt pesters me. I have a habit of showing up at his workplace with life-changing news, and he's still in his provisional period. *Maybe I should wait until he gets home...* My phone buzzes in the cupholder.

> **TREVOR**
>
> Hey, Gem. About to head into a meeting. How's your first day back?

> **ME**
>
> Good. I'm actually outside right now. Can I come up?

> **TREVOR**
>
> Yep 😵 I'm just suffering through a conference call. Stop by the front desk for a guest pass. I'm on the third floor. Directly to your right when you leave the elevator.

With a hand on my belly, I sway my hips while I wait for the receptionist, hoping it will ease the dull ache in my groin from walking across the parking lot. My nerves are buzzing as I secure my guest pass sticker to my shirt in the elevator. *Will Trevor be as excited about this as I am? Should I have waited?* The doors slide open, and my steps propel me forward before my mind is made up. Ready or not, he needs to know.

A dozen offices surrounded by glass walls are the first thing I see when the elevator opens. I turn down a long corridor as instructed, and I'm about to slide my phone from my crossbody purse when Trevor slips out of the double wooden doors in front of me. He smiles like he didn't just see me at home a few hours ago, and I feel silly for second-guessing this decision. Of course he wants to know about this. He's been all in since the beginning.

He pulls me into a hug when he reaches me. "This is a nice surprise. What's up?"

I look at him for a beat, taking in the dimples in his cheeks and the lovable look in his eyes while his smile threatens to burn me up. "The doctor's office called."

His face falls. "Is everything okay?"

"Yeah. I'm fine."

"...And the baby?"

"She's good too."

He blinks at me, exactly three times. "*She*? It's a—we're having a girl?" The question barely makes it out of his mouth before he's twirling me around. *How did I get this lucky*? Having this man as the father of my daughter is the best mistake I've ever made. The excitement radiating from him is palpable. When he sets me down and kisses me, I thank all the stars in the universe for conspiring against me to bring us together. "I'm so fucking happy, Gem."

"Me too." He wipes the tears sliding down my face and gives me another quick kiss.

"Hey..." We turn, and a tall, curvy woman flips her curly hair behind her shoulder as she steps around the door. Her eyes sweep over our emotional embrace, and she squares her shoulders. "Trevy, you're up."

Trevy? I stifle a laugh.

Trevor nods and tucks me under his arm. "This is Marla," he says to me. "Marla, this is Willa."

Marla gives me a professional smile. "It's nice to meet you." She looks back to Trevor. "You ready?"

Trevor turns back to me and nuzzles my nose. "I have to go,

but I'll see you when you get home from the studio tonight." He gives me another peck, squeezes my hand, and follows Marla back into the conference room.

I UNDERESTIMATED MY ABILITY TO LAST THROUGH A full day at work. The guest photographer I hired while on bed rest did an amazing job and was very thorough, but I still have so much administrative paperwork to sort through. Three weeks away from my business left me with a stack of bills and a reorganized studio.

"You look exhausted, Boss Lady." Emily settles into her favorite spot by my desk, tugging at her sleeves.

"Yeah." I yawn. "I think I'm going to call it a night."

Nodding, she turns back toward her desk.

"Hey, Emily?"

"What do you need? Food? A footrest? I can get any—"

"Whoa. Chill. I'm fine," I say with a laugh. "I just wanted to thank you for taking care of everything while I've been out. I couldn't have done it without you."

She blushes and shrugs, using both hands to tuck her short black hair behind her ears. "Just doing my job, Boss Lady. Let's lock up so you can get your baby girl home."

I spilled the beans to everyone in the studio once I got back from lunch. My high from finding out is just now fading. I'm going to be a mom to a baby girl, and I can't wait to meet her.

When I pull up to my house, my feet are killing me. The doctor warned me about swelling, and it's like her word of caution wrote a prescription for my body to retain water. My belly isn't huge yet, but I'm already seeing cankles forming. Add in the round ligament pain, and I'm a hobbling mess. The walk to my door takes almost all the energy I have left.

Delectable scents waft through the air, dancing right to my nose with the beat of the soft R&B music playing from the kitchen speaker. Trevor's back is to me, and he's whistling along to the song while he finishes up the dishes. With the tea towel casually draped over his shoulder, his movements are relaxed and familiar, as if he's at home in my kitchen. It's my future cemented into canon. I can see us doing this every single day, and the thought both thrills me and sets me on edge. *What if he changes his mind? What if, after all is said and done, the baby's born, and he's no longer excited about all of this? What if I don't measure up to his expectations? What if—*

"Gem? You okay?" Trevor's worried tone snaps me back to my entryway.

I hang my purse on the hook by the door and slip out of my shoes. When I shuffle into the kitchen, a pink It's a Girl! Mylar balloon wrapped around a vase of pink tulips greets me on the countertop. A small pink teddy bear lounges against the side of it, holding an envelope. I glance with guilt at the struggling orchid just beyond the display. *When was the last time I watered that thing?* "Yeah, just tired." I sigh. "What's all this? And how did you know tulips are my favorite flower?"

"Ashlie is a wealth of knowledge." He dries his hands with the towel and tosses it on the counter behind him. "I thought we should celebrate this milestone after how stressful the last few weeks have been." My fears from moments ago are nudged away as he closes the distance between us. Smiling, he sweeps the twists off my shoulder. *What was I even worried about?* After seeing how he completely spoiled his nieces at Christmas, how could I ever question his excitement for his own baby girl? Trevor will be the most attentive father, and I have a sneaking suspicion that the pink teddy bear is just the beginning.

"Celebrate how?"

"With all your favorite things: dinner, a foot rub, *Deserted Desire...*" He smooths his palms over my shoulders with a smirk. "And me."

I snort, settling against his chest. "Oh, okay, *Trevy*. I see you."

His grimace makes me giggle. "I can't believe she fucking called me that. I set her straight after the meeting."

"You want me to start calling you that too, my big Italian fountain of a man?"

"Hell, no," he murmurs, dusting my lips with a kiss. It's soft and sweet, despite the passionate hold his hand presses on my lower back. When he pulls away, his eyes sweep over my face slowly. "You're so goddamn beautiful, sweetheart; I can't stand it sometimes." Heat surges everywhere in my body. My ears burn, my cheeks flush, and if I thought I could do it without being obvious, I'd cross my legs to relieve the pulsing between my thighs. He's doing a damn good job of changing my mind about those pet names. *Maybe I spoke too soon about the "no dick" thing.* "Go put your feet up. I'll bring everything over." He kisses me again, spins me around, and nudges me toward the couch.

After dinner, we're two episodes into a *Deserted Desire* marathon when my mind wanders to my baby girl. *Our* baby girl. I pause the TV.

"Hey!" He turns incredulous eyes on me with a laugh. "Dalton and Kimberly were just about to make an alliance..."

"What do you think she'll be like?"

"Kimberly's going to be a complete menace." He answers so quickly, I don't realize he's messing with me until he winks.

"You like this show more than I do at this point."

He pinches his fingers together. "Maybe a little." Then he reaches over and puts a hand on my foot. "I think she'll be smart like you."

"We're both smart, Tre."

"Yeah, but I hope she has your mind. Your passion. I hope she notices all the small things and finds inspiration in the mundane."

Is that really how he sees me? What he's describing feels too elegant to be used for me. "Thank you," I whisper, grabbing my camera charm.

"It's all true. I've never met anyone like you, Gem, and I

doubt I ever will." He squeezes my foot, then extends my leg so it rests in his lap. "Except for our daughter."

"I hope she's kind like you. And happy."

"She will be." His thumbs knead my sole. "She'll have us to make sure of it."

Shit. This foot rub might be better than the glazed pork chops he just fed me, which is saying a lot. I'm steadily sinking into the cushion with each delectable circle, so relaxed I'm barely able to keep track of the couples on *Deserted Desire*. A moan slips out of my mouth as I drop my head to the arm of the couch. Another firm swipe has me falling into a state of ecstasy. I'm halfway gone when his fingers still. I pop my head up, shooting him a glare. "*Nooo*, why'd you stop?"

"Come here." His husky baritone matches the lust in his eyes, dousing my annoyance. I don't even hesitate, scrambling across the couch. My usual instinct to challenge him is swallowed up by my body's reaction to his deepened rasp. Before I can straddle him, he spins me around and pulls me onto his lap, gripping my hips as he grinds into me. I moan again, pressing my back against his chest. It's been so long since I've felt him like this. I'm about to throw the medical advice out the window. *No dick, my ass.*

"Feel that?" he asks. His fingers ghost over my nipple, and I whimper, arching my back to search for more. "Your moans are making me squirm, sweetheart, and I can't do anything about it..." He drops a kiss on my neck. I slide a hand to his head, keeping him there. His tongue soothes after each nibble, sucking lightly until my hips roll in time with his. *I need to touch him.*

"I can help you do something about it, Tre," I pant, sliding my hands down his thighs. If this man only knew what he was doing to me right now, how fast I'm ready to drop to my knees and gobble him up, he wouldn't be playing with fire.

"You're aching for me too, aren't you?" He teases my other nipple with a pinch, his devilish snicker rumbling when I groan his name. His hands slide to my thighs, cracking them open so quickly I gasp in surprise. "Tell me." He knows *exactly* what he's doing to me. I'd have something to say about the teasing if it didn't feel so damn good. Biting my lip, I nod against his chest instead. "I need your words, Willa…"

"You're driving me fucking crazy," I whine.

"Fuck, I miss these." His hands caress my inner thighs, then slowly brush against the wetness seeping into my leggings. "This." Softly, they slide over my belly until his thumbs brush my nipples. "Definitely these."

I'm squirming all over him, trying to get something, *anything*, to give me relief. Gripping my hips, he angles just a fraction so I can really *feel* him, and a string of indulgent obscenities falls from my lips. "*Please.*"

"We *can't*," he whispers, nipping my ear. "Not yet. I just wanted to remind you what you do to me." He chuckles when I struggle against his hold on my waist. "Now we can suffer together."

CHAPTER FORTY-TWO

TREVOR

Tossing another pink giraffe in the cart, I smile at the eye roll Willa sends my way.

"Yeah, because five isn't an excessive number of pink giraffes for a newborn to have…" Her sarcasm is clear, but the fake scowl gives way to a cute little smirk.

"You're right. Let's balance it out with some pink elephants." I wink, and she pushes the cart past me.

Last night, I suggested we spend our Saturday morning looking at baby clothes and nursery items now that we know we're having a girl. Willa's transitioning her home studio to make room for the baby, and we've cleared enough space to decorate. After being stuck in the house for the last few weeks, she eagerly jumped at the opportunity to run errands. I haven't seen her wince at the steadily growing crowd once. Reaching for the shelf, I snag an elephant.

"Tre, you're going to spoil her."

"Good. Then she'll grow up knowing she deserves to be spoiled." I dodge another eye roll by dropping a kiss on her forehead. "A lesson her mama still needs to learn."

"Oh, and you think you're the one who's going to teach me?"

"All part of my master plan." I cover Willa's hand on the shopping cart, and she spreads her fingers, letting mine fill the space in between. We round the corner and face a wall full of diapers. "Do you think it's too early to start stocking up?"

A puff of air wheezes past her lips as she settles into a pout. "I don't even know. I've read every single baby book in the house and still have no idea what I'm doing."

"I mean, you're not supposed to know everything, Gem," I tease.

"Sounds fake." She laughs, but the smile falls from her face. "I don't know the first thing about babies. Hell, I don't even know how to be a good mom."

"Whoa. Hey. Nope." I angle the cart to the side and turn her to face me. "We're not doing that."

"It's true! You've seen what I grew up with. What if I'm just like her?"

"You won't be."

"I might..."

I tug her toward me. "You won't, and the fact that you're worried about it now shows you won't. You know what it was like to grow up in that environment. You overcame it. I have no doubts you'll do everything in your power to give our daughter all the love and support in the world."

"I don't even know how to change a diaper, Tre." Tears well in Willa's eyes, and I wrap my arms around her shoulders, pressing a kiss to the top of her head.

"Good thing they have classes for that. We can sign up for one when we get home."

"I should probably call my therapist..."

"That's a good idea." I nod. She looks up at me and sniffles, smiling a little when I wipe the wetness from her cheeks. "Just to help you feel a little more confident in yourself. You've got this, sweetheart. *We've* got this, and you don't have to figure everything out on your own anymore."

Willa snuggles into me and sighs. "It still feels like I do."

"Well, you don't." I stroke her back, hoping to ease her mind.

"You have me now. And Ash and Hunter, and your therapist. Sam. Even the girls at the studio have your back. We're all here for you, and we're all cheering you on."

She props her chin on my chest to look up at me, and despite the red-rimmed eyes, she smiles. "I have you."

Wholly. Entirely. If only you knew. "You have me." I smile back and nod.

She tips on her toes and graces me with a peck on the lips, then turns back to the cart. "Let's go. I'm starving."

HAND IN HAND, WE STROLL ACROSS THE PARKING LOT toward the red-brick Lunch-a-Bunch building. I pull Willa in close to steal a kiss before we reach the door.

"What was that for?"

Shrugging, I smile at the flushing on her neck. "Just wanted to."

Her reaction to me when I surprise her with the most basic acts of affection is extremely adorable. I know she's not used to being treated well in relationships, but that I'm the one who gets to show her how it feels to be cherished—the fact that she *lets* me —means the world.

"*There they are*," Hunter calls across the parking lot. "My two favorite people."

Willa pulls away like she just got caught with her hand in the cookie jar, but I hold her at the waist to keep her close. I know her past makes her hesitant with me in public, but she won't get used to the idea of us together unless she moves past the discomfort. She sends me a small grin, as if apologizing for the impulse to hide, and I pull her closer.

"Favorite?" she asks Hunter.

"Yeah. You two are looking at the newest LA Frost season

ticket holder."

"Nice," I say, raising a fist to his. "Let me in on one of those games."

"I haven't purchased them *yet*..." Ashlie rolls her eyes and hip checks Hunter.

"But you will. You're just mad you have to sit through every hockey game with me, and I have *them* to thank." He turns to us with a smart-ass smirk on his face. "Thanks for boning before New Year's. I owe you one."

"*Ugh*! You're so annoying." Ashlie pushes his shoulder and takes a step toward us, yelping when she's pulled back by Hunter's hand around her waist.

"That's not what you were saying this morning..." Hunter wraps his arms around her from behind and snuggles into her neck, inducing a round of giggles from the both of them.

"Ew. I didn't need that visual." Willa grimaces.

Ashlie throws a glare at her sister. "*Okay*, little Ms. Oops, I'm Pregnant. You two owe me a pair of shoes for not being able to keep it in your pants."

Hunter laughs and leads the way to the door. It's only a few minutes before we're seated at a booth against the large picture window. The powder blue and sage green walls are lined with plants and macramé tapestries. Willa snuggles into my side while she looks over the menu. The smirk that settles across my face while I watch her feels like a reflex at this point. Whenever I see her, even if it's only the milliseconds between blinking, I grin. I can't help it. She's chiseled out a spot in the middle of my heart, and I'm so in love with her I can't do anything but smile about it.

Ashlie clears her throat, and Hunter snickers, snapping me out of my daze. They laugh like they heard every single one of my thoughts. My cheeks flush. I don't care about them knowing. I'd shout this from the rooftops if it felt like the right time. But Willa's a delicate diamond, strategically placed on a pressure-sensitive platform. If I don't carefully swap the gem with those three little words at the same exact time, it'll all be gone in a puff of smoke, with lasers and alarms blaring.

"So, the baby's good?" Hunter asks, his eyebrows dipping.

"Yep," I say. "Everything looked good at the appointment a couple days ago. That's actually why we invited you two to lunch..."

Willa's eyes meet mine, and we share a smile. Without breaking eye contact with me, she says, "We're having a girl."

"Woo!" Ashlie shimmies in her seat with a victory dance, holding her upturned palm in Hunter's face. "Pay up, Hunt."

Hunter sighs as he leans to the side for his wallet. "Man, I really thought it was a boy."

"You two had a bet on my kid?" I chuckle, shaking my head at the money exchange happening in front of me. Hunter slaps a twenty-dollar bill in Ashlie's hand. My eyes grow wide when he slides another twenty across the table to Willa. "*You* had a bet going on our kid? When was this?"

Willa shrugs and pockets the money with a smirk. "Mama was bored on bed rest."

"Good luck, bruh. Willa and Willa Jr. are gonna give you a run for your money."

"Oh, I know." I wink at my love, eliciting a playful side-eye from her. "I'm looking forward to it."

CHAPTER FORTY-THREE

TREVOR

"For the third time, we'll be fine."

"But I won't be back until *February*!" I whine, playfully using a technicality to garner her sympathy. Today's the last day of January; I'll be back tomorrow, but still.

"You should win an Oscar..." Willa walks to her front door with a hand on her belly, extending her other arm with my computer bag dangling. Her head falls to the side, resisting the eye roll I know she wants to give. "It's less than twenty-four hours."

I just got in from work and had enough time to hop in the shower and throw a bag together. One of my flex teammates broke her foot, and my team needs me to step in earlier than planned and take over her session in San Diego. Saying I'm stressed is an understatement. Not about the training aspect—that'll be a breeze—but leaving my girls. In the two weeks since we found out we're having a girl, my protective instincts have skyrocketed. My sole focus has been staying three steps ahead to anticipate Willa's needs. That's kind of hard to do when I'm a few hours away. Not to mention, it'll be the first time in a month I won't have her next to me in bed. Grimacing, I rub the back of my head.

Willa's eyes soften as she watches me. "Tre, we'll be okay."

"Yeah, but what about me?" I joke despite the dread rifling through me. Shuffling over to her, I reach out to caress her face. "I'm gonna miss you, Gem."

She leans into my hand. "I'll miss you too, sweetheart."

My heart shoots to the moon. *Sweetheart.* It's not a new thing, but ever since she's started using it, I get butterflies like I'm back in middle school. I take my bag from her and slide it over my shoulder.

"If it makes you feel better, you can video call me to say good-night. Might even get a little show, if you're lucky."

"Don't threaten me with a good time," I murmur, pulling her to me for a long, slow kiss. Willa's still on pelvic rest, and it's getting harder each day to keep our hands off each other. There's two weeks until her next check-up. If she isn't cleared by then, I might need to sleep out on the couch just to put myself on ice. Even kissing her like this has me squirming to adjust my jeans.

Willa pulls back and places a palm on my chest. "Sweetheart, you need to get on the road." *Sweetheart.* I can't take it and dip down for another kiss. She puts on a brave face, but the fistfuls of my shirt in her grasp tell me she's as nervous about tonight as I am. Once I finally let her go, she takes a step back and eases out a whistle of air.

"You call me if you have the nightmare. I'll answer on the first ring."

"Go..." She turns me at the shoulders and nudges me toward the door. "I'll be fine, and you'll be back tomorrow. Good luck on your first day on the road."

When I open the door, she grabs my ass, giggling when I jump in the air. "Hey!"

"For luck." She shrugs, smirking playfully.

Laughing, I step out onto the porch. "Luck, my ass."

"You're right. Your ass *is* pretty lucky." She gives me one more kiss and eases the door closed. My dramatic trudge to the truck takes double the time it should.

The drive to San Diego wasn't terrible. I got caught in the tail end of rush hour traffic, which added almost an hour to my arrival time. But now I'm checked into my hotel and ready to review the employees' files in the design department I'll be training tomorrow. I let Willa know I made it with a quick text and pull up the email from my supervisor, Miles, with tomorrow's bullet points. It's all generalized professional development, seeing as the design team in the San Diego office had a major overhaul in quarter three. They're dealing with a bunch of freshly graduated designers who need some corporate structure. I skim to the end of the email and Marla's name jumps out at me. *What the hell*? The best part about this trip is being away from her at the office. Scrolling back up, I actually read Miles's message in its entirety.

The dark cloud that settles over me is menacing as I read. He's sending Marla down to be on hand for this training. I understand his reasoning—it's my first session in the field—but the storm threatens to downpour with every new word I read. Knowing Marla, she probably suggested this impromptu trip under the guise of "guidance for the new trainer." I want to throw my laptop at the wall and say every curse word slamming into my brain right now. I want to block out every Marla-filled memory flooding over me.

I want Willa.

Even just hearing her voice would work to calm me down right now. The urge to disclose to her that I'll be forced to spend the day with my ex is immense. I don't want her to ever think I'm keeping secrets from her. Reaching for my phone seems like the best course of action right now.

"Hey, sweetheart," Willa says, stifling a yawn. My anger cools just from that. "Hang on." I hear shuffling in the background before the call switches to video. Her twists are tied back by her scarf, and she's wearing one of my old Coast Guard T-shirts. She yawns again. "I wasn't sure I'd make it."

"Yeah, sorry. Had to review some things Miles sent over. Uh, so…" *We talk about things, even scared shitless.* "I have some news." Willa tilts her head, waiting for me to continue. I focus on my thumbnail under the screen as the grip on my phone increases. "Apparently, Miles is sending Marla down for the training tomorrow. I just found out, and I—"

"Tre?"

"Yep."

"Take a breath."

I do, exhaling a frustrated groan. "If I would have known, I'd have told you earlier."

"You've already said there's nothing to worry about. Has that changed?"

"No. Never. I just don't want you to think I'm keeping things from you."

"I know the kind of man you are, Trevor. You're more bothered by this than I am."

"Understatement of the year. She's doing this on purpose."

"Doing what?

"Messing everything up!"

Willa laughs, "Like what? Besides your attitude."

"I don't know."

"Tell me what happened with her, Tre. Why do you hate her so much?"

"I flew halfway around the world to propose to her and found her in bed with her boss."

"That'll do it."

Shaking my head, I sigh at the memory. "We'd been together for two years. Had been talking about marriage for months. When she got a temporary job transfer to France, she called me every day, crying about how much she missed me. I felt bad for taking so long to propose, and she was so sad every time we talked that I took a few weeks off work and flew out to seal the deal. She was busy sealing deals of her own."

"That's why you went to France?"

"Yep. Spent the rest of my time there drinking in my room. Not my finest hour."

"Tre, that's horrible..."

"Yeah, that's why I don't drink much anymore."

Willa shakes her head. "No, I mean Marla. Did she say anything when she got caught?"

"Oh, just the standard. 'It happened one time. It was a mistake. He means nothing.'"

"I get it. You were busy planning on forever while she was in the process of blowing up your life."

"Seems to be a running theme with her. She's still actively trying to ruin my life."

"I didn't realize you were so dramatic," she teases, giggling. "Don't let her ruin this for you, Tre." Yawning, she plumps up the pillow under her head. "She took something away from you back then, but she doesn't have the ability to do that now. You've worked too hard to let her get in the way of something you've wanted for years. Don't give her that power." Yawning again, her eyes rest as slits while she fights to keep them open.

"Go to sleep, Gem."

"No." She shakes her head. "I want to keep hearing your voice."

"Okay, how about this? Prop up your phone on the nightstand. I'll stay connected until you fall asleep. Yeah?"

She nods and sets up her phone before collapsing back onto the bed.

"Hey, that's my pillow!" I tease.

"*Duh*. It smells like you, and I miss you," she mumbles while snuggling into it, eyes fully closed now.

"I miss you too," I say, even though my head and heart are screaming *I love you...*

CHAPTER FORTY-FOUR
WILLA

Oh, I'm definitely staying up. I slept horribly last night. All I wanted was Trevor's arms around me. He's my comfort, my safety, and my reassuring furnace when I wake up in the middle of the night shivering. Slowly, he's becoming everything I associate with home. Even though I act unflappable, I'm a mess inside. *God, these fucking hormones.*

I know I could get ready for bed and wait for him in there, but he's been on the road now for four hours. I want him to come home to a freshly cooked meal. This domestic side is new to me. One I've never felt safe to explore in the past, but Trevor's fostered it. He handles me gently, whether I'm emotional and fragile or bullheaded and fierce. I didn't realize that was a need for me—

tenderness. I'm getting so fucking sappy, but embracing my soft side with him feels really damn good.

So I pull out the ingredients for his favorite meal and set a pot of water on the stove to boil next to a warming skillet. While chopping the veggies, I think about his dimples that interrupt the skin on his rugged face when he smiles at me. I mince the garlic and onions and slide them into the pan while imagining his arms wrapping me in a blanket of security. As I reach for the bag of pasta, silly little butterflies waltz in my belly at the thought of him kissing my shoulder like he does when he thinks I've fallen asleep in bed.

No, not butterflies.

It's more like tiny bubbles bursting. I drop the pasta in the pot and stare down at my bump. *That's my baby girl...* I giggle, putting a hand on my belly. *This is so bizarre.* Feeling her move for the first time—it's amazing. It's been twenty-two long weeks, but somehow, everything up till now is nothing compared to how monumental this is. A tear slips down my cheek, and I don't even hurry to wipe it away. Those tiny bubbles just solidified the new title that's steadily being woven into my heart. I laugh again as I remember my worry a few weeks ago about being able to do this. Between Trevor's reassurance and a couple of appointments with my therapist, I feel more capable. Right now, I have no doubts as determination sparks inside me. I'll be the best damn mama to this little girl, if it's the only thing I accomplish for the rest of my life.

Stirring the boiling pasta, my mind drifts to the centering rumble of Trevor's voice. The sensation in my belly starts again, as if she senses my excitement at seeing her dad. I press a hand against my stomach, rubbing back and forth slowly to soothe her. "Daddy will be home soon," I say quietly, carrying the boiling pot to the sink. I've barely plated the food when the lock turns on the front door.

Trevor's eyebrows dip as his gaze sweeps the room. "What are you still doing up? It's almost ten o'clock."

I shrug, my heart suddenly pounding like I haven't been sharing a space with this man for months. "I just thought you might be hungry since you've been stuck on the road after a full day of work..."

He slowly drops his bags on the floor next to the couch and walks toward me with a smile. "It smells good. What did you make?"

"Pasta primavera."

Something flickers in his eyes that makes those butterflies join the popping bubbles in my belly. "My favorite," he says, reaching up and taking my face in both of his hands. I'm only slightly sure he's talking about the food. He holds me there, staring straight into my soul like he's scouring over the *Book of Secrets*, trying to memorize everything inside. Staring back is my only choice. *Could I love him?*

I've never been in love. Not really. I've had the cheapened pseudo-love I thought I deserved, but never anything like this. Never something so pure and all-consuming. Never something that has me eager to give parts of myself no one's ever seen. Trevor keeps his eyes on me as his forehead rests against mine. "I love you, Willa."

Everything around me stills except for the pounding in my chest. Even though I just had the fleeting thought, I don't trust myself with it. *How can it be this easy? What if it all changes after the baby?* I hardly feel like myself most days as it is. When everything settles and hormones aren't making me soft anymore—when I'm back to my old self—will he really put up with me? *Will I let him? I don't know.* Breathless, I drop my head, and just as fast, he lifts my chin.

"Just...breathe." He grins at my sharp inhale, then chuckles when shallow breaths take over. "There we go... Sit with it. *Feel* it." His gaze holds mine until my breathing slows, a soft smile gracing his lips once he senses my calm. He leans in and kisses me like I'm a long-lost memento he's found after too many years. It kneads into my psyche, clings to my bones, and vibrates through my chest, amplifying all of my apprehension. Those who've claimed to love me in the past have only ever weaponized it. Why would this be any different?

He strokes my cheek, and must see the anxiety in my eyes. "It's okay," he whispers. "You don't need to say it back, don't need to earn it, or even reciprocate. Just...hear me when I say I love every single part of who you are. Each eye roll and sarcastic comment. All the teasing at my expense. Your philosophical rambles. That thing you do with your hands when you're nervous. The quiet ways you show affection. I love all of you." He presses a soft kiss to my lips. "You'll say it whenever it feels right to you, and that's okay."

What if I can't ever say it back? My gaze falls. His confidence in me is astounding, considering I have none in myself right now. Turning to the stove, I hand him a plate, then step away for a fork. "We should eat before it gets cold."

"...Willa..."

I brace my hands against the counter, dropping my head with a sigh. "I know. I'm sorry."

"You don't need to apologize." His arms wrap around me from behind. "Just talk to me. Please?"

Even when we're scared shitless...

Turning in his arms, I fix my eyes on his. Despite the intensity, I don't look away this time. "No one says those words without some expectation to hear them back. I don't know when I'll be able to do that...*if* I'll be able to, considering my track record."

"Okay." He shrugs, and I scowl at his nonchalance. "I'm not saying *I love you* just to hear it back. I'm telling you because it's true. I'm not going anywhere, and I'm *not* changing my mind. If it takes an eternity and a day for you to feel it, I'll still be here waiting for that day after forever *because* I love you." He kisses me again, slowly this time, as if he's pouring a wax seal over my heart for safekeeping. "I don't want to disturb your peace, Gem," he whispers. "I want to be a part of it."

You already are. The realization hits so suddenly, I can't deny the truth in it. Despite all the chaos, he's only added to the peace I've so carefully crafted in my life. There's no separating him from my newfound harmony. So even though I can't find the courage to say those three little words yet, in this moment, I feel them.

CHAPTER FORTY-FIVE

WILLA

"And there's been no bleeding or cramping?" Dr. Quentin asks, her red sequined heart headband glinting in the fluorescents as she drops the sheet from my pelvic exam over my legs. She spins in her stool and fiddles with the ultrasound machine. My eyes sweep the heart filled exam room, perfectly decorated for the day of love. It's Valentine's Day, and her office goes all out, complete with everyone wearing red and pink scrubs.

"Nope. Nothing."

"You're over the halfway mark. Are you feeling the baby move?"

"More and more every day. It's such a relief."

"It definitely can be after months of stress." She smiles and squirts the gel on my belly. "Tell me how much of a relief it is when it keeps you up at night."

The bubbles in my belly have steadily grown into jabs these last few weeks. It's amazing and only a little jarring when I'm about to snap a photo in the studio and get surprised by a kick. My hand steadily stays on my not-so-easy-to-hide bump now. It's safe to say the cat is officially out of the bag.

When we hear the heartbeat, Trevor slides a hand over my shoulder. I nuzzle my cheek against it without any thought. It's been two weeks since he told me he loves me. Two weeks of him showing me what that means—which isn't any different from how he's always been. I think he's loved me for much longer than I've realized. I'm accepting how easy it is with him. How right it all feels.

"Well, everything looks good to me." Dr. Quentin points at the screen. "Your SCH was here, and it's gone now. And since you haven't had any bleeding, you're officially free from restrictions. Just in time for Valentine's Day." She balances a knowing smile between Trevor and me like she knows we've been struggling to keep things above the belt. "Any fun plans?"

"My sister's hosting a party tonight that we'll probably check out," I say.

"Ooh. Just stay away from any meat on those sharkoochie boards."

Trevor laughs and slaps a hand over his mouth.

"Charcuterie, Doc," I say, trying to keep from giggling.

"Listen..." She laughs along with Trevor, wiping the gel off my stomach. "It made sense to me. I'll see you in four weeks. You two stay out of trouble."

After checking out at the front desk, Trevor walks me to my purple crossover. He opens my door but pulls me to him before I can climb in. "Are you sure about that party tonight?"

"I think Ash will crash out if we don't show up, since we missed the New Year's Eve party."

"Let her. Say the word, and we'll stay home. We can start that new *Dater or Hater* show."

My heart flutters at the out he's trying to give me. He's really spent the time to learn all the little details about me, and I love him for it.

Oh.

Maybe it really *is* supposed to be this easy.

I love him.

As I bite my lip at the realization, Trevor takes it as hesitation about the party.

"I'm serious, Gem. We can skip it."

"I think we should go. I'm kind of excited to get out of the house."

His eyes dance around my face skeptically. "Okay then... I'll see you after work." He pins me in place with a kiss, hesitating to let me go when he pulls away. "I love you," he whispers, our foreheads pressed together.

I love you too.

I keep my confession under lock and key, as if letting it fly will send me spiraling across the parking garage. I've barely come around to hearing myself say it in my head. Who knows what saying the words out loud will do?

Trevor helps me into the car, giving me another peck after I've buckled up. When he strolls to his truck, I marvel at the love of my life going on about his day while I panic over something I know I need to get used to. I'm in love with Trevor Jones. *I just need to find the guts to tell him.*

ASHLIE PROMISED TO HAVE TAQUITOS WAITING FOR ME at the party, and as we pull into their neighborhood, my mouth waters at the thought. I got home from the studio late, with just enough time to change into something that fit the requested dress code—red, pink, and fancy. My blush velvet dress is stretchy enough to be comfortable and matches the tie Trevor coordinated with my outfit. I reach for the door handle as soon as we pull up to Ashlie and Hunter's house, but Trevor puts a hand on my arm to stop me.

"Wait a minute." Leaning across me, he reaches for the glove box, and I guard my belly with my hands as the compartment door pops open. He grabs a wrapped package small enough to fit in my palm, sticks it in my lap, and smiles at the surprise on my face. I'm even more confused when I open the box to find two sleek, noise-canceling earbuds attached to the end of gold earrings. Looking at him, I tilt my head, waiting for his explanation. "I know how much the noise gets to you at these parties. I saw these online a few weeks ago and thought they might help. And we can leave whenever you want. Just say the word and we—"

"Iloveyou." The declaration flies out of my mouth, and I suck in a hiss of air in its wake. I stare at him with wide eyes, not sure what happens next. The smile hasn't left his face while he watches me accept the full weight of what I just said to him. "I...love you, Tre."

"I know you do." He brushes a knuckle over my cheek. "I feel it whenever you look at me." Leaning across the center console, he cradles my face in his palm. "But God, hearing you say it is better than anything I could have imagined, Gem. I love you too." Our lips meet in a searing kiss as we twist against the car seats, accommodating for my growing belly while trying to get as close as we can. Every swipe of a tongue is met with wrestling lips, and when I suck his lower lip in between mine, I'm met with a moan filled with weeks' worth of desire. We've done all of this in the messiest way possible—a one-night stand, a baby, family conflict, and trauma—but as inconvenient as it is to be making out in the front of his SUV right now, it feels like the most fitting way for us to admit our love. A surprise declaration and a meeting of hearts while nostalgia plays on the radio in the background.

After fixing our clothes and digging under the passenger seat for the earbuds that fell while we took our fill of each other, we walk to the front door. Trevor pauses before going in, checking to make sure the earbuds are tight in my ears. He kisses my forehead, and we walk into the party with timid smiles and entwined fingers.

"Took you long enough." Hunter snorts from the door. "Thought you were trying to make another one out there."

"We can leave," I say, cocking my head to the side.

"Don't you *dare*, Wills." Ashlie peeks her head around the

corner. "Hunter's just mad because I told him I want to wait another year before we try for a baby."

"Damn, Ash. Let's just tell everyone our business, huh?"

"Oh, whatever. They're family." Ashlie grabs my arm and pulls me away from the door. "Now, if you'll excuse us, we need to have a sister chat."

Confusion pulls into the guys' faces simultaneously as they look at me, and I respond with a shrug. I have no idea what a "sister chat" entails. Ashlie and I don't have those regularly. She marches me through the handful of couples in the living room, under the pink streamers hanging from the ceiling, and straight back to the kitchen, guiding me onto a stool at the counter. "*Sooo…*"

"Look, can I get some food first? I'm starv—"

"Yeah, yeah, here." She grabs a heart-shaped paper plate and reaches into one of the slow cookers lined up on the counter. When she presents me with the steaming taquitos, I chew them with an open mouth, trying to cool them down while I scarf. "So, are you cleared? Did you have a quickie before you came over?" She gasps, wide-eyed, whispering, "Were you doing the nasty in his truck just now?"

I finish the food in my mouth, hoping a pause will calm the madness. "No, Ash. Not everyone's comfortable with getting it on in public like you and Hunter."

"Hey, don't knock it 'til you try it, sis."

"Well, I'm not trying it, so…"

"Whatever. Are you cleared at least?"

I take another bite. "Yep, this morning."

"And you haven't jumped his bones yet?"

"What are all these euphemisms you keep coming up with? No, I haven't *jumped his bones*. Some of us have businesses to run."

"Then what were those bedroom eyes you two walked in with?"

My ears burn, and I wave a hand in the air as a distraction. "I don't know what you're talking about."

"I do. Either you're freshly fucked or you..." She peers at me, then gasps again. *Dramatic ass.* "You love him!" she squeals.

"So what? I'm having his baby. It was bound to happen."

"Have you told him yet?"

"Of course I have. And before you ask, he said it first."

She shakes my arm, making the food roll around on the plate in my hand. "Girl! If you don't get your ass home and go service your man..."

"What?" I scoff. "You're ridiculous."

"Wills, he's been in love with you for months, and crazy about you before that. You've just been clueless. You're going to tell me after eight weeks, you're not busting?"

She has a point there. Apart from the steamy dry humping lap ride I took on him weeks ago, we've kept it pretty tame. I'd be lying if I said I hadn't thought about throwing caution to the wind and crawling on top of him in the middle of the night. "Okay, maybe I am, but we can stay for the party."

"Ten bucks says you leave early."

"Twenty bucks says you're annoying."

Trevor walks into the kitchen then, and Ashlie and I freeze like we just got caught with state secrets. He gives us that same confused look from before. "Just came to check on you. Everything okay?"

"Yep!" Ashlie turns on her heel and flits across the kitchen. "I was just leaving."

I roll my eyes at her exit and smile back at the dimples grinning down at me. "How are the earbuds?"

"They're fantastic. I could barely hear Ashlie's nonsense," I joke, biting my lip and dropping my eyes at the intensity in his stare. "What?" I ask nervously.

Trevor steps forward until his thighs hit my knees. He leans in and plucks an earbud out of my ear. "I just can't wait to get you home so I can do all the things I was imagining doing to you in the truck."

My cheeks burn, and he straightens with a snicker, knowing full well he's responsible for me squirming on this stool. The tip of his tongue peeks out at the corner of his mouth, his head shaking while his eyes rake over me slowly.

For once, I think my sister might be right. "We, um...we made an appearance," I trill. "It's probably safe to head out. If you want to."

He smirks, his gaze flaming with an all-consuming hunger that prompts me to stand before I can second-guess myself. Maybe it was the "sister chat" or the steam in the truck, but my singular focus right now is getting Trevor home. He's on my heels as soon as I slip past him, weaving through the living room. I don't even bother finding Ashlie. I'll text her later.

"What got you so eager to leave?" Trevor teases as he ushers me to the passenger side, loosening his tie.

"*Me*? You were the one whispering sexy sweet nothings in my ear."

"I'll take the credit for..." He pauses, eyes dipping amusedly and back up. My breath catches when he leans in, guiding me against the door with a grip on my waist. "I was gonna say *for making your panties wet*, but you're not wearing any, are you?" Biting my smile, I shake my head, unable to tear my eyes away from the lips I want all over me. The tutting click of his tongue while his thumb caresses my hip sends a shudder through me. I'm already dripping, and he kisses me like he knows it, plunging his tongue past mine with the type of lust that feels obscene out in the open. "You're playing with fire tonight," he rasps. "Wait till I get you home."

TREVOR

Willa's fingers caress the back of my neck the entire drive home. Each scrape of her nails on the base of my scalp zings straight through me. I'm a live wire once we make it to the front door. We're on each other as soon as we step inside, our thighs wedged together while we stumble through the darkness. Our shoes land somewhere near the couch in our clumsy dance. We don't even make it past the kitchen, using the indigo sky glowing through the window as our guide. She untucks my shirt while I palm her ass, lifting her onto the countertop. Her fingers fumble on my button-up as our tongues fight for dominance, and I'm two seconds away from popping all the buttons myself just to feel her hands on my chest. "Why the hell did you wear this?" She huffs through the struggle.

I take over, deftly working my shirt open while she grabs my belt buckle and pulls me closer. "Didn't think you'd be ripping it off—mmm, *fuck*." I don't know how she got my zipper down so fast, but her fingers are wrapped around my dick before I have time to drop my boxers. *I need to be inside her.* Her dress falls to her waist when she cinches her legs around me and brings me to her soaking slit.

"The bedroo—*shit*." I gasp when her heels drive my hips

forward, fully filling her drenched pussy with my hardened length. Our moans meet in harmony as I drop my head to hers. I'm dazed and highly turned on by this possessive hold she has me in. She's finally got some control over her body again. If stuffing herself full of my dick is what she wants, I'll gladly hand it over. Who am I to take it away from her? She rocks me into her again, and my lips find her neck. "Fuck, Gem...I don't want to hurt you."

"You won't," she sighs, tipping her head back to give me better access. I leave sloppy kisses along her collarbone, my mind melting as I give up control. She hungrily takes all of me, and it's the best fucking feeling.

"I never want to hurt you," I murmur, sucking on her skin. "I wanted to make tonight special..." My thumb swirls over her nipple until the stiffened peak pokes through her dress. She arches into my touch, whining at my teasing tug before I drop my hand. This need to feel her everywhere, all at once, is all-consuming. She rolls her hips, fucking growling as if her pussy demands revenge for my absence, and I'm like putty in her hands. I'll be her goddamn prey all night if she wants me to. "*Shit...*" I pant, "You keep having your way with me like this, and I'm not gonna last longer than a few minutes."

Her legs propel me forward, and she fists my shirt, grinding her slick clit against my skin. My head falls back with a groan as she lets me retreat slightly. "Mmm, Tre," she whimpers. Sliding fingers around the back of my head, she directs my gaze to where I'm still half-buried inside her. "Look what you're letting me do to you."

Holy shit. This better not be a fucking dream. Slowly, she eases me in, then out, and in again. I'm dead. That's the only explanation for this ecstasy. Gone to glory from dirty words and Willa's pussy.

I'm so stuck in the haze, all I can do is stare, slack-jawed, following the movement in the dusky glow streaming through the window. My breath stutters when she slips a hand to her clit, stroking herself confidently. It's so damn hot watching this woman get herself off with my dick, I can't move. Can't think. Soon, she's a panting mess right along with me. Her walls flutter around my length, and I grip the back of her neck, a string of labored *fuck-shit-goddamnits* falling from my lips.

"I don't want you to last," she croons in my ear, her fingers still strumming furiously. "I want you to fuck me." A tremor travels through my body as goosebumps scatter down my neck. *Need her. Right now.* Slowly, I cant my hips, unconvinced I won't completely lose myself to her. "Good-*fucking*-boy." Her triumphant smile as that praise leaves her lips sends me spiraling. Clutching her hips, I thrust into her so quickly; she barely has time to grip the edge of the counter with her free hand. My desperate rhythm is accented by grunts each time I drive into her. "*Yes*, Tre!" she whines, her hand jerking over her slickened bud like it's the last thing she'll ever do. "You feel so fuck—*GAH*."

The orgasm racks her body, her voice trilling wildly as each wave crashes into the next. I feel every single one of them as she quakes around my dick, stunning me into stillness while I watch her fall apart...watch her *let go*. She's clearly holding nothing back right now, finally giving me all of her, and warmth floods my chest. The relief easing into her face, her sated whimpers, my name falling from her lips—I'll remember everything about this moment for the rest of my life. The moment when I finally believe she's mine. Her body goes slack, and I hurry to catch her, holding her against my chest as I slip out of her. The baby bump knocks into me, so I adjust my hips backward, tucking myself back into my boxers.

Chest heaving, head burrowed against me timidly, her body trembles. "You're shaking, sweetheart," I whisper, as my fingers caress her shoulders. "Did I hurt you?"

"N-no... I think I'm... C-can you just..." Her breath comes out in spurts, and her head shakes against my chest. "Hold me, please?" she whispers.

Smiling, I encase her in my arms tightly and press a kiss to her forehead. "For as long as you want me to. What else can I do?"

She takes a beat and wraps her arms around me, tilting her head back to look into my eyes. The demure flutter of her lashes in the pale moonlight sets my heart pounding. I'm so in love with this woman; I'll do anything she asks. "Show me how to make love to you, Tre."

Especially that.

CHAPTER FORTY-SEVEN

WILLA

Trevor sets me in the bedroom and flips on the lamp. I reach behind me to take off my dress, but he stills my hand. "Don't you dare touch that zipper, Gem. I've been dying to unwrap you all night."

Anticipation rushes through me. *It's never been like this with anyone else.* Words alone have never made me crave someone's touch, but his hands on my body are all I can think about. A whimper slips from my lips when I turn around to find him stripping for me. My eyes course down his thick biceps and rigid sepia abs, taking in the first man to ever hold my heart. Running a palm down his chest, I stifle my smile at the irrational urge to follow it with my tongue. "What?" His voice has dropped an octave, taking my coyness with it.

"I want to lick you," I say, shaking my head. "Kiss you. Taste you."

"Me first." Spinning me away from him, he kisses my neck as he unzips my dress, sending it falling to the floor. I slump against him as pleasure zings through my body. His lips move to my shoulder while he fiddles with my bra, fingers trailing to each breast once I spill free. Trevor's arms circle my bump as he walks me to the bed, peppering my neck with kisses the entire way. "Sit.

I need a taste of that pussy. It's all I can think about." His voice is a whisper, but it reverberates through my crumbling resolve.

I sink to the bed, eyes fixed on him as he slowly kneels before me. A hunger blazes in his stare, as if I'm his last request before demise. He lifts my leg, lavishing it with soft kisses up to my thigh. The drag of his stubble leaves a trail of yearning in its wake as he hooks my knee over his shoulder, repeating with the other side. He grips my thighs, and with one voracious tug, he's on me, tongue spearing my pussy like they're having a debate over who's more needy. "*Fucking* hell," I whine, dropping my head to the bed. The way he's sucking on my clit twists my insides as if I didn't just come apart in his arms. "I've missed your mouth," I say on a breath. "Missed you." Reaching for his head, I anchor him firmly against me. I take and he gives—pulsing, sucking, nibbling—until I'm screaming his name through the erratic waves ravaging me. "*Please*, Tre, don't stop." The firm pressure of his tongue as he keeps his pace sends me spiraling through an ocean of searing magma, drowning me until I'm a floppy, satisfied mess. One look at him, face glistening from feasting on my pussy, and I need him inside me again. I drop my legs from his shoulders and pull him into a kiss so deep, we're wandering aimlessly in a passionate void, our beating hearts the only sound.

"I'm not done showing you," he whispers, sweeping his knuckles across my cheek before climbing on the bed next to me. Leaning against the headboard, he pulls me onto his lap, facing him. "I want full access to this," he says with a rakish bite to his lip, thumb rubbing my nipple. His head dips to suck it into his mouth, and my moan echoes across the room. "And this." He blesses the other, sending a new pool of heat between my thighs. I'm so turned on by his dick twitching between us, I don't notice he's watching me. "Touch me, sweetheart. All you want." *Yes sir.* I wrap my fingers around his shaft, teasing him with a slow glide until the muttered words *fuck* and *God* slip from his lips. He's melting in my hands like it's the first time we've ever been together, his hips swaying in time with my touch. I'm aching to watch him fall apart, but not like this.

Gripping his shoulders, I adjust to give him entrance. Our eyes lock as he slides into me, an intimacy I didn't know I craved until now, when blinking feels too long of a separation. My head falls back when our hips fully seat, my desperate whimpers surging with the rocking of his hips.

"Look at me, beautiful." The rumble from his chest makes me comply with his gentle demand, pinned in place by the devotion in his stare. It feels curated, just for me. He rocks at a glacial pace, the unhurried friction winding me so tight, my hips sway with his to relish the sensation. And it hits me that I have no desire to control what's happening right now. *I'm okay with letting go.* With a strong hand on my back, he presses me toward him and gives me a slow, sweeping kiss. "You're mine, Willa," he whispers.

I nod, sinking my teeth into my bottom lip.

"Say it."

The sensual way we're keeping time, this intimate dance between us, it's like seeing a world of color after a lifetime in the darkness. "I'm yours."

"And I protect what's mine." He pulls another moan from me when he takes my nipple between his teeth. "Unravel with me, Gem." He pinches my other nipple, and I cry out, digging my fingers into his shoulders, ready to do anything he says. The tension twists in my core, and he slips a hand between us, circling my clit with his thumb. "Let yourself fall apart."

I ease out a breathless moan, giving in to his words. "I love you."

"Always will." His lips crush mine, and he grips my ass, bucking into me. I'm plummeting, toppling over the edge while my climax rifles through my entire body. He holds me close, whispering my name as he tumbles after me. Synchronized hearts beat while we drift back to reality together.

The energy shift in our lovemaking was absolutely earth shattering, and every word he said remains imprinted on my heart. "That was..." My chest heaves as I try to catch my breath.

"Soul melding," he whispers, caressing the back of my arm. "Are you okay?"

Nodding, I steal a kiss. It seems like such a silly thing for him to ask after experiencing the divine together. How we just shared the deepest parts of ourselves and he believes I didn't love every single second is unfathomable. *I'm his.*

CHAPTER FORTY-EIGHT

WILLA

"Guess what, guess what, guess what!" I rattle off quickly. My hands flap excitedly when I ambush Trevor at the door. He just got home from his overnight work trip to Santa Barbara and barely has time to drop his bags before I drag him to the kitchen. "*Look!*"

He follows my finger and squints out the window. "Huh. They moved that bulldozer. Guess they really are done with those house—"

"Not *that*!" I jab my finger at the teensiest bud shooting out from the previously barren plant on the windowsill. "I didn't kill her! Apparently, orchids thrive on neglect because I haven't touched her in months and she's *blooming*!" My cheeks ache from the wide smile on my face until I see him wrinkle his nose.

"About that..." He grins nervously, then presses a kiss to my temple. "I've been taking care of her."

"Wha—when?"

"When you go to bed, usually. I started after Thanksgiving... You didn't notice the new pot?"

I whip my head back to the pot on the sill that's definitely purple and filled with holes instead of brown. *Damn it*! I was so fucking proud of myself for not killing that stupid plant too. But *nooo...* Super Dimples saved the day because, of course, he did. Huffing, I trudge past him and flop onto the sofa dejectedly. He follows, sliding me onto his lap once he settles on a cushion. I pout, despite the warmth spreading through me at his casual intimacy. "So you, what? Whispered sweet nothings to her every day and fed her artesian cloud water?"

He throws his head back and laughs. "She's not that high maintenance."

"She's a bitch!" I purse my lips to stifle my giggle, relaxing into him.

"No. She just knows what she likes. Water once a week, a high-quality substrate mixture, indirect sunlight"—he brushes a thumb across my cheek—"room for her roots to do their own thing, space to breathe. Peace and quiet." He smiles, and by the fluttering in my chest, it's clear we're no longer talking about a finicky plant.

"That's not high maintenance to you?"

"She's perfect..." His eyes twinkle as he pulls me closer. "Just needed to be understood."

Our lips barely touch when my damn phone shrills with my assistant's ringtone. She closed the studio today, so the only reason I answer is to make sure everything's okay. As soon as I do, her words fly a mile a minute.

"Whoa. Breathe, Emily. It's fine. I'll do it. Have fun at the show." I roll my eyes as I end the call and turn to Trevor. "Emily forgot to set the studio alarm again, so I have to drive over there." He shifts me onto the cushion next to us and digs in his pocket for his keys. "Tre, no. You just got home and look exhausted. It'll take me forty-five minutes, tops."

"You know, for someone so smart, you sure have a hard time understanding that I want to spend all my free time with you, whether I'm tired or not." He flashes those dimples. My insides turn to goo as he pulls me up from the couch and nestles his lips against mine. "Now that I'm holding you, I have all the energy in the world."

The hormones are making me lightheaded or something. I definitely didn't swoon just now. But it takes a minute for my head to stop spinning before I can stumble to the door for my purse.

THE PARKING LOT IS PACKED WHEN WE PULL INTO THE strip mall, leaving exactly one spot open in front of the studio. The nickel arcade at the end of the mall is a bustling spot for date nights on Thursdays, but I've never seen it this busy before. Trevor comes around to open my door, and I play with my keys while we walk hand in hand to the studio. *At least Emily remembered to shut the lights off this time.* He shifts behind me, ever my protector in the darkness while I fiddle with the lock. I don't miss the gentle hand he's pressed to the small of my back as I reach for the lights. And then my mouth drops. I'm met with the smiles of everyone who's important to me as I blink against the sudden brightness. *Silent smiles. No yelling.* Trevor presses a kiss to my neck and whispers, "Surprise, Gem."

I turn wide eyes to him, and he smirks, steering me into the pink streamer-covered studio. Our small pod of friends and family mill around the room, moving out of crouched spaces toward the tables set up in the middle. Chase ushers Kayla and her large belly to a seat. Hunter hovers over a wireless speaker, while Ashlie chats with Trevor's mom and sisters excitedly. Even Sam is here, entertaining my three employees at the front desk. "When did you plan all of this?"

"After we went shopping for baby clothes. I asked our sisters for help. Emily too." He squeezes my hand as I look around the room again. "You were just so down on yourself. I wanted to remind you how much support you have now." He drops a peck on the top of my head.

"Okay, T, you can't hog her all night," Maya says. She and Lainey loop their arms around each of mine.

"Yeah, she's got presents to open and people to hug." Lainey sticks her tongue out at her brother, eliciting a chuckle from him as she pulls me toward the food table. "Please tell me he's lightened up…"

"Not in the slightest." I laugh at the faces the two sisters make at each other. They're tired of his antics for me.

"He was so worried we wouldn't be able to pull this off without you finding out," Maya says.

"I think pregnancy brain helped with that. I feel like the dumbest person lately."

Maya smiles, nodding knowingly. "How are you feeling otherwise? Twenty-five weeks, right?"

"Yeah. All good. Everything's going smoothly now." I glance back at Trevor, who's laughing about something with Sam. He catches my eye with a smile, winks at me, and returns to his conversation so smoothly, I doubt Sam even realized.

With a plate full of food, I make my way to the table where Kayla and Chase are sitting. Chase presses a kiss to her temple before he stands and heads toward Hunter.

"Twins! You've got to be more exhausted than I am," I say, slipping into the chair on the other side of Kayla. "But you're glowing!"

"Girl, I'm *sweating*." She laughs, her deep bronze skin glistening as she fans herself. "This whole pregnancy thing is kicking my ass. I just hope they stay in there as long as possible…" Turning in her seat, she searches my face. "How are you feeling? I heard about everything. That must have been so scary!"

"It was, but the bed rest was the worst part."

"*Ugh*. I can't even imagine." A grimace scrunches her face as she sweeps her dark locs over one shoulder. Kayla's about as much of a workaholic as I am, so I know she understands how hard it was. She grew up with us in Fort Bender, and even though she's my sister's best friend, we've always gotten along pretty well. "The studio looks great, Willa. I haven't been since you repainted. It's completely you."

"Thanks, girl." My eyes sweep the lavender walls as I nod at my pride and joy, landing on the neon logo right above my employees at the front desk. Having everyone I care about in the space I've worked so hard to build brings tears to my eyes. *How did I get this lucky?* I may not have the best relationship with my parents, or a squeaky-clean past with relationships, but I have this, and I have every single one of them.

"*Heyyy,*" Ashlie sings. Hunter and Chase follow behind her. "I just wanted to thank you both for making me an auntie. You need more food? Water? Whatever it is, Hunter will grab it for you."

Hunter sucks his teeth. "I will, but only to show Ashlie how good I'll be when it's our turn..."

"*Hunt,*" Ashlie growls, bumping him with her hip. "You said you'd drop it."

"Naw. I said I wouldn't ask you anymore. And I didn't." He throws an arm over her shoulder and kisses her temple. "You guys think I'll be a good uncle, right?"

"Sure, man," Chase squeaks out, avoiding his gaze.

"Won't be watching my kids," Kayla mumbles before taking a sip of her water.

Hunter's face falls into a scowl, and Ashlie laughs, patting his chest. "You'll be great, love."

"Don't worry, Hunter. I'll let you babysit," I say.

"See! Willa's got some faith in me." Hunter claps me on the shoulder. Everyone is so tough on him, but he's one of the most observant people I've ever known. He plays it cool, acts like nothing fazes him, but I think he'll do great as an uncle *and* a dad.

"Will!" Sam whispers loudly from across the room, beckoning me with a head tilt. I excuse myself to see what's been so funny. He waits for my nod before pulling me into a hug, his familiar woodsy scent wrapping me in nostalgia, back to the days when he was the only one I had. "I was just warning Trevor that you might be hearing from your parents soon."

"Sam's gutsier than I am." Trevor laughs. "Called them out in the middle of the grocery store."

I chuff. "They knocked you down a peg, huh?"

"Of course they did." Sam laughs. "You know your mom's teacher look? I felt like I was back in junior high. Gave them the best lecture I could though. Told them how stupid they've been."

Amusement pops my eyes wide. "You called my mom stupid?"

"Well, no. Not exactly." He wrinkles his nose. "But I thought it real hard. I don't know if it did anything, seeing as they're not here, but I tried."

"I'm just surprised you didn't get your tongue snatched out of your mouth after back talking Jackeline Willis." I nudge his side with my elbow.

Trevor shudders. "You're a brave man, Sam. I thought I was pushing it by setting them straight in their own home, but in public? Props." He holds up a fist and taps Sam's knuckles.

"Where's Maci?" I ask, looking around the room for that cute, chubby scowl.

"She's home with Claire. Ear infection and pink eye. But Claire sent me with her 'new mom' survival kit and detailed instructions for everything." He grips my shoulder. "Speaking of *detailed instructions*, how's the Phalaenopsis?"

"You'll be happy to know Trevor nursed CC back to health."

"My man!" Sam pounds Trevor's fist again, and they chat about business at the flower shop. Watching them interact so casually puts a smile on my face. Trevor slipped into my life so effortlessly, it's as if he was always meant to be a part of it. This man is one of the best things to ever happen to me, and that's saying something. But the longer I watch my favorite person joke around with my other favorite person, the more I'm hit with an unexpected wave of inadequacy.

Trevor's built for connection and intimacy. He's always

wanted a wife, kids, and the white-picket fence. I've known this since the day I met him. He'll be a great father and a fantastic husband someday, but he deserves someone who can give that back to him tenfold. I'm independent, stubborn, and I'd never considered sharing my life with someone else permanently before all of this. What if I can't measure up? Or worse, what if I end up being too much for him?

TREVOR

I hear a knock on the front door and check my phone. Mom, Maya, and Lainey are only in town until tomorrow morning, but they're about thirty minutes early for our brunch outing. At the baby shower last night, all three essentially begged me and Willa to take them to the beach today. I took the day off in anticipation of their visit, and Willa's employees are handling the studio so we can show them around. February in LA is a hell of a lot warmer than the freezing temps they're used to in Nebraska. I wouldn't be surprised if Lainey shows up in shorts and flip-flops.

When I open the door, I'm steeling for a sarcastic comment from Maya. Instead, Robert and Jackeline Willis shift uncomfortably as they take me in. My jaw clenches tightly, and I'm having a hard time relaxing it.

"I didn't realize you two were shacking up," Jackie reproves.

"Can I help you?" I ask, crossing my arms as I lean against the doorframe. The attitude radiating from her sets off all my protective instincts. I'm not giving them access to Willa today.

"We wanted to speak with Willa. With both of you," Rob says gently, a complete reversal from his wife.

"She's in the shower now, and we're heading out shortly..." My words are calculated and clipped. Over my dead body are they stressing out the mother of my child after the joy she experienced last night from being surrounded by people who care about her.

"Maybe you could meet us for dinner, then?" Rob urges.

"Busy then too."

"This is ridiculous, Trevor. We came to see our daughter, and that's what we intend to do." Jackie huffs.

"What's ridiculous is you two showing up here with demands after months of silence. No checking on her. No questions about the baby. Did you even know she's been on bed rest?" That makes the scowl fall from Jackie's face, and Rob's intake of air gives me my answer. *How shameful.* "Didn't think so," I say, biting back the string of profanity I want to unleash on them. *What kind of fucking parents treat their child this way?* "Willa's busy today. I can tell her you two came by. If she wants to talk to you, she'll reach out."

"What about breakfast in the morning?" Rob offers.

"That's entirely up to Willa. If she says no, the answer is no."

I turn to go back inside, ready to leave their nonsense and shock out here on the porch.

"Trevor." Rob's voice trembles, and I pause. "Is—are they okay? Willa and the baby? We heard it's a girl."

I blow out a breath of frustration. "They're both fine now. Everyone's happy and healthy."

Rob nods quickly and looks down at the ground with a face full of remorse. "We'll wait to hear from Willa about tomorrow. Come on, Jackie." He tugs on her arm, and after a stubborn back and forth, she allows him to lead her down the sidewalk.

When I close the door, Willa meets me with a misty gaze. "Uh." I rub the back of my head, scrunching my nose. "Your parents are in town..."

"Yeah, I heard."

"How long have you been standing there?"

"Long enough to watch you enforce some boundaries." She closes the gap between us. "No one's ever done that for me before you."

"Done what?"

"Cared..." Her hands smooth over my chest until soft fingers frame my face. "Pretty fucking sexy, if you ask me." She pulls me into a mind-numbing kiss. I clutch her waist and let her guide the pace. Between my aggravation at the exchange on the porch and her sudden desire, we're melding into a pit of passion that has me considering undoing the shower she just took. Her libido has been sky high the last few weeks, and we haven't had our daily romp yet this morning. "Bend me over the couch," she pants.

"We don't have time." I groan, diving back into her lips.

Tugging me with her, we stumble into the living room. "We can make time. That's what quickies are for."

She grabs the back of the sofa and bends at the waist, sticking out her ass with an enticing wiggle. *All logic: gone.* My hand is under her dress, fingers gliding through her soaking slit so fast, I don't have time to think through unbuttoning my pants. I sink two fingers inside her right when someone knocks on the door. Willa stills in my arms, giggling at the growl rumbling through my chest. *If it's her goddamn parents cockblocking me right now, I'll fucking lose it.* There's another knock, and I painstakingly slip out of her with a groan. She turns to face me with a smirk. "We should probably answer it, yeah?" I say, diving in for another kiss.

She smiles against my mouth, nodding. "I can hear Lainey talking a mile a minute through the door."

"Good. She can keep them entertained while I take care of something." I nibble her neck, her little giggle-moan hitting me straight in the dick. *They'll be fine outside for a minute.* She gasps when I grip her thighs, lifting her onto the back of the couch. She braces her hands on the sofa as I spread her legs wide. "Just a little taste," I mumble, preparing to drop to my knees. Willa stops me with a hand on my chest, and I whimper shamelessly. *"Please..."*

"Ew!" Maya yells. "If you can hear us, we can hear you, dummy!" The doorbell rings, but I'm too keyed up right now to care.

Willa's eyes twinkle with amusement. *"One* taste," she whispers. Gripping my wrist, she guides a finger through her arousal. A needy moan leaves her lips when I brush her clit, and she lets me linger there. "Mmm, you be my good boy today..." She brings my finger to my lips. My tongue darts out for a taste, and the sinful way she stares as I savor her essence has me bricked up. "... And I'll be your good girl tonight." She leans in, ghosting my lips. "*All night long.*"

Fuck me. I groan as a shiver rolls down my body. I'll be thinking about her dirty little mouth the entire time we're out today, just like she planned. She smirks, moving off the couch, and I head straight down the hallway.

"Where are you going?" She laughs. I don't know why she's acting like I'm not busting through my jeans right now.

"You can't tease me like that and expect me to open the door to my family."

"Again, *ew!*" Maya calls from outside.

Willa cackles, and I shake my head, calling over my shoulder, "I gotta go calm the fuck down. Gimme a minute."

AFTER A FULL DAY OF FOOD AND SIGHTS, AND MORE pink onesies than I think is possible for a baby to wear in their infancy, we're strolling along the beach. Maya pulls me back, the cool breeze ruffling her curls as Willa, Mom, and Lainey walk ahead. I smile, just watching them huddle together for warmth. The sense of completeness at seeing my lady get along so well with my family strikes me out of nowhere. This feeling is undeniable, accompanied by thoughts of Willa walking toward me in a white dress. *Shit. Back up.* We're not even close to talking about that...

Maya's smile quirks her lips, a knowing look sparkling in her eyes.

"Are you gonna say it, or just keep staring with that stupid smile on your face?" I ask.

"Trevor's in *love...*" she teases in a sing-song tone. Even though it's true, my cheeks heat. Another look at me and she's laughing like it's the most hilarious thing to witness.

"You having fun, My?" I chuckle, kicking a shell in the sand as we follow their footsteps.

"It's cute, T!" Her face falls with a grimace, and she bumps into me. "Except for this morning...ew."

"How 'bout you stop bringing it up, huh?" We share a laugh, and she hooks her arm around mine.

"We've never seen you like this. Even with Marla, it wasn't like this."

"Yeah, well, Marla didn't make me feel like this so..."

"So...love? You love Willa?"

I look up, and Willa quickly glances over her shoulder before the three of them giggle about something else. It's likely at my expense, but I light up inside. "Wholeheartedly. She's everything."

"Good. I like seeing you happy. And at this point, I think you'd be voted off the island if you got rid of her."

"I don't doubt that." I bump her shoulder playfully, and she pushes back like she's trying to knock me off course. "You know I'm not above throwing you in the ocean, right?"

"Then you'd definitely be voted off the island, seeing as *I'm* the favorite." She sticks out her tongue in a taunt.

"Favorite pain in the ass, maybe. Who's the one Mom's always begging to come home though?"

"Oh yeah? Watch this..." She puts a hand to her mouth. "Mom, T just pushed me," she calls.

"Trevor Anthony, you better not."

"She pushed me first!" I defend myself, somehow transported back to childhood. Maya jogs to catch up with them.

"You're twice her size. We'll vote you off the island, Trevor."

"What is this island?" I ask.

"It's from a show," all four of the women in my life shout

back at me. Laughing, I quicken my steps to catch up to them, feeling that light inside me glowing brighter by the second.

Once we get back to the house and say our goodbyes, Willa pulls out her phone. "I think I'm going to meet up with my parents tomorrow," she says.

"You sure?"

"Yeah. I had a talk with your mom today, and she told me laying out my ground rules with them now, before the baby comes, was something she wished she did with her parents. I think she's right."

My grandparents were definitely the steamrolling type, so Mom's advice makes complete sense to me. "Whatever you want to do, that's what you should do, Gem."

"Yeah...but could you maybe come with me?" She bites her lip, and even though she's holding her phone, she still manages to strangle her fingers.

I slip my hand between hers and pull her toward me, right into a kiss. "Of course, sweetheart. I'll go with you anywhere."

She presses another quick kiss to my lips, takes a deep breath, and scrolls through her phone while walking toward the bedroom. I watch her, feeling like the luckiest bastard on the Pacific coast to have landed her. Stopping at the door, she gives me a sultry look. "Don't think I forgot about being your good girl tonight..." The hooded look in her eyes and the bite of her lip spring my dick into action. I don't know why she keeps leaving me in the entryway with a hard-on, but this better be the quickest damn phone call of her life.

CHAPTER FIFTY

WILLA

"Gem…" Trevor turns to me after parking his SUV, leaving the engine running. We pulled into Honey Brunches thirty minutes early so I could feel like I have the upper hand with whatever is about to happen. Dark storm clouds rolling in over the half-full lot seem like an omen, but I'm trying to ignore it. When my parents arrive at ten, there should be enough people inside to stave off any potential of Mom making a scene. He turns down the comfort playlist he made for me, then grabs my hand. "I'll support you either way. If you still want to go in there and say your piece, I'll be right by your side, giving them the stink eye until you're finished. But if you don't want to do this anymore, if it's too stressful right now, that's okay too. You don't owe them anything, and you're allowed to change your mind."

Changing my mind has been villainized for so long, his reminder gives me more courage than he'll ever know. Giving him a small smile, I squeeze his hand. "Thank you. But I want to get this over with today."

He leans in and presses a kiss to my forehead. "Then let's do it."

As we walk hand in hand toward the brick café, my other hand settles protectively over my belly. I'm only doing this for my little girl. She deserves a support system that will show up regardless of whoever she decides to be. I'm willing to give my parents the chance to be a part of it, but some things drastically need to change.

Trevor and I have time to order and finish half of our breakfast by the time my parents walk into the brown and black accented café. Bronze pendant lights hang from the ceiling over wooden bistro tables. The whir of coffee grinders mixes with the easy jazz playing softly. Dad trudges past the dark vinyl booths lining the windows, looking worse for wear as he drags Mom behind him. "Hey, Willabean. Trevor." His tired smile barely reaches his eyes. I haven't heard that nickname since I was a kid, and it hits me right in the chest.

"Hi, Dad." I return his smile, and he takes a seat. "Hey, Mom."

"Hay is for horses, Wilhelmina." Her eyes narrow on my plate as she sits in the wooden chair across from me. "My grandbaby's going to come out as big as a house if you keep feeding her bacon and pancakes."

Everything in me tenses, but Trevor squeezes my thigh, bringing me back down immediately.

"*Enough*, Jackie!" Dad snaps, and I tense again. "You've been running your mouth since we landed on Friday. Be *quiet*." My eyes shift between them cynically. Never in my thirty-one years have I seen him stand up to Mom. She purses her lips, fixing her eyes on the black condiment caddy. "Willa, I'd like to apologize for Thanksgiving. It was out of line for us to question your choices like that, and I think *we*"—he glances at Mom who sits still as stone—"have forgotten." The lines around his dark brown eyes crinkle as warmth fills his expression. "I've spent the last few days researching everything you've accomplished out here. Your partnership with TAILA, the studio, your home—you've really made a name for yourself." He reaches for my hand and gives a squeeze. "I'm proud of you."

What the fuck is happening right now? I blink away my

surprise. "Uh...thank you? Um, I just wanted to set some expectations when it comes to the baby."

Mom chuffs, patting her afro, and Dad's jaw hardens. "Jackeline," he says through gritted teeth.

"*Oh,* I'm allowed to speak now?"

"Don't start." He sighs.

"She's talking to us like we don't know how to raise children, Robert. It's insulting."

I glance at Trevor, and he looks just as perplexed as I feel watching my parents bicker like this. Mom sneers at our exchange. "Please give us some privacy, Trevor. Your services aren't needed."

"Services?" I hiss, seeing red. This is already off to a horrible start. Less than ten minutes, and the rapid cycling through anxiety, anger, and confusion is making me regret meeting up with them.

"Yes. *Services.* Honestly, Wilhelmina, what made you think you'd need a handler when meeting with us? This is a family matter."

"He *is* my family," I say cooly, leaning into him. "And it's called support. The only one who needs handling here is you."

"You hear that, Robert?" she huffs, hitching her purse higher on her shoulder. "Now we're not supportive. She's completely ignoring all of those expensive math and science courses she used us for." Her cold brown eyes settle on mine. "Seeing as we're so easily replaced, there's no need for us to be here."

"You mean the courses I was forced into? The ones I took to keep you happy? Make you proud for once? I never wanted any of that."

"*Ooh,* well excuse me for trying to cultivate your God-given talents. Most people would be thankful they had parents dedicated to their education. But it's always something with you."

"Jackie," Dad warns.

"What is *that* supposed to mean?" The baby kicks at my heightened pitch, and I soothe her with a caress as I adjust in my chair. "What did I ever do that was so wrong?

"You know exactly what it means, Willa. You've never needed me the way your sister does."

The bite in her confession knocks me back with surprise, and my mouth drops. "What child doesn't need their mother?"

"YOU!" Mom's chair scrapes across the floor as she stands, pointing a finger in my face. Several eyes around the café dart to our table as Dad reaches for her arm, but she snatches it back. "Since the day you were born, you made it clear I wasn't enough for you. Never slept for me, never took to my milk, never returned my smiles. You threw horrible tantrums whenever I'd try to play with you. And then you'd hide from me. *Hide*. Like locking yourself in a dark closet was easier than looking me in the eye."

I'm speechless. This tirade is the first time she's ever explained where her issues with me stem from. *She actually hates me.* Tears well in my eyes, and I glance at Trevor. Eyebrows cinched in concern, he clears his throat. "Did you ever talk to someone about it?"

She slices a glare at him, but her hatred fixes back on me so quickly, it's clear she truly resents me. "There's nothing wrong with her, *Trevor*, except for being contrarian and hardheaded. Everything has to be her way. She'll cast you aside too, as soon as she gets whatever it is she wants from you."

"Not Willa," Trevor says, his calm voice soothing the agitation burning inside me.

I focus on it, let it wash over me as he strokes my knee. In the past, I would have flown off the handle and matched her energy. But now, all I see is a woman who never took the time to understand herself. There's nothing I could have done—nothing I *can* do—to get into her good graces. She may hate me, but the issue lies within herself. The realization is freeing.

"I'm asking if *you* talked to someone for the way you felt back then," Trevor continues. "That's a lot of resentment to hold over a child."

"Don't you dare patronize me. You think impregnating my daughter out of wedlock gives you the right to—"

"You're making a scene." Dad yanks on her arm, and the rest of her sentence is swallowed up when she lands in the chair with a thud. "Sit. Down."

Pursing her lips, she jerks her arm away, glowering at me like I'm the one who forced her to sit. "Just say whatever you have to say so we can leave."

My eyes lock onto hers, and the smugness pinching her face tempts me to lay into her. But then the baby moves. *My daughter.* Her kick is the enlightenment I need right now. I don't want to be anything like the woman crumbling in front of me. Stooping to her level will only validate her, and I need to get my message across clearly: this behavior won't be allowed around my child. So I breathe deeply, emulating the calm assertiveness radiating from Trevor.

"When this baby is born, she'll be surrounded by love and genuine support. We won't hesitate to keep her away from anyone who speaks to her the way you speak to me. Anyone who blames her for things beyond her control. I'm not doing this for me, Mom. I don't give a damn if you think I'm the devil incarnate, but if you want the chance to know your grandchild, you'll do the kind of soul-searching you should have done when I was young. Things need to change. Until they do, I'm not comfortable having you around her."

"Who do you think you are?" She sneers. "I'll do whatever I damn well please, including seeing my grandbaby *whenever* I choose."

I turn to Trevor, and his eyes are already on mine, offering the protection he always has. The faintest smile quirks his lips, his reassurance washing over me. He squeezes my knee, and I slip my hand over his as I face my mom. "Fucking try me."

"I don't have to sit and listen to this." Mom bolts from her chair, her heels clipping on the dark herringbone flooring all the way to the exit. As soon as she's gone, I feel as light as a feather. She's made her choice, and I've made mine.

"I have a lot of regrets, Willa." Dad's shaky words pull my

attention from the door. "You've suffered through too much because of my silence, and it's something I'll be fixing for a long time. But that's what I'll do because I want the chance to know her." His eyes glisten as he reaches across the table for my hand. "I'd like the chance to know you too, Willabean. As you are."

I've always seen Dad as a silent antagonist, ready to enforce Mom's bidding. Until today, there's been no evidence of his backbone. If I hadn't seen their interaction with my own eyes, I'd never believe it. But the sincerity in his voice and the emotion in his eyes are undeniable. If he's committed to changing, I stand by what I said. "Let's take it slow and see how it goes. But I'm serious about Mom. She can't act that away around the baby, and I won't let her anywhere near us as long as she does."

"I agree." Dad glances out the window at Mom pacing the sidewalk, a chagrined frown on his face. "She needs to come to her senses on her own or face the music. I'll let her do just that." As if on cue, thunder rumbles. The slightest smirk settles on his lips as raindrops patter against the roof. He pulls his rental car keys from his shirt pocket and sets them on the table, then lounges back in his chair with his hands settling over his stomach.

"If you have to go rescue her, that's okay, Dad. I understand," I say, nodding toward the door.

He gives a mischievous grin. "Like I said, she needs to come to her senses. As for me, I'm long overdue for a coffee with my daughter and her boyfriend."

CHAPTER FIFTY-ONE

TREVOR

"Hey, Trevor. Take a seat." Gabriela from HR welcomes me into her office. Her dark hair is pulled into a tight bun settled against the collar of her black pinstripe power suit. She gestures to the empty leather armchair next to my supervisor, Miles, whose hulking frame barely fits in his. His salt-and-pepper goatee stretches around the smile he beams at me as I sit, bald head gleaming under the recessed lighting.

"How are you liking the team so far?" Miles asks.

Slinging my arm over the chair back, I turn to face him. "They're great. I think we all work pretty well together. Can't complain." Despite having to deal with Marla every so often, her main focus has been putting out fires across the various training departments. I've had ample space to focus on building rapport with my teammates for the last two months.

"That's great! I've only heard good things about you from everyone. How has the overnight traveling gone for you?"

"Again, no complaints. The overnights have all been simple to navigate."

"Well, if you're still interested, we'd like to finalize your permanent contract. I hear you have some stipulations we need to negotiate. Let's hear them."

"I really just need to be close to home until the baby's born, and a guaranteed paternity leave with health care benefits for the duration."

Gabriela nods while tapping on the tablet in her hand. "It doesn't look like that should be a problem. You've been with the company long enough to qualify for all benefits. As for the traveling, that's up to Miles."

Miles clears his throat. "I'd really like you to have the full flex experience under your belt before paternity leave so you can hit the ground running when you return. How far along is she?"

"Uh, twenty-six weeks."

"If we started you on the midweek travel schedule now until your wife hits the thirty-five-week mark, would that work for you?"

Wife? I try to consider this compromise, but everything gets tangled up in the word. Over the last few days, I've thought about marriage more than I'd like to admit, but hearing someone else refer to her as my wife does something to me. Nothing has ever felt more natural. *Does she feel it too*?

"Trevor?" Miles shifts in his seat, pulling me back to the HR office. "We'll have to adjust for any team needs of course, but unless something crazy happens and every single person comes down with COVID at the same time, I don't anticipate you needing to be far from LA when that time comes. Does that work for you?"

Wife. "Yeah. Yep. Sounds good." Does Willa even want to be a wife? Would she want to be *my* wife? We've made some giant leaps in our relationship, but this is in a different realm entirely.

"Excellent!" Miles stands and offers me his hand. "I'll leave you and Gabriela to finalize the paperwork. Welcome, officially, to the team, Trevor."

I turn to Gabriela, who hurriedly scrawls the additional terms we agreed on just now. She walks me through all the parts of the contract, has me sign what feels like a thousand times, and finally shakes my hand before I'm able to walk out the door.

As soon as I step out of the elevator and onto the training floor, my coworkers, Bryant and Jared, swarm me. "Hey, Trev. Wanted to run something past you." Bryant throws an arm over my shoulder as we walk down the carpeted hallway in between the glass partitioned offices. His dark brown skin and black fade is a complete contrast to Jared's pale complexion and bald head. Oddly enough, they wear matching glasses.

"Let me guess. You need help swapping out the toner in the copier again?"

"Don't remind me." He shudders. The last time he tried it on his own, he was covered in toner. "It was in all my crevices, man. *All. My. Crevices.*"

"I'm pretty sure talking about your crevices at work is a straight shot to HR..." Jared chimes in, knocking his fist into Bryant's shoulder.

"Naw, we wanted to know how you'd feel about a team baby gift," Bryant asks.

"It's kind of a tradition we started," Jared adds. "We'll take care of everything. Just wanted to check with you and your wife. Don't want to overstep."

Wife. What is this? I've never heard the word *wife* so much in my life, and every time someone says it, Willa's smile fills my mind.

"*Please* let us do one." Bryant's eyes light up. He and Jared both have kids, but I'm surprised how excited they are about this. "Run it by your wife, of course, but babies gotta be celebrated, man."

There it is again, thrown into my orbit so casually, like it's meant to be there. I could correct everyone—*should*—since I don't know how she'd feel if she knew I'm letting people think we're married. But with the way I feel about Willa, the longer I mull it over, the more the word *wife* doesn't even come close to describing her position in my life.

"Uh, yeah. I'll check and get back to you on Monday."

THE REST OF MY DAY IS UNEVENTFUL, EXCEPT FOR THE incessant droning in my head about marrying Willa. It was all I could do to focus on my reports for the week without my mind drifting to rings and weddings and every single lyric on my comfort playlist.

Driving home isn't too much better, and after ten minutes, I click to my worry tunes just to get a break from my thoughts. It works long enough to get me home, but walking in to see Willa lounging on the couch with a smile just for me ramps it all back up.

I make a beeline to her, dropping my computer bag somewhere between the door and the sofa. Once I'm sitting on the cushion, she shifts to climb into my lap. It feels so effortless, so *right*. I can't shake the thought that's been hammering in my head.

Her forehead creases as she stares into my anxiety riddled face. "So...are you going to tell me what's wrong?"

I smile, loving how she can sense my apprehension without my saying a word. "What makes you think something's wrong?"

"Well, you haven't kissed me yet, for starters. Did something happen with the contract?"

"Nope. That's all settled. I got everything I asked for, with a small caveat to step in if there's an emergency."

"Okay...so why do you look like you just signed away your smiling rights?" She reaches up and strokes my cheek. "Seeing those dimples is my favorite thing at the end of the day."

My heart pounds as a handful of doubts smack me in the face. I pull her in for a kiss so she can't see it in my eyes. She's never once mentioned marriage, not even in passing. She owns her own business, her own home. Before the baby, she'd set herself up for a life on her own. It would make sense if she didn't want to be tied down in that way.

Willa pulls away, placing a hand on my chest. "Why are you kissing me like that?"

"Like what?" I stall. I'm not ready for this make-or-break conversation, especially the *breaking*. Not now, when we're finally together.

"Like this is the last time you'll ever kiss me."

Shit. I drag a hand down my face. "Because it might be, and I'm scared shitless, Gem." We said we'd be honest with each other. This is as honest as it gets. I kiss her again, but that hesitant palm on my chest pushes against me. She watches me, scrutinizing the sullen expression on my face as I trail my thumb across her cheekbone. "I want everything, Willa. Kids, a house, marriage. I want it all with you..."

She juts her head back. "Sweetheart, where is this coming from?"

"Me, mostly." I let out a nervous laugh. "A couple people called you my wife at work today, and the thought has been festering ever since. It doesn't need to be now, or anytime soon even, but I can't shake how it felt hearing someone call you my wife. I crave you in a way I've never imagined was possible, but I just don't know if that's something you even want."

With a pinched expression, she bites her lip. "It's not that I don't want it. I've just never...considered it..."

I tuck my chin, eyes dropping. That's about what I figured, but the disappointment still twists like a switchblade to the gut. My eyes swirl around the narrow space between us as I reel in the pleading words forming behind my tongue. She's made leaps and bounds for us to get to this point. I could try to convince her to consider it, but I respect her too much to pressure her like that. If it means keeping everything else just like it is now, maybe giving up the marriage thing could be okay. *This can be enough for me.*

Willa's fingers slide up my jaw, and she presses a chaste kiss to my lips. She smiles sweetly. "Until you, Tre. Never, until you. I have thoughts about it now, I'm just unsure of what they mean..."

"Yeah?" Hope springs inside me, just hearing she's thought about it. She leaves another kiss on my lips, and I latch on for dear life.

"Someday," she whispers, snuggling into me. That's something I can hold on to. It's tangible. Willa needs time. I can give her that.

WILLA

I slip my phone into my bag and gather the rest of my things from my work desk. My damn stomach knocks my water bottle to the floor, right next to the pen and notepad I dropped earlier. I'm almost thirty weeks pregnant, and bending over hurts. All that shit down there is dead to me now. My phone buzzes, and I check to see if it's Trevor.

ASHLIE

Mom wants to know if you're going to breastfeed.

ME

Mom can take a flying leap.

ASHLIE

You want me to tell her that? 🫢

ME

Nope. I'll tell her when she gets the guts to call me.

The breakfast with my parents was a month ago. Dad's gotten into the habit of checking in every Sunday, and I can really see him putting in the kind of effort he never did before. Mom's still on her bullshit. I can't say I didn't try. *I'm going to be late.*

"I'm heading out, Emily," I call toward the front of the studio as I power down my computer. "And I have that birthing class tonight. If you forget to set the alarm again, call Cara."

"Sure thing, Boss Lady. But I won't forget. Wrote it down." Emily holds up her hand where the bright green word *alarm* is written on her skin. "It's permanent marker, so I'll remember tomorrow too."

"Doubtful," I tease, stopping in front of her at the front desk. "Tomorrow's Saturday anyway. I'm locking up."

"Oh yeah…" She laughs sheepishly. "I forgot."

Rolling my eyes, I head out the door, pausing in the mid-March warmth. How she can be so good at her job and such a space case is beyond me. You gotta love her though. My phone buzzes again as I'm digging for my keys.

TREVOR

Let me know when you're outside. I'll walk you up.

ME

You think my legs stopped working while you were gone?

TREVOR

Nope. Just wanna make out in the parking lot 😉

ME

Trevor's been on his full flex training schedule for several weeks now, flying out on Sundays and flying back home Thursdays—basically the same schedule we followed when he was still in San Francisco. But it's harder now. I've gotten used to having him around. Usually he gets in early on Thursdays, but he got back so late last night, we didn't have much time together before bed. I'm bringing lunch to his office to make up for it.

I slip behind the wheel and shoot him a text, letting him know I'm on the way. He sends back a bunch of lips emojis, and I bite mine, giggling at the silliness. The way I've missed him this week is borderline unhinged. Making out in the parking lot sounds fantastic.

When I pull into the EdTechU campus, Trevor's already standing outside waiting for me. He strolls across the lot to my car, and once I've put it in park, my door flies open and he's unbuckling my seat belt. I'm pinned to my headrest by his lips, giggling at the giddiness fluttering around in my chest. "Hey, Gem," he mumbles, smiling against my mouth like breaking apart just to say hello is unbearable.

I give him another peck. "I thought you wanted to make out in the parking lot, not the car."

He presses a kiss to my stomach, then helps me out of the driver's seat. "Technically, the car's *in* the parking lot." He grabs the Subbies bag on the console and closes the door. "But if you insist…" Pulling me to him, he leans against the side of my car. With a hand on my belly, he says, "I'll kiss you out here, too. Oh—"

Right before our lips meet, he jumps at the kick against his hand. "Damn! That was—did that hurt?" His eyes are a mix of excitement and concern. With all the traveling, he hasn't been able to feel the baby kick yet, despite weeks of me feeling her move around on the inside.

"Nope." I press his hand into the spot where she kicked. "She did that last night, too, when she heard your voice. Say something else."

His excitement turns timid. "Like what?"

"Anything." I take the Subbies bag from him. "Say hi. Tell her a joke. I don't know. You're the talker here."

He squats so he's at eye level with my bump and frames it in his hands. I give him a reassuring grin when he flicks hesitant eyes up at me. "Hi, sweet pea. I can't wait to meet you."

The baby lands a hard kick right on his palm, and the look of awe on his face as he stares at my bump has me melting like a popsicle. We might be outside in a bustling parking lot, but it feels like it's just the three of us sharing this moment. He presses another kiss to my stomach before standing, shaking his head with wonder. "You feel that all day?"

"Mostly. She usually sleeps while I'm at work, but as soon as I eat something, and whenever you get home, she perks right up and stays that way all night."

"Amazing." He kisses my forehead. "Let's get inside."

Trevor's hand stays on my lower back until I'm settled in the leather swivel chair in his glass partitioned office. All the other offices are empty.

"They went out for lunch today," he says, sitting in a metal chair across the desk.

"Oh. You could have gone with them, Tre. This isn't impor—"

"I'm right where I want to be." He winks, then digs into the Subbies bag. While he figures out which sandwich is my veggie sub, I gaze around his office. It's mostly bare, just like his apartment was in San Francisco, save a few file folders stacked neatly next to the computer on his desk, a filing cabinet in the corner, and a couple of shelves.

I spin in the chair to the bookshelf behind me and gasp at the framed pictures on top. There are only two, but something about seeing them in his ascetic office brings me near tears. The bigger one is a horizontal four-paned wooden frame with a progression of ultrasound pictures—the first all the way to our latest gender scan. But the smaller photo catches me by surprise. It's a profile of me, bundled up in my winter coat with a smile as I aim my camera at a snow-covered tree. I had no idea this picture existed, and even though it's the most mundane pose, it means the world.

"That's the happiest I'd ever seen you," Trevor says quietly. "And I just wanted to remember it... I, uh, hope that's okay."

Spinning to face him with tears in my eyes, I smile and reach for his hand. "More than okay. It just surprised me. You can't do that to a pregnant lady," I tease, fanning my face with my free hand. He leans forward and brushes a tear from my cheek, then kisses me softly. When he pulls away, I see forever in his eyes, and our conversation about marriage rings in my ears. Maybe *someday* is a lot closer than I realized. As the smile grows on his face, his gaze memorizing mine, I'm pretty sure I want everything with him too. Who knows if I'll be good at it? But goddamn it if I don't want to try.

CHAPTER FIFTY-THREE

TREVOR

"Please tell me you're kidding, Miles." Leaning back in my office chair, I stare at the towering suit standing in front of me. I shake my head as his face moves into a grimace.

"Afraid not. That potluck yesterday wiped almost everyone out. Jessica's the latest one to call in sick."

The irony of food poisoning taking out the entire team isn't lost on me. The only reason I was spared is because I was out of the office for Willa's thirty-seven-week appointment yesterday. Despite it all, I feel completely betrayed by the universe. How could the one stipulation in my contract collide with the one exemption *right now*? It's the middle of May, I've only been off the flex schedule for a week, and Willa's already having Braxton Hicks. This is a fucking nightmare and a half.

"Look, I know it's horrible timing for you, but even I have to jump in and help. It's only a two-day training. We fly out to Salt Lake City tonight, and I booked return flights immediately after we end on Thursday."

I'm so pissed off I can't even speak, so I sit with my jaw clenched, eyes roving over my workspace. It takes me a couple of seconds to accept that I have to do this. I signed a contract saying I'd step in for this exact scenario. Walking back through everything he just said, I get stuck on a word. "Almost everyone? Who else didn't get sick?"

"You and Marla. That's it."

Of fucking course.

"It's too late of notice to pull someone from a regional office, so I'll be tagging along too," he continues. "The Salt Lake office is a big one. We'll need all hands on deck."

I blow out small puffs of air as I come to terms with having to leave tonight, knowing Willa could go into labor any day. "I get it. Are you good with me leaving now to pack?"

"Yep. I'm headed out myself. Emailed you the itinerary. Flight leaves at eight."

Nodding, I log out of my workstation, and by the time I look back up, he's gone. It's just past ten now. I'm not even going to give Willa a heads-up. I'll just show up at the studio with flowers in hand and groveling.

When I walk into Framed Orchid, Willa's standing on a step stool, securing the top of a summer themed backdrop. My heart stops, and I drop the bouquet of tulips at the empty front desk before rushing across the studio. "I swear you're gonna be the death of me, Gem," I grunt, wrapping an arm around her legs. "Why the hell are you up there?"

"Emily stepped out for a coffee run, and I need this up for the rest of my popsicle mini shoots today." She puts a hand on my shoulder and steps down.

Her independent streak has been off the charts the last couple of weeks. Between nesting and insomnia, it's like the bigger her stomach gets, the more determined she is to do things on her own. Being back home every night this past week has been an adjustment for both of us. I had to threaten to strap her to the bed so she'd relax, which only made her push me down for a steamy quickie on the couch. The libido's back too.

"Don't you have interns for this?" I ask, helping her down.

She throws one hand on her hip while rubbing her belly with

the other. "Do you see an intern, Tre? What are you even doing here?"

"Saving your life, apparently." I pull her toward me and hold her in my arms. She tilts her head back expectantly for my kiss. Our lips meet in a casual sweep, and I'm dreading telling her why I'm here.

She pulls back, eyes narrowing. "What's wrong?"

"What makes you think something's wrong?"

"You kiss weird when something's wrong. What is it?"

"Can I show you the flowers I brought you first?"

"Tre...

"Okay." I take a deep breath. "I have to fly out tonight for a training in Utah."

Willa's eyes bug out of her head. "You're leaving? *Now*?"

"The team's all sick from the potluck I missed out on yesterday, so Miles, Marla, and I have to step up."

Her face drops, and the slump of her body in my arms wrecks me. I never want to be the reason for the terrified look on her face right now. "How long?"

"Two days. I fly out tonight and get back Thursday night."

"I could have the baby by then," she whines.

"Okay, well, do me a favor and don't," I tease, but she's too busy staring blankly at my chest to return it. Willa squirms out of my hold and trudges back to the step stool. "Gem—"

"I'm putting it away!" she snaps, folding it up. Her cute little pregnancy waddle as she walks to the back room would make me smile if it wasn't for the frustration steaming off her. I take a few quick steps back to the front to grab the flowers and meet her at the doorway. She glances at the tulips with a scowl, but I give her a little smile, hoping to melt some of the frostiness. I hold out the bouquet with a bite of my lip, and that's when she breaks into a little smile. Tugging her to me, I wait for her eyes to meet mine. "You better train the hell out of those people and get back to me ASAP, Trevor."

"First plane back. I promise."

"God, you better not miss the birth of our child..."

"Not for the fucking world."

Joining Miles for a quick dinner when we landed didn't seem like a bad idea until we bumped into Marla and he invited her along. Now I'm trying to network with my supervisor while fuming inside from being stuck at a table with my ex. She keeps trying to engage me in conversations I don't want to have. We've just placed our food orders, and I'm kicking myself for not getting it to-go.

"So, Trevor"—Miles turns to me—"tell me about your thoughts on the EdTechU expansion."

EdTechU has been slowly expanding into the Educational Technology market overseas. Everyone's been making bets on the next region we'll land in. I take a sip of my water to clear some of the aggression from my throat. "I think Germany's the next logical step, considering how well the expansion into the UK was."

"I think we'd do better in Spain, personally, but Germany's a smart choice too." Miles's entirely too loud ringtone blasts from his shirt pocket. He squints at the screen as he brings it to his face. "This is about tomorrow. I'll be right back."

Marla's mouth is moving before he even steps away. "You've been to Germany, right, Trevor?" she asks as if she doesn't already know the answer. Rage buzzes in my ears. This ploy she's using for interaction is bullshit.

I nod curtly and slip my phone out of my pocket. "Yup. Been to France too... Excuse me. I have to check this." There's nothing on the screen but a thumbs-up text from Hunter, confirming he can check in on Willa at the studio over the next couple of days. I open it anyway, acting like I've just received a message from on high. If it gets me out of her direct line of questioning, I have no qualms about faking it. A text from Willa buzzes through during my charade.

WILLA

You sent my sister over here to babysit me?

TREVOR

Nope. Just to make sure you weren't climbing anymore ladders.

WILLA

It was a damn step stool!

ME

Same diff.

WILLA

She showed up with bags, Tre...

And she won't shut up.

And now Hunter's texting me

ME

Just go to bed early, Gem.

WILLA

Call off your hounds, Jones.

ME

Nope 😳

I can't help but chuckle at her outrage. Ashlie said she'd check in on her tonight, but turning it into a sister sleepover makes me feel a little more at ease. If something happens, Willa won't be alone.

"You really love her, don't you?"

My spine snaps rigidly at her voice. I'm about ready to stalk off to my hotel room, dinner order be damned. The last strand of patience I have is stretched so tightly, it's threatening to snap. When I look at Marla, she has an easy smile on her face, and it catches me off guard. "Completely," I say before clearing my throat, eyes dropping back to my phone.

"Good. I'm happy you're happy, Trevor. I—" Marla stops mid-sentence, and I look at her again as her well wishes filter through my annoyance. "I'm sorry. About everything. I know that's not even close to making things right, and I've been trying to give you space like you asked. But I just really feel like I owe you this apology. I treated you horribly. You didn't deserve anything I put you through. I know it doesn't mean much coming from me, and I'm not looking to give any excuses. I just want you to know that I'm sorry, and I'm genuinely so happy you're happy."

Nodding slowly, I accept her words for what they are, but I'm unwilling to give her an inch. I could say thank you back, but what's the point? It would only get her hopes up that we can be friendly. I appreciate the apology, but it doesn't change anything. It might feel a little better on the inside, hearing her take the responsibility she refused to take before. Other than that, I have no interest in revisiting it or establishing an amicable environment with her. It's in the past, and she needs to leave it there.

The waiter's upturned palm carrying sizzling plates arranged on a tray prompts me to sit up straighter and flash him a friendly smile. He doesn't know how welcome his interruption is. Just as he sets the last plate on the table, Miles slides back into his chair, and I'm spared from having to address Marla for the rest of the night.

Willa's video chat is connecting before I even lock my hotel room door. She answers with a sleepy yawn, her phone positioned so I can see her body stretched out on the bed, on my pillow, in my T-shirt. My empty arms ache. *I should be next to her. Not here, and definitely not now.* "Were you asleep?"

"No." She yawns again. "Close though. I was waiting up for your call. How was dinner with your ex?" Willa's eyebrows wiggle playfully, and the ache in my arms shoots to my chest.

"The best." I roll my eyes, and she laughs at my sarcastic tone. "It was fine. She apologized for everything."

"And now you're getting back together so you can have all her Trevy babies."

"The fuck I am." I chuckle, a grimace scrolling down my face. "I'm taken."

"Damn right." Her yawn eats up the last word.

"I love you, Gem. I'm gonna let you get to sleep."

"Love you too..." Her mouth sets in a scowl as her hand rubs the side of her belly.

"You okay?" I try to keep the panic out of my voice, but she clocks it just the same.

"I'm fine, Tre." She scrunches her nose and rubs her stomach again. "She's just really active tonight. I'm okay."

"I hate this."

"Yeah, me too. I'll talk to you in the morning."

"Love you."

"Tre?"

"Yeah, I'll stay on while you fall asleep."

Willa snuggles up to my pillow and gives me one last sleepy smile as she closes her eyes. She's out within minutes, but I plug in my phone and stay on the video chat, just watching her. I take it all in—the way her lips part while the heavy breath of deep sleep pushes through them, the curled shadow of her eyelashes on her cheekbones, the peaceful expression on her face. All of it tears my heart to guilty shreds from not being home. I fall asleep to the soft sounds of her breathing, and when my alarm goes off in the morning, she's still sleeping peacefully on the screen.

CHAPTER FIFTY-FOUR

WILLA

"Oh, so you're ignoring me now?" Hunter quips, strolling into Framed Orchid. I roll my eyes at the stupid-ass smirk on his face. It's a little past three, and between Hunter, Ashlie, and Trevor, my phone's been pinging nonstop. I'm grumpy, sore, and woke up with indigestion. It's still waging war this afternoon.

"Don't start with me." I take a deep breath through the lingering burn that slides across my stomach. "My back hurts, and I've been dealing with your fiancée all night."

Hunter's face drops as he whips toward Emily at the front desk. "How long has she been breathing like that?"

"Eh, since she came in." Emily shrugs. All the humor drains from his body. I'd cuss her out for being a snitch, except another pull across my stomach makes me press my hand into my bump with a groan.

"Willa, you need to go home..." he says.

"Or I can stay here and take care of my business, and *you* can go home."

His arms cross over his chest as he continues to block the door. "Naw."

"*Ugh*! Go home, Hunter! I'm fine." With my free hand, I reach behind my back and clutch at the aching there.

Hunter smirks. I'd punch him in the face if my hands weren't occupied. "Naw, I'll take you home though. You shouldn't drive when you're in labor."

"I'm. *Not*. In. Labor," I grit out, slumping against the wall for support.

"Willa, how long have you been grabbing at your stomach like this?" Hunter's serious face is back.

"Off and on since last night. Nothing's consistent. She just has no room in there, and her dad is a fucking giant. It burns whenever she moves."

He slips his phone out of his back pocket and taps away. When my next groan turns into a whimper, he glances up, eyes circling around me like he's trying to calculate something before tapping some more. "Get your stuff, Willa."

"No," I growl. "I have work to do."

"Yeah. Like having a baby. You're in early labor."

"*Okay, Hunter*," I scoff. "What do you know?"

"I remember when my mom was in labor with my sister. Anyway, let's go." Hunter turns to Emily. "Ashlie said you have a maternity plan for this?"

She nods slowly, her eyes growing as she realizes what's happening. "Yeah. We have the guest photographers all set up in our system."

"Great. You can handle the studio?"

"*I* can handle the studio, Hunter," I say through gritted teeth. "I'm only thirty. Seven. Weeks-*uh*." The words stutter out of me, followed by a stifled wail. "It's too early."

He ignores me and waits for Emily's nod.

"Good. Don't bother Willa about anything studio related until you hear from Ashlie. We don't want her stressed about work through all of this."

Emily shakes out her shoulders and sits up in her chair. "Got it. We have it covered."

"Where's your stuff?" Hunter asks me. I stare at him, annoyed that he walked into my studio, bossed around my employee, and called out the cramping I've been dealing with for what it really is —labor pain. As the realization dawns on me, the intensity of my glare fizzles out, and I relent.

"It's all at my desk," I say, turning toward the back of the studio.

"I got you. Car's unlocked."

"Did Trevor put you up to this? I'm fully capable of getting my own shit."

Hunter's eyes dance with mirth as he shakes his head. "You think we don't all know that, Willa? You're a fucking badass. Now get in the damn car. You're not doing this"—he waves a hand toward my bump—"on your own." Stepping closer, he puts a comforting hand on my shoulder and levels me with a stare that's equal parts compassion and assertiveness. "You're not alone anymore," he says softly. "Stop acting like it." Tears well in my eyes, and I don't even bother to wipe them away as I nod. Hunter pulls me into a quick hug and whispers, "I've already talked to Trev. The only thing you need to worry about is my niece, alright? I got you."

CHAPTER FIFTY-FIVE

TREVOR

Apparently, massive Utah snowstorms in May aren't completely unheard of. We had to end the training a couple of hours early due to the approaching storm. Getting from the office, back to the hotel, and then to the airport was such a headache. All the ride share apps were canceling on us left and right like we were problematic celebrities. Once we made it to the airport, any extra time we would have gained from leaving the training early was eaten up by waiting for available drivers.

HUNTER

Just saw about the storm. Your flight still on?

ME

As far as I know. How is she?

HUNTER

Bruh, she's grumpy as hell.

ME

Bro…

HUNTER

> She's okay. Still at home. Contractions are
> tearing up her back, but they're not
> consistent.

Shit. My worst fucking nightmare is unfolding in front of me, and I can't do a damn thing about it. I promised her I wouldn't miss this, promised I'd be there for her every step of the way. It's eating me up inside that I'm failing at the one thing I told her to count on.

Miles, Marla, and I get through security and rush down the terminal, only to find a huge uproar at our gate.

"Sorry, folks. We'll have hotel vouchers at the desk, but all flights are grounded as of five minutes ago."

Fuck. This isn't happening. There's no fucking way this is real life right now.

"Well"—Miles claps my shoulder—"guess we're here another night..."

I turn to my colleagues, and my rage makes both Marla and Miles take a step back.

"Fuck this shit." Hitching my bag on my shoulder, I stalk back the way we came.

Hurried footsteps follow me, and Marla grabs my wrist. "Trevor, where are you—?"

"I'm renting a car!"

"You can't drive in this."

"I'm from Nebraska, Marla." I rip my arm out of her grasp. "You think I don't know how to drive in the damn snow?"

"The storm's due to stop by morning. We'll get one of the first flights out." Miles tries to appeal to my logic.

"I don't have that kind of time. I shouldn't even fucking be here, Miles! Willa's in labor. I have to get to LA, and the more time I waste standing here talking to you two, the angrier I get." Turning around, I stomp through the terminal. The singular thought in my head propelling me forward is getting to Willa, no matter what it takes.

I convince the rental desk that I'm aware of the liabilities of driving in the storm, pay the outrageous insurance fees, and finally settle into an SUV. This feels like the first breath I've been able to take all day. Early labor with first babies can take days. I remember this from all the documentaries Maya made me watch growing up. There's still a chance I can make it in time. I reach for my phone and press Hunter's contact info. As soon as the call connects, I hear Willa groaning, and it punches me in the gut. *We're supposed to do this together. I need to get to her.*

"Heyyy," Ashlie's voice makes me pull my phone back to look at the number I just called.

"Hey, so my flight got canceled."

"Shit. Trev—"

"I know. I just rented a car, and I'm on my way. It'll be about twelve hours with the storm. Can I talk to her?"

"I don't know that she'll do much talking, but I'll put the phone up to her ear."

Another wail, and everything inside me crumbles. Panic shreds through my composure. I hit the steering wheel, trying to expel some of my frustration. *This is my fucking fault.*

"Tre..." Willa's shaky voice rattles through me. "I don't think I can—" Another whine interrupts her sentence. *"I need you."* Her voice breaks, and an avalanche of guilt collapses in on me. This incredibly strong woman of mine is telling me she needs me, for maybe the first time since all of this began, and I'm not fucking there.

"I—Willa, listen to me, okay? I'm on my way. I'm driving, but I'm coming straight to you. Ashlie's going to keep me updated. I'll be there as soon as I can. I love you, Gem."

"Always will?" she asks tearfully, just tearing what's left of my heart to shreds.

"Al—" My voice cracks, eyes burning. "Always."

"Hey, Trev," Ashlie says. "You on the road yet?"

"As soon as I hang up. Keep me posted, Ashlie, about every-thing. Contractions, water breaking, when you leave for the hospital. I'll have my phone hooked up to the car system. I need to know everything."

"Of course. Drive safe, okay?"

I nod like she can see me, and the line goes dead in the middle of another groan from Willa. After hooking up my playlist, I set the GPS and barrel through the worst of the raging storm. It's bad out here, but the skills ingrained from growing up in the Midwest winters are like muscle memory.

By the time I've reached the halfway point, my body's stiff, and my mind is in shambles. Ashlie just let me know that they're taking Willa to the hospital after laboring at home for six hours. I feel like the worst kind of failure right now. It's not healthy to think like this, but driving through a pitch-black snowflake vortex for hours has given my mind way too much freedom to wallow in the guilt eating me up inside. I've already crossed into Nevada, and while the snow cleared a while ago, I still have six more hours on the road, at least.

Every single time I've had to stop for gas, food, or the bathroom, I've rushed in and out to get back on the road as fast as possible. My mind is focused on getting home, in between the berating thoughts screaming louder in my head with each update from Ashlie.

It's just after one in the morning when I stop in Vegas to fill up and stretch my legs. When I walk into the convenience store, I come face-to-face with a wall full of stuffed animals wearing *Welcome to Fabulous Las Vegas* shirts. The slot machine flashing rapidly in the corner briefly distracts me from my relentless mental battle. *I'm about to be a dad.* An actual father to a living, breathing person. My eyes land right on a pink giraffe, and I smile as Willa's amused scowl appears in my head. *You're going to spoil her.* My breath stutters as I reach for it, and I'm suddenly frozen next to the energy drink stand. *This is really happening.* The anticipation for the last nine months is about to be realized, and while I'm up for the challenge, I don't know that I've stopped to think about how much everything's about to change. I don't get a chance to think about it now, either, because my phone rings in my pocket. Seeing Willa's name flash across the screen drops me back into a panic.

I press the little green phone, and before I can say a word, Willa's going in on me. "I hate you so much right now, Trevor Jones!" She makes a low whine, akin to something caught in a trap, and my heart shatters.

"Gem—"

"I'm not done. I hate you so much"—she says through what sounds like gritted teeth—"I'm making you sleep on our hard-ass couch for a week."

"Willa—"

"They want to shove a needle as long as your fucking arm in my back, Trevor! They want to impale me to make the pain go away, and the only thing I can think about are the stupid dimples on your stupid, handsome face."

I chuckle despite the anguish twisting my insides. "So, you finally admit I'm handsome..."

"Yeah, and I"—she screeches, and I pull the phone from my ear with a grimace—"I hate that most of all.'

"I love you, Willa."

"Alway—*ughhh*." Her voice trembles, and I swallow back the thick coil of emotion in my throat so I don't break down in the middle of this convenience store.

Ashlie comes on the line, talking so fast my feet match her cadence as I head to the register. Willa's only at five centimeters, but she's so exhausted, they want to give an epidural so she can rest. I set the giraffe and an energy drink on the counter, pressing my phone against my shoulder as I reach for my wallet. The clerk watches me like I just hopped out of a UFO. I'm sure I look a wreck.

Back on the road, hope sparks in my chest at the four-hour mark. *I might actually make it.* Three hours left, and I'm a little worried I haven't heard anything from the hospital. Between Hunter and Ashlie, I've been updated every hour or two, but it's been hours since I left the convenience store. No calls. No texts. I reach over to the radio display and pull up Ashlie's number. It rings for the longest eternity before going to voicemail, and I hang up and try Hunter. Same thing. Thirty minutes later, I'm cussing as I toggle between calling the two people with the only information on my wife. *Shit. Not my wife.* She feels like my wife though, in every way that matters. *Fuck.* I drag a hand down my face and pin my eyes to the road. There's no time to unpack any of that right now.

By the time I get to the hospital parking lot, I'm a motherfucking mess. My stagnant muscles are screaming as I park the car. I grab my phone and the pink giraffe, and despite the exhaustion settled into my body, I run. The elevator takes two seconds too long, so I sprint up the three flights of stairs to the maternity floor. When I reach the nurses' station, they look at me like the madman I feel like inside.

"Willa Willis?" My breath comes out in heaving waves. I gulp as I take in the bubblegum pink strip of paint across the white walls.

"You are...?"

"Trevor Jones. I'm the—"

"Dad!" A short nurse with graying coils peeks around her computer, smiling. "Willa will be so relieved. Room 315."

I nod, skipping the pleasantries as my adrenaline sends me rushing down the hall.

Room 309. A monitor beeps rapidly behind the closed door.

Room 311. I narrowly miss a nurse rushing into the chaos.

Room 313. A baby wails, filling me with dread.

Room 315. I bust through the door, hoping to hear screaming, crying, *anything*. But no.

Silence.

My eyes sweep the darkened room, landing on a sleeping Willa, still very much pregnant. Ashlie's snoring lightly, lying across the bench under the window with her head in Hunter's lap. He's sitting up, head slumped back against the wall, knocked out.

With a relieved sigh, I close the door quietly behind me, and the click of the latch makes my last thread of composure snap. Tears stream down my face, relief mixed with mental and physical fatigue. I slump against the door, covering my mouth with my hand to stifle the ridiculous noises ripping out of my throat. *I made it. I didn't miss everything.*

"Sweetheart, are you crying?" The amused lilt in Willa's voice makes me pop my head up.

Wiping my eyes with an emotion-filled chuckle, I nod quickly. "Yeah. I'm just—thank you for still being pregnant." I shuffle over to her, and she homes in on the stuffed animal in my hand. "I couldn't help it," I explain, sticking it on the table next to her hospital bed.

"You were about to be in so much trouble..." The IVs dangle from her hands as she holds her arms out to me, welcoming me home. *She's my home.* I lean down and interlace my lips with hers. Every shattered piece of me knits back together as I dust kisses on the swell of her cheekbones, the tip of her nose, her lips. This silent apology is all I can muster right now, and she accepts it, clinging to me.

"I didn't think I'd make it," I whisper, choking back emotion as her soft fingers caress my cheek. "I thought I was going to miss it all."

"I know you, Tre." Tears glisten in her eyes, and she shakes her head with a smile. "You wouldn't miss this."

"Not for the fucking world, Gem." I kiss her again, and she clutches to me as if she's scared I'll evaporate through her fingers. *I'll never leave her side again.* "Let's meet our little sweet pea."

Welcome Home Baby Lyla!

THE GROUP CHAT

ASHLIE

My niblings miss me, I can feel it. GIMME MY
BABIES!

WILLA

Call my child a nibling again…

KAYLA

You could just have your own babies instead
of hounding us for ours.

HUNTER

Look at my little sister sticking up for me!

KAYLA

I take it back…

HUNTER

ASHLIE

You all promised daily auntie pics.

TREVOR

image unavailable

ASHLIE

Trev, for the love of everything in this world, get rid of that damn Pro-Phone.

TREVOR

✨No✨

CHASE IS CALLING
MISSED CALL FROM CHASE

CHASE

Ahhh, sorry! Both boys had blow-outs. Up the back. Dropped my phone getting them in the tub.

HUNTER

🤮 Bruh, TMI.

WILLA

Lyla got me good last night at dinner. Bright yellow. I swear she saves it for when I'm wearing my favorite pajamas.

HUNTER HAS LEFT THE CHAT
ASHLIE ADDED HUNTER TO THE CHAT

ASHLIE

Naw, Hunt. This is what you're asking for. Get used to baby shit.

HUNTER

🖕

TREVOR

Are the boys out of size 2 diapers yet? Lyla's almost there.

CHASE

😭We just sized up. They'll be driving soon.

KAYLA

🙄 Don't mind him. We had to buy bigger socks for the boys and he's having a hard time with it.

CHASE

It's all happening too fast. They used to fit in
my hands!

HUNTER

Don't let him watch that penguin movie, or
he'll never stop crying.

CHASE

That happened ONE TIME…

CHAPTER FIFTY-SIX

TREVOR

September

"Uh-oh!" Bryant calls when I get off the elevator. "Here comes Mr. Reed Award."

Head shaking, I chuckle as I pass his office. Across the hallway, Jared shouts from his desk, "You've only been back for a month, and *bam*! The most coveted award in the technology sector."

"We are not worthy!" Bryant chants.

"Oh, *mighty* Trevor. Teach us your ways!" Jared bows his head.

Bryant and Jared set their offices up in a way that they can see and talk to each other without having to do more than lean back in their chairs. I swing my head back and forth, trapped between their good-natured taunting. "For starters, you have to actually *do* your job…" I say, choosing to stop at Jared's door.

"Sounds fake," Jared scoffs, while Bryant boos at me.

"It's clearly rigged. Good looks can get you anywhere these days," Bryant jokes.

Chase and I got word about receiving the Innovations in Tech Sales Award right around the time my paternity leave ended a month ago. It turns out the automated reporting system we developed as a last-ditch effort to help our new associates wasn't as simplistic as we thought. The chief information officer had summoned us to her office, where we found out she'd sent our work to the board at the Edward Reed Technology Foundation. They created an entirely new category just to give us this award. Honored doesn't even begin to cover how I feel. Chase and I were featured in yesterday's newsletter from corporate, and as soon as the congratulations died down, Bryant and Jared laid it on thick. This is just the tip of the iceberg with these two.

"The Office Slacker Award nominations were already full," I say, tapping Jared's doorframe with my palm and turning to look at Bryant over my shoulder. "Nice pictures, by the way."

Bryant laces his fingers behind his head, leaning back in his chair with a hearty laugh. "Oh, he's got *jokes*?"

"Nah, but I do have work to do." I give a head nod and stroll down to my office.

"Come on, Trev. It's Friday," Jared calls after me. "Live on the wild side!"

Laughing, I flip on the light and drop my phone and laptop bag on my desk. I settle into my chair while my computer boots up, and my phone vibrates with a "good morning" picture of my Lyla Belle. Her sleepy smile, complete with a singular dimple in her left cheek, is offset by her copper-colored curls sticking straight up like they do on most mornings. I don't know how it's possible, but my heart bursts every time I see her deep brown doe eyes. Lyla Isabelle Willis-Jones is the perfect mix of Willa and me.

WILLA

Morning Daddy!

ME

There's my sweet pea 😍 Now where's her beautiful mama?

Willa sends back a picture of her rolling her eyes. She's getting back to her old self more and more every day, and all it does is make me fall deeper in love. This is the Willa who had me crushing for years, only now I'm living the best of both worlds. I get to kiss and hold her. Tell her exactly how I feel. She only gives me a little bit of a hard time about it now. No sex though. At least, not yet, anyway. She hasn't felt ready. With all the changes her body has endured over the last year, I want to give her the time she needs. But it's getting hard to hide how much I miss our physical connection. Her body was incredibly sexy before—curvy and full in all the right places—but now, it's a goddamn masterpiece. A shrine that was the lifeblood of my most precious treasure, and I'm near frothing at the mouth to fall to my knees and worship every single inch.

ME:

So sexy.

WILLA

Flattery will get you everywhere right now. Lyla just puked in my hair.

ME

My sweet pea would never...

WILLA

You two probably conspired against me before you left this morning.

ME

It was all her idea, Gem. Love you.

WILLA

You better.

ME

MILES FELT SO BAD ABOUT THAT SALT LAKE TRIP, HE'S keeping me on local flex for several months so I can be close to home. I told him it wasn't necessary, water under the bridge and all that, but he insisted. Who am I to refuse that gift? Coming home to my girls every night is the best thing I've ever experienced. Exhaustion and all, I wouldn't change a thing.

Willa's slumped against the kitchen counter, wiping the back of her hand across her forehead, when I drop my bags by the door. She doesn't look up, instead closing her eyes as her head falls back, stretching out her shoulders. I take a few steps through the living room and wrap my arms around her, hugging her from behind. She melts into me when I nudge her hair off her shoulder and kiss her neck.

"Hi, Gem." I press kisses along her skin, and she lets out the lightest moan. "Rough day?"

Leaning her head back into my chest, she nods but doesn't say anything. I walk her to the couch, keeping my arms wrapped around her waist, and pull her into my lap facing me, waiting for her to let me in. "Lyla's teething, for sure. Soaked through five bibs. The good ones with the waterproof layer in the middle. And she was ornery as hell. She just now went down for a nap."

"Come here." I sweep her twists behind her and anchor her head in my hands, pulling her forward until our lips meet.

She pulls back abruptly and shakes her head. "I still have puke in my hair. I haven't had time—"

"I don't fucking care," I mumble, crashing into her lips. As I try to keep the heat out of my kiss, she returns it like she's been thinking about it all day too. And when she shifts to straddle my lap, I'm done for. My hands grip hard on her waist, sliding slowly down to her hips to bracket her over the bulge growing in my pants. She scratches my scalp with her fingernails as she urges me closer, my hips bucking in response. Willa stills, and I want to smack myself in the head.

"I'm not... I don't think I'm ready." She looks into my eyes, and I track the vulnerability as it slides onto her face.

Am I disappointed? Hell yes, but I don't want her to feel bad about it. "It's okay. Take the time you need. I'm not going anywhere."

She kisses me again, just as feverishly as before, with an added roll of her hips. *Fuck.* "You keep grinding into me like that though, and I'm gonna need to excuse myself."

Willa sits back with a sigh. "I know. I'm sorr—"

"Nope. You're not apologizing for this. You don't owe me a thing. I'll be ready whenever you are."

Lyla's cry crackles through the baby monitor next to us, and frustration slumps through Willa's body. She drops her head against my chest and groans. "How can I ever be ready when she won't *fucking* sleep? I love her. Really, I do, but I'm about to send that baby monitor right out the window. I look like garbage. Smell like puke. And every time she cries, this intense demand to fix it twists in my stomach. I just..."She finally takes a breath, and I give her a small smile.

"I'll get Lyla. You jump in the shower." I give her a quick peck on her forehead, but she doesn't move from my lap. "Unless you want help in the shower...?"

Willa's laugh makes me smile, and I smooth my hands over her back as she leans into me. "I don't think I'm ready for that either," she says, even with the slightest movement of her hips.

I lean forward, and she shudders at my whispered breath in her ear. "I know you can feel what you're doing to me right now. You're gonna have to walk away first. There's no way in hell I'm leaving this spot while you're grinding all over me. I want you too much."

She takes another deep breath, bites her lip like she's contemplating taking it all back, and slowly rolls off my lap. If my dick could talk, the protest would be louder than a jet engine.

I take a few deep breaths before heading into the baby's room, not bothering to turn the light on. Hearing her cry breaks my heart too, so I quickly scoop her in my arms. As soon as I do, her whining turns to happy babbling, and all is calm inside. I shift her in my arms to grab the pink Las Vegas giraffe from her crib before heading back to the living room.

CHAPTER FIFTY-SEVEN

WILLA

"Hey, sweet pea," Trevor coos at Lyla when he enters the nursery. I melt. Goo on the floor, completely dissolved. I know I should hop in the shower and get ready, but hearing the love for our daughter come out of Trevor so easily always pins me in place. He doesn't hold back his feelings about being a father, and Lyla has him wrapped around her cute little fingers. "I'm jealous you got to spend all day with Mama."

Lyla laughs, and I melt again. *What the hell have these two done to me?* For the last few months, my insides have been all ooey-gooey. I can't control it.

"I know, Lyla Belle, but you can't *spit up* on her." Trevor walks out of the room and smirks right at me as if he knew I would still be standing here listening to him talk to the baby. "She *is* beautiful, huh?" he asks Lyla in a high-pitched, cutesy voice, eyes still locked on me.

Biting my lip, I walk to the bedroom, ready to wash this baby puke out of my twists. It's about time for Ashlie to pick me up anyway. Just as I'm zipping up my sheer lilac dress, the front door slams.

"OH MY GOD!" Ashlie's voice travels through the closed

door, and I rush to the living room in a panic. *Where's the baby?* "Have you seen the news?"

Lyla's calmly settled on Trevor's chest, babbling to herself. My heart's pounding so hard, I could slap my sister. "Stop yelling," I huff, arms settling across my chest. Ashlie grabs the remote and turns on the TV, but I'm too busy juggling glances between her and the baby to worry about whatever the hell has her dramatic ass in a tizzy.

News Reporter: Carter Zane, a partner at the prestigious Johnson and Associates, has been arrested on charges of felony assault and indecent exposure. In the complaint filed by the Los Angeles County District Attorney's Office this morning, Zane has been accused of multiple assaults spanning three years, involving three women identified in court documents as Jane Doe one, two, and three."

My head whips to the TV, mouth gaping as I watch shit-for-brains being led from his office in handcuffs. He struggles as they try to duck him in the back of a waiting patrol car, hitting his head on the door.

Johnson and Associates has been a champion against domestic violence in the community for fifty years. The charges follow an Equal Employment Opportunity Commission investigation into allegations stating Zane sent explicit photos of himself from company devices. According to court documents, this investigation prompted the anonymous victims to come forward. We've reached out to Johnson and Associates for comment but have yet to hear back. This is a developing story.

I cackle so loudly, it makes Lyla jump. *Dumbass.* Caught sending puny dick pics from the law firm. In all the messages he sent me, I'm glad I never had to see *that* again.

"Should I turn in the mall video?" Ashlie asks through her giggles. "Maybe they'll put his ass under the jail."

"Nope." I laugh, heading back toward the bedroom. He stopped messaging me after our run-in at the mall. The video we have is pretty damning, but I've moved on and he's clearly being taken care of. "I just never want to hear his name again. Let me get my shoes."

Trevor is hooking up a gaming system to the TV when I come back to the living room. Ashlie and Hunter are on the sofa, fawning over baby Lyla with animated smiles on their faces. Auntiehood suits Ash, and Hunter's taken the uncle role to an extreme. I regularly get demanding messages from both of them requesting baby pictures during the day. It's annoying and adorable, but nice to know my little village of people is legit. For the first time in forever, I actually believe I'm not alone.

"Ash, stop hogging the baby!" Hunter leans over her lap, putting his face in front of Lyla.

"Get your big-ass head out of her face, Hunt. You get to see her all night."

"That doesn't mean you get all the quality time right now."

I step forward and reach for Lyla, who's fussing tugs at my insides like the last dissolvable stitch in a healing wound. "How about you two have your own baby and stop fighting over mine?" Cradling her in my arms, I sway my hips in a figure eight, hoping to settle her before the wailing starts again.

"Sounds good to me." Hunter's eyebrows dance suggestively at Ashlie, who rolls her eyes back at him.

"Don't get him started, Wills. Do you know how many times a day he tells me Lyla needs a cousin?"

"Five?" Trevor offers from across the room, squatting low to reach behind the entertainment center.

"Today it was seven," she says.

"That's it? I need to up my game then." Hunter flashes her a grin and sneaks in a kiss.

"Whatever." Ashlie uses Hunter's thigh to help her stand from the couch. "You ready, Wills? I'm not trying to keep you out too late. I know how much of a lightweight you are." She shimmies her shoulders as she backs up toward the door.

"What exactly are you getting her into, Ash?" Trevor asks.

I shake my head at him, switching to bouncing Lyla once the swaying proves ineffective. "It's just dress shopping and dinner. I don't know what her little happy dance is for."

"Oh, that's just a thing she does whenever she knows I'm right about us having a bab—"

"*Ugh*! Hunter!" Ashlie shoots him a glare, but the smile on his face grows.

Trevor slips the baby out of my arms, hands her to Hunter, and wraps his arm around me. She wails immediately, and I try to wiggle free. "Maybe I should stay. Lyla's been fussy like this all day and—"

"Nope." Trevor pulls me into his chest. "You deserve a break, Gem. She'll be fine." He tips his forehead down to mine with a smile. "Have fun, and good luck dress shopping." His kiss lingers on my lips, and as much as I say I'm not ready to be intimate with him, the tingling between my thighs reminds me it's a bold-faced lie. I am ready. I'm just scared.

"Okay, *Dad*. You gonna give her a curfew, too?" Ashlie mocks. We ignore the sass being thrown at us from the open door and lean in for another embrace.

"Damn, Lyla, you might have a sibling before we get you a cousin," Hunter says.

Pulling away, I scowl at Hunter. Mostly because he's cussing in front of my child, but also because I know—with absolute surety—I won't be having any more babies. I love Lyla more than anything, but I have zero interest in repeating any of this. One and done. *And another reason I'm scared*.

"Willa, come *onnnn*. We have to find you a gala dress before your social meter runs out."

"Okay, okay. Keep your pants on," I say to Ashlie before turning back to Trevor. "Don't you spoil her by letting her sleep on your chest." I poke him right in the spot I'm talking about. "She sleeps in the crib tonight, Tre."

"But what if she does the lip wobble thing?" He puffs out his lower lip, making a near identical face to Lyla's.

"She can barely lift her head. *You're* the boss."

"Mmm, nah, I'm pretty sure she is. She's even got Hunter whipped into shape." He tips his head over to the couch, where Hunter's making her laugh with another animated look on his usually schooled expression. *It really is adorable.*

"Willa!"

"I'm this close to staying home, Ash, I swear…"

"Nuh-uh. Nope. You're going." Trevor presses a peck to my lips and turns me toward the door. "I love you. Have fun. Relax."

"We will!" Ashlie cheers loudly, arm shooting into the air as if she's still on the cheer squad.

"Not likely." I scrunch my nose, and she bumps my hip before yanking me out the door.

"So, how's it going, really?" Ashlie asks, thumbing through the circular rack at Dress Designs Depot.

"Good. Really good."

"Like wedding bells on the horizon, good?" Her eyes glisten with excitement.

I grimace and shake my head. "No."

"You just said everything was going well. You don't want to be married?"

"It's not that I don't want to. It's complicated. The kid thing was something I dreamed about, but I always envisioned doing it by myself, just like everything else. I knew I'd have my own career and house and child." I pull a black sequined sheath dress from the rack and fold it over my arm. "As great as he is, it's an adjustment envisioning a life with a man I couldn't stand a year ago, who's more actively involved than I ever could have imagined possible from a partner."

"But you're already living it, Wills. You already have all of that, plus a life with him. You have for months."

"I know." I sigh. This sounds like a weak excuse, even to myself. It is one. Right before having Lyla, I had frequent thoughts of marriage. But now that everything's settling, doubts follow each hope for the future. "I can't imagine not having him in my life going forward."

"So, you do want to marry him?"

"I...don't know."

"Girl, don't give me that. You *do* know. You're just using your logic to crowd out your emotions. The question is *why*?"

"I'm just...not convinced he's going to like me..."

Ashlie cackles, fully doubling over and hissing like a cat trapped in a burlap sack.

"I'm serious, Ash! Now that the hormones are settling, and I'm starting to feel like myself again, who's to say he's going to keep feeling the same? I'm not the easiest person to live with— you know this. And don't get me started on how my body has changed. I find a new consequence of pregnancy every time I look in the mirror."

"Girl. I say this as your loving sister... You're the dumbest smart person I've ever met. That man has been captivated by you for years."

"Yeah. *Okay.*"

"Oh, you don't believe me? Hold this." Ashlie shoves her collection of dresses into my arms, and I have to steady my feet to keep from tipping over. "Look. He sent this the night we were at dinner before the music festival last year."

TREVOR

What do you think Willa would do if I called her pretty?

ASHLIE

Why don't you do it and find out?

TREVOR

Because I think she'd leave, and I really don't want that to happen.

ASHLIE

You could offer to walk her back to the hotel... win-win.

He did ask if he could walk me back to my room that night. I remember thinking I'd rather choke on a dry biscuit.

"How far back do you want me to go, Wills? He liked you before anything happened. It's been years. I doubt falling in love and sharing the cutest baby ever would change his mind about anything." She puts a hand on my shoulder and squeezes. "You had a baby, not a lobotomy. I'd say you were more authentic when you were pregnant than you ever have been. You didn't hide yourself, Wills. We got the full range of you for nine months, and it was beautiful."

I shrug and stare at the fancy gowns in my arms. "I'm just scared, I guess. Everything's great right now. I don't want that to change. Not when I'm finally..." My breath catches, my eyes darting to hers to see if she heard.

"*Happy*?" She gives a knowing smile. "It's okay to say you're happy. Saying the word won't make Trev and Lyla evaporate into the ether." She nudges my elbow. "Say it, girl. You're happy."

"I'm happy." I smile, the sequins gleaming with little starbursts as a watery puddle fills my eyes. Extremely happy. We've gotten to a comfortable place, Trevor and I, and I've never felt so cherished and understood and...happy.

Ashlie glances at her buzzing phone and rolls her eyes. "Not to burst your bubble, but Mom has been asking how you're doing." She holds it up, and reading the message takes away all the warm fuzzies I had a second ago.

"That's the whole problem, Ash. Instead of fixing things herself, she's trying to do it through you."

"That's what I told her when she called me yesterday, asking for pictures of Lyla. I didn't send any, by the way."

"*Oh*? Is the golden child feeling a little tarnished?"

"Maybe a little. Mom won't shut up about the wedding, and I'm so close to jumping on a plane and eloping."

"Is that why you're so interested in me getting married? To get Mom off your back?" I squint at her.

"No, Willa. Some of us just really like seeing you happy for once and want it to become a regular thing."

"You wanted to be the maid of honor, huh?" I tease.

"Shut up, *okay*?" she wails, fanning her face to keep her lovey-dovey tears from spilling. "I just *love* love, and you and Trevor are so cute. And yeah, maybe I do want to be the *MOH*." She pronounces it like *Moe*. "Is that a crime to want to be there for my sister?"

"Come on, *MOH*. Help me decide which one of these is gala worthy so I can go home." I giggle at how emotional she is over this hypothetical wedding. Trevor and I have only ever had one conversation about it, and he hasn't brought it up since. Maybe he's okay with things staying just as they are too.

CHAPTER FIFTY-EIGHT

TREVOR

"Fatherhood looks good on you, bruh." Hunter furiously taps the GamePlay controller, keeping his eyes on the TV screen.

"Bro, it *feels* good." My eyes drop to my Lyla Belle snuggled up on my chest, staring for so long I crash into a wall on the racing game we're playing. I can't help it. She's perfect. "Being a dad is my favorite thing."

Hunter leans back on the couch and smirks at the baby. "You think you'll have any more?"

"Nope. I mean, if Willa really wanted to, I'd do it. But I'm good with one."

He nods and tips his head over the back of the couch, stretching out his back. "Things still going good there?"

"Yeah." Except for the fact I want to lose myself in her, but she doesn't want me to touch her. "I think."

He pops his head up with a quirk in his brow. "What you mean, *you think*? I saw you two before she left. You're gonna tell me that's not good?"

"Man, I don't know. It's all fine, but we still haven't…" I hesitate to share this. I'm not into giving details of my sex life, even to friends.

"Haven't what? Joined bank accounts?"

"We haven't had sex since before the baby. She hasn't been ready, and I'm trying not to be that guy." Lyla shifts and turns her head to the other side, making the smiling koala on the back of her onesie wiggle side to side. "It's so hard, bro. All I can think about is getting that connection back, but she doesn't want it."

"Naw, this isn't about you."

"How do you know?"

"Because Willa and I have a lot of the same issues," he says. I tilt my head, eyebrows dipping. "Hey, I go to therapy too. I know I have problems." He laughs and sits forward to slide the controller onto the coffee table. "Bruh, trust me when I tell you, she's in her head, and it has nothing to do with you."

The front door opens, and I turn my head slowly, knowing I'm about to get in trouble. Willa takes one look at Lyla on my chest and crooks a pointed finger at me with an annoyed glare. I tip up a shoulder with a grimace. "Look at her!" I say defensively. "She's so comfy. How could I move her? Just look at how cute she is."

"She is pretty cute, Wills." Ashlie perches next to me on the sofa arm and sweeps a thumb over Lyla's curls. Hunter starts unhooking the game from the TV.

"Great," Willa says to Ash. "So when she wakes up in the middle of the night screaming, I'm calling you to remind you just how cute she can be."

Willa's purple sundress hugs her waist, and my heart thumps wildly, just imagining my hands all over her hips. I'm so thirsty for her, it's ridiculous. Like I'm kneeling at a trickling stream in the forest but too racked with fear of what's in the trees to guzzle for survival. I just need to know what's in the trees. I have to talk to Willa about this, make sure I'm not missing something.

Lyla stretches and blinks up at me before that lip quiver starts. Willa rushes over from the front door and swoops the baby in her arms, then walks her into the kitchen. I watch the sway of Willa's hips, hung up on her silhouette and what's underneath. *No panties*? "Did she eat anything while I was gone?" Willa asks, popping open the fridge for some thawed breastmilk. We have so much stored from her overproducing days, Willa's no longer breastfeeding. She slides the bottle into the warmer and sways those hips while she waits. *I need to get a fucking grip.*

"Nope." I clear my throat, swatting away my dirty thoughts. "She slept the whole time."

She puffs out a breath. "Of course she slept for you." She smiles down at Lyla. "Can Mama get that same courtesy sometimes? Hmm?"

Hunter packs up his gaming system and stands behind Ashlie. "Well, we'll leave you to it." He smirks at me, and Ashlie shoots a sly grin over to Willa. "Maybe check your condom for holes this time, though." He dodges a shove from Ashlie.

"Bye, Hunter." Willa rolls her eyes and, with warmed bottle in one hand and Lyla in the other, turns toward the nursery. "I'll see if I can get her back down," she calls over her shoulder. I lock the front door and take the temporary freedom to hop in the shower.

Adjusting the top of the towel around my waist, I step from the bathroom and nearly walk into Willa, her fingers clutched tightly. "Everything okay, Gem?" I ask nervously. The worry etched on her face sets me on edge. But then she steps toward me and smooths her hands over my ribs. Her touch sends a frisson across my body, igniting at the tips of her fingers. Gripping the back of her neck, I tug her toward me. I just need to get lost in this —*in her*—for a fraction of a second before my worries take over again. Her breathless moan into my mouth sends my body into overdrive, and I crush her to my chest. The towel on my hips threatens to fall, but how bad would that be, really?

"Tre," she whimpers around my lips when I graze her nipple through the sheer bodice of her dress.

We need to have this conversation, but I can't find the motivation to unlatch myself from her. "Is it me, Willa?" I ask, trailing my lips from hers, across her jaw, until I reach the coconut scented pulse on her neck. "Did I do something?"

"What?" She pulls away enough for me to see her mouth gaping. "No. You're...perfect, Tre. This is me. It's all me."

"Please talk to me. I'm floundering here."

She bites her lip, her eyes sliding down to the space between us. "I'm scared shitless."

"About what?"

She puffs her cheeks as she breathes out. "So many things." I brush a knuckle over her cheek, and she leans into my hand, shaking her head. "I don't want more kids."

"Great. Me either."

Her eyes pop wide, and she searches my face. "But before, when we were talking about future things, you said you always wanted to be a dad."

"Good thing it only takes one kid to make that happen." I smile, pulling her back to me. My thumbs caress her back. "What else?"

"How do you know there's anything else?"

"Because I know you, Willa," I say, dipping down to kiss the tip of her nose. "So tell me. What else?"

"I'm starting to feel like my old self again. I can be a lot to deal with..."

Staring into her eyes, I take in the full weight of her fear, and it's devastating. *She thinks I'll stop loving her.* "Gem, the people who convinced you that you're hard to love were never worthy in the first place." I press a kiss to her lips, then her chin, and down to her neck. "Loving you is easier than breathing," I whisper across her skin, smiling at the goosebumps rising. "I was crazy about you before Lyla. Now that I finally have you, there's not a chance in hell that's changing." Sucking on her neck earns me a moan filled with desire, and she tips her head back to give me better access. "What else?" I murmur. I know that's not it. Those things aren't what's actually stopping her from dragging me to bed like she used to.

"I'm not the same as before. My body, I mean. Things are

stretchier and lumpier." She looks down at her chest. "Lower. I just don't want you to be expecting an unblemished body."

I jut my head back and scan her face. *That's what this is all about?* She purses her lips, curling her hands into fists to quell that finger habit. She's worried I'm not attracted to her anymore, and I'm so speechless I do the first thing that crosses my mind. I spin her around and march her to the full-length mirror across from the bed.

When I rest my chin on her shoulder, we stare at each other through the reflection, neither of us blinking while we take each other in. I slide my hands over her shoulders, then caress the soft skin on her upper arms. "Willa, all I've wanted to do is melt with you, touch you, feel your sweet body shuddering around me. This body"—I whisper in her ear—"is a goddamn masterpiece. It handcrafted my greatest treasure. If you think, for one second, I don't love every single part of you...well, I guess I'm gonna have to show you." She inhales sharply, eyes fluttering when my hand slips under her dress. I trail up her thigh, stopping when I reach her ass. *No panties.* "Do you like when I touch you like this?"

She nods, biting her lip.

"Do you want me to keep touching you?"

She nods again, eyelids hooded to slits as my thumb brushes her nipple. Hissing a breath, she leans back against my chest, giving my towel the last bit of permission it needs to break free of the knot and drop to the floor. "I need your words."

CHAPTER FIFTY-NINE

WILLA

"Touch me," I gasp. Trevor slides my dress zipper down to the small of my back, his touch slow and tender, as if he's holding the most delicate stardust in the universe. He eases the straps over my shoulders, replacing every inch of fabric with light brushes of his lips before doing it all again to remove my bra. I've missed this feeling coursing through my body, his yearning for me skirting over my skin, piercing straight into my soul.

My dress drops to the floor next to his towel, and his fingertips trail down my sides until his hands grip my naked hips. "Just look at yourself. You're my fucking dream." His warm breath fans over the crest of my ear, and I shudder.

What the hell was my problem? Why keep myself from this— from him? "*Please* don't stop," I whine.

He pulls me against him, palming one breast while I grind into his erection. "You without panties has me hard as a rock, Gem." He walks me backward, and when his legs hit the bed, he sits on the mattress and pulls me into his lap. I melt into his sturdy chest supporting my back as his orange, clove cologne wraps around me. "Eyes on the mirror, Willa." His warm, broad hands glide over my stomach, sending hot shivers through my body. He tugs my nipples, and I gasp in surprise as he soothes them with a caress.

I silently thank the little pep talk from earlier because *this* is something I've been missing fiercely. He takes his time stroking my body, like I'm the first thing he's ever touched in his life. Each gentle swipe of his fingers awakens the desire I've been scared to unleash. "Tre, don't stop."

"Never, sweetheart." He nips at my neck, the sensual tug sending my eyes to the back of my head. A jolt of pleasure shoots right to my core. "Watch me worship you." Still tugging and soothing my nipples, he dusts kisses across my shoulder, and I rock my ass against him. "You're perfect." His hands slide to my thighs, easing them apart. When his thumb brushes my swollen clit, everything goes hazy. "Every single part of you." I cry out when Trevor dips a finger into my pussy. Then another. He lightly swirls my sensitive bud, his other hand grazing the front of my neck. Watching him touch me through the mirror is the hottest damn assault to my senses. It's all I can do not to shatter in his arms. With slow precision, he keeps his rhythm, sinking his fingers inside me, then circling my clit with the wetness. The pressure in my core winds tighter with each stroke, and my eyes fall closed in pleasure. He stops. "Eyes on me, beautiful." I pop them open, staring at him through the mirror as he lifts his fingers to his mouth and sucks my arousal. "*Goddamn*, Willa," he moans. "You're my favorite fucking flavor."

"*Oh shit*," I sigh, my cheeks flushing. I might come on his words alone. When he gets like this, sweet Trevor and his dirty words will always find a way to make me squirm. Squeezing my thighs, I try to find some relief. His hand darts to my leg, and he grips my thigh firmly, the carnality in his eyes absolutely feral.

"Open."

My legs fly apart, and just as fast, he's pumping two thick fingers inside me. His thumb swirls over my sensitive bud, and my head falls back with a moan, unable to control my racing breath from the relief unwinding inside me.

"You're the best thing to ever happen to me, Willa." He sucks the skin on my neck with a delicious pinch. "Now shatter for me."

I do, his name trilling from my throat as I writhe against his hand. Chest heaving, I ride wave after delicious wave through my climax. His fingers drag up to spoil my clit with my soaking arousal, dropping me into a cloudy haze. "Look at the mess you made," he tuts, holding up two glistening fingers. A growl rumbles in his chest as he slips them past my lips, nipping my tongue in place. "Suck." I lazily draw them into my mouth, still catching my breath as his dick twitches against my back. "Taste how perfect you are?"

Twisting my head around, I steal a deep, sweeping kiss, sampling my claim on his tongue. I plunge into his mouth as my fingers stroke his hardening length. It's indescribable how much I need him inside me right now. I break the kiss and push him back on the bed, then tuck my legs behind me on either side of him, still facing the mirror. Holding the base of his dick, I slide onto him. "God. *Fuck*. You feel incredible." He moans, fingers pressing into my hips tightly, eyes stuck to my ass bouncing in his lap.

"Watch, Tre," I say. "Watch how well I take all of you." Gripping his knees, I shift forward, taking him to the hilt. The fullness is a familiar ache I've been craving. He props on an elbow, watching me in awe through the mirror, as if he's never been inside me before. It sends glimmers to my heart, and I'm overcome with the urge to tell him what he means to me. "I love you, Trevor." I roll my hips, and he bucks to meet me with a grunt. My slow grind makes his eyes roll back, a guttural *fuck* leaving his gritted teeth as his hips stutter against my ass. "You're my all, my everything, and I never want to know a day without you." Pouring out the depths of my heart, I wind him into his own release, smiling at the rhythmic way he pulses inside of me. He clutches my waist with a possessive grip, pulling me back and holding me to his chest as he collapses on the bed.

He slips out of me and rolls us face-to-face. That vulnerability is back in his eyes as he brushes a thumb across my chin. "Please don't hide from me, Willa... I can't take it."

Placing my hand on his cheek, I give him a smile. "Never again."

"I love you."

"Always will," I say, giving him a kiss.

"We didn't use a condom," he mumbles against my mouth.

"Birth control." I kiss him again, but as the post-sex daze dissipates, I can't help but circle back to the kids conversation. "You really don't want any more babies?"

"Nope. We made one perfect little girl, and that's enough for me." He pecks my nose. "I'll set up an appointment on Monday to get snipped, as long as you're positive."

"You'd do that? Why would you do that?"

"Your body's been through hell and back, sweetheart. Let me do this for our family." He smiles, and my heart finally accepts what's been so hard for me to wrap my mind around. Trevor's my forever. Him and Lyla, they're my family. And I finally have somewhere I belong.

CHAPTER SIXTY

TREVOR

"Trevor, thanks for meeting with me." Miles stands from his desk and motions for me to sit in a chair across from him. "You ready for tonight?"

"Pretty sure. I have to dip out early today to grab my tux."

"Of course. That's not a problem at all." His eyes dart toward the door before he gives me a nervous grin. "You know, I wanted to apologize again for pulling you away from your family for that training in Utah."

"Hey, it's water under the bridge. Lyla's good, Willa's good. I made it back in time. We can forget it."

Miles nods and looks at the door again.

"So what did you need, Miles?" I have a lot of work to do before clocking out at lunchtime. The gala doesn't start until eight tonight, but after I pick up my tux, I have to get home so we can take Lyla to Hunter and Ashlie's. They're watching her overnight so Willa and I can have some much-needed alone time. I'm sure after spending the day with my parents, she'll need it.

"Well, this award of yours has put you on corporate's radar, digging in your file, and I'm not sure about your position on the team."

My head juts back. "What do you mean? Did I do something?"

"No, nothing like that." He shifts his eyes back to the door, and this time, I turn and look. There's no one there. "You've been a great asset to our team."

"So, what's the problem?"

Miles stands again, and when I turn, I'm met with the smiling founders of EdTechU. They also happen to be the fathers of my two best friends, Chase and Hunter, so seeing them in suits like this is a little weird. "Russell, Kendall, come on in," Miles says nervously.

I stand and shake both of their hands, and Russell tracks my confusion immediately. A friendly grin lights up his ivory face, his full head of gray hair professionally coiffed with a side part. "Sit. Sit. We'll explain in a minute," he says. They take the seats on either side of me, and I settle back into my own.

"We don't want to keep you, seeing as you have a big night to prepare for." Kendall claps my shoulder, a bright smile flashing from his deep umber skin. "We've been very impressed with your work, both here and in San Francisco, and we have a proposition for you."

The smile never leaves his face, despite my knitted brows raising in surprise while he and Russell give me their pitch. It's a once-in-a-lifetime opportunity that I would be insane to turn down. While I hear everything they're saying, all I can think about is Willa and Lyla.

"Now, we know you just had a baby"—Russell tacks on—"and we want to make this worth your while."

I nod, my breath shallow while I try to juggle the information with the panic rising in my throat. This could be the perfect solution to a problem I thought was so far in the future I didn't need to worry about it. But here's the solution, just the same, and I think the timing might be just right. Maybe. *Hopefully*.

"This wouldn't start for a few months, but you'll need that time to get all of the paperwork submitted. You could take the weekend to think about it, talk to Willa, and get back to us on Monday if you nee—"

"I don't need to think about it." I shake my head, wetting my lips with sudden clarity. "I'll take it."

Miles nods with an easy smile that matches the CEO and CTO of EdTechU. All three take turns shaking my hand, and I feel like I'm walking on a cloud, thinned air and all. I turn to Miles. "Do you think I could clock out now? I have some things I need to prepare for this new...career path."

"Of course. Of course. We'll see you on Monday."

I nod, and my eyes dart around the room, trying to focus on anything that makes sense. *Did this really just happen?* I'm so sleep-deprived, maybe I'm dreaming. I'm still nodding as I turn out the door and head to my office to clock out. When I get to my desk, however, the first thing I do is dig my phone out of my pocket and dial.

"T? Is everything okay?"

"My," I say to my sister. "I need you."

WILLA

I've never been to something so fancy before. The Reed Tech Gala is all swanky chandeliers and candlelit banquet tables, and I feel out of place, despite my black floor-length chiffon gown. I fiddle with the pins securing my twists in a low bun and smooth a hand over the deep slit in my dress for the seventeenth time. If I didn't have this clutch in my hand, I'm sure I'd have a death grip on my fingers.

Trevor grabs my free hand and pulls me toward him. "You're beautiful, Gem." He smiles, his calm easing into me. Giving me a sweet kiss on the lips melts the rest of my tension away. The elevator opens, and we head to the main ballroom.

Trevor's mom and dad are already at the table when we get there, beaming at him like he's the absolute light of their life. I can't help looking at him the same way, considering he's the light of mine. Asa and Adele flew in last night and spent today catching up with me and Lyla. All day, they gushed over how much she resembled Trevor when he was a kid. Lyla spent the time laughing at Asa's silly faces and cuddling with Adele. I love how they've welcomed me into their family, but I can't help but feel sad Lyla won't get a double dose of grandparent affection.

Trevor pulls my chair out for me, and once he takes his seat,

Asa starts with the jokes. "See, Adele? Being raised in a barn didn't affect him at all. He's wearing a tie and everything."

"Asa, honey, if you embarrass our son on his big night, I'll pinch the living daylights out of you."

Asa leans to the side like he's digging in his back pocket. "Well, just make sure you even it out on both cheeks, dear. Lord knows it's the most action I've seen in weeks."

My hand flies to my mouth to cover the cackle threatening to escape, while Trevor's shoulders shake wildly next to me as he tips his head back and laughs. Adele swats at Asa's shoulder with her program, then quickly uses it to hide giggles of her own. Asa Jones and his jokes are nothing less than a national treasure.

As the laughter dies down, we're joined by Chase and Kayla, who look happily exhausted as they tuck into the chairs next to us. "Hey, Willa!" Chase says with a wave. I give a little wave back as he passes behind me to greet Trevor and his parents. The bright smile on his face never falters. It suits him, but I've known Kayla long enough to know she's not a social butterfly.

"He always like this?" I ask Kayla, who pulls her phone out of her clutch and sets it in her lap—a telltale new mom anxiety habit. I know because I did the exact same thing.

Kayla leans in her chair to give me a side hug. "Worse, usually. I don't know where he gets his damn energy from. He was on baby duty last night." She looks at me and offers a smile. "You look great, Willa. Happiness looks good on you."

I nod and smile back. "Can you believe we're here? From small town Fort Bender to a ritzy LA gala?"

"Better get used to it, girl. I doubt Trevor's letting you get away."

I doubt it, too. After we broke through my body image barrier last week, I've let myself completely give in to him, and he's met me with the most enthusiastic protection. I can't believe I ever doubted him wanting me. Ever doubted him staying.

Once the dinner plates are cleared away, the lights dim, and the excitement in the air makes me wonder how Trevor's taking all of this. I reach for his thigh under the table and squeeze to get his attention. When he smiles at me with that dimpled grin, I know two things. One: he's not nervous at all. He was made for success like this. And two: he has my entire heart. He presses a kiss to my cheek, whispering, "Thank you for everything."

He's thanking *me*? After all the things he's had to give up and adjust to over the last year, he's smiling at me with gratitude like I'm the prize here. All my words scramble in my head as I gape at him in confusion. "What are you thanking me for? You did all of this yourself, Tre."

"Maybe. But it definitely helps having you next to me."

I want to tell him he's crazy for putting me on such a pedestal. That, if anything, I've made it harder for him to get to where he is now. But the pure adoration in his eyes shuts down every conflicting thought. Leaning forward, I press a soft kiss to his lips. "I love you," I whisper as silence washes over the room.

He smiles and gives me a quick kiss back. "Always will."

After dinner and the award ceremony, we skip the dancing and head straight home. Trevor seems just as eager as I am to have a night to ourselves. He tucks in behind me as I unlock my front door, hands curling around my hips while he nips my ear. My giggling is swallowed up by a gasp when the door swings open. There's a pathway of candles through my house. He nudges me inside with a sexy chuckle in my ear.

"What's all this?" I ask, turning to face him. He's busy digging in his work bag, so my eyes sweep over the romantic setup again. Even on his special night, he planned all this for me?

"Willa..."

When I turn around, his fingers grip a small black box, and I shake my head as if it will make it disappear. "W-why do you have that?"

Trevor inhales deeply and steps toward me. "Because I was offered a position in Germany, and I want you to come with me..." He takes another hesitant step, and my body forgets how to move, how to breathe. "It's a short assignment—just a year. I know this all sounds crazy right now. Rushed. Unorganized. But come with me, Willa." A hopeful grin slides across his lips. "*Be with me.* Traveling through Europe is your dream, and you're mine. Let me support your dreams, sweetheart. Just...let me come along for the ride too."

Eyes wide, I glance at his hand. "That doesn't explain the box, though."

Trevor turns back and grabs some paperwork from his bag, thumbing through it until he finds what he's looking for. I blink at the words on the paper. *Spouse.* "The easiest way for me to keep my promise and give you your dream trip to Europe is if you're my wife...German visa guidelines are pretty strict about that. I spent most of the morning trying to sort out all the rules." He chuckles nervously, but it doesn't touch the fear in his eyes as he takes another step toward me. "Willa, we've done all of this backward. Every single part of our story has been out of order, but there's no denying the timing has always been right." Another step, and he reaches for my hand, placing it over his chest. "You're in here. You're a part of me in a way I don't ever want to be without. You're the sound waves rippling across the ends of the earth and back, calling to that secluded place in my heart. You're the ocean that swept me up, molded me, gave me new purpose. It's you, and it's been you for so long, I can't remember a time before you." He places a soft kiss on my hand, then drops to his knee. "Marry me, Willa. I promise we'll work out all the details with the studio and anything else. Just...marry me?" His eyes plead, and it breaks my heart that he looks so scared right now. Scared of my answer. Scared that I'll walk away from him.

My heart pounds in my chest, beating so fast I'm worried it'll fly across the room. Taking this leap with him is something I've considered multiple times over the last few months. It's terrifying to put all my trust in someone else when I've worked so hard to make sure I never needed to. Scared shitless doesn't even begin to cover it. But as much as the old me wants to fight this, she's wrong. This is the next step for us, and it feels right. "I'm trying to dig up the courage to say yes," I whisper.

"Yeah?" His shoulders collapse, his face the picture of relief when I nod quickly. A cautious grin slides across his face as he flips the box open, revealing a simple round cut, solitaire ring with a twisted gold band. I stretch my left hand toward him, and the closer I get, the deeper those dimples go. As I stand here in front of a man who I couldn't stand a year ago, I know without any shadow of a doubt that I long to be his wife. He pulls the ring from the box and hesitates before pushing it on my finger. "I'm gonna need some words, Gem."

"Yes, Tre," I say, tears falling despite the smile on my face. "Yes, and yes again. When do we leave?"

He slips the ring on my finger. Everything that happens next moves in warp speed and slow motion all at the same time. Trevor pins me against the wall and kisses me with a tender passion. I meet him with just as much enthusiasm, grabbing at the lapel of his tux to pull him closer. We move slowly through the house, never breaking our connection on the way to the bedroom.

When we drop on the bed, fancy clothes rumpled all to hell, he brackets me with his arms. I slide a hand behind his head, finally giving myself permission to let go and rest in him completely.

"You're sure?" Trevor asks. I prop my chin on his bare chest and smile at him as we lay together, feeling perfectly at home in his arms. Our gala clothes lay crumpled at the foot of the bed.

"Why do you keep asking me?"

"Because I know you didn't ever envision yourself being

married, and we were in the heat of the moment. It's okay if you've changed your mind or you—"

Stopping him with a kiss, he sighs like it gives him the answer to a million other questions. I pull back, my heart leaping at the crooked smile on his face. "I'm sure, Tre."

He strokes my back with his fingertips. "I don't want you to feel pressured. You didn't want marriage before."

"That was before you—before I knew what it was like to be yours. You're the only one it could be, and there's nothing I want more." I hold my hand up, admiring my new ring. "You did *good*, Dimples."

"Yeah?" He chuckles, pulling me closer. "Maya helped me pick it out over video chat... We'll have to do it pretty soon—the wedding. They want all our paperwork in before November so everything hopefully goes through by the new year."

"That's okay. I don't want a big wedding. I don't even want a wedding. Or a fancy dress. I'd be fine at the courthouse."

"Then let's do it." He smiles, tracing my lips with his thumb.

I give it a peck. "Won't your family be upset by not being there?"

"Naw, not really." He shrugs. "They're used to my surprises by now, and they'll just be happy I'm happy." Trevor's phone chirps in the pants at our feet, and he cranes his neck to look at the time on the alarm clock. He bites his bottom lip, which does nothing for the smile playing at his lips. "It's midnight," he says, stretching to open the nightstand. He pulls out a small blue velvet bag, identical to the one that held my camera necklace all those months ago. Dangling it in front of me, he says, "Happy birthday, sweetheart."

With a shake of my head and a smile on my face, I grab the bag out of the air. I should have known he'd do something for my birthday. "You remembered."

"I remember everything about you. It's kinda my thing." He presses a kiss to my temple. "Open it."

I untie the satin strings cinching the bag closed, and the

skinny golden cuff that slides out makes my heart burst. My thumb swipes over the *Always Will* inscribed on the inside curve. His fingers tangle with mine when he turns the bracelet around, revealing the etched pattern of sound waves. "It's just a way for you to remember my promise to you. I love you, Gem."

Dropping the bracelet on his chest, I prop myself up to reach his lips, a kiss backed with all the emotions swirling inside. Excitement. Peace. Love. *Happiness.* I palm his jaw, hoping to convey how much this simple gift means to me—how much *he* means to me, as I whisper, "Always will."

ABOUT THE AUTHOR

Layna James is a romantic at heart whose stories feature diverse characters navigating the complexities of life while falling in love. Angst, yearning, and swoon-worthy banter are her favorite things to write.

COMING SOON

Single Dad. Christmas tree farmer. Lumberjack. Flower shop owner. Samson's got way too much going on. So why can't he get the small town librarian out of his head? And why does she look so sad? Meet Vanessa and Samson in the fourth and final book of the Fort Bender series, coming Winter 2026.

ALSO BY LAYNA JAMES

Some Kind of Forever (#1)

Sunshine with You (#2)

Always Will (#3)

When Love Blooms (#4)—Coming in 2026

ACKNOWLEDGMENTS

As always, I have to give the biggest thanks to my wonderful family. None of this would be possible without their support and patience. And to my bestie for lifer—Kenz, you're the best hypewoman!

A huge thank you to my editors, Kourtney and Jessica. From beginning to end, you've helped make this story everything it is today, and I couldn't ask for a better editing team.

To my early readers and sensitivity checkers, I can't thank you enough for helping me craft this story with care. A special shoutout to Anna, Olive, Olive's Brothers, Melissa, Aria, Emmy, Giuliana, Jessica, and JB for sticking with me through my third book!

Last, but not least, I want to thank my writer's club for being the best resource and comedic relief when I needed to take a step back.

—LJ